A WINTER BRIDE

Other titles by Isla Dewar:

Keeping Up with Magda
Women Talking Dirty
Giving Up on Ordinary
It Could Happen to You
Two Kinds of Wonderful
The Woman Who Painted Her Dreams
Walking with Rainbows
Dancing in a Distant Place
The Cherry Sundae Company
Secrets of a Family Album
Rosie's Wish
Getting Out of the House
The Consequences of Marriage

Available from Ebury Press:
Izzy's War

A Winter Bride

Isla Dewar

EBURY
PRESS

1 3 5 7 9 10 8 6 4 2

First published in hardback in 2011 by Ebury Press,
an imprint of Ebury Publishing

This edition 2011

A Random House Group Company

The Random House Group Limited Reg. No. 954009

Addresses for companies within the Random House Group can be found at
www.randomhouse.co.uk

A CIP catalogue record for this book is available from the British Library

The Random House Group Limited supports The Forest Stewardship
Council® (FSC®), the leading international forest certification organisation.
All our titles that are printed on Greenpeace approved FSC® certified paper
carry the FSC® logo. Our paper procurement policy can be found at:
www.randomhouse.co.uk/environment

Typeset in Galliard by Palimpsest Book Production Limited,
Falkirk, Stirlingshire

Printed and bound in Great Britain by
Clays Ltd, St Ives plc

ISBN 9780091938147
To buy books by your favourite authors and register for offers visit
www.randomhouse.co.uk

To Bob and Adam

Chapter One
Teenage Kicks

Saturday night at the Locarno and the heat was on; the place was heaving. The air reeked of booze, cigarettes and cheap perfume. The atmosphere was shrill with drama. Girls were screaming; boys were shouting. How could people be like this? Nell wondered. So frenzied, so wild – all raw emotion. She wouldn't behave so badly. Well, not in public anyway. Still, it was thrilling to see. She was a watcher from the wings. She never joined in but what she saw made her gasp. Anything could happen here.

There was a wall of people packed round the bar. At the door, two men were fighting, red-faced, spitting blood and fury. Somewhere near the bandstand a man had punched his girlfriend. She was on the floor wailing that she loved him and she hadn't done nothing. Her friends were screaming that the puncher was a bastard. Upstairs, a girl was dancing on the parapet of the balcony. Boys below were looking up her skirt. Some people were just running about holding drinks aloft and bawling; letting off steam. A man was standing right in front of Nell looking glazed, as if he'd temporarily lost contact with his brain. Someone had slit open his back pocket with a knife and removed his wallet; blood oozed down his leg. He hadn't noticed.

Nell watched it all in awe. This was where she and Carol came to get their weekly kicks; to see people let their hair down. Their mothers would be shocked. This place was strictly out of bounds. 'Don't you *ever* go to the Locarno,' Nell's mother, Nancy, said. 'That place is heathen.' Nell was grateful, though. If her mother hadn't so vehemently forbidden her to darken the Locarno's doors, she would never have come. She'd had to see what all the fuss was about.

Yeah, heathen, Nell thought, it's great. People left their inhibitions at the door and went wild. Who could resist? Saturday nights were a reason to be alive – a few glistening, rowdy hours of laughter, booze and endless possibilities. If only life was always like this, but it wasn't. Real life, she glumly told herself, was what happened in the boring bits between Saturday nights.

It was April 1959. Nell had turned seventeen earlier in the year and was too young to be at the Locarno, which was for eighteens and over on account of it being licensed. She thought that she was in her prime but that Carol, at eighteen, was past it. Well, for a teenager, anyway. Women had two primes, according to Nell: one at seventeen and another at twenty-five. She didn't go beyond that. She couldn't imagine being thirty but was sure it would be dull. Carol was definitely too old to be coming to the Locarno. She should be settling down. A girl, Nell was convinced, should have a good time at seventeen, have met her true love at eighteen, be engaged at nineteen and marry at twenty-one. Somewhere along the line she should also lose her virginity. Nell was planning to do this in the next six months. She hadn't yet met anyone to do it with, though; that was a bit of a worry.

Right now the dance floor was packed with people pressed close – groin to groin, cheek to cheek – shuffling on their few square inches of space, hips swaying in time to the song. Above, the glitter ball swirled slowly, flickering splashes of light across the sea of bobbing heads. A cloud of cigarette smoke shifted, curling towards the ceiling. Nell leaned against a pillar, watching the action.

The band was playing 'Heartbreak Hotel', one of her favourites. She hated this version, though. The musicians, all wearing evening suits with bow ties, had stripped it of its raw passion and turned it into a cheery ditty. The singer – who was dressed like all the other men in the band, aside from his white jacket – was pronouncing every word of the lyrics as if he was reading the BBC news. This made finding a new place to dwell down at the end of Lonely Street because his baby had left him sound like a jolly fun thing to do. He was also doing strange things with his eyebrows, raising and lowering them in time to the music. Nell curled her lip. God, these people understood nothing. They're old, too old for rock and roll, she thought.

She took a sip of her vodka and lime and made a face. God, she hated vodka and lime but it was the thing to drink so she drank it. Carol was dancing with a man with a quiff of greasy hair, a long jacket with a velvet collar and a black shirt with a white, shoelace tie. Not Nell's type at all. Carol had her arms round his neck and his hands, which had started the dance on her waist, and were now slipping towards her bum. Carol wasn't objecting, though.

He'd come up to them, given them the once-over, chosen Carol, and had held out his hand. 'Dancin'?' he'd said.

Carol had said, 'OK,' as if she didn't care if she did or didn't. She'd taken a swift sip of her drink, handed it to Nell, and had followed him into the throng.

Nell checked her watch. Half-past twelve. Not good. She had thirty minutes left before the last dance; thirty minutes to find someone who'd ask to see her home. If she didn't, the night would be a failure. That was the point of the evening: meeting someone who might be *the* someone who would turn her life into an endless round of Saturday nights.

This place was full of young men on the hunt for sex, or at least a snog and a grope: the perfect end to a wild night. They prowled the edges of the dance floor, sizing up the talent. Right now two of them were giving her the once-over. She was at the wrong end of a critical leer. One boy jerked his thumb towards her and said to his friend, 'Fancy that?'

His mate stared at her. 'Nah.' They moved on.

Nell shrugged and curled her lip at them, making a show of not caring. Even though she did.

Sneering was a big part of Saturday night. Nell was good at it. She'd had a lot of practice. Surviving the Locarno with her self-esteem intact meant perfecting the disinterested look and the superior sneer.

Sometimes Nell and Carol would spend an evening sneering in Nell's bedroom. They had lip curling and dirty look routines that made them cry with laughter. They'd sing 'Bird Dog', rolling their eyes and raising the corner of their upper lips, perfecting their scathing disdain. They drank Coke, ate chocolate biscuits and discussed men. Nell was an expert. 'They don't have as many feelings as women,' she said. 'That's why they can't be faithful. They don't feel love the way we do.' She sighed and rolled her eyes. 'Love.'

'Love's everything,' said Carol. 'You'll never be truly happy if you don't ever know love.'

'Nah,' said Nell. 'That's not true.'

'So what do you think brings happiness?' said Carol. 'Money?'

Nell said she thought happiness came from knowing what you want. 'And making sure you get it.'

'And what do you want?' Carol.

'Money,' said Nell. They sniggered and drifted into their favourite what-would-I-do-if-I-had-a-million-pounds conversation. Nell wanted a huge house with rolling lawns and peacocks walking about. 'And inside would look like a magazine.'

'I just want to lie in bed till after ten every morning and never go to the office again.' Carol worked in a typing pool, battering at the keys of an Olivetti from nine to five, Monday to Friday. She thought it a classier way to make a living than being a shop girl like Nell.

Nell shrugged. She liked her job. One thing was for sure: you didn't find many rich men hanging about typing pools, but you never knew who you'd come across standing on the other side of the counter in a stationery shop. Rich men, or at least men who gave Nell the impression of being rich, often came in to buy cards with padded hearts to give to some lucky woman.

Sometimes they bought posh pens. Nell would take them from the glass display case and lay them on the counter. 'A pen like this will last a lifetime,' she'd say. 'This is the Rolls Royce of pens. Beautiful ink flow.' She told herself she could tell a lot about a man from the pen he used. Nell knew the exact requirements of the man she planned to marry. He'd be rich, have a car and wear Buddy Holly glasses.

When the band struck up the last dance, Nell headed for the cloakroom. No doubt about it, she was down-hearted. Another Saturday night, another failure. She hadn't got off with anyone, unlike Carol, who'd been so close to the boy she was dancing with it was almost obscene. They'd been draped over one another, her arms round his neck, his hands on her bum and his face buried deep in her neck. She'd be wearing high-necked tops all next week to hide the love bites. Sometimes Carol went too far.

Nell teetered to collect her and Carol's coats, taking tiny steps in her six-inch heels and a tight black skirt, then went to the ladies' room to join the queue for the loo. It was hell in there. The thick fug of hairspray and cigarette smoke, the shrieks, the yelling and swoons of women newly in love with someone they'd met ten minutes ago, the mingling perfumes – it was difficult to breathe. Women preened, furiously backcombed their hair, smoked and discussed the night's adventures simultaneously.

The queue to the loo was long and rowdy but moved along swiftly as girls went into the cubicles two or three at a time. They didn't see any need of privacy to relieve themselves, and group peeing meant they could continue uninterrupted their fervent and busy conversations.

Peeing wasn't easy either – Nell had to sit on the loo with one foot up holding the door shut – as there were no locks. And, she had to balance two coats and a handbag on her lap. It wasn't safe to put things down here. Well, not only was the floor suspiciously wet, but the rumour was that someone would reach under the huge gap between the door and the floor, grab your bag and run. By the time you pulled up your knickers, the thief would be long gone. The skills a girl had to master, Nell thought. They don't teach you nothing like this at school. But then, they hadn't taught anything interesting at school. If there had been an exam in surviving the ladies' room at the dancehall, she'd have gotten an A.

Carol was outside, standing by the front door with her new love and a geek.

'This is Johnny,' said Carol, pointing at the new love. She jerked her thumb at the geek. 'And Alistair.'

Nell nodded.

'They're going to see us home.'

Nell nodded again. She scanned the geek with a full head-to-toe scathing look. He was wearing grey flappy trousers with big turn-ups, a green shirt with a tweed tie, old man's shoes – brown with little holes over the toecap – and a duffel coat. Oh God, Nell thought, a student. And not an interesting student who'd wear a corduroy jacket, but a boring one who probably studied something incomprehensible like maths or physics.

They started the long walk home, Carol and Johnny in the lead, Nell and Alistair trailing behind. She noted that he walked on the outside, nearest the road. A gentleman, Nell thought. A man should always let the woman walk on the inside. She checked her watch. She gave Johnny ten minutes before he took Carol's hand.

Alistair asked if she went to the Locarno often.

'Every week,' she told him. 'It's great.'

'It's a bit rough.'

'Yeah, but it's fun. How often do you go?'

'Never. I just went along tonight to keep my brother company. His usual mates are on holiday.'

Nell pointed at Johnny. 'He's your *brother*?'

'Yeah.' He smiled. 'Chalk and cheese, eh?'

'Too right.'

'He only looks like that on Saturdays. Rest of the time he looks more like me, only smarter – no duffel coat. Actually our mother hates him going out like that. She says he looks common. But he likes it. He thinks it makes him look hard.'

'What does he do?'

'Works with our dad at the garage.'

'He's a mechanic?'

'He did his apprenticeship. Now he's in sales. He has to wear a normal suit and white shirt for that. When he's twenty-five, Dad'll take him into partnership and, eventually he'll take over the business.'

'The garage?'

'Yes. It's on the Queensferry Road. Rutherford's.'

'The big one? That sells Jaguars?'

'Yes.'

'Goodness. What about you? Don't you want to work there?'

'Nah. Not interested in cars. Couldn't fix one. Couldn't sell one.'

'But you could have one.'

'Getting one soon,' he said. 'I passed my test yesterday. Johnny's already got one, but it's getting fixed at the moment. He drives like a maniac with two speeds: fast and very fast.'

Alistair had just risen hugely in Nell's estimation. In front of them, Johnny slipped Carol's hand into his. Nell checked her watch. Yes, spot on.

'Am I boring you? You keep looking at your watch.'

'Course not. I'm checking how long it took your brother to take Carol's hand. I'd bet myself it'd be ten minutes. I was right.' She punched the air in triumph.

He smiled, said, 'Great,' and asked how long she thought before the couple in front kissed.

'Oh, he'll put his arm round her first. That'll be in

another five minutes. Then he'll kiss her when we're further down the road, maybe about Calton Hill.'

'Bets?' said Alistair.

'OK.'

'Bet you five shilling he kisses her five minutes from now.'

'Nah, it'll be more like ten.' She took the bet, and noticed Alistair was now walking a lot closer to her. She decided she'd let him take her hand and kiss her when they got home. After all, he'd soon have a car. She wouldn't let him grope her, though. He wouldn't respect her if she did, and with a boy who had rich parents and his own car, respect was important.

He asked what she did.

'I work in a stationery shop. Little's. There's a lot to know about stationery – weights of paper and the like. And all the different sorts of cards. And pens. I love pens. One day, I'm going to have my own pen shop. I'll sell nothing but pens . . . and ink, of course.' She'd just decided this but it sounded like an awfully good idea.

Ahead, Johnny let go of Carol's hand and slipped his arm round her shoulders, pulling her close. She put her arm round his waist. Nell checked her watch. Five minutes. She shot Alistair a smug look.

'Where do you live, by the way?' he asked.

'Restalrig.'

'That's miles.'

She shrugged. 'You don't have to come. I can make it alone, no problem.'

'Couldn't let you do that. Can't let you wander the streets unprotected.'

She smiled and stepped along beside him, six steps to his two, her high heels clicking on the pavement. She supposed it was better to have someone to walk with. Usually, she trailed along slightly behind Carol and whoever she'd picked up. Carol was the good-looking one: blonde; fond of low-cut dresses; pouty lipped with pick-up techniques she'd learned from magazines and movies; a knack of tilting her head and looking fascinated by what boys said; a certain way of lowering her eyelids – and she never got spots. She did well with the opposite sex. Nell didn't. Brown haired, pale, dreamy – she was always the dowdy best friend.

She liked it best when she and Carol walked home together, boyless and happy. On summer nights, they'd slip off their shoes and tread the pavements in stocking soles. They'd link arms and sing, mostly Buddy Holly. They were both in love with him and had agreed they'd like a bloke with horn-rimmed glasses. 'So sexy,' Nell said. 'And intelligent, too.'

They would never discuss what they would sing. As if by telepathy they'd both start on the same song, 'Rave On', an all-time fave. Sometimes they'd stop, do a little jive together, and then carry on, arms linked once more. They'd interrupt their small concert with squeals: 'Oooh, did you see that bloke drinking a whole pint in one big gulp?' or 'There was a couple having sex outside the loo. Real sex, all the way. Didn't even notice me watchin'.' Then they'd resume their singing.

Even though the night would be almost over, and they'd be going home, which was never Nell's favourite journey, she'd be in heaven. She was young, she was out in the night, she had a little bit of money in her pocket and all the songs on the radio were about her.

She asked Alistair if he liked Buddy Holly.

'Who couldn't like Buddy?' he said. 'We lost a genius there.'

She told him she'd cried when she'd heard he died. 'The saddest day of my life.' She sang 'That'll Be the Day'. She had the quirks and turns of the chorus perfected. He nodded approval, brought out his horn-rimmed specs, did a small pavement jive singing 'Peggy Sue', accompanying himself on the air guitar. Nell was impressed. In specs like that, she could almost forgive him his awful clothes.

She asked what he usually did on Saturday nights, since he didn't go to the Locarno.

'I go to a jazz club or a folk club up the High Street. Or just to the pub.'

By now they'd reached Princes Street and were heading towards Calton Hill. Johnny and Carol were so close, so entwined, walking was becoming difficult. First kiss coming soon, Nell thought.

The couple in front stopped, and turned to one another. He put his arms round her waist, pulled her to him. Kissed her. For a moment, she stood, arms by her sides, receiving the kiss but not participating in it. Then she slipped her arms round his neck and kissed him back. She had one foot on the ground; the other was sticking out behind her. It was a move she'd seen in the movies.

'Oh, the leg-bent-behind-you kiss,' said Nell. 'The passion of it.' Then, 'You owe me five shillings.'

They walked past the embracing couple, moving now further and further away from the thrum of city nightlife. This always saddened Nell. She hated going home. Loved the city after dark, the rustle of taxis, the tide of people shifting from one night spot to another, or hanging about looking for somewhere to go, hoping to find a party because they, like her, didn't want the night to end.

Alistair said, 'You never asked what I did.'

'You're a student.'

'It's that obvious?'

She nodded and smiled. 'What are you studying, anyway?'

'The law.'

'You're going to be a lawyer?'

'That's the plan,' he said.

A lawyer. My God, a lawyer. Nell's imagination went into overdrive. Lawyers made pots of money. They could have a big house, rolling lawns, film-set interior, a Jaguar (from his father's garage) at the door. Of course, it would be tough at first. They wouldn't have much money and would live in a small flat – hopefully somewhere off the West End. He'd be studying night and day. She pictured him sitting at the kitchen table, books piled high; he'd be burning the midnight oil, sipping coffee, wearing a crisp white shirt open at the collar, sleeves rolled up. She'd come to him wearing only a long silk robe, slightly open. She'd rub his shoulders. 'Come to bed, darling. It's late.'

'Soon,' he'd say. 'I've just got to finish this first.'

'You're tired. You'll work better after some sleep.'

He'd lean back and run his fingers through his hair. Then he'd reach for her and pull her to him. 'What would I do without you,' he'd say. She'd seen all this in films.

When he graduated, she'd give him a pen. At first, he'd work for a reputable law firm. But after a year or two he'd branch out on his own. He'd have an office on George Street and a secretary: an older, plumpish woman with crisp permed hair, lumpy tweed suits and a fine line in wisecracks. He'd make his name taking on famous cases, defending people whose lives were in ruin after being falsely accused of murder or fraud. He'd win them all. When film stars, international sportsmen, Nobel Prize-winning scientists and world-renowned business leaders found themselves in trouble with the law, they'd turn to their aides and hiss, 'Get Alistair Rutherford.' She'd be the beautiful wife in the background, always there, always supporting him. She'd look like Audrey Hepburn. She'd throw parties every-body longed to be invited to. She'd have her photo in the society columns of newspapers. Yes, Nell decided, this man was rich, had a car and wore Buddy Holly glasses. She would marry him.

Chapter Two
Emotionally Itchy

It was late when they reached Nell's home. She sat on the low wall beside the front gate. He stood in front of her, hands in his pockets. She wondered if he'd kiss her. But, worryingly, he wasn't making any moves. Perhaps he doesn't think I'm kissable, she thought.

'So, a lawyer,' she said. 'Your mum and dad must be proud.'

He kicked the ground with the toe of his old man's shoes. 'The day will come when they'll be glad of a lawyer in the family.'

Nell asked what he meant by that.

He shook his head and said, 'Nothing, really.' He turned, looking for his brother and Carol, but passion had delayed their long walk home.

'Does your friend live near here?' he asked.

'Round the corner,' said Nell. 'I'll see her tomorrow.'

'To compare notes?'

'No,' she said. A lie. She was desperate to compare notes. 'By the way, you still owe me that five shillings.'

'I'll buy you dinner next Saturday instead,' he said.

She thought about this. Dinner on Saturday would mean missing the Locarno. And she'd never been to dinner with a man. Dates were usually a night at the cinema or the pub. This seemed awfully sophisticated. Still, if she was going to marry this man, she'd better get used to such things. So she said yes.

Ten minutes later, lying in bed, too thrilled to sleep, Nell planned it all. She would, of course, have to change his appearance. He'd have to get tighter trousers and ditch the old man's shoes. She thought he'd scrub up well. He was quite handsome if you screwed your eyes and imagined him with a decent haircut. *And,* he had Buddy Holly glasses and almost had a car. You could forgive him the duffel coat if you thought about that.

In the morning, Nell went round to Carol's to compare notes. Her friend was still in bed, lying sprawled between her pink sheets, hair spread over her pink pillow and surrounded by her menagerie of soft fluffy toys. Carol was indulged by two doting parents who were better off than Nell's. She had everything, including, years ago, a Mickey Mouse watch that Nell still envied.

Nell sat on the end of the bed and watched her friend yawn and stretch.

'Great night,' Carol said.

Nell agreed.

'What was yours like?' Carol asked.

'He's nice. He's going to be a lawyer.' She didn't mention getting married to him. Too soon, she thought.

And if I say I'm going to marry Alistair, she'll just say she's going to marry his brother.

'I'm going out with Johnny tonight,' said Carol. 'He's going to borrow his father's car and we'll go for a drive.'

'Alistair has a car. Or, at least, he's getting one,' said Nell.

'Johnny has a sports car,' said Carol, 'but it's getting fixed.'

Nell was about to say she knew that but Carol wasn't to be interrupted.

'He's really handsome,' Carol said. Her glistening words tumbled out. 'I told him straight out not to wear that long jacket when he comes tonight. And he said he wouldn't. He said his mum didn't like it either. He's going to take over the family business when his dad retires. Though that's not going to be for ages yet. Years and years. Still—' she turned to gaze at Nell '—he's really, really rich.' She sat up, took her favourite toy – a soft little pink spaniel that was also a pyjama case – held it to her and kissed it. 'He looks a bit like a film star when you see him up close. A bit like James Dean. Sort of sulky and moody. I always wanted someone who looked like that. I think he may be The One. I think I'm in love. It's wonderful. It can happen just like that.' Carol sighed. 'A look across a crowded room, a kiss and your life is changed forever.'

It all sounded so romantic, a whirlwind of love and starlight, that Nell felt downcast. She'd been upped. Carol had a moody hunk with a sports car. She had a student who wore old men's shoes and a duffel coat. She pointed to the red row of lovebites on her pal's neck and said, 'Better hide those.'

The following Saturday, Alistair drew up outside the house at half-past seven and blasted the horn. Nell had been watching for him at the window. She picked up her coat, shouted goodbye to her mother and father and ran out. She didn't want him to come in; he might mention the Locarno, and then she'd be in trouble.

The car was, at first, disappointing. She'd been hoping for a Jaguar, but what she saw was a Morris Minor convertible. However, as they drove into town, roof down, she revised her thoughts. This was fun. People in the movies had soft-top cars. Also, this was right for now, while they were young. They'd get a Jaguar after they'd been married for a couple of years and had bought a big house with a drive.

They went to a small Italian restaurant not far from the university where Alistair studied. There was a wine bottle coated in dripping wax and a candle in the neck on every table, plastic flowers adorned the doorway and spread up the fake trellis on the wall. 'This is lovely,' Nell said. Alistair said he came here often. He ordered a bottle of Chianti. Nell thought it amazing – a bottle that was wrapped in a basket. She asked if she could take it home.

Alistair ordered for her. 'When in Rome,' he insisted and asked the waiter for two plates of spaghetti

Bolognese. 'You'll love this,' he told her. She did. At least she'd loved the small amount she'd actually managed to get into her mouth. She decided that this was why Italians were the way they were. They weren't excitable. They were just hungry. Their food was hard to eat.

He asked her what her parents did. It was always a tricky question for Nell, and usually she lied when answering. She liked to give her mother and father a tragic past. Her father had fallen while painting the Forth Bridge and was lucky to be alive. Her mother, once a talented dressmaker, had gone blind due to the intricacy of her work. Or her father had been an important businessman in Warsaw; her mother had been an opera singer. They'd had a marvellous life – a beautiful house filled with music, wine and interesting witty friends. But when the Nazis invaded, they'd fled the country escaping with nothing but the clothes they stood up in. Her mother had never recovered from the horrors she'd seen and had lost her exquisite voice. Now they lived in a council house on the east side of Edinburgh. This story had been adapted from a magazine serial she'd read, but Nell could see it all as she told it.

Obviously, Nell couldn't tell any of her stories to Alistair; a person couldn't lie to her future husband. He'd meet her mum and dad at the wedding. So, she told the truth: her dad had been a coalman, but heaving heavy sacks from the lorry and lumbering to customers' cellars to deliver his burden had done nasty things to his back. Now, he was retired and spent a deal of time lying flat on the sofa dealing with the pain. Her mother worked in a cake shop.

'Good honest salt-of-the-earth people,' he said. 'No greed, no shady dealings, no back-stabbing.'

His comment surprised Nell, but she agreed. She sneaked a peek at her watch. Nine o'clock. The Locarno would be humming now. Fights and screams and dancing; booze flowing; boys and girls on the hunt, looking to grab a quick shot of love in doorways on the way home. God, she missed it, and was a little jealous of Carol, who'd gone there with Johnny.

Alistair suggested they go on to a folk concert after dinner.

'Folk singing?', said Nell. She didn't think so. The only folk songs she knew were the ones she'd been forced to sing at school. She remembered with heavy heart the dreary rendition of 'The Skye Boat Song' her class had moaned out on Thursday afternoons when they'd suffered double music in Miss Penny's overheated room. *Speeee . . . . eeed bonny bo . . . . at like a burd on the wee . . . . . . eeeng . . . . . .*

'Yes,' he said. 'You'll love it.'

It was in a tiny café in the High Street – wood panelled walls, wooden tables, wooden floor and no drink. Nell wasn't sure about this. Alistair bought them Cokes. Nell looked round. The people here all seemed very sure of themselves despite their worn clothes, quite tatty, she thought. She felt out of place in her pink frilly blouse.

The band, wearing fishermen's jumpers, was hearty. They played guitars, opened their throats and belted out rebel songs. They shouted. All this would have shocked Miss Penny. People stamped their feet, whistled and yelled for encores. Nell couldn't stop her toes tapping.

Before she knew it, it was eleven o'clock and she had almost forgotten about the Locarno. There were songs about lonesome rides on trains, people sailing away to far-flung lands, the lure of whisky, drinking in empty bars and drinking in crowded bars. Her favourite was a woman with blonde hair that fell past her breasts who sang sad ballads about waiting for death or having lost her man at sea. Her voice was like crystal, so clear it reminded Nell of the loch near the village where she and her parents had taken the only holiday they'd ever gone on. It was all very surprising.

The best bit, though, was when it was over. The audience poured into the night, songs pounding through them. It was September, and the first bite of autumn was in the air. People pulled their jackets round them, hauled up their collars, shivered and started their slow journeys home – on foot, walking, shanks' pony. Nell and Alistair crossed the road and climbed into the car. Smirking, Nell thought, ha, ha, have that, confident tatty people. She couldn't help but feel a little smug.

Driving Nell home, Alistair asked what she'd thought of the concert.

'Great,' she told him. 'I wanted to stamp my feet

and join in. Only it's all old songs. The people that wrote them are dead and the things they're singing about happened long ago. I still prefer the songs on the radio. They're my songs. About getting out of school for the summer, or going to the hop, crying in the rain or falling in love with someone who doesn't even know you exist. They're about me.'

At the traffic lights, he gave her a long look and said that perhaps she was right, and then asked if she was in some unrequited affair.

'No. I just hear a song like that and I know what it would feel like. And I feel sad. I like feeling sad.' She thought about this. 'Well, when it's over and I don't feel sad anymore, I look back and think I quite enjoyed it.' She sighed. 'Sometimes I imagine that the song's about me. Someone's in love with me and doesn't tell me. A secret admirer. And I feel sad for the person who's in love with me and feels too shy to tell me. And I feel sad for me having love I don't know about.'

Alistair thought he might have to stop the car so he could lean back and sort out this onslaught of emotions. He was glad he wasn't a woman. They seemed to have an awful lot to cope with. He liked to keep his life and thoughts as simple as possible. He agreed that he thought a secret admirer sounded good. 'Someone who adores you from afar. Maybe someone does adore you from afar. Do you get loads of Valentine cards?'

She got two every year regular as clockwork. One was from her dad; the other she sent to herself. She only did this to keep up with Carol, who always got at least six cards. But Carol was pretty, a shiny person who stood out in crowds. Boys chased her. Often they'd befriend Nell just to get a little bit closer to Carol. It had been demeaning. Nell thought she was one of the shadow people who always walked a few paces behind the adored ones but she didn't mention this to Alistair because who would want to marry a shadow person?

'I usually get a couple of cards,' she said, and then confessed that one was from her father. 'Although I think my mum buys it.'

'I never get any,' said Alistair. 'Unlike my brother, who gets piles of them. He was in the first rugby team at school, was head boy, always had the prettiest girl-friends and used to get loads then.'

Ah, Nell thought, you're a shadow person, too. At last, I've found something we have in common.

So when he asked if she would like to see him again next Saturday she said she'd love to. She would have agreed anyway, since this was her chosen husband, but now she meant it.

The next morning, Nell went to Carol's house to compare notes. 'We went to a restaurant and ate spaghetti with wine. Then we went to a folk concert.'

'Folk music?' Carol sneered. 'Yuk.'

'It was great! People stamped and clapped and the songs were rowdy. Some of them were dirty. About sex.'

'Maybe I'll get Johnny to take me to a restaurant.'

Nell's heart sank. She just knew that the restaurant Carol went to would be bigger, better and more expensive than the one she had visited with Alistair. 'How was the Locarno?' she asked.

'It's not the same going there with a boy. You have to dance with him all the time so you can't eye up other boys or flirt and look around for someone you fancy. It's not a place to go on a date. The Locarno's where you go to find a date. It was rubbish.'

Nell's heart leapt. For the first time in her life, she'd upped her friend.

On Saturday, Nell and Alistair went to a film. She had been hoping to see the latest Doris Day movie, but no. 'This is in French,' she said. 'I won't understand it.'

'You can read the subtitles,' Alistair told her. 'This is a great film.'

In the end, she didn't follow the dialogue. She stared at the clothes and the décor of the sets. It was the start of something: the long, slow sophisticating of Nell McClusky. Because in the end she didn't change Alistair at all; he changed her.

She stopped wearing the pink swirling skirts that spun out revealing her knickers when she jived and started wearing tight jeans with long jumpers, or skimpy tops shaped to her body, all in dark colours. She moved from pink to black.

He insisted she read *Bonjour Tristesse, On the Road* and *Catcher in the Rye*. Much to her surprise, she enjoyed them. Though, as she told Alistair, she felt that Holden Caulfield needed a good slap. 'A night at the Locarno would sort him out. He'd get drunk, get sneered at, have a fight or two and run about yelling his head off. It'd stop him thinking so much. That's this guy's problem – too much thinking, too much longing.'

'Longing?' said Alistair. 'What do you mean?'

'He's longing for something but he doesn't know what. That's why he's so sneery. And if you want to sneer, the Locarno's the place to do it. Everybody sneers there. It's because they're too young to be really young and not old enough to be grown up. Full of feelings that they don't understand. They're emotionally itchy.'

He asked if that was why she went. 'Were you emotionally itchy?'

'For God's sake, no. I sneered because everyone else was sneering. I wanted to fit in. But I never screamed. I didn't have the longing. That feeling of wanting something, only you didn't know what. I've always known what I wanted. I went to the Locarno to watch the show. It was great.'

He was so taken with the notion of being emotionally itchy he didn't ask Nell what it was she wanted.

Just as well, really, she thought, as she wouldn't have told him. She wanted him; she was going to marry him. She knew not to mention this so early in their relationship. It might frighten him off. According to the rules that she'd picked up in magazine love stories, he had to ask her to be his wife but she had to put the notion into his head. And she wasn't quite sure how to do that yet. In the meantime, she would cake her eyes with black eyeliner and paint her lips white and stop wearing her hair in a beehive.

At supper one night, her mother asked if she was a beatnik.

'I am against convention,' Nell said. 'I am simply expressing my feelings of negativity about the bourgeoisie through my clothes, Mother.'

Her mother smacked her wrist. 'Don't you dare call me mother. That's rude. I'm your mum.'

On nights out, Nell and Alistair went to the cinema to see foreign films, to poetry readings in a candlelit dive in the High Street or to folk concerts where men in fishermen's jumpers sang lusty songs about battles and long roads to travel. Sometimes, they drove in his Morris convertible to Queensferry for a drink. They also drove to quiet spots where they'd have long deep kisses and exploratory fumblings that after a while got more and more intimate. The car windows got steamy.

Eventually, after six months of romance, they did it. Went all the way, as Nell put it. It wasn't as wonderful as Nell supposed it would be. Stars didn't sing in the sky. The earth, or in this case, the Morris Minor, didn't move. But it was fine. The deed was done. And not only was it done in time with Nell's losing-her-virginity schedule, it was also done with a man who had a car and wore Buddy Holly glasses.

With practise, as the weeks passed, it got better and

Nell began to enjoy it. 'We're getting good at this,' she said.

The Locarno was never mentioned again but Nell never forgot it. She promised herself she'd go back for one last look at the emotionally itchy.

The chance came when Alistair was sitting his Christmas exams. He needed to study. 'I know it's Saturday night,' he said, 'but when it's all over I'll take you somewhere special.'

Nell phoned Carol. 'I'm free on Saturday. Fancy the Locarno?'

'You bet,' said Carol. She told Johnny she had 'flu, knowing he'd keep well away from her.

'He can't stand illness,' Carol told Nell. 'He's not sympathetic like Alistair. He's good-looking, though. Girls stare at him. So that's all right. Good-looking, rich and a car . . . what more could you want in a bloke?'

On Saturday night, the girls took the bus into town, had a few drinks and hit the Locarno. They were both quivering with excitement at the prospect of revisiting the reckless abandoned nights of what they now considered to be their youth – this was going to be great. The Locarno was all it ever had been: the same frenzy, the drink, the fights, the yelling, boys stamping through the crowds, girls jiving on the balcony and the same old staid band taming Eddie Cochrane and Elvis.

Nell was wearing her pink dress, which was tight at the waist then flared out and her white stiletto heels. Her hair was piled on top of her head. It felt odd. 'I don't feel like me. I feel like an impostor,' she said. 'And, to be honest, I'm finding this a bit scary.'

'You've got old,' said Carol.

'Nah,' said Nell. 'Everybody here has got young. All the girls look about sixteen.'

'Christ,' said Carol. 'I'm eighteen and past it.'

They got a couple of drinks and stood at the edge of the dance floor looking disinterested. They revived the old sneer when a couple of passing boys gave them a dismissive glance and said, 'Christ, it must be grannies' night.' They danced together, got jostled, couldn't make themselves heard above the shouts and squeals, and felt horribly out of place. Eventually, they retired to a table on the balcony and sat looking critically down at the mayhem below.

'It was never like this in our day,' said Nell. 'It's got wilder. Drunker. There're men fighting in the middle of the dance floor. They used to take their battles outside. And girls are fighting, too.'

'There were always girls fighting,' said Carol.

'Yes, they'd hit one another with their handbags, scratch and scream and cry. But look, they're actually punching one another, actual fists flying. I don't know . . . the youth of today are out of control.'

'Yeah,' said Carol, 'but the band's still rubbish. It's good to find something hasn't changed. Don't think I'll come back, though.'

'I think I'll go home. I need a pee first, coming?' asked Nell.

Carol said she'd have one last trip around the edge

of the dance floor; one last look at the glitter ball. 'I'm just going to say goodbye to it all. I'm a grown-up now. See you at the door.'

Nell tottered down the stairs and into the corridor leading to the cloakroom. A couple of men were fighting; it was an intense and bitter struggle, heavy breathing, no words, only the thick sound of grunts and gasps of pain. Fighting in real life was nothing like Hollywood fighting. In films men danced round one another throwing punches that landed neatly on their opponent's jaw. But actual fights weren't like that. These two men were locked in a heaving grapple. It was hard to see what was going on. Still, this wasn't an unusual sight at the Locarno on a Saturday night.

Nell ignored them and went to the loo. She did her usual skilled peeing, keeping her handbag on her knee and her feet off the floor. She sprayed fresh lacquer on her hair and applied a layer of pink fizz lipstick and gazed at her face. Tonight she didn't look beautiful; she looked tired and disappointed. And sex had done something to her face. It was thinner; more knowing. She liked that, though.

As she came back out she glanced at the fighters. Now one man was slumped on the floor. The other man was standing over him. He stared at Nell. He was one of the hard men, as she called them. There was always a gang of them at the Locarno. Bigger and broader than the normal boys, they moved their shoulders as they walked, shoving people aside. They wore sharp suits, tailor-made. They were the best sneerers and drinkers. They swore. They swaggered. They carried knives. Nell had danced with one of them once. He'd shoved his hand up her skirt, stroked her in her secret place, leaned into her and whispered, 'I'll give you the best fuck of your life.' He'd laughed when she ran away.

There was something odd about the way the man on the floor was lying – something silent and final; a weird dull stillness. Nell's blood curdled, a thick chill ran over her scalp and a shrill wave of nerves shuddered through her stomach. The man on the floor was dead. Nell just knew it.

For a moment, Nell and the other man stood, eyes locked. They didn't speak. Then he ran, pushed passed her and disappeared into the throng on the dance floor. Nell stepped nearer to the man on the floor and bent close. He wasn't breathing. His mouth was open and his eyes were staring. Her hand hovered over him but she couldn't bring herself to touch him. She turned and ran.

When she found Carol at the front door, she grabbed her arm. 'Let's get out of here.'

Outside, Nell hailed a taxi that was drawing up. 'My treat. I can't face walking home.' As they climbed in, the man who'd ran away into the crowd came out, grabbed the door handle, yelling 'Hey, this is my taxi, you stupid bitch.' The driver locked the door and pulled away from the kerb. Looking out the back window, Nell could see the man standing in the middle of the road still shouting and throwing curses at them.

Nell spent the ride watching the road behind them, checking they weren't being followed. She convinced herself that the killer had gone to find his friends. They'd come after her and threaten her. She'd seen such things in the movies. She told the driver to drop them several streets from her house. She said she needed some fresh air. But actually, she didn't want any followers seeing where she lived. She couldn't see anyone behind her, but you never knew. These sorts of hoodlums were good at sneaking after people without being spotted.

On Monday, Nell read the newspaper but could find nothing about a death at the Locarno. Nor was there anything the next day, or the next. The police were probably keeping it quiet as they investigated. Perhaps someone had seen her. Now the police might be looking for a woman in a pink dress and white shoes who could help them with their inquiries. Nell shoved the dress and shoes into a paper bag and, on the way to work one day, dropped them into a litterbin. For weeks she kept looking behind her, fearing that *the man* was coming after her. At night she peered out of her bedroom window, checking that he wasn't lurking in the shadows across the road, watching the house. She worried that the police would trace her and turn up at her door. She would deny she'd been at the Locarno.

She never told anybody about what she'd seen. She shuddered to think of herself caught up in such a sordid affair. In films, she'd seen terrible things happen to witnesses. They were humiliated and harangued in the witness box. She imagined herself sobbing as a bewigged and begowned man pointed at her, 'Admit it, Miss McClusky. You are a slut and a harlot who only goes to the Locarno to pick up men.' Her mother, father and Alistair in the public gallery would gasp in shock. Worse, that man, *the man,* might find her and threaten her. He'd hold a knife to her throat. 'Squeal and you're dead.' Every night, lying in bed, clutching her pillow, she ran these scenarios through her mind and lay staring wide-eyed with fear into the dark, working herself into a panic.

All that, and Alistair would find out where she'd been. He'd think she'd gone to pick up a boy for the night. Why else would anyone go there? He might drop her. He surely wouldn't want to be involved with a woman who was caught up in such squalid dealings. All her plans would be lost. All her hard work – the black clothes, the books read, the nights at poetry readings and French films – would have been for nothing. 'To hell with that,' she said, and decided never to tell anybody what she'd seen.

Chapter Three
Late

The Boheme, a coffee bar, was now *the* place to be seen on a Thursday night. The walls were adorned with huge multi-coloured murals of people – young people – jiving. The booths were red mock leather. A spiral staircase led to the inner depths, and descending it, one hand on the rail, Nell felt special, like a film star. Tonight she wore her tight black pants and a huge cream turtleneck sweater. Though it was February, and cold, she didn't wear a coat; it would have spoiled the look. She went to the bar to buy two frothy coffees while Carol slipped into a booth. The jukebox played Del Shannon.

When Nell joined her, Carol didn't even give her a chance to gaze round the room, eye the faces in other booths, check the boys, or make sure that none of the girls looked more interesting than she did.

'I'm late,' Carol said.

Nell didn't understand. 'Late for what?'

'What do you think? I haven't had a period for two months.'

Nell leant forward and gasped a dramatic intake of breath. 'No. Oh, shit, Carol.'

'I know. It's awful. Every morning I wake up and I feel OK for a minute or two, then I remember and I'm a wreck. I'm shaking.'

Nell put her hand on Carol's. 'Poor thing.'

'Then I'm sick every morning and my tits are sore. I feel like I'm living in a black tunnel. I'm scared. I've got constant butterflies in my tummy.' She put her hand on her stomach, demonstrating where the over-active butterflies were. Grimaced.

Nell asked what Johnny thought of all this.

'He says it's a fine time to have lots of sex. Now I'm up the spout, I can't get more up the spout.'

'Well, that's true, I suppose,' said Nell. She didn't think he sounded very sympathetic, but it was interesting to note that being pregnant was indeed an excellent contraceptive.

'We're going to do the hot bath and gin thing on Saturday night. His folks are going to a charity ball. Won't be back till late.'

Nell had heard girls at work talking about the hot bath and gin thing, but wasn't sure what it entailed: sitting in a bath filled with heated gin?

'What if it doesn't work?' said Carol. 'I could end up in the Bellamy.'

Nell cupped her hand over her mouth. Ending up in the Bellamy was just about the worst thing that could happen to a girl.

Bellamy House was set back off the road and the end of a short drive. For years, Nell and Carol had walked past it on their way to school. A large green

sign at the gate read MATERNITY HOME. It was well
known that this was where unmarried mothers ended
up. That neither Nell nor Carol had the slightest idea
what went on in the home didn't matter; they could
imagine. In time their imaginings became real. Women
in that home were a disgrace. They had to wear rough
smocks and scrub floors. They were fed on bread and
water. When their babies were due, they were tied to
their beds. The cries of women in labour could be heard
for miles around. They hadn't heard any cries, but
assumed that was because they happened at night when
most babies seemed to be born.

They had, on their journey to school, talked about
the business of giving birth. Their conversations spurred
to great heights of fantasy since they knew nothing
about it. They knew how babies got in to their mother's
wombs. But the details of how they actually came out
were a mystery. From the information they'd gleaned
from the movies, they knew it involved some sweating
and screaming. The films they'd seen mostly showed
fathers pacing and smoking and looking pale with
anxiety. Sometimes the father was drunk. If the birth
was in a remote cabin, it involved a plump bossy neighbour boiling gallons of water. Nell and Carol shuddered
to think what that water was for. 'Do they pour it over
you? They can't dunk the baby in it?' Carol said. Both
decided they didn't want to experience the horrors of
the labour ward. They didn't want babies.

Nell drifted off, dreaming of life in Bellamy House.
She imagined herself there. She'd look like Audrey

Hepburn in *The Nun's Story*: pale but exquisitely beautiful. Suffering would give her eyes a mysterious wisdom. The itchy smock mightn't look too bad if it was cut low round the neck. She looked across at Carol who was pulling on her coat, sniffing and trying not to cry.

'Let's get out of here,' Carol said. 'This coffee is making me nauseous. I should have had a Coke. I've got a craving for fizzy drinks.'

They walked along Princes Street gazing into shop windows sighing at things they couldn't afford – mostly shoes since other things made Carol realise that if the gin and hot bath didn't work, she wouldn't be able to get into them. They stopped to stare at some people getting out of a chauffeur-driven car and strolling past the uniformed doorman into the North British Hotel, and dreamed of the plushness awaiting them. 'Thick carpets, drinks with ice in, a phone by your bed,' said Carol. 'One day that'll be me.'

They walked down Leith Walk and decided to spend their bus money on chips from the Deep Sea.

Once they'd paid for their chips, a bag apiece, they headed home, eating in comfortable silence. When they'd finished, they linked arms, and with unspoken mutual consent burst out singing 'Bye Bye Love', which was a favourite they'd long practised harmonising. There was comfort in cherished songs.

The next Sunday, Nell's mother stopped her as she was going out the front door.

'It's February! You'll catch your death going out like that.'

Nell said she was fine and, anyway, she was just going round the corner to see Carol.

'But sandals?' It's freezing out. And that jumper's hanging off you.'

'That's the style.'

'I don't care if it's the style. What's the point of a jumper if it doesn't keep the cold out?'

Nell sighed, shoved her hands in her pockets and looked down at the floor. Her mother reached forward, took hold of the jumper and hauled it up over Nell's shoulder.

Nell pulled it back down again. 'It's *meant* to be off the shoulder.'

'You can see your bra strap. It's almost indecent. And sandals at this time of year? Your feet will get filthy and you've painted your toenails. Only sluts and hussies do that.'

Nell sighed again. She jiggled her knee impatiently, desperate to get away. There were important goings on in her life to be discussed. Things she couldn't possibly tell her mother. The two stared at one another. There was no understanding between them. They didn't speak much.

The kitchen smelled of cooking fat and the sausages the family had just eaten. And bleach. It always smelled of bleach. Mrs McClusky went through two bottles a week. She waged a daily war on filth and germs. The room was as it had been all Nell's life. Never in this house (except for the television a couple of years ago) was anything new added or anything old thrown out. Every evening, within minutes of the meal being finished, the dishes were cleared, washed, dried and put away, the draining board vigorously wiped, dishtowels neatly folded and hung up on the rail beside the sink. 'There,' Mrs McClusky would say, 'I can relax now.' She was a violent vacuumer, fierce duster and energetic wiper. Her life revolved round things she understood: the cake shop, gossip and cleaning. Her daughter was a mystery.

Everything about Nell – the girl's clothes, musical taste and strange notions – took Nancy by surprise. Last night at supper, over fried egg and chips, Nell had said, 'We never talk when we eat.'

Her father had pointed at his mouth, busy with a couple of yolk-dunked chips, and said, 'Eating's too important to bother with talking. Besides, it's rude to talk with your mouth full.'

Nancy had helped herself to a slice of bread, and said, 'What would you like to talk about, dear?'

'We could discuss philosophy,' said Nell. 'Like Simone de Beauvoir and Jean-Paul Sartre.'

'Who?' asked Nancy. 'Do they live around here? They sound French.'

'They are French,' said Nell. 'They are philosophers and writers.' She imagined them drinking wine, eating fabulous food and intently discussing art and life. She didn't suppose they ate fried egg and chips very often. She didn't imagine they ever said anything ordinary like we need more toothpaste, or is there anything good on telly tonight?

Nancy and Stewart looked at one another and raised their eyebrows and Nancy said, 'Pass the tomato sauce.'

In fact, Nell's very existence baffled Nancy. How did she get here? How did she happen? It was a surprise. It certainly wasn't planned. Mrs Lowrie, two doors down, was to blame.

In 1941, Stewart McClusky was working as a coalman. War was raging in Europe, but he was too old to fight. Instead, he joined the Home Guard. Nancy did her bit: she grew vegetables in the back garden and worked with the Women's Voluntary Service, gathering books, cakes and other goodies to send to troops overseas. In the evenings, she knitted socks, also to be sent to overseas, while listening to the wireless. The pair had been married for fifteen years by then and hadn't produced a child, They'd finally given up trying, which was a bitter disappointment to Stewart and a bit of a relief to his wife.

One night Stewart rolled into bed at four in the morning. He'd had a hard night. There had been a raid on the Forth Bridge, bombers droning overhead, but, tired as he was, he couldn't sleep. He'd turned to Nancy to tell her about all he'd seen and done.

Earlier that day, Nancy had invited Mrs Lowrie, whose husband was at home on leave, into the house for a cup of tea. Mrs Lowrie had complained of being exhausted. 'Didn't get much sleep last night. But you know, there's a war on, men are fighting for their country and us women have to do their bit to keep them happy.'

In bed, as the first glimmer of dawn seeped round the edges of the curtains and Stewart reached for her breast, Nancy McClusky remembered her neighbour's words and allowed her husband his first bit of intimacy in years. It lasted only minutes, but he rolled over and slipped into a deep, satisfied sleep. She lay awake watching the day arrive, wondering what all the fuss over sex was about.

Three months later Nancy went to the doctor. 'I haven't had my monthlies for a while,' she said.

He asked how old she was.

'Forty-seven.'

'Well,' he said, 'I think you know what that's all about. You're going through the change. Just have a rest if you get all hot and flustered. When it's over you'll be right as rain and full of energy.'

Five months later, Nancy once again went to the doctor. 'I've got terrible heartburn,' she said. 'Can't sleep for it. And I'm putting on weight even though I'm hardly eating.'

He told her to pop up on the bench while he took a look at her. He checked her blood pressure, pummelled her stomach. And, to her horror, gave her an internal examination before congratulating her. 'Well done, you're pregnant.'

'I'm what?' she said.

'You're going to have a baby. Bit late, I know. But it happens.'

Mr McClusky had reacted in the same way as his wife, 'You're what?'

'Pregnant,' she told him again. 'I haven't thought about having a baby in years. I'd forgotten I ever wanted one.'

A month later, Nell was born, red and screaming and bursting with life. And there she was standing now in the kitchen, which was exactly as it had been when Mrs Lowrie had stood in it drinking tea and complaining about how exhausted she was.

Nell, with her sandals and her painted toenails and her man's jeans bought from the Army and Navy stores and her jumper that slipped off her left shoulder and showed her perfect young skin and her bra strap and her long hair that hid her lovely face. Who was she? How did she happen? And why was she nothing like the little girl who had worn pink frocks and stood on a chair by the sink helping with the dishes? God, she'd loved that little girl – the feel of her body against hers when she carried her. And how she'd carried her, never wanted to put her down, the soft breathing in her ear, the child's endless questions, and the little hand in hers. The way that little girl had trusted her completely. Now she was rarely home; a stranger who seemed to disapprove of her.

'Oh, away you go,' said Nancy now. 'But don't come crying to me when you catch double pneumonia after traipsing about the streets in the freezing cold dressed in nothing at all.'

Nell fled.

*

Carol's house smelled of carpets. They'd just been fitted, wall-to-wall, in every room. They even stretched all the way up the stairs, soft under Nell's feet as she climbed to Carol's bedroom. She burst in. 'Well?'

'Didn't work,' said Carol. 'I'm still up the bloody spout.' She considered Nell. 'Look at you. Jeans and a long black jumper. Your hair's all straight and hanging down. You're hardly you at all these days.'

'I know. I'm more like Juliette Greco.' Seeing Carol's baffled face, she explained. 'A French singer. Sort of bohemian. Anyway, some men find this look very sexy. They ask if I'm French and they think I'm mysterious.' She sat on Carol's bed. 'Your mum says she'll bring up coffee and biscuits.'

Carol's mum was Nell's idea of a perfect mum. She was pretty and always cheery. 'Carol's in her room, love. Just pop up. I'll bring you coffee in a while,' she'd said. It always touched Nell somewhere in the depths of her to be treated so affectionately. There was no tenderness in her own home. In the evenings, they watched television in silence. Then, at half-past ten her mother would make a pot of tea and bring it through to the living room. After that, and after the cups had been washed and put away, it was bedtime. Fire tamped down, lights out and upstairs they all went. Nell would lie in bed, blankets over her head and listen to Radio Luxemburg. It was her favourite time of day – her dreaming time – listening to songs on the radio.

'And what do you say,' asked Carol, 'when men think you're French?'

Nell was sitting on the floor, legs stretched out in front of her. 'I don't say anything. If I did they'd find out I'm not French and I'm not mysterious at all. They'd find out that I'm just me.'

'So what do you do if you don't speak?'

'I have this little smile. Took ages to get it right. But I look sort of pleased and knowing.' She demonstrated the smile.

'Great smile,' said Carol. 'I don't know why you do it, though. What's wrong with being you?'

'I need to be more than just me,' said Nell. 'Being me isn't enough.' She turned to gaze at herself in the dresser mirror, and did the smile again. When she turned back, Carol had hitched up her skirt and was running gentle fingers down a row of savage blisters on her legs.

'Jesus, your legs are all burned,' Nell looked at them in horror.

'I did it in the bath. The blisters on my bum are the worst. Johnny held me in while he kept the hot tap on. I didn't feel it at the time on account of being drunk on gin. Didn't work.'

'Didn't you use anything, you know, when the pair of you . . . you know?'

'Johnny won't. He says it spoils it. It's like washing your feet with your socks on.'

Nell said that was plain stupid. 'You can't take chances.'

'I've tried everything,' said Carol. 'I've been lifting heavy boxes at work. I've jumped off park benches. Then last night, in Johnny's house, I sat in a boiling hot bath drinking gin. I drank almost a whole bottle. And I was so drunk and hot I couldn't get out of the bath. My head was pounding. I was in that bath for two hours. Burned my legs it was so hot.'

'Carol, that's awful.' Nell was glad this wasn't happening to her.

'So,' said Carol, 'I was crying and crying and screaming out. But Johnny kept telling me to stay put while he added more hot water. Then, when I did get out, all blistered and drunk and crying, I had to clean up the bathroom. It was all steamy. My hair went lank and my mascara ran. After that we had to drive about with the roof down in his car, so I'd sober up. It was freezing. . . And I'm *still* up the spout!'

'So now what are you going to do?'

They heard the soft fall of Carol's mum's footsteps coming up the stairs with a tray of coffee and biscuits. Carol pulled her skirt down, jerked her head in the direction of the door. Time to shut up.

Mrs Anderson shoved the door open with her hip, stepped into the room and looked at the two. 'Guilty faces. What have you two been doing?'

In unison they answered, 'Nothing.'

Nell took the tray, as it would have been painful for Carol to stand up, and set it on the floor. She desperately wanted Mrs Anderson to go away; she was, after all, in the middle of the most fascinating conversation of her life. Mrs Anderson obliged, but the two remained silent, staring at one another, bursting to talk, until they heard the living room door downstairs shut.

Carol leaned forward, whispered, 'I'm going to see this man Johnny found out about. Dr Low. He can fix it.'

'You're not going to have an abortion?'

'Nah,' said Carol. 'He wouldn't do it anyway. He says he'll see me and give me something. Forty pounds. Johnny gave me the money.' She took a tight roll of notes out of her skirt pocket. 'You've got to come with me.' She started to eat a chocolate biscuit. 'I can't stop eating. It's the worry.' She looked at Nell. 'That's all I do – eat and cry. I'm scared.'

'Why doesn't Johnny take you? He got you into this.'

Carol shrugged. 'He hates doctors. He hates all this. He hated last night – all the crying and the mess. You come, please.'

Nell couldn't resist. It was an adventure. Besides, her friend needed her. She said of course she'd go.

Carol took another biscuit. 'This has got to work. What am I going to do if it doesn't? I'll have to tell my mother.' There were tears when she said this. 'She'll go off her head.' Carol chewed her biscuit, her face crumpled. Shoulders heaving, melted biscuit seeping down her chin, she gave into serious weeping.

Two days later, they met after work and took the bus to Leith. They sat on the upper deck, Carol jiggling with nerves, complaining about butterflies in her stomach. 'What do you suppose he'll give me?'

'A pill, I expect,' said Nell.

'Then the baby will just go away?'

'I expect,' said Nell. She had no idea what she was talking about.

The doctor's house overlooked the Links, and was, to Nell's surprise, large and elegant. She'd been expecting a small sleazy flat up a dank stairway, ill lit and reeking of damp. But this place was behind a wall and had a wide gravel path leading to the front door. Nell rang the bell. They heard steps coming nearer and nearer from what seemed like a long way off and giggled nervously.

Dr Low was small, round, white-haired and, Nell thought, like a kindly uncle or Santa Claus. He patted Carol's hand and told her not to worry. 'I've helped hundreds of young ladies in your condition.' He indicated to Nell to wait in a small front room while he and Carol went for a little chat. As she was led away, Carol looked back in alarm at her friend. Nell waved, and then felt foolish.

She sat on a cracked and creaking leather sofa, thumbing through a copy of the *Reader's Digest*. A clock ticked, buses passed by on the road outside, from some distant part of the house came kitchen sounds – the clink of crockery, pots banging. The faint waft of onions cooking drifted up the hall. A small, slightly shrivelled old woman appeared at the door. 'All right, dear?'

Nell said she was.

The woman told her the doctor would be with her soon.

Nell was shocked. 'Oh, this isn't me. I'm not here. I mean it's my friend who is seeing the doctor. I'm just keeping her company.'

The woman nodded and disappeared as silently as she'd arrived. Nell started to worry. This place was unnerving. The clock seemed to be ticking louder than it had been before. She started to sweat. Carol was in trouble. She should find her and help her escape. What if that man murdered her? The police would come and she'd be arrested for being an accomplice in seeking an illicit abortion. She could be sent to prison. She stood up and was considering running away when she heard the two coming back down the long lino-covered hall.

When the doctor entered the room he signalled for Nell to sit down again. 'A wee word,' he said.

Behind his back, Carol stuck out her tongue and jabbed her finger into her mouth, feigning being sick. Nell revised her opinion of the man. He looked nothing like Santa Claus. His face was red and glistened with sweat. He wheezed. His black suit was stained and old. He was creepy. This house was creepy. Nell wanted to get out.

The doctor opened a large dresser behind the sofa, took out a small brown bottle and gave it to Carol. 'Three months,' he said. 'You've left it a bit late. I'd have been happier with two, but this will do the trick. This will shift it. It's stronger than my usual mix and I don't give it out often but I hate to see you young ladies in such distress. That'll be forty pounds.'

Carol pulled the money from her pocket and handed it to him.

'Now you must understand the effect this will have on you. Don't touch a drop till you get home. And take the lot all at once or it won't work. Don't go out after you've taken it, and make sure you have access to a lavatory. Don't be alarmed at what happens. It's just the way of things. Life is messy. And don't tell anybody where you got this mixture.'

Carol said she understood and headed for the door.

'Not yet, young lady. I think we must have a little chat about how you got into your current condition. I don't want you coming here again. May I suggest that in future you and your young man—' he turned to Nell '—and indeed *you* and your young man, if you have one, refrain from sexual intercourse?'

Nell blushed. Carol's jaw dropped.

'There are many ways of pleasuring yourselves without going all the way. I suggest you restrict yourselves to mutual masturbation for the moment.'

The two girls gasped, looked at one another, wide-eyed in horror. They never spoke about things like this to anyone, and certainly not to anybody as old as this man. Old people shouldn't know about this. It was disgusting. Nell's blush deepened. They barged towards the door. Didn't pause to say thanks.

Arm-in-arm, they fled down the drive, walking faster and faster, till they hit the pavement. Then they ran. Nell was in front, heels clicking, puffing silently at first.

Then, a squeal from Carol, a shriek from Nell, and

they were both sprinting and screaming. They hurtled through the chill evening away from the doctor's house. Every so often, they stopped to pant and heave and clutch one another and squeal, 'Oh God!' Then they were off, running again, working off their shock and putting some distance between them and the disgusting old man.

Spent, they flopped onto a park bench, and sat side-by-side, gasping. Their throats were raw from squealing. They could hardly speak. They looked at one another, panting and swearing, 'Jesus, oh God, bloody hell.'

'He was a dirty old man,' Carol said when at last she could speak.

'I know,' said Nell. She squirmed in disgust.

'He made me lie on this bench thing while he pummelled my tummy. Then he poked at me.'

'What do you mean, poked?'

'With his fingers. Down there. Inside.' Carol buried her face in her hands and drummed her feet on the ground, exorcising the memory.

'No,' said Nell. 'He didn't. He's not meant to do that. It's not right.'

'He said I was about fourteen weeks gone and shouldn't have left it so long before coming to see him.'

'Well, at least he gave you something.'

Carol fished the bottle out of her bag, opened it and held it to her nose. 'Doesn't smell of anything.' She handed it to Nell who took a sniff and agreed.

Carol took the bottle back and peered at the contents. 'It's very oily. It looks serious.'

'It'll do the trick,' said Nell.

'Definitely,' Carol agreed.

The night was cold; the air damp and smelled of coal fires. Across the park some children were playing, calling through the gloom; buses lit up against the dark rumbled past. The first stars were out.

'I'll be fine, now,' Carol said quietly. 'This will work.'

'For forty quid it better.'

'Too right,' said Carol. They stood up to go home and linked arms.

'Let's get some chips first,' said Nell.

Chapter Four
They've Had Their Fun

Eleven o'clock the next night, Carol's mother and father, Margaret and Norman, walked up the garden path to the front door. They'd been to the cinema to see *North by Northwest*. Margaret was wondering where she could get Norman a grey suit like Cary Grant's. Norman was looking forward to a cup of tea and a slice of sponge cake before bed. The house was dark, not a single light burning. Margaret thought that odd, but didn't remark on it. Carol must have gone to bed early.

She froze when she stepped inside the front door, sniffed the air. 'Something's wrong.'

She was a woman who lived by instincts and intuition. She could taste and smell trouble. She could feel it on her skin. She could interpret a hundred different types of silence, just by listening and breathing it in. 'Something's definitely wrong,' she said. She took off her coat, handed it to Norman and took the stairs two at a time.

Carol was in bed, curled up, clutching her stomach, shivering and groaning.

Margaret went to her, put her hand on her forehead. 'You've picked up something awful.'

Carol threw back the covers, dragged herself to her feet, and shouted, 'Not again.' She rushed past Margaret, out of the room and down the hall to the loo.

Margaret followed her, rapped on the bathroom door. 'Don't be sick in the sink.'

She went downstairs, put on the kettle. 'Poor girl's got some sort of tummy bug.'

Waiting for the kettle to boil, Margaret considered the bottle Carol had left on the draining board. She held it to her nose, sniffed. Touched the rim with her finger and cautiously tasted the tiny drop she'd collected. 'Castor oil.' Her bewilderment lasted but seconds.

She stamped back upstairs, shouting, 'Carol! Carol!'

Her daughter, drained, pale and shivering, was crawling towards her bedroom. Margaret blocked her way, held up the bottle. 'Have you taken this?'

Carol nodded. She pleaded for her mother to get out of the way. 'I need to get to bed.'

'Castor oil,' said Margaret. 'You've drunk a whole bottle of castor oil.'

'It's not castor oil,' said Carol. 'It's . . . medicine.'

'Don't tell me what is or what isn't castor oil. I know castor oil when I see it.' She bent down, heaved Carol to her feet and helped her to bed. 'And I know why young girls take it. How far gone are you?'

'Three and a bit months.'

'You stupid, stupid, stupid girl.'

*

It was two days before Margaret phoned May Rutherford. First she had to calm down, drink umpteen cups of tea, pace the living room, arms folded, quizzing her daughter. 'Why didn't you come to me,' she asked.

'There are some things you don't tell your mother,' said Carol. 'Being pregnant's one of them. It's the main one.'

'But going to that man on your own? It must have been awful for you.'

Carol shrugged. 'It wasn't so bad.' She never did admit to her mother that Nell went with her. It wasn't so much that she didn't want to get Nell in trouble. More, she didn't want to confess to anything that might dilute the sympathy she was getting. She rather liked the image of herself, scared, numb with nerves and desperate, going to see a dubious man to buy an even more dubious remedy for her condition.

Eventually, Margaret took Carol to see Dr Bain, the family doctor. She sat in the waiting room staring at peeling wallpaper, leafing with disinterest through a three-year-old magazine while Carol was in the consulting room. When the doctor appeared at the door and beckoned her with his finger to join him and her daughter, she knew she was going to be a grandmother.

When she did phone May Rutherford, she was curt but polite. 'It appears,' said Margaret, 'that our Carol is three months pregnant. Your son is the father.'

May said, 'Johnny? Is your Carol sure? I mean, she might have been seeing someone else.'

'Of course she's sure. And he's sure too. He gave her forty pounds to go see some quack who took the money in exchange for a bottle of castor oil.'

May was silent for a few moments, and then said, 'Oh God, the old castor oil trick. Brings back some hellish memories. It's always the women who suffer.'

'Indeed.' Margaret heard May remove the receiver from her ear and yell, 'Johnny, get your backside down here. Now!'

A week later, the two sets of parents met at the Rutherford's house to discuss the situation. Carol and Johnny were not included as their opinions were immaterial. They'd had their fun, May Rutherford said, 'Now, it's up to us to pick up the pieces.'

They ate roast beef, drank red wine from crystal glasses while Johnny Mathis crooned in the background. A huge fire roared in the fireplace. Margaret Anderson said the house was lovely, that the roast beef was perfect, and that, no, she didn't want any more Brussels sprouts. She thought May bossy and a show-off, and Harry too jolly by far.

Nobody mentioned the castor oil.

'Well,' said May, refilling everyone's glass. 'This is a fine mess our two children have got themselves into.'

'Happens all the time,' said Harry. 'They were having a bit of fun. Nothing we didn't do.'

May glared at him and told Margaret and Norman

to help themselves. 'There's plenty more and apple pie for afters.' She put down her fork. 'I've spoken to the hotel down the road and they'll give us a discount on account of it only being March and things are a bit quiet. The wedding business hots up next month. Now, what I thought was, if you two pay for the wedding, we'll put down the deposit on a bungalow for Johnny and Carol to live in. There's one for sale round the corner, so I'll be nearby to help with the baby.'

Margaret said nothing. The house was too hot. The room was too bright. These people knew nothing about grief and young ruined lives. She did. Had this not been her almost twenty years ago? She knew well the black tide of gloom and worry that came with being unwed and pregnant. She remembered the days of waking every morning gripped by nerves, raddled with shame and guilt and dread.

In 1940 Margaret had conceived a child to a soldier called Angus. Oh, the heated pleasure of those nights with him: the touching; the whispering; the kissing. He was all she thought about. And once she'd discovered sex, she'd wondered how people could go about their day-to-day business when they could be doing that instead. Sex was wonderful; it was magical. It had made her heady. The passion had lasted for two weeks before Angus was posted to North Africa.

A month later, Margaret had missed a period. A worm of worry had gnawed at her. A month on, she'd missed another period. Now, she'd been sure. The worry had flared into full-time fretting. She'd written to Angus telling him there was a baby on the way. He'd written back telling her to hang on; he'd marry her as soon as he got back. *A baby,* he'd written. *I hope it has your looks and your brains, too.*

Norman had brought Margaret the news. Angus had died. He'd taken her for a walk, sat her on a park bench, held her hand and told her the telegram had been delivered to Angus' mother that morning. He'd watched her weep, given her his handkerchief and waited for the sobbing to stop.

'Angus wrote to me,' he'd said. 'Told me to watch out for you till he came back.' Then, 'I'll marry you, if you want. I'll say the baby's mine. Nobody need ever know.'

A quiet, kindly soul, ten years older than Margaret, he'd raised Carol as his own, with never a word of complaint. She hadn't told anybody, not even her own daughter, about this.

Margaret wondered if getting pregnant outside of marriage was a family trait. Perhaps reckless passion was in the blood. If Carol had a daughter, would it happen to her, too? Some women thought getting married and having a child was the beginning of everything. It was what life was about. Margaret thought it had been the narrowing of her world. She'd dreamed of travelling, had hoped she might become a teacher. But her life had become a series of routines: washing, ironing, dusting, cooking and shopping. She thought she'd become dull. For almost twenty years she'd been grateful to Norman. Sometimes she'd catch him looking at her; it was the gaze of someone too much in love, weakened by adoration. She knew he thought he was not worthy of her, that he was second best. Lying awake at night, listening to him breathe, she thought they were fools. They'd spent their married lives being polite. They should have talked more. They should have explored each other, taken time to fall in love. They should both have looked for, and demanded, passion.

Now her beautiful daughter was to marry that conceited boy with his flashy car and his silly clothes and his revolting way of pulling his comb out of his back pocket and slicking it through his stupid hair. He was a bit of a lad for getting a girl into trouble. Carol, who'd allowed herself to get into trouble, was now a woman of low repute: a hussy who'd let a man have his way with her. How unfair it all was.

She glanced at Norman, and saw from the slight smile he gave her that he knew what she was thinking. He always did.

Now, May reached for the wine bottle, refilled her own glass and waved it at her guests, snapping Margaret from her thoughts. 'Top up?'

Margaret shook her head. She feared getting drunk and speaking her mind; she didn't trust herself to be diplomatic.

'I've made up my guest list,' said May. 'Twenty people.'

Margaret thought that excessive, but still kept her mouth shut.

In the end there were thirty guests at the wedding; it wasn't as small as Margaret would have liked. She'd hoped for ten. The reception was in a hotel near the zoo, champagne flowed. The gathering was fed on shrimp cocktail, roast duck with orange sauce and chocolate mousse.

Nell, dressed in a dark-blue velvet suit, was the bridesmaid and Alistair best man. Carol, in a white silk suit and a large white hat bedecked with flowers, looked radiant. But Johnny stole the show. He was jaw-droppingly handsome. The groom was prettier than the bride. He'd recently had his rock'n'roll quiff cut off. Now his hair was short: a flat top he called it. It suited him. It showed off his cheekbones and full lips. Margaret noticed Carol noticing women in the room noticing her new husband. There will be trouble, Margaret thought.

Johnny drank too much. His speech was short and to the point. 'Thanks a bunch for coming,' he said before turning to Carol and spreading his arms to her, smiling and embracing her. 'Thanks a bunch for marrying me.' He raised his glass to her, drained it and sat down. Carol beamed.

Before that, Alistair had said how lucky his big brother was to have such a beautiful bride and he hoped they had many years of happiness before them. He'd sounded doleful. Harry, Alistair and Johnny's father, had saved the day even though as father of the groom he was not meant to give a speech. 'The Rutherfords,' he said, 'are a close and happy clan. We eat, laugh, work and play together. Now my randy son has added not one, but two new Rutherfords to the family.' He'd lifted his glass. 'Nothing keeps a Rutherford down.'

Everyone laughed except Carol's mother who whispered to her husband that she thought the speech inappropriate. She added it was normal to toast the bride and groom, not the groom's family. She was starting to dislike the Rutherfords.

Chapter Five
Family Nights

Thursday nights were family nights at the Rutherford's. Everyone gathered round the table in the dining room and discussed the business: how much money had been made since the previous Thursday; how to make more money; and how to cut corners and spend less money making the money they were making. Neither Nell nor Carol was ever invited.

It was a Thursday in September when Carol went into labour. She'd been having twinges all day and had phoned the hospital, but had been told not to come in till the pains were twenty minutes apart. Her mother had come over for a while in the afternoon, but had gone home before five to cook the supper. 'It could be a false labour,' she'd said. 'Happens all the time. Babies are awkward little things. They never arrive when you expect them to; they pick the most inconvenient moment.'

Half an hour after her mother left, Carol's twinges developed into pains. She paced and put her hand on her lower back. Worried, she phoned the garage to tell Johnny to come home immediately. He wasn't there;

it was his family night habit to go straight to his mother's house where she'd serve vast amounts of food as business was discussed.

Carol phoned the Rutherford home. Nobody answered. No phone calls were allowed to disrupt the important matters of eating and talking money. So Carol walked to the house – slowly, painfully, stopping every now and then to clutch her stomach, keeping the baby in. She feared she might give birth in the street.

Eventually she reached the Rutherfords and rang the bell. Nobody opened the door. The rules about not answering the phone also applied to the doorbell.

Carol let herself in. She shuffled up the hall and burst into the dining room. 'The baby's coming.'

Everyone turned to stare at the interloper. Cigars were being smoked, brandy drunk. The food had been cleared away but the aroma of roast chicken lingered.

The money caught Carol's eye. Bundles and bundles of it stretched the length of the table. Carol stared at it, then at the gathering before shouting, 'For God's sake. I need to go to the hospital.'

Johnny remained motionless, gazing at her, mouth open.

Alistair stood up and came to her, took her arm and led her to the living room.

May was hot on his heels, shouting at Johnny to get up off his backside and take his wife to the maternity unit. 'You're going to be a father.'

Johnny appeared looking pale and glazed.

'He's drunk,' May said, 'Alistair, you'll have to drive.'

They bundled Carol into Alistair's car. There was fuss. There was panic. They left Johnny standing at the front door, still looking pale and glazed. In the rear-view mirror, Alistair saw May smack him on the shoulder and point to the car, plainly chastising him for not getting into it and accompanying his wife to hospital.

At the front desk of the hospital it was obvious why Carol and Alistair were there. She was hugely pregnant, in pain, sweating and anxious. Alistair looked awkward. Carol was trundled off in the wheelchair. Alistair was shown into a waiting room.

He was sitting nervously on an uncomfortable chair when the matron of the maternity ward stuck her head round the door. 'Mr Rutherford?'

'Yes?'

'Why did you leave it so long? Your wife should have been here hours ago. Having a baby is nothing to be casual about.'

Alistair opened his mouth to say that he wasn't Carol's husband. The matron – a woman who rarely allowed herself to be contradicted – raised a silencing hand. 'Your wife wants you to stay. We'll let you know as soon as the baby arrives. Won't be long.'

At two in the morning Alistair was ushered into the ward. Carol was sitting up in bed, looking tired, but beautiful, he thought. The baby was in a bassinette beside her. A nurse lifted her out and handed her to him. 'Say hello to your daughter, Mr Rutherford.'

He glanced at Carol.

'Please,' she mouthed. She wanted a husband here. Right now, anyone would do.

He held the child, whispered hello. Kissed her head. Marvelled at her tiny fingers.

Carol watched. How gentle he was. And so handsome. Some people's beauty grew on you. It wasn't a matter of cheekbones and lips. It was the kindness and intelligence in the features that made them beautiful.

Carol had always envied Nell's taste in fashion. Now she realised that it wasn't just clothes that Nell chose wisely. It was also men.

Alistair came over to her, kissed her cheek, and told her the baby was gorgeous. 'You'd better sleep now. You'll be tired.' He said he'd better let everybody know there was a new little girl in the world.

Watching him go, Carol knew then she'd married the wrong brother.

Chapter Six
What's in the Green Cupboard?

By the time Carol and Johnny became parents Nell had been dating Alistair for almost a year and a half and was a regular at the Rutherford home. 'You're one of us,' they told her. 'Part of the family.' She stayed over at the weekends and often went to their house straight from work on weekdays. Compared to the Rutherfords, the McCluskys were dowdy.

Everything in the McClusky house was old. The meals, nourishing but bland, were eaten in silence. Nancy's culinary repertoire extended to ten recipes – one for every day of the week, one for birthdays or for when visitors appeared, one for Christmas and one for New Year's Day. The family loved one another. They just didn't show it, or mention it.

The Rutherfords were different. New things appeared in the house – kitchen gadgets, towels, lamps, bed linen – almost on a weekly basis. Their meals were lavish. May was a messy, flamboyant and extravagant cook. She presented Nell with food she hadn't known existed: stroganoff; chicken curry; pork cooked in milk. She used ingredients that were strangely new and mysterious to Nell: tomato purée; garlic; turmeric; herbs. May crushed, pounded, chopped, stirred, and flambéed with gusto. Hair tumbling out of her bun, face glistening with sweat, she'd expound to Nell about the state of the world, the battle of the sexes and the wonderful weakness of men.

'Women,' May declared, 'operate from here and here.' She thumped with clenched fist her heart and her stomach. 'Heart and gut. It's all intuition and feelings. Men operate from here and here.' She tapped her head and pointed to her groin. 'They use their minds and their cocks. Nothing more. And they've the cheek to laugh at us women and call us fragile. Hah.'

Nell was dumbfounded. She didn't know that people over the age of twenty-five talked about such things; certainly her mother didn't.

The Rutherfords gathered every evening round the table in the dining room, toasted the back lot, ate, drank, laughed and told exaggerated stories about the day they'd just lived through. Like the McCluskys, they loved one another but the difference was that they showed it. They touched. They hugged. They called each other love or darling or honey. They took Nell's breath away. She wasn't sure if she loved Alistair, but she was infatuated with his family.

She first visited the Rutherfords in the November after she'd started dating Alistair and had been over-awed. 'Ma wants to meet you,' Alistair had said. 'You've to come to dinner on Saturday.'

She'd said she would. But when Alistair had advised

her not to wear anything silly – 'You know, like that jumper that slides off your shoulder' – she'd suspected that this wasn't an invitation. It was a summons. May Rutherford liked to inspect any girlfriends that lasted longer than six months. At the time Nell and Alistair had been together for almost eight.

Nell had gone straight from the shop and had changed out of her working outfit into a simple red dress and black patent leather shoes in the cloakroom before meeting Alistair. 'Good meeting-the-boyfriend's-mother outfit,' he said. 'You'll be fine. Just let her boss you about and she'll love you.'

Nell said she wasn't awfully keen on being bossed about.

'But my mother is good at it. It's her calling. She was born bossy. She bosses everyone and everything. She bosses the plants in the garden, wags her finger at them and dares them not to grow. She's a maestro. Bossing is her art form. People feel privileged to be bossed by her. In fact, if you are in her company, and she doesn't boss you, you feel left out, sort of neglected.'

May had barged up the hall, arms spread. 'Nell, here you are. We've been dying to meet you.' She'd held her by the shoulders, looked her up and down and smiled. 'You're just lovely.' She'd turned to Alistair. 'You've got yourself a good one this time. Alistair says you like Italian, so it's lasagne for supper with baked Alaska for afters. We're going all international tonight.' May was in the habit of announcing her menu to guests as soon as they arrived.

Nell had been swept up the hall and into the living room and introduced to Alistair's father, Harry. He'd stood up, strode to her, and had pumped her hand. He prided himself on his handshake: a firm grip and crisp up up-and-down movement. 'Good to meet you at last, Nell.' He'd waved Nell into a seat by the fire and had said to Alistair, 'She's a corker.' He'd turned back to Nell. 'What'll you have?'

Nell had floundered. She hadn't known what to ask for. At home, her parents kept a bottle of whisky and a bottle of sherry, which were opened once a year, at five to twelve on New Year's Eve. If you were female you got sherry, whisky if you were male. Anyone deviating from this rule caused consternation.

Alistair had said, 'She likes a rum and coke, Dad.'

Harry said, 'Excellent,' and went to the huge drinks cabinet that took up most of the far wall, 'May?' he asked.

'Oh.' She'd flapped her hand. 'I'll have a wee G and T.'

This room was vast, high ceiling, bay window. It was chintzy. May Rutherford was fond of a frill or two. A huge fire had blazed in the hearth. The central heating had been on full blast.

May was taller than Nell had imagined. And she was forceful. She expected nothing more than to get her own way at all times. Her hair had been pulled off her forehead, fixed at the back of her head in an untidy bun; wisps escaped and had hung either side of her face. Her lips had been painted alarmingly red. She would have been daunting, but for her smile and for the concerned way she'd sat on the sofa, hands folded neatly in her lap, leaning towards Nell and asking how her day had been. She'd seemed genuinely interested.

'Good,' Nell had said. 'We were very busy. I like that; you don't notice the time passing.'

May had clapped her hands. 'Good girl. You enjoy a bit of hard work. Nothing else for it in this life. The only thing that'll get you anywhere is good old fashioned down-and-dirty hard graft.'

There was something about this family, Nell had thought. They were down-to-earth, energetic, enthusiastic, easy to get along with and utterly, fabulously rich. May, though, was clearly the boss: a throaty-voiced, over-active despot in this chintzy, overheated world.

As they had taken their seats at the dining-room table, Alistair had nudged Nell. 'Ma must like you; she's put out the posh glasses.'

They were May's pride and joy, fine gold-rimmed crystal glasses that only the privileged drank from and the very trustworthy were permitted to wash.

Before they'd started eating, May had filled everybody's glass and had sat back nodding to Harry. He'd risen, lifted his glass, looked round at the gathering and shouted, 'To the back lot.' Everyone repeated the toast, Nell included, though she hadn't a clue what they were talking about.

The meal had gone well. May had fussed. She'd bustled to and from the kitchen carrying overflowing dishes, heaping food onto plates, insisting that everyone eat. 'C'mon, Nell, have some more lasagne. Put some meat on your bones. You're too thin.'

She'd kept glasses topped up, and all the while, had quizzed Nell about her family.

'We're not well off,' Nell had said. 'Compared to you, we're poor.'

Alistair had sighed, slapped his forehead and said, 'Don't mention poor to my mum. She's a world expert on being poor.'

May had taken a swig of her wine, and then had pointed at Nell with her fork. 'Do you have electricity? Is your bathroom indoors? Do you eat regularly?'

Nell said, 'Yes.'

'Then you're not poor,' May had replied. 'Me, my mother and three brothers lived in two rooms. My father buggered off when I was three. Never saw him again. We'd no electricity. The bathroom was two floors down and across a muddy back yard. If you needed to go in the middle of the night, you didn't. You crossed your legs and hung on. There were rats. Often the only thing I had to eat was a slice of bread and the top of one of my brother's boiled egg. I went barefoot in the summer. In winter, I wore hand-me-downs. We burned the furniture to keep warm and when that was finished, we burned the door. Cold; I've known cold. I'll never let myself be cold again.' She glared at Alistair who was playing a melancholy tune on a pretend violin. 'Oh, you can mock me. You've never been cold or hungry in your life. If you had, you'd know the fear of being poor. It's humiliating. Nell, eat your lasagne and have some more salad. And leave some room for your pudding.'

When the meal had ended, May had waved Harry and Alistair away from the table. 'Take your coffee and drinks through to the living room. Nell and me'll clear up. C'mon, Nell. I'll wash, you dry.'

Until that evening, Nell hadn't thought about kitchens. She'd never considered them to be beautiful, and had never thought of lingering in one. In fact, it was a relief to leave the kitchen at home. Walking out of that room meant that the dreary business of preparing food and clearing up after that food had been eaten was over. It was time to relax.

May's kitchen was large. She'd swelled with pride as she stepped into it. 'This is where I'm really me,' she'd said. 'This room makes me happy.'

Food was cooked on a huge range. Copper pots hung from the ceiling; herbs grew in pots on the window sill. One wall was lined with shelves containing over two hundred cookbooks. Nell's mother had one cookbook, a battered, splattered collection of wartime recipes, which she rarely opened.

May was a passionate cook. Food and love were one for her. A well-fed family was a happy family. The surest route to anyone's heart was through the stomach. 'Well, most of the time,' she said. She had nudged Nell and winked. 'But, your children would grow to walk away from you, if you made them face the day on nothing more than the top of a boiled egg.' Hungry families fought. She knew this; it was a knowledge that moved through May's veins, beat with her heart and rested in her bones.

The far wall of the kitchen was made up of floor-to-ceiling cupboards, each one with a door painted one of the colours of the rainbow. They were packed with food. Nell had never seen so much in her life.

The yellow cupboard had been filled with packets of pasta, rice, flour, sugar, lentils, packets of tea, jars of coffee; the red full of tins: meat, tuna, fruit and vegetables; the blue, jams and jellies; the orange door fronted a fridge stuffed with cream, butter, cold meats, milk, and wine. Behind the violet door was a packed freezer. The green door was locked. Nell had asked what was in this cupboard. May had replied that it was her little secret.

'I like to see my family fed,' she'd said. She'd filled the sink with hot water and set about washing the plates. 'What do you think of Alistair?'

'He's very nice.'

'Nice? Nice? Don't mention nice to me. I don't like it. It's a mean little word, tepid, means nothing. Alistair's a good, kind, gentle soul. He is a bit logical, I admit. But then most men are. It's one of their failings.'

She'd told Nell to pile the dried plates on the counter. 'I'll put them away later. See, men think in straight lines. Women think in curves. It makes them rounder people. Do you like men, Nell?'

Nell had said she did.

'I like men. They're handy. I like a man in my bed. But I don't like them in my kitchen when I'm cooking.

They always want to know what I'm making. And they hang about watching me and nibbling at things. I like a clear run between the sink, the chopping board and the cooker. And I don't like men to see my mistakes, like if I drop something on the floor and pick it up and put it on the plate. Men don't like that. Men are afraid of two things—' she'd held up two fingers encased in orange Marigold gloves '—bossy women and germs. Remember that.' She'd started washing the cutlery. 'When we're done, I'll show you my family albums. And leave them glasses. I'll dry them myself. They're precious.'

Before looking at the albums, May had beckoned Nell upstairs. 'Come, I'll show you my collections.'

She'd led Nell into her bedroom. A massive four-poster bed complete with thick floral drapes had been centre stage and the carpet had been white shag. 'I love this room. This is where I come to find peace. I just sit by the window and relax,' she'd said, crossing to the floor-to-ceiling louvred doors on the wall opposite the bed 'Look. My precious shoes.'

Nell had gasped. There had been rack upon rack filled with shoes – all colours, all styles.

'I love shoes. Never could resist a pair I like. Got over five hundred pairs.'

It had been plain to Nell that quite a few of them hadn't been worn.

'Then there's my handbags. Got one or two of them. Always good to know there's something in the cupboard to match whatever I'm wearing.' She'd opened another door. Handbags had been neatly stacked side-by-side from carpet to ceiling. 'Got quite a few now. Nothing lovelier that a soft leather handbag. Beautiful to touch.'

Nell, proud owner of three pairs of shoes and one handbag, had been impressed.

Then they'd gone back downstairs to the dining-room, where May had brought out many family albums, all stuffed with photos of Alistair and Johnny.

'You know what people are going to be like from the minute they are conceived,' May had said. 'Harry and me were drunk the night I copped it with Johnny, so he's the wild one. But we snipped up to bed one quiet Sunday when we both wanted a bit of a cuddle and that's when Alistair came along. He's the quiet, thoughtful one. Hardly kicked at all in the nine months I carried him. He was too busy sitting in there thinking.'

On the drive home, Alistair had said, 'Christ, she asked you to help with the washing-up. She never does that. She must like you. What did she talk about?'

'Men. Then she got out a bottle of brandy and poured us both a huge glass and showed me the family albums. Pictures of you naked on a rug when you were a baby, and the like.'

'Christ.'

'Have you taken many girls home to meet your folks?'

He shook his head. A small thrill buzzed through Nell. This must mean he was serious about her.

She asked him what happened on Thursday evenings, as May had said Thursday nights were family nights and Nell was never to expect to see him then.

'Me, my brother, mother and father all have a big meal and talk business. We discuss how to make money, then discuss how to make more money.'

Nell had said, 'Gosh.' When her family got together with relatives they mostly discussed the price of coal. She leaned back, smiled to herself and asked what was in the locked cupboard in the kitchen.

'Don't ask,' Alistair had said. 'It's another of her collections; her most important one.'

It only took a few weeks for Nell to be fully sucked into the dazzle of Rutherford life. They called her name when she stepped over the front step. 'Hey, it's Nell.' She was thrilled by their welcome. It made her feel special, and this was new to her.

In time, she started to stay over with them at weekends and slept in the spare room. She'd lie listening as the house slipped into silence, waiting for Alistair to pad barefoot along the corridor, down the stairs to her room and into her bed. Telling him to keep his freezing feet away from her, she would slide into his arms. This was perfect, so much warmer and more comfortable than making love in the car; no more steamy windows. In the morning, Harry would wink at them. Of course he knew what was going on; his son was only doing what he would have done when he was his age, if he'd had the chance. It was natural, he thought. It never occurred to him that Alistair might, like his brother, make his girlfriend pregnant and have to wed. Alistair was the cautious one. And Johnny was simply a casualty of passion. That's what happened. It was life.

And even though Johnny's mischievousness had led to him and Carol having to get married, Harry knew that each man was responsible for his own actions and that it wasn't his place to warn Alistair from making the same mistake as his brother.

May took Nell under her wing, and bought her gifts: a new handbag; a watch; a cashmere jersey. 'I saw it and thought about you,' she'd say. She'd regularly turn up at the shop where Nell worked. 'Just passing. Thought you might like to go out for a spot of lunch.' Nell was flattered. She'd never been taken out to lunch in her life. Her family never ate any meal out, ever. May would take her arm and together they'd walk to the North British Hotel, a plush, expensive and comfortable place where May's face was known and always welcome. 'Table for two for Nell and me,' May would say. No matter how busy the place was, she was never denied. Waiters bowed their heads, pulled out their chairs, fussed round them with menus and the wine list. Nell had her first taste of being important – one of the privileged people – and she loved it.

'You would think your mother would be careful with money considering her childhood,' Nell said to Alistair once. It was late. They were in bed, speaking quietly in the dark. 'I thought people who'd known real poverty saved a lot, in case it ever happened to them again. They want to feel secure.'

Alistair had agreed that she had a point. 'My ma loves money. She likes to keep it close. She loves cash and hates banks.' He'd sighed, 'That's what she keeps in the green cupboard in the kitchen. A stash; thousands of pounds.'

'Really?'

'Don't tell her I told you. It's a secret. A secret stash.'

Nell promised not to tell.

'She loves to spend money because for years and years she never had any. She didn't have friends at school on account of how she looked. Not exactly raggy clothes, but pretty close. Now she loves to buy things for people. Probably she's buying their love and friendship, but I don't like to think about that. And she can't resist buying things for herself and for the house. She gets a kick out of splashing cash around. She loves that shop assistants fuss round her. Plus I don't think she can quite get over the fact she can afford to buy whatever she wants. She sees something. She likes it. She buys it. She's happy.'

Nell said she still thought May should save for a rainy day.

'Oh, there's plenty in the green cupboard for a rainy day. There's money enough in there for years and years of rainy days,' Alistair had told her.

In time, Nell was allowed into the inner sanctum. May let her into the kitchen when she was cooking. Nell learned to chop, slice and mix ingredients, and, as the room filled with the aroma of garlic and onions hitting hot olive oil, she listened to May's opinions on men, love, money and the family.

'Nothing is more important than family. Romantic love, pah.' May had flapped her hand wafting it away. She'd told Nell how she thought romance was an annoyance. It made your heart beat too fast. It disturbed your sleep. It stopped you thinking straight. 'It's nothing; lasts a year, maybe two. Then you're left with affection and companionship if you're lucky. Money matters, of course, but only if you use it properly. It can buy you lovely things and that's fine. Mostly you should use it to buy respect. Make no mistake, money can buy you happiness, but family should be the heart and soul of your life.'

Chapter Seven
The Second Saturday in January at Two O'clock

By November 1961, Nell was nineteen and content. She hadn't forgotten the vow she'd made on the night she'd first met Alistair over two years ago. She still planned to marry him someday. He had exceeded all of her expectations. When he'd graduated she'd smiled when she'd given him a Parker pen on the day of the ceremony, thinking of the promise she'd made on the first night he'd walked her home. He was working as a lawyer but wasn't earning a huge amount. Though Nell knew that would come eventually. Meantime, she could eat and sleep in his comfortable family home, and she did so often that the drab two-bedroom council house where she'd been brought up became a stopping-off point for her. Her mother made the occasional pointed comment but that didn't stop Nell. Her old home soon became the place where she kept her clothes and where she slept on the nights she didn't sleep in the Rutherford's spare room. This convenient arrangement went on for almost two years.

Carol, now mother of a one-year-old and a self-proclaimed expert on relationships, had suggested to Nell that she and Alistair were in a rut. But Nell had denied it. They were a couple, she'd said, and this was how couples behaved. They went to the cinema, had the odd drink together in their favourite bar, and ate out now and then, trying new restaurants. 'We're comfortable,' Nell said, and then quoted May, 'Romantic love, pah. It disturbs your sleep. Stops you thinking. What you want in the end is affection and companionship. Alistair and I have that.' Still, it bothered her that she was knocking on and hadn't achieved her goals. She should get engaged this year. She should be getting married the year after next. There was no sign of either of these things happening. Perhaps she should mention this to Alistair. But she didn't want to upset him. Magazines and movies were full of the dire things that happened to women who were too pushy.

It was bitterly cold outside, rain streaming down the window. Nell and Alistair were curled up, entangled on the living room sofa watching *Casablanca*, their favourite movie. They could speak along with it, and usually did. 'Of all the gin joints . . .' Alistair was saying, when May bustled in.

'Brought you something to keep you going till supper time.' She put a tray with a couple of mugs of hot chocolate and some almond cake on the coffee table in front of them. They both thanked her, and took a mug, cupped it in their hands.

Nell sipped the hot, sweet drink and smiled up at May.

'Just the thing on a day like this.' She had a thin chocolate moustache on her upper lip.

'Look at the two of you,' said May, critically considering them and folding her arms. 'You're like a couple of teen-agers, huddled up watching a daft film.'

Alistair protested it wasn't daft. 'It's a classic.'

'I don't care what it is,' said May. 'I think you should be doing more than just sitting watching TV. You're a grown man now. A lawyer working with Hepburn, Smith and Rogers, you've got your own office with a desk and a telephone. You shouldn't be living with your mother and father.'

'But the food's good here,' Alistair said. And winked at Nell.

'No matter. Strikes me that you two are too comfort-able. You're being waited on hand and foot, getting everything done for you. You're getting up to all sorts in that spare room. Don't deny it. I know what goes on under my own roof. It's time you both grew up and settled down.'

Both Nell and Alistair looked embarrassed but neither said anything, though they knew this was true.

'So,' said May, 'since it doesn't look like either of you are going to do something about moving on with your lives, I've done it for you. I've booked the church for the second Saturday in January, two o'clock. The reception's in the George Hotel. You're getting married.' Arms folded, she bustled out.

The film played on, but Alistair and Nell had stopped watching. 'She's joking,' said Nell. 'Tell me she's joking.'

Alistair shook his head. 'That wasn't her joking face.'

'But she can't do that. She can't arrange our wedding without asking us first.'

Alistair said. 'She's just done exactly that. Do you mind?'

'Yes, I mind. If I'm going to get married, I'd like to choose when and where.'

'And to whom, presumably,' he said. He was mortified. He ran his fingers through his hair and looked at Nell. 'Well, will you?'

'Will I what?' she said.

'Marry me on the second Saturday in January with a reception in the George organised by my bossy mother?'

It was probably the almond cake that did it. It was awfully good. Taking a bite, feeling it melt in her mouth, Nell realised that if she said no, she was saying goodbye to the good life: the food; the gifts; this fabulous family. She couldn't do that. Besides, she'd become accustomed to Alistair. She liked his quiet ways; his thoughtfulness. He made her laugh. So she said, 'Why not. Yes, I'll marry you on the second Saturday in January with a reception in the George. Why not? I'm not doing anything else on that day.'

He put down his cup, reached for her and kissed her. 'I was going to ask you. I just hadn't got round to it. I took too long thinking about it.'

It wasn't the proposal she'd imagined. She had fond notions of the question being popped over a candlelit dinner, or perhaps as they strolled along the shores of a tranquil lake bathed in moonlight. Obviously that wasn't going to happen. He'd been thinking about it too much to actually propose. He was behaving the way his mother said he behaved ever since he'd been in the womb.

He took her hand. They returned to the film. Then he kissed her fingers and whispered, 'Thank you.' They watched a few more minutes of *Casablanca* before they both started to giggle. In the circumstances, it seemed the only sane thing to do.

Two days later they bought a ring. After that, the wedding plans rolled on. May was in charge. Nell and Alistair let it all happen.

But Nancy McClusky wasn't happy. She took the news badly. 'January? Nobody gets married in January. It's not lucky. Married in January's hoar and rime, widowed you'll be before your time. And, don't you know about winter brides? A winter bride always goes back.'

Nell laughed. 'Back to where?'

'Where they started from. Well, don't you go thinking you can come back here after you're married. It'll be up to you to make a go of it.'

Nell laughed, 'These are old wives tale. Superstitious nonsense. This is the modern age. The age of television and the radio. We are exploring outer space. We don't believe any of that stuff anymore.' My God, she thought, what would Simone de Beauvoir and Satre make of all that?

As the wedding loomed nearer, Nancy had regular outbursts in the kitchen, which was the venue for all serious family discussions. 'You've become a stranger to us. You're never here. You're not a McClusky anymore. You're a Rutherford. You've gone over to them.'

Nell was sitting at the small Formica, fold-down table. Nancy bustled around washing, drying, and putting away the supper dishes. She could never complain, nag and fuss while sitting still; there had to be movement, a rhythm to her fretting.

A second outburst followed a few days later. 'That May Rutherford went with you to pick your dress. That was my job. A mother should always help to choose her daughter's wedding dress. I've been looking forward to that all my life.'

Nell said that it hadn't been May's idea to take her to the bridal shop. It had been Harry's. 'He thinks I wear strange clothes. He worried about what dress I'd wear. He thought I might come down the aisle looking like a beatnik.'

'Cheek of him,' said Nancy. Although she'd had the same worry.

May had turned up at the shop where Nell worked. 'Thought it time you picked out your wedding dress,' she'd said. Nell had been flustered by this. She knew a wedding dress was necessary but had been putting off buying one. She didn't have the money to buy the kind of dress that would meet the Rutherford's expectations. Recently she'd been thinking that the groom would be better turned out than the bride. But she never did know how to say no to May so she'd gone with her.

They'd gone to the bridal department of an upmarket Princes Street store. The atmosphere was hushed, almost holy. The only sounds were the whispered tones of reverential sales women and the silken rustle of frocks being pulled from displays and laid out for inspection.

May had swooned over a multi-layered confection of lace, frills and bows. But now upstairs in Nell's wardrobe was a simple long-sleeved dress, cut low at the front with a bow at the back. She visited it daily, stroking it, holding it to her face, breathing it in. Sometimes she stood staring at it; she couldn't believe she owned such a beautiful thing. She'd even kept the tissue paper and glossy carrier bag the dress had been wrapped in. She'd thought them too beautiful, too expensive, to part with.

Insisting that this was what she wanted wear on her wedding day was the nearest Nell had come to falling out with May. There had been glaring, tight lips and a bit of tugging to and fro of very expensive dresses. Eventually, encouraged by the assistant who'd clapped her hands in joy when she'd seen Nell emerge from the changing room in *the* dress, May had pulled her purse from her handbag and forked out the money. 'Cash,' she'd said. 'Can't be doing with banks.' Thanks and gratitude had tumbled from Nell's lips but May dismissed them, saying, 'Don't be daft.'

Two days later, when Nell was at the Rutherford's dining table, she heard May's rewritten version of their shopping spree. 'Nell wanted the full meringue,' May had said, 'but I steered her towards this simple sophisticated frock. Knew it was the one soon as I saw it. Very Audrey Hepburn. Nell looks a treat in it.'

Nell had opened her mouth to protest at this description of their outing, but Alistair, having heard what had really happened, kicked her shin under the table. For a week, the dress-buying business festered in Nancy's mind.

Soon after there was another kitchen outburst.

'I'll tell you why the Rutherfords were so worried about you not looking like a beatnik on your wedding day,' her mother said. 'It's because this isn't a wedding for them. It's a bit of showing off.'

'Is it?' said Nell.

'Of course. They sent out the invitations, not us. And look who they've invited: councillors, the chief of police, business clients and relatives, three hundred and six of them. And only fifteen McCluskys.'

This surprised Nell. She hadn't realised her mother and father knew fifteen people.

The resentment went on. Nancy complained that May Rutherford had chosen the flowers for the church and the reception. She'd booked the band. She'd chosen the menu of smoked salmon, beef Wellington and crème brûlée. 'That food's too rich for me. I'd have been happy with a sandwich.'

The next day Nancy was incensed that May was having the viewing of the presents at her house. 'She says her house is bigger, with more room for everybody. She's serving sherry and canapés, and acts as if I don't even know what a canapé is. Bloody rude.'

By this stage, Nell had stopped listening to her mother's outpouring of rage. Instead, she tuned in to the songs in her head. As Nancy ranted, Nell let 'Stand by Me' rip through her mind. Ben E. King sang and she swayed slightly in time with him.

'I feel like an outsider,' Nancy said one evening. 'An onlooker at my own daughter's wedding. It's not right. Your father and me have been shoved aside as if we don't matter. I tell you, these Rutherfords with their fancy ways, flashing their money around are going to get found out for what they are. One day they'll get what's coming to them and they'll fall flat on their faces. You'll see.'

But Nell had moved to a new tune. Horns, bawdy-voiced backing singers and Ray Charles' aching, rasping growls, 'Hit the Road, Jack', were playing in her head and she didn't hear the warning.

Chapter Eight
The Youngest and the Sanest

It was after the meal and the speeches at the wedding when Carol upstaged Nell. Johnny, the best man, said that Nell was the most beautiful bride he'd ever seen. 'The bridesmaid's pretty cool, too. But then I have to say that; she's my old lady.' Everyone laughed. He shoved his hands into the pockets of his pinstriped pants. 'Alistair and Nell. Look at them. Young, in love, with a flat in the West End. The world is at their feet. They're going to be the grooviest couple in town.'

Alistair leaned over and whispered in Nell's ear. 'He's jealous.'

Looking up at Johnny, seeing a slight twist in his lips as he spoke, Nell agreed and wondered why.

Since Nell's father was pale and nauseous at the thought of giving a speech, Harry gave one in his place. He thanked his wife for organising this wonderful party. He thanked Carol for being a marvellous bridesmaid and he thanked everyone for coming along. Then he turned to Nell and Alistair. 'A lovely couple. You'll be happy. Now, get busy doing what you've been doing in our spare room for the past few years and make some new Rutherfords to join the clan.' Nell blushed, but not as much as her mother, who looked scandalised.

Alistair smoothed things over when he finished his speech by thanking Nancy for having such a beautiful daughter and allowing him to marry her. When Nell looked at her, Nancy was smiling. It was the first time Nell had seen her do that in months. She wished she would smile more often. It really suited her.

Sitting in her fabulous dress watching the room relax as people finished their meals, swigged brandy, lit cigars and cigarettes, it occurred to Nell that she hardly knew anybody here. The room was a blur of strange faces. They were, however, faces in full wealthy bloom. This place swaggered with money. Men opened their jackets, leaned back in their chairs and guffawed at their own jokes. Women with immovably lacquered hair leaned towards one another, smiling discreetly, and discussed their latest gadgets and holidays. People gleamed, comfortable in the knowledge they were right about everything from the political party they supported to their taste in shoes or kitchen curtains. Nell could breathe in the confidence. She wished it were infectious; she could do with some of that.

However, someone who could do with it more was her mother, who was wearing a navy-blue suit bought from a catalogue. She was paying it off by the month, and would still be paying it off this time next year. The skirt was too big and hung limply from her hips. The jacket was too small. It strained at her armpits and there was still a crease along the back from lying folded in its box. She was sitting staring ahead, raking in her mouth with her tongue for stray bits of food and thinking of something to say to the woman sitting next to her; Nancy never was very good with strangers. Nell watched as she turned and spoke. The stranger looked surprised. Nell wondered what her mother had said, and decided it was something about the price of coal. It was still a popular topic in the McClusky household. After that, her mother gave up and resumed her quiet staring ahead. Her father joined her. They gazed mournfully at the braying mass, looking confused. Her father put his hand over her mother's, patted it. She smiled at him.

It made Nell smile. She was glad they had each other. They were mutually lonely, companions in awkwardness. Nell wanted to rush over and hug them, but she didn't. Now that her mother knew of her secret shenanigans with Alistair in the Rutherford's spare room, Nell was too embarrassed to look her in the eye, far less put her arms round her and hold her close. Besides, the McCluskys didn't do such things. Spontaneous displays of affection were not their style.

So instead she turned back to Alistair and asked why Johnny was jealous.

'My brother wanted to do what we're doing – renting a flat in town. Except his dream was to have a bachelor pad, leather sofa, modern prints on the wall, hi-fi, huge bed to entertain the chicks. He had it all planned out. Now he's got a mortgage, a wife and a baby. He feels he's old enough to really enjoy being young and young enough not to be old. But he can't do the things he wants to do: flirt with girls, sleep around a bit, fritter money on booze and clothes. He feels trapped. He and Carol fight all the time.'

'He told you that?' said Nell.

'He tells me everything,' Alistair told her. 'Everyone in my family turns to me with their troubles.'

'But you're the youngest,' said Nell.

He told her he was also the sanest.

Nell snorted.

'No, really,' said Alistair. 'Haven't you noticed that my family is ever so slightly mad?'

Nell said she hadn't; she thought his family wonderful. She looked across at May who was deep in conversation with a man and a woman. She was decked out in pink and was gesticulating as she spoke, bursting now and then into a throaty laugh. Nell was sure they were talking about something fabulous, probably to do with making money.

Harry brought the room to order, tapping on his glass with his spoon. 'Ladies and gentlemen, would you please repair to the lounge while the floor is cleared for dancing? First drinks are on me.'

Nell said it was a good time to slip off for a pee. She went to the room booked for her to change into her going-away outfit, and when she emerged from the loo, smoothing down her dress, Carol was sitting by the mirror, applying a fresh layer of lipstick, leaning forward, pouting and admiring herself.

'I'm looking OK,' Carol said. 'You'd never know I was a mother.'

Nell agreed.

'So,' said Carol, 'how are you enjoying your wedding?'

'It's great.'

'Of course, you're having the wedding I should have had,' said Carol.

Nell looked at her in surprise. 'But there wasn't time to plan a big do for yours – you were pregnant.'

'I always wanted something like this. Posh frock, church filled with flowers, red carpet, big meal, lots of people, then dancing with a band, and me the star of the show. The Rutherfords have spent a fortune on you.'

'Christ, Carol. You got a house and all your furniture from them.'

'I got a bungalow that I don't like and a sofa I hate,' said Carol. 'My mother-in-law chose everything. I wanted this, the big wedding. I've always wanted a big wedding. I'm so jealous.' She flounced out.

Nobody could flounce like Carol, Nell thought. She wondered if she practised it.

The dining room had been cleared by the time she got back. Tables and chairs were set round a huge open stretch of polished floor; the dancing was about to begin. In the corner, the Billy McGhee quartet – a piano, guitar, accordion and drums – were setting up. Nell joined Alistair at a table on the edge of the floor. 'Brought you a drink,' he said. 'Dutch courage for the dance ahead.'

'What dance?' said Nell.

'The first waltz. The bride and groom take to the floor first. It's traditional.'

'But I can't dance,' said Nell. Since May had arranged almost everything to do with the big day Nell hadn't thought much about what would be expected of her. A red blotch appeared on her throat. It always turned up when she was nervous. 'Well, I can shimmy to music. I can jive, do the twist, but only on crowded dance floors where I'm hidden by the throng.'

Alistair said he couldn't even do that.

'All the things we've done together, concerts, films, meals as well as, you know, sexual positions.' She blushed, and looked round checking nobody was eaves-dropping. 'We never thought to dance.'

'I just don't like dancing,' said Alistair. 'Didn't you get it at school?'

'Yes, but I never paid attention.' She looked away, troubled by sudden painful memories. 'We used to get rehearsals for the school Christmas party. We had to do country dancing – eightsome reels, the gay Gordons and that. But when the teacher shouted, "Take your partners . . ." all the boys would swarm over for Carol. A great kicking scrum shoving and elbowing – she was the class sweetheart. When she was taken, the boys just picked anybody. But never me, I sat at the side. I never danced.'

Alistair took both her hands in his and kissed them. 'The swine,' he said. 'The bastards. Give me their names and I'll track them down, every single one of them and sort them out. A vendetta.'

'You'd do that for me?' asked Nell, and laughed. 'That's so kind. You could leap on them from above wearing a cape and swishing a sword. You could cleave a deep Z in their foreheads, like Zorro.'

'Only, I'd do an A for Alistair or an N for you.'

'Splendid,' said Nell. 'We'll start after the honeymoon.'

The band played a few chords, tuning up.

'The ordeal is approaching,' said Nell.

Harry walked into the middle of the floor, clapping his hands, 'Ladies and gentlemen, the bride and groom will lead the company in the first waltz.'

Alistair and Nell stood up, looked sheepishly around.

'I have a plan,' said Alistair. 'I'll grab your waist and we'll strike up a Ginger Rogers and Fred Astaire pose, then I'll step back on my right foot and you step forward on your left foot and we'll take it from there.'

'Good plan,' said Nell. 'Christ, they're playing the Tennessee Waltz. I hate that song. This is not an auspicious start to our marriage.'

He took her hand, 'This is our first trial as man and wife. If we can get through this, we can weather any storm. Stride boldly with me to the middle of the floor.'

They took up their Astaire and Rogers pose, looking deep into one another's eyes. The band played. Alistair stepped back on his right foot, but Nell never had gotten the hang of right and left and she put her right foot forward, treading on his toe. He lost his momentum, twirled her round, stepping on her toe. She winced. They stumbled, bumped into one another, tripped and painfully trod on each other's feet. The guests watched in silence.

May, who by now had drunk too much, shouted, 'We all know there's something the two of you are good at, and it isn't dancing.'

The red spot on Nell's throat turned a deeper crimson. Alistair smiled and pulled her closer. 'What we do is so much more fun.'

And then the mood changed. The wedding guests started to clap, and a whispered 'aww' rippled through them. 'Sweet,' someone said. And the clapping got louder.

Alistair said, 'We're getting the hang of this. We're getting audience approval.'

He twirled her once more, and as they whirled, he saw the objects of admiration. Carol and Johnny were waltzing perfectly. So expert was their dance, anyone could see they had rehearsed this. And to complete the one-upmanship, they held between them Katy, their baby daughter. She was laughing in delight. She was also dressed in a miniature version of Carol's bridesmaid dress.

'We've been upstaged,' said Alistair.

He and Nell stopped their bridal waltz and stood hand-in-hand watching the perfect three twirl and glide over the floor.

'The swine,' said Alistair. 'It's an N on the forehead for them.'

'Let them. It's what Carol always wanted. To be the star of the show. Besides, we're off to Florence, and they're not.'

Chapter Nine
Florence

It was late afternoon on the day after the wedding when Nell and Alistair arrived in Florence. They'd taken an early morning flight to London, a second flight to Pisa and then a train the rest of the way. At first the speed and whoosh of the planes taking off and landing had bothered Nell. Alistair, seeing her upset, had held her hand and whispered that this was really exciting. Nell comforted herself by thinking of Grace Kelly, Frank Sinatra and Tony Curtis. They did things like this all the time. She'd seen pictures of them looking relaxed and waving as they boarded planes. If they could do it, so could she.

The hotel was small and in the centre of the city. The bed was wrought iron with a pale blue eiderdown, and the walls were pastel green. It had a tiny en suite with a deep bath that had ancient brass fittings. Nell thought it perfect. This was how she'd decorate the bedroom when she and Alistair bought their house with the sweeping lawns.

'This is wonderful,' she told him. 'You must have been saving for ages to afford to come here.'

He shrugged. 'It's our honeymoon. A once-in-a-lifetime experience we'll remember when we're old. We can tell our grandchildren about it.'

In fact, May had given him the money. She'd pressed a roll of banknotes into his hand and told him to take Nell somewhere exotic. 'The girl knows nothing about marriage. It'll be a shock when reality kicks in. She'll need some good memories to fall back on.'

Alistair had asked his mother what she meant. 'Marriage isn't all getting into bed together. Suddenly Nell will have to cook supper and wash clothes and clean the flat. She'll have to shop and, oh, all the things she's never even thought about doing. There will be bickering. She'll not take kindly to coming home from work and having to peel potatoes and chop onions.'

Alistair had said he'd imagined Nell would give up work and become a housewife. 'I don't want anyone thinking I can't support my wife.'

May had told him not to be so old-fashioned. 'She'd be bored alone all day in that flat.'

'But she'll have the baby,' Alistair had protested.

'What baby? She's not pregnant, is she?'

'Not yet. But I'm hoping she will be when we come back from the honeymoon. I want to start a family right away.'

May had asked if he'd spoken to Nell about this.

'No, but we agree on everything. I didn't think I needed to talk to her about it.'

May had told him he'd better, and had left it at that.

After they'd unpacked, the pair set off to explore. They meandered, walking down one street, turning into another without knowing where they were going. It was busy. Eventually, they found themselves looking at the river. The light was golden, a lone rower skimmed along the water. Alistair sighed. This place was amazing. 'Do you realise the people who have lived here . . . Dante, Botticelli, Leonardo da Vinci, Michelangelo. History was made here.' He leaned over and whispered in Nell's ear. 'Our baby will be made here.'

Nell was alarmed. 'I don't want a baby. Not yet.'

'Isn't having kids the point of being married?'

'I want to wait for a couple of years. I want to have some time when it's just us. I thought the point of being married was so you could grow old together.'

'Yes, but I want children, too. Three at least. A boy first, then a girl and I don't care what the third one is.'

'You've taken me by surprise. This is the first time you've mentioned having a baby to me.'

They walked on, both quiet. The late-afternoon sun drenched fabulous buildings they moved past; young boys on scooters whizzed by; people chattered in Italian, and they noticed none of it.

Eventually Alistair suggested they find somewhere to eat. 'We'll talk about this like grown-ups.'

Nell thought there was nothing to talk about: she didn't want a baby.

They found a small bustling place and were given seats by the window. He ordered *bistecca* for both of them. 'They sear the meat in charcoal,' he said. 'It's a local speciality.' They drank Chianti. He'd been studying travel books about Florence for months and had even learnt a smattering of the language.

He smiled at her, took her hand and said they mustn't argue. 'This is our special time together.'

She agreed. 'No arguing.'

He took out his itinerary. 'I've made a list of things I want us to see. The Duomo, Michelangelo's *David*, the Ponte Vecchio, the Botticellis at the Uffizi Museum, the Boboli Gardens—'

'The shops,' added Nell. 'I want to buy shoes.'

'Italian shoes are a must,' he agreed.

The place smelled of coffee and searing meat. There was the babble of foreign voices. Waiters fussed over them and flirted with Nell. They got a little tipsy on the wine and the grappa they drank with their coffee. They held hands as they walked back to their hotel. But even though they made love, the matter of baby making niggled away at both of them, unresolved.

Over the next few days, they followed Alistair's itinerary. Nell marvelled and stared and wondered. 'Do you think there's anything ugly here?'

Alistair doubted it.

But it wasn't the tourist spots that fascinated Nell. It was the people. They were, she decided, born stylish. She wished she lived here. She could stop for an espresso on the way to work. Pop out for another at odd times of the day. She loved the little cups of strong dark coffee. She'd heap in two spoons of sugar, and then, when the cup was empty, she'd dip her finger to gather the sweet traces at the bottom and lick it.

'We could move here,' she said.

'What would we do?' Alistair asked.

'There's bound to be pen shops here. Or I could work in any shop selling anything. They're all lovely.'

He said they'd have to learn Italian.

Nell was sure she'd quickly pick it up. 'I can already say, "Two coffees please," and "Good morning," and, "Thank you." We could get a little flat and I could keep you while you studied Italian law.'

'Thanks for that,' he said.

'Don't you love the way people dress their kids here?'

'No reason you can't dress them like that back home, though.'

Oh, no, she thought, I've brought up the subject of children.

He drained his cup, and sat back in his chair. 'How do you see us in ten years time? Where do you think we'll be?'

Nell said she thought they'd still be the same. 'Just us. Only we'll have our own house. Quite a big one with long lawns and a couple of children and . . .' she trailed off. She hadn't planned beyond the big house; she had no other thoughts on the future. 'I just want to be happy.'

'You've no plans of your own,' he said. 'Don't you want anything other than a big house? You don't seem to be ambitious for yourself. You left school, got a job in the pen shop and haven't moved on. Me, I can stay where I am, move up through the firm. I could start my own law practice. I could try to become an advocate. I have options. I have plans. Mostly, right now, I'd like to start planning a family.'

'Usually it's the woman who wants a baby.'

'Yes, but I was moved when I held Carol's baby when she was born. Something happened. I wanted one of my own.'

He'd seen Carol sitting in bed, leaning on a pile of pillows. She'd looked exhausted but glowing. When the baby was placed in his arms, he'd marvelled. It had been amazing, a whole new person in the world – tiny, yet perfect. He'd been close to tears.

'Think of it – a little bit of you, a little bit of me all bundled into a whole new person. Doesn't that excite you?'

'Well, yes,' said Nell. 'I just want to have a couple of years enjoying being married first. Going out and coming home to our own place. Eating when we want. Watching television together in the evenings, that sort of thing. A baby's a lot of work. I don't think I'm ready yet.'

Alistair was adamant that nobody was ever ready for a baby. 'They take you by storm, but we'd manage. We would do it together. Share the load. I'd do my bit, change nappies, do some of the night feeds, all that. And when the baby grew up a bit, I'd take him out, play with him. We'd be a family.'

Nell sighed. 'OK, but just not yet.'

He ordered two more espressos. 'I don't mean to be rude, Nell, but you're not exactly chasing a career. You're a shop assistant. You could easily leave your job and take care of a baby. I want to provide for you. I want to take care of you.'

He was ashamed to tell the people he worked with what his wife did for a living. Most of his colleagues' wives were housewives.

'But I like my job,' Nell protested. 'I'm good at selling pens. I don't want to stay at home all day.'

She was afraid of getting pregnant. She'd seen Carol growing larger and larger and more and more tired. She'd watched her friend sit slumped on the sofa, legs apart, complaining about heartburn and how coffee made her nauseous. She was afraid of looking ugly and she hated the maternity clothes. She looked away from him. She was hurt. She loved this place – buildings so ancient the street names carved on their walls were unreadable, narrow streets, wide squares, markets, traders selling ice cream, shops filled with exquisite things. She'd been anticipating this holiday for weeks. Alistair nagging her about having a baby had not been on her itinerary, and she was finding it unbearable.

Tears glazed her eyes. She turned to him. 'Do you have to go on and on about having a baby? Here we are in this fabulous place and I can't enjoy it. I mean everything's beautiful and fabulous people have lived here. I might have stood on the very spot Leonardo da Vinci once stood on. Famous people must have come here. Sophia Loren's Italian. She might have come to Florence. She might have even come to this café and sat at this table.' Nell lifted her cup. 'She might have drunk from the very cup I'm drinking from. This is only the second holiday I've ever had in my life. Can't you let me daydream?'

Alistair said he was sorry. 'Daydream away if it makes you happy.' It wasn't something he understood. He didn't understand the joy of standing where da Vinci had once stood. Did Nell think the man's genius was catching? It would start at her feet and move up to her brain? He doubted very much that Sophia Loren had ever come to this café and drunk from the cup Nell was using. And if she had – so what? Then, he picked up on what she'd told him. 'You've only had one other holiday?'

'Yes, when I was little we went to a little village up the west coast called Catto. It was lovely. I paddled in the sea and built sandcastles. We stayed in a big house that had a monkey puzzle tree in the garden. It was a bed and breakfast, so we had to buy our evening meal. We had fish and chips every night.' That was all her mother and father could afford. Now she thought about it, she remembered that on a couple of occasions her mother had gone without. For lunch, they'd bought a loaf of bread and some slices of spam and her mother had made sandwiches. They were always gritty with sand. But in Nell's mind they'd been heavenly. She'd worn a swimsuit made of some kind of seersucker that had left square marks on her bum. She'd shrieked at the cold as she ran into the sea. Her mother and father had gone in too, but only till the water reached their ankles. Her mother had lifted her tweed skirt above her knees; her father had rolled up his trousers. She'd had her parents' undivided attention and had felt loved. All that and there had been cornflakes for breakfast. Never in her life before had she eaten anything so exotic. What more could a little girl want?

Alistair was swamped with guilt. He'd gone on holiday every year of his childhood, usually to France where his mother studied the cuisine. He promised not to mention babies again. 'Not till we get home, anyway.'

By their last day, they were both looking forward to going home to the flat they'd rented. It had two bedrooms and a cosy living room, and was near the West End of Edinburgh. Alistair had bought a leather Chesterfield sofa and a matching chair that was to be delivered in their absence. Johnny had agreed to let the deliverymen in and had been given strict instructions on where each item was to be placed. Alistair had also arranged for the walls throughout to be painted white. He had a selection of Picasso prints he planned to hang on his return. Nell hadn't been consulted on the décor, but was excited about how it might look. As the flat was partly furnished, they hadn't needed to buy a bed, but Nell had bought brown sheets, blankets and a

Spanish bedspread and rug. They were, they thought, a thoroughly modern couple.

On their last day, they hit the shops and bought presents for everyone and shoes for Nell.

Sitting on the plane home, Alistair had lifted Nell's hand to his lips. 'Now our journey really begins.'

Chapter Ten
The Real Woman

'Of course,' said Carol, 'you didn't marry Alistair. You married his family. That's what you're in love with.'

Nell denied this. 'I love Alistair. It's just not the passionate love you and Johnny have. It's a love full of trust and companionship. It's what makes a marriage.' The gospel according to May.

Carol curled her upper lip. 'Marriage,' she scoffed. 'It's rubbish. And any passion me and Johnny had died ages ago.'

They were in Carol's living room, sitting on the chintz sofa May had chosen. Lined up on the coffee table in front of them were six dark-blue wine glasses, Nell's gift for Carol from Florence. She had been going to buy the decanter that went with them, but she hadn't quite forgiven Carol for upstaging her at her wedding.

Nell looked round the room. It wasn't to her taste. The sofa was floral patterned, as was the carpet and curtains. Nothing matched. The wallpaper was striped gold and cream. May had gone to town here. Thinking she was doing a good thing, she'd put a deposit on the bungalow and furnished it for the young couple. It was an act of generosity that came from the heart. Only May's heart was wildly flamboyant – no subtlety at all. There was no comfort, just a cacophony of colours.

'I'll get a little something to christen my new glasses,' said Carol. She disappeared into the kitchen and returned with a bottle of Blue Nun and filled two glasses.

Solemnly they each raised a glass. 'To the back lot,' they said in unison. It had become a habit.

'Have you ever been to the back lot?' asked Carol.

'Only once,' Nell said. 'Ages ago.'

She had gone with Alistair to collect his car after it'd had new tyres fitted. Harry had welcomed them. He'd put his arm round her and told her this was the best place in town to buy a car. It had been the first time Nell had seen him in such bright light. Up to this point her meetings with him had been at his home where he'd been dressed in his casual clothes – twill trousers, checked shirt and slip-on shoes. On this day he'd been wearing his working outfit. He wore an immaculate bespoke suit, pale blue shirt and dazzling pink tie. His hair had been combed into style and held in place with a lavish helping of Brylcreem. With a sweep of his arm he'd proudly shown off his sales area. 'You won't find anywhere like it. We serve coffee, have comfortable seats for the customers and newspapers for their relaxation. Our workshop is immaculate, not a drop of oil on the floor. Our mechanics wear the Rutherford uniform.'

There had been six Jaguars in the main showroom.

They'd glistened. The place had smelled of polish and new cars. Nell had, up till that moment, never really been interested in cars, but suddenly she'd wanted one. She'd lusted after the red Jaguar that had been mounted on a stage that was slowly revolving, light bouncing off its gleaming body.

'No doubt you'll want to see the back lot we all toast,' Harry had said to Nell.

Alistair looked sheepish, hands shoved in his duffle-coat pockets. 'Not the back lot!'

But Nell had insisted. 'I'd love to see it.'

Harry had led Nell through the back door to a large courtyard lined with cars. A banner buffeted by the breeze had read QUALITY USED CARS. The cars, about thirty of them, had glistened. Some had been yellow, some blue, some green; many had been red. There had been Alfa Romeos, Renaults, Rovers – some big, some small.

'We cater for everybody. Whatever your motoring needs, we can provide the car for you.' Harry had led Nell to a red Alpha Romeo sports car. 'Now if I were to choose a car to match your current needs and your personality, I'd pick this one. It's nippy, a lovely drive, stylish and you'd turn heads as you whizz along. This is a cult car.'

Nell had pointed out that she couldn't drive.

Harry had opened the door of the Alfa Romeo, indicating that Nell should slip in behind the wheel. 'But doesn't this car make you want to learn? Isn't it to die for?'

Alistair had stepped forward, taken Nell's arm and had pulled her out. 'Nell doesn't want a car,' he'd said. 'Especially not this one.'

'I'd love that car,' Nell had protested. 'It's beautiful.'

'It's an illusion. It's a dream. You don't want it. Believe me.' He'd asked if his car was ready. When Harry had replied that it was, he'd walked towards the workshop. On the way they'd passed a row of rusting bangers, hidden from view round the corner. Some had no wheels, some had smashed windscreens, doors hanging off and some had obviously been crashed. Nell had asked about them.

'Just some old things,' Harry had said. 'Handy for spares.'

Alistair had found his car, opened the passenger door and ushered Nell in. 'C'mon, we have to go.'

Nell had said she wanted another look at the sports car. 'Your dad could probably do me a good deal.'

As they had driven off, Alistair had told her there was no such thing as a good deal on a car like the one she fancied. 'Not that long ago it looked like one of the ones that are kept out of sight. Trust me, you don't want it.'

'The cars were lovely,' Nell told Carol. 'Rows and rows of them, all shiny. I fancied an Alfa Romeo, but Alistair wouldn't let me buy it.'

'You still can't drive,' said Carol.

'I would have taken lessons if I'd had that car,' said Nell. 'It was beautiful.'

'Do you think the Rutherfords are crooks?' Carol asked Nell.

'Nah,' said Nell.

'Only, when I was in labour with Katy, I went round to the Rutherford's house to get somebody to take me to hospital. It was a Thursday. You know, family night. They were all sitting in the dining room and there were piles of money on the table. What was that about?'

'It would have been their weekly takings,' said Nell. 'They probably bring it home to count it. That's what people do.'

'I don't know,' said Carol. 'They looked shifty. They couldn't wait to get me out of the room.'

'You were in labour. They'd have been worrying you'd have the baby on the spot. They're definitely not crooks. They're too nice. May's so generous and Harry's all heart. Crooks are nasty.'

Carol said she thought May was a pain. 'I wish she wasn't so generous. She chose this house and this furniture, and I hate them both. She comes round everyday with stuff for Katy that I'd never dress her in. Sometimes she brings casseroles for our supper, so I'm even eating food I don't like.' She sighed. 'Johnny goes out every morning at eight o'clock and comes home after six. Apart from visits from Old Mother May, I'm alone all day. I pretend this house isn't mine, and I pretend I'm looking after Katy for someone else. I try to make life perfect for this make-believe woman's baby.'

Nell didn't understand. 'Why do you do that?'

Carol shrugged. 'Dunno, it just appeared in my head. I didn't plan it. But it works. I clean the house. I look after Katy. It makes it easier if I pretend that the real woman who lives in this house and has a baby will come home and be pleased with what I've done.'

Nell looked round. There was a pile of plastic toys heaped on the floor by the sofa and a trail of more toys led to the kitchen. Katy's shoes were lying in front of the fire beside a couple of cups half-full of cold coffee. Katy's tartan skirt, pink jumper and white socks were draped over a chair. Her teddy bear was lying under the television.

'The real woman doesn't come round on Sundays then,' said Nell.

Carol shook her head and smiled. 'Nah. Don't know what she does at the weekend. She probably has a better time than me, though.'

'Where's Katy, anyway?' asked Nell.

'At my mum's. She sometimes stays there Saturday nights so Johnny and me can go out. She'll be home soon; my dad'll bring her round.'

'And where's Johnny?'

'Fishing. He said he'd be back for lunch, but he hasn't turned up and the roast beef's gone all dry and wrinkly.'

Nell had already smelled the dark brown smell of burned meat filling the house. She noticed too, as Carol put her feet up on the coffee table, that she was wearing odd socks and her big toe was sticking out of one of them. The house was oddly quiet. Usually Carol had the radio on, or if the she couldn't find something to please her – she thought programmes that were all talk and no music so boring she'd run across the room to switch them off – she'd be playing records. This silence was unnerving.

'Are you all right?' Nell asked.

'Just ever so slightly fed up,' said Carol. 'God, I miss going to the Locarno. Wild nights, flirting and dancing, hoping to meet someone new . . . I was happy then.'

'And you're not happy now?' asked Nell.

'Of course I'm not happy! Who would be happy living here? Look at the carpet! A mass of pink daisies – makes me dizzy just looking at it. And this sofa's like something your granny would choose.'

'Lots of people would envy you,' said Nell.

Carol snorted and said that lots of people, whoever they were, could have all this if they wanted it. 'Except Katy, I'll keep her. One night of passion, one little mistake, one sweaty grope and kiss in a cramped car with the gear stick poking into your left leg and this is what happens.' She slumped lower in her seat. 'Except it wasn't even a night of passion, was it? It was five minutes . . . or less. It was nothing, a fleeting moment, then he lay slumped on top of me and I couldn't breathe. And now I'm a mother with a husband I hardly ever see and I'll never go dancing again.' She turned to Nell, eyes blurred with tears.

'You will,' said Nell. 'Johnny could take you dancing. You could go to the Cavendish.'

'The *Cavendish*?' Carol spat out the word. 'That's for old folk who do proper, serious dancing. Tangos and foxtrots and that. The women have fierce haircuts and frocks strewn with sequins and the blokes wear penguin suits with shiny shoes. They do twirls and glare into the distance. And they're all old. I just want to jump and jive and get sweaty and forget I'm me.'

The last few words hung in the air. Nell didn't know what to say. She had just returned from a honeymoon, wandering hand-in-hand through Florence with her new husband. She'd drunk wine and sipped espresso in pavement cafés. What did she know about depression? So instead of delving more she said, 'Do you suppose the real woman goes to the Cavendish?'

'Definitely,' said Carol. She laughed, though the tears never quite faded away.

Nell loved to be touched. The soft weight and warmth of someone's hand on her arm or shoulder pleased her, made her feel wanted, but it wasn't an art she herself had mastered. Reaching out didn't come naturally. All Carol needed was a hug, but Nell hadn't got the hang of the intricacies of tenderness. All the touching, hugging and arm linking had come from Carol. Nell lifted her hand, stretched it towards her friend, clenched her fist, let it hover in the gulf between them, and then softly let it rest on Carol's arm. 'You should tell that real woman to get out of your house. She's driving you nuts.'

They sat in silence for a minute, lost in their private musings.

Suddenly Carol said, 'You know, the thing I liked best about going to the Locarno was walking home.'

'Yeah,' said Nell. 'I loved that. 'Being seventeen and out in the night singing a song was the best thing in the world. If you weren't doing that, you were sad and old.'

'Yeah.' She started a slow rendition of 'Will You Still Love Me Tomorrow', swaying slightly, lost in the song and in memories of long walks home, footsore from dancing, heady from a night on the town drinking vodka and looking for love, arm-in-arm with her best friend and singing. That had been wonderful.

Nell joined in. They faced one another, earnestly working at perfecting their performance, enjoying the harmony and the fleeting few moments when the only thing on their minds was the song. All doubts and fears were banished.

It didn't last long. The front door burst open and Carol's father came in, carrying Katy. Carol jumped up and took the child, held her and kissed her. Still with the child wrapped round her, she twirled round the room. 'I missed you!' She was so lost in the joy of this reunion, Nell and Carol's father felt forgotten.

Carol looked round at her audience, noticed the expression on Nell's face, kissed Katy again and said, 'Don't worry. This will be you before too long.'

But it hadn't been maternal longing Nell had been feeling. It was guilt. She'd been a small child again, running into her mother's arms, swept up, kissed, and hugged. Oh, the welcome Nancy had always given her when they'd been reunited. Back then, her mother's arms were the safest place to be. There had been love.

Nell had realised that the only person she hadn't contacted since she'd got home was Nancy. It hadn't crossed her mind to do so. Last night they'd phoned May who'd insisted they come for a meal. 'Come over tomorrow and tell us all about it. We want every detail. Well, almost every detail.' After that Nell had phoned Carol and arranged to drop in on her before going to May's.

This morning, she'd lingered in bed with Alistair. They'd eaten breakfast there, revelling in their new two-bed flat in Grosvenor Crescent.

'Our love nest,' Alistair called it. Almost everything was new – the sheets; the plates their bacon and eggs glistened on; the towels they'd dried themselves with after they'd shared a bath. It had all been so exciting that Nell hadn't given her parents a thought. She felt awful about that.

'Soon you will have one of these,' Carol said, looking at Katy with love.

'Actually, Alistair wants three,' Nell said. She checked her watch. 'I have to be going. May's cooking dinner. You know what she's like if you're late. She takes it as a personal insult if you're not at the table when the meal is at its peak of perfection.'

The Rutherford's house was only a five-minute walk from Carol's. Late afternoon, five o'clock sparrows bickered in suburban hedges, and the drifting smells of Sunday cooking filled the air. This was Nell's favourite time of day. She watched her feet moving over the pavement in their new patent leather Italian shoes with long pointed toes. She loved her winkle-pickers and was a little miffed that Carol hadn't mentioned them. Mostly, though, she thought about her mother. She'd have been expecting a call. Not that she would have sat by the phone. She'd have glanced at it hopefully every time she passed it in the hall. She wouldn't mention her disappointment at its silence to Stewart, though.

May was at the window when Nell arrived. She waved, beckoned Nell in.

'Come away in. We've been wondering if you'd got lost. Oh, thems lovely shoes. Did you buy them in Italy? I've done a lovely ham with a honey glaze. We'll have it with salad and some white wine. There's chocolate mousse for after.'

She held Nell by the shoulders, admiring her for a few seconds, then kissed her. 'I've missed you.'

The family was gathered in the living room, and a fire crackled in the grate. Alistair patted the sofa. 'Here,' he said, 'beside me.' He put his arm round her, pulled her to him.

The house was full of the sweet smell of May's ham. May and Harry fussed over her, and Harry fetched her a glass of Italian wine. Thoughts of Nancy started to slip away.

Nell was surprised to see Johnny in the room. He was watching a football match on television, drinking beer.

115

'Thought you'd gone fishing,' she said.

'I did. Now I'm back. Popped in here for a beer and to say hello. How's my wife, anyway?'

'She's a bit depressed at being on her own all day. And she'd burned your dinner.'

Johnny turned to May. 'In that case I'll stay to eat.'

May said that was grand. She nodded to Harry. 'Time for the champagne.'

Harry brought the bottle from the kitchen along with five flutes.

'We're celebrating,' said May.

Harry opened the champagne, filled the glasses and handed them round. Johnny protested that he was already drinking beer.

'You'll put it aside and raise a glass with the rest of us,' said May. 'We're drinking a toast to our new venture.'

Alistair said he'd thought they were celebrating the return of the honeymooners.

'No,' said May. 'Not that. Well, a little bit. But we've been busy when you were away. We've bought a hotel.'

'You've what?' said Alistair.

'You heard,' said May. 'We're going into the hotel business. There's money there. It's going to be a family business, with everyone involved. It'll be a restaurant first. Then we'll expand into having staying guests. We're all going to have to muck in. But it'll be the best hotel in the country. Luxury bedrooms, top cuisine, a swimming pool. Oh, it'll have everything. I've got it all planned.'

Johnny, Alistair and Nell were too stunned to speak. Even if they did have misgivings, they knew not to mention them. May was giving them 'the glare'. It was a look that told all doubters to hold their tongue.

Harry raised his glass. 'To the hotel and to the Rutherfords.'

They held up their glasses and shouted, 'To the Rutherfords.' They drank. Harry took the bottle round the room. 'Top up? Top up?'

'A hotel,' said Nell. 'Goodness.' Her mind filled with dreams of plush carpets, glistening rows of exotic bottles on shelves behind dark mahogany bars, velvet-covered chairs, a candlelit dining room with a single white rose on every table, sophisticated diners, and a swimming pool – deep blue and tempting. It would be like the sumptuous hotels she'd seen in the movies. The sort of place films stars haunted. Audrey Hepburn and Rock Hudson might turn up there. Unlikely, but Nell was an unlikely dreamer. She was bedazzled. Thoughts of her mother vanished.

Chapter Eleven
Carol

Carol knew where Johnny was, and why he didn't come home. He'd be at his mother's house; the food was better there. No doubt Nell would have told him that she'd burned the roast beef.

Johnny would return sometime after ten, but he wouldn't spend time with her, chatting, telling her about his day. He'd go straight to bed. She'd sit up till after midnight, watching television or reading. They rarely communicated. Almost as soon as they'd married, they ran out of things to say to one another. But then, when Carol thought about it, they never had spoken much. She realised that her relationship with Johnny hadn't been about conversation. When they were alone together they'd been too busy making love to chat. On dates they'd gone to the pub where Johnny was a regular. He'd talk to his mates about sport and cars. She sat beside him looking beautiful. This was all he asked of her. But she couldn't complain; all she asked of him was that he was so good-looking girls in the pub would gaze at him and envy her.

She carried Katy to the kitchen where she fed her.

'Don't think your dad's coming home anytime soon. It's just us again. You'd think they'd invite us round if they're celebrating the return of Nell and Alistair. But they didn't.'

She scooped a spoonful of mushy cauliflower cheese into Katy's mouth. 'Made it myself. What do you think?'

The child stared at her and opened her mouth at the approaching loaded spoon.

'We'll take that as an excellent, then,' said Carol. 'Awfully quiet here. I think we should put the radio on.' She stuffed a third spoonful into Katy's mouth, got up and switched on the radio then returned to the task in hand. 'Didn't think you'd be so hungry.' She sighed then apologised. 'Sorry, huge sigh. It isn't you. I'm just not happy. One, your father's hardly ever here. Two, when he is here he's sleeping.' She leaned towards her daughter. 'You don't mind me dumping all this on you, I hope, only I've nobody to talk to. You know what the problem is, don't you? He's still a kid. And, after having you, I became a woman. That's the problem.'

Katy grinned. She didn't talk much yet but was a happy baby.

'You think that's funny? I think it's a bit dire. There's mushy apples for pudding. Your father gets dressed up every Friday and off he goes into the night looking for a good time like he was seventeen. And don't tell me there aren't women involved in this good time. There are. There has to be.'

She fed Katy the puréed apples and told her, 'I don't

think there's any actual sex. Don't repeat that word to either of your grannies. But there will be fondling and kissing. He needs constant reassurance that he's still good-looking.' She absently ate a couple of spoonfuls of apples. 'I can't complain about money, though. He gives me more than enough.'

Every Friday evening, before he went out on the town, Johnny would take a wad of notes from his pocket, peel off several ten-pound notes and give them to Carol.

Once she'd suggested they open a bank account and start saving.

'What for?' Johnny had wanted to know.

'For a house.'

'We've got a house.'

'One day we might need a bigger one.'

He had shaken his head. 'No we won't.'

Carol had pointed out that they might have more children. 'A brother or sister for Katy.'

'We've got three bedrooms. That's enough for any family.'

Carol had gone on to suggest they might need to replace the carpets and the sofa one day. 'To be honest, I don't like them. I want to pick my own furniture.'

He'd told her that his mother had picked their furniture and would be hurt if they threw it out and bought something new. 'I'm not going to get on the wrong side of my mother, and neither are you. I don't like this house either. It's not what I'd have chosen. But then, I don't like my job. It was always assumed

I'd work with my dad. Nobody asked me what I wanted to do. I hate selling cars.'

Carol had asked what he'd wanted to do.

'Something in sport. Perhaps a physical education teacher or a coach. Look, none of this is what I wanted. But I did the right thing. I married you, and I do love my little girl. So here we are. The hideous carpets don't bother me as much as they do you. I've been living with my mother's taste all my life.'

Carol had pointed out that if he'd sorted the sofa and the carpets, faced up to May, maybe he'd be able to sort out the rest of his life. 'Your job, for example.'

He'd waved the suggestion away. 'Here's the deal. We stay here. We suffer the carpets and the sofa. Friday nights I go out. I need to relax. I give you money. You can buy what you want. Only no new houses, no new furniture and no bank accounts. You pay for everything with cash. OK?'

'OK,' she'd agreed. But it was only said quietly to avoid an argument.

She removed Katy's bib, wiped her mouth, heaved her from her high chair and took her back to the living room. 'Yes,' she said, 'Johnny is still a kid. He's angry. You can see it in the way he walks and the way he prowls about the house or sits in front of the television drinking beer. He even mumbles furiously in his sleep. And it's why he buys all the clothes. Every week a new shirt or shoes or trousers. He's clinging to his time as a single guy.' She put Katy down on the rug and handed her several bright red bricks. 'Build me something. A new house would be good. Maybe you'll grow up to be an architect. You can do anything you want when you're big – just don't get pregnant before you're married.'

She poured some of the wine she'd brought out to christen the new glasses. 'Good glasses. They're just about the only thing in this house that I like. Did you see Nell's new shoes? God, they're lovely. Wish they were mine. Still, I didn't mention them. Didn't say they were great. God, I'm such a bitch. I'm jealous of my best friend and her life and her new husband.'

She got down on the floor beside Katy and put one brick on top of another. 'Now you put one on top of my one.'

Katy swept the brick away. 'Down!' she cried jubilantly.

'Ah,' said Carol, 'you're feeling destructive. Well, that's OK. Gets rid of the anger. Johnny should do that – express his rage instead of bottling it up. You know what's going to happen, don't you? He's going to explode one day. Or I might explode. One way or another an explosion is coming.'

Chapter Twelve
Isn't Life Fabulous?

The hotel was not as Nell had imagined. But then, nothing ever was. She'd dreamed of a huge mansion fronted by spreading lush lawns either side of a long drive. But this was an old coaching inn set a little bit back from the main road. It looked lonely.

The white walls were now grey, a searing black damp stain rose from the base of the front wall up to the first floor windows. There were tiles missing from the roof, stringy ivy crawled past the main door, paint peeled from the window frames, the small car-parking area at the front of the inn was layered with scruffy gravel. May declared it beautiful, and since nobody disagreed with her – they didn't dare – she assumed everyone thought so too.

Stepping inside, the word that came to Nell's mind was rubble. She was reminded of the aftermath in disaster movies. That moment when the survivors of some horrendous explosion emerge from a collapsed building, look round at the destruction, scarcely able to believe they are still alive and not sure, really, if they want to be among the living if this was what they had to contend with.

What Nell saw was dust. A dense cloud floated in the few rays of sunlight that came from the broken windows. There was a scattering of abandoned furniture – bar stools, tables, tattered lamps – and more dust. A forlorn moth-eaten stag's head loomed over the doorway. A couple of pigeons perched on one of the exposed beams that stretched overhead from one end of the room to the other. They cocked their heads, eyed the intruders with suspicion. After all, they'd had the place to themselves for the past seven years.

Everyone was here. May had insisted the whole family come with her for her first inspection of the new property. She'd brought a picnic.

'It's a bit run down,' observed Nell.

'Of course it is,' said May. 'That's why it was so cheap. I'm not daft.'

She turned a full circle, arms spread. 'This area will be the bar, with a big roaring log fire and a fine range of whiskies. Then through there—' she pointed to a room off the one they were in '—will be the dining room. It'll be exclusive. You'll have to book a table in advance. The bedrooms, all done out in luxury, will be upstairs, of course.' She looked up, contemplating the gorgeousness to come. Her entourage – Harry, Johnny, Carol, Alistair and Nell – followed her gaze, but saw only the pigeons and a ceiling with lumps of plaster missing. 'It's going to be lovely.'

She walked past the bar, opened a door at the back of the room. 'This is the kitchen and out there's the garden. There will be a covered walkway leading from the French windows in the residents' quarter to the swimming pool.'

The kitchen was small. There was a grease-encrusted commercial range, a long table and beside the door was a selection of bins. The garden outside was mostly brambles and nettles.

Nell wasn't impressed. 'What are you going to call the place?'

'Something French,' said May. 'France is where you get the best cuisine. People will be expecting that sort of food. Chateau House, I thought.'

Alistair looked thoughtful. 'Chateau means big house in French. So you're calling your hotel House House?'

May gave him the glare, and then continued enthusing. She folded her arms, looked round and announced, 'I have a vision.'

Alistair followed her gaze and said, 'A vision is good. You've got to have a vision.'

'Yes,' said May. 'I have a vision. It'll make us a pile when we get going.'

'You'll need a lot of staff,' said Nell, 'for the bar, dining room and kitchen, as well as people to look after the bedrooms – chambermaids and the like.'

'We'll keep it in the family,' said May. 'There are Alistair's aunts, uncles and cousins. There's you and Carol. We'll manage. I've got it all sorted in my head.' She tapped the side of the head, proving how sorted it was up there.

Nell said she didn't want to be a chambermaid. 'I'm happy selling pens.' Taking part in the new venture hadn't been what she imagined. She'd thought she'd enjoy dropping in at a bar where people knew her name and asked if she'd like her usual. Being one of the Rutherfords would give her automatic admission to the in crowd. Scrubbing out lavatories and making beds had no appeal.

It was her turn for the glare.

'No, you're not happy selling pens. You just feel safe doing it. You've never tried anything else,' May told her. 'There's no future in it. You're a Rutherford now. You're life isn't about you anymore. It's about us, all of us. You'll have to roll up your sleeves and muck in like the rest of us. It's your duty.'

Alistair put his arm round Nell and said he was sure she'd like to help but they were planning on starting a family.

Nell looked at him in horror.

May gripped Nell's arm. 'You're not . . . ?'

'No,' said Nell. 'I'm not. I don't want to have a baby yet. I want Alistair and me to spend time together first. Alistair wants to have a baby. He keeps nagging me about it. He said he'd stop, but soon as we got back from the honeymoon, he started again.'

May slapped Alistair's wrist. 'You leave Nell alone. She'll have a baby in her own good time. The notion will grab her soon enough. It grabs most women, after all. It's a curse.'

Alistair looked sheepish.

May put her arm round Nell. 'This girl needs time to enjoy being a wife before she becomes a mother.

Once you're a mother, you're a mother for life. The worrying and the caring goes on and on and on.' She hugged Nell. 'You stick to your guns. You have a baby when you want. It's you has to carry it and you that gives birth. Then it'll be you doing the midnight feeds and the nappies and dealing with the teething and you taking them to school and you helping with the home-work and you sitting up worrying when they're out late.'

Nell thought that this woman alone could solve the world population problem. She'd certainly put her off motherhood, but she loved May for taking her side in the ongoing baby dispute.

'Still,' said May, 'you can both help with the decor-ating at the weekends. Do you no harm to get familiar with a brush and a pot of paint.'

Johnny said that it'd be a while before they got to the actual decorating. He had his hands in his pockets and was looking down at his shoes, lifting them from time to time, examining them, worried that the muck on the floor would ruin their shine.

May said, 'Your Uncle Dave will see to all that. He's got contacts in the trade.'

Harry's brother Dave was in property. He owned a huge number of flats across Edinburgh that he rented out. Whenever something in one of his flats needed fixed or replaced, Dave got in touch with one of the many workmen he'd met in pubs on the outskirts of town – plumbers, joiners, roofers, painters and many more who were prepared to work for cash. He had names and phone numbers listed in a small red note-book that he kept in his desk at home.

It was Sunday, a month exactly since May had made her announcement. She'd picked up the keys on Friday. This was her first trip out to view her new property.

'I'm itching to get started, but I have to wait till your cousin Derek draws up the plans. Then we'll get going.' May made her way back to the front door, looked up at the pigeons. 'The pair of you will have to find a new home. Your days here are numbered.'

Alistair followed, pointing out that Derek had not long passed his final exams. 'He's fresh out of university. Don't you think you need someone with a bit of experience?'

'This will be his first commission. He's got to make a go of it. Can't mess up your first job – your future depends on it. Besides he's family.'

'This venture is all about family,' said Harry.

Nell stopped worrying about the effects of dust and rubble on her beloved Italian shoes as she was hit by a sudden inspiration, 'Then that's what you should call this place.'

'What? Family?' said May. 'I don't think much of that.'

'No,' said Nell. 'You should call it Rutherford's.'

May swooned. 'It's so bleedin' obvious, I never thought of it. Rutherford's. That's perfect. Says it all.'

They trooped back to the parking area outside where May unpacked her picnic basket, pulling out a selection of sandwiches, an almond cake, a bottle of Sauvignon and glasses. They uncorked the bottle (May would never forget something as important as a corkscrew). They shouted their toast. 'Rutherford's,' they cried. The sun shone, birds sang and May looked round at the small company, eyes aglow with joy. 'Oh, isn't life fabulous?!'

Chapter Thirteen
The Famous
One-Legged Kiss

By late spring, work on the hotel was underway. The rubble was cleared, the walls plastered, the roof retiled and the pigeons sent on their way. May visited every day. Scarlet-lipped and eyes thick with blue shadow, she tripped through the building on six-inch stilettos, hugging her fur coat round her. She beamed at the workmen, telling them to carry on and keep up the good work. She fussed over details, itched to get busy choosing wallpapers, curtains, carpets, 'and taps,' she said. 'Good taps are a sign of a classy hotel. Mine will be gold-plated.' Always she looked round and sighed. 'This is going to be lovely.'

Every Friday at four o'clock, Harry stopped by the worksite and pulled a pile of cheap brown envelopes from his briefcase. He paid his tradesmen in cash. He'd tap the side of his nose. 'Good money for good work and the taxman doesn't know a thing. Let's keep him out of it.'

Thursday nights were as they'd always been. The family had their meetings. Alistair went to eat and discuss business with his parents. Nell wasn't invited.

It was so much part of her life with Alistair, she didn't think about it. Besides, he'd told her it was boring. 'Just business, business, business and a lot of bickering.'

'But the food will be good,' said Nell, because the food wasn't so good where she went on Thursdays: home to eat with her mother and father. Thursday nights were egg and chips nights. In fact, Nell didn't really mind. She was beginning to find comfort in the familiar.

She'd go directly from work. The food was always ready and put in front of her as soon as she'd taken off her coat. Every week Nell's mother would glance at her stomach to see if it was swelling, then the glance would move up to Nell's face. Their eyes would meet. Nancy would raise her eyebrows, silently asking if a grandchild was on the way. Nell would sigh and shake her head and say, 'Not yet. Give me a couple of years.'

She and her mother and father would sit at the fold-down Formica-topped table politely passing round the tomato ketchup and sliced and buttered bread. The teapot in its green cosy sat centre stage, and, now that Nell was married, living away from home, and was, therefore, a visitor, they drank from the good china. The place still smelled of cooking fat with an undertow of bleach. These days, Nell found it rather calming.

The conversation was mundane – the weather, Nell's day at the pen shop, Nancy's day at the cake shop and things Nell's father had seen from his vantage point on the sofa. Today it had been a dog peeing on the front gate and Mrs Livingston next door buying fish from the van that came round every Thursday morning. Not a lot, but he made it sound interesting.

Afterwards, her father would go back to his sofa to watch television while Nell and Nancy washed up. As they did, they'd talk womanly talk. Nell noticed that now she was a married woman, her mother spoke of married things. For Nancy this meant instructing her daughter in the importance of cleaning. 'A day set aside for every chore. Monday for washing, Tuesday ironing, Wednesday the bedrooms, change sheets and . . .'

Nell lost interest. She'd heard all this many times, and always found it boring. She wondered if there had ever been passion in this immaculate house. Had her mother and father rushed home every evening after a day delivering coal and serving in the cake shop to hold one another, to kiss deeply and swear eternal love? Had they made it a mission to make love in every room in the house as she and Alistair had? Had they shared baths, bickering about who would sit at the tap end? Did they have a song that was *their* song? Had her mother ever stripped off in the kitchen when a sexy tune had come on the radio, abandoning the lamb chops under the grill as she wriggled and pranced and peeled off her clothes? Nell had done this last week. The chops burned. Watching her mother vigorously wipe plates and set them on the draining board for Nell to dry, jaw clenched, determined not to let a scraping of egg yolk escape the fevered scouring of her dish cloth, Nell decided no, Nancy had done none of these things. The way she bustled and wielded the bleach, she certainly didn't look like she'd ever done any of these things.

Nell slowly, slowly dried a teaspoon and gazed out into the garden. Late spring, and light was fading. Tulips were in flower. Not in clumps, but in splendid regimental order, shoulder to shoulder, braving the breeze. Nell stopped drying the spoon. She looked out the window in amazement. The garden was small. She hadn't noticed that before. In fact, for years she'd thought it huge. Well, she thought, it *was* huge when I was three.

She looked round the room. It was small. When did this happen? Had it shrunk, or had it always been this size? And her mother suddenly was so much smaller than Nell thought. She had to stretch on tiptoe to reach the back of the draining board. Had she always done that? Nell gazed into the distance, wondering at this new revelation.

Her mother snatched the tea towel she was using and waved her towards a chair.

'Give me that. You've been wiping that spoon for the last ten minutes. You've drifted into a dream. You're always dreaming. Too much dreaming and not enough doing, that's you.'

Nell turned arms spread, taking in the kitchen. 'Has this place got smaller? Have you got smaller?'

'Don't be daft,' Nancy said. 'That's the silliest thing anyone's ever said to me. This place is the same size it always was. I'm not getting smaller. It's you is getting bigger.'

'No, I'm not,' said Nell.

'Of course you are.' Nancy flapped the dishtowel at her. 'You've moved out. You live in that fancy flat; go fancy places with that man of yours. Your world's expanding. I knew this day would come. When you'd look at me and your dad and notice what we're really like – plain and ordinary, a bit dull. Well, that's what happens to you when you've been married for years. It's the routine does it. Anyway, I like being dull. It suits me. I know what's happening everyday when I get up. No surprises, that's what I like.'

Nell sat on the top deck of the bus going home. She watched the world slip by, catching fleeting glimpses of passing front rooms. Families watching television, a man polishing his shoes, a woman ironing – these things pleased her. She loved to speculate about other peoples' lives. Tonight, though, she cursed herself for her stupid remark about her mother getting smaller, and wondered if, now she was married, she was on her way to being plain and ordinary and a bit dull. Certainly Carol was up in arms about how dull her own life had become.

Last week Carol had phoned Nell. 'I'm lonely.'

It was nine o'clock at night. Nell and Alistair had just taken up their television-watching positions on the sofa. Alistair had been slouched in the corner, Nell lying with her head in his lap. She'd heaved herself to her feet and, complaining bitterly, stumped to the kitchen to pick up the receiver.

'Why are you lonely? Isn't Johnny there?'

They always launched straight into conversation. Announcing themselves, saying hello, it's me, would have taken up precious gossiping time.

'Yes, he's here. But he's sleeping in front of the telly. That's what he does every night when he's home. He never talks to me.'

'He's tired.'

'So am I. Really tired. It's exhausting looking after a little one all day. I look forward to a little adult conversation at night, but all I ever get is him snoring.'

Nell had said nothing. She hadn't needed to speak; Carol had been working up to a full rant.

'He comes home, throws down his jacket, eats, then goes off to watch the TV. Hardly says a word. This isn't right. I'm not putting up with this. He goes off every Friday night, and says it's his relaxing time. But what about me?'

'What about you?'

'I need relaxing time, too. I need a night out. Remember when we used to go to the Locarno? I was happy then. Out on the town. Dancing. Having fun. I was really living then. Now my life is really boring. I'm fed up and I'm eating too many biscuits. Ever since I left school, it was my big ambition to get married. And my mother was forever saying that one day I'd have a husband and children and live in a house of my own. She never mentioned how awful it is – cooking and cleaning and that. I'm bored and I'm lonely and I'm getting fat.'

'So what are you going to do?'

'I'm going to go out and find some fun for myself before I get any older and fatter.'

Nell had heard Katy start crying in the background.

'Bugger. Katy's awake. She's probably had a bad dream. I'd better go.'

Nell had gone back to her television-watching position with Alistair. 'It was Carol complaining that she's bored and she's getting old and fat.'

Alistair had yawned. 'Aren't we all?'

Now the bus trundled into Princes Street. Nell got off; she'd walk the rest of the way home. The city was busy tonight. She made her way through the crowds, stopping now and then to window gaze and people watch. She liked looking at the young men who strutted along the middle of the pavement eyeing passing girls. Thursday night was just for flirting. The drinking and swaggering would come tomorrow after they'd been paid. Nell was good at observing from the sidelines without being noticed. It was a skill she'd learned at the Locarno.

Still she was glad she was no longer part of this parade. Time was, she and Carol would walk, arms linked, secretly watching the boys while pretending to be more interested in the shop windows. They'd nudge one another if they spotted someone they fancied, giggle if he noticed them and winked, whistled or smiled. Back then Carol had been the one who got the admiring glances. She'd been queen of the street game, the one who'd mastered the fine art of noticing she'd been noticed and acting coy. Nell had been the dowdy best friend. She never got the boy.

Remembering this, she sighed and quickened her pace. She wanted to be at home and hoped Alistair was already there waiting for her. She reached the West End and glancing across the road at the Caledonian Hotel, saw Carol standing at the entrance. She was laughing. Nell stepped toward the kerb, raised her hand to wave and was just about to call her friend's name, when a man came out. He too was laughing.

The man put his arm round Carol, pulled her to him. Kissed her. Nell lowered her hand. That wasn't Carol. It couldn't be Carol. But there was something about the kissing stance that was very familiar. The woman across the road had her arms round the man's neck and was standing on one leg, the other bent behind her. Carol's favourite street kissing position copied from a film she'd seen years ago. The kiss ended. The woman gazed up at the man, stroked his cheek then put her lips softly to his mouth for a little finishing-off mini kiss – one of Carol's trademarks.

Nell stepped back, hid in a doorway. There was no mistaking it. That woman across the street, laughing and kissing, was her best friend. Carol was out on the town having fun before she got too old and too fat.

Heels clicking on the pavement, handbag banging on her side, Nell ran home. She had to tell Alistair about this. He was calm, steady and reliable. He could mend fuses, change plugs, fix flat tyres – he could do just about everything. He'd know what to do. He always did.

She burst into the flat, bristling with her news, calling his name. He was in the kitchen, sitting at the table with a bottle of whisky in front of him.

'Well,' he said topping up his glass, 'that's it.'

'What's it?' said Nell.

'I've left the family. Told my ma and pa I don't want to know about their business dealings. I don't think we'll be seeing much of them in future.'

Nell's face said it all. She was confused, worried and disappointed.

'There are things going on,' said Alistair. 'My mother and father's dealings aren't exactly legal. I'm a lawyer; I can't be in on that sort of thing. I'd lose my job. My whole career would go down the plug. To be a lawyer you have to be a fit and proper person.'

'What sort of dealings?'

'Illegal ones,' said Alistair. 'I'm not going to tell you about them. What you don't know can't hurt you.'

'But you can't do that. You can't leave your family.'

'I just have,' he said. He smiled. 'I have you. You're all I need. We'll be fine.'

Nell was struggling to take in this dreadful news. She was sure the dubious dealings Alistair mentioned couldn't be *that* bad. She was totting up all the things that were about to drop out of her life: the elaborate meals; the flowing wine; the lavish Christmases; the out-of-the-blue gifts. She'd been hoping she and Alistair would get a Jaguar soon.

This was awful. Why, the family was part of the reason she'd married Alistair. It broke her heart. The fabulousness would go on – the roaring fires, the food, the glistening glasses kept constantly topped up with wine, the laughter – and she wouldn't be there to enjoy it.

Chapter Fourteen
A Running-away Fund

Rutherford's opened in August. May and Harry had put up a huge dark-green sign outside with their name in gold lettering. The building was bedecked with fairy lights. They celebrated by throwing a party for over two hundred people. The hospitality was lavish: champagne and a buffet table laden with gleaming glazed hams, lobsters, chickens and an array of salads and multi-tiered cakes. May had wanted a roasted hog's head complete with apple in its mouth as a centrepiece but Harry had told her no. 'People will think it's giving them the evil eye.' She'd opted instead for a huge shimmering ice sculpture of the Eiffel Tower. 'Since we're to be serving French food.' She'd sighed when she saw it. 'It's shiny. It's magnificent. When it comes to Rutherford's, that sculpture says it all.' She'd taken Harry's arm and put her head on his shoulder. 'We're shiny and magnificent.'

The guests mingled, marvelled and sweated. It was hot; one of those nights when the heat of the day lingers deep and thick long into the evening and seems to suck the oxygen out of the air. The heat was intensified by the roaring flames in the huge hearth – May insisted that the place didn't look inviting enough with the fireplace empty and dead. 'You need flickering flames to give the place sparkle.'

Alistair and Nell were there. They hadn't been invited – they'd been summoned. *Don't you dare not turn up,* May had written along the bottom of their embossed official invitation, *this family has to present a united front to the world.* So, dressed in their best clothes, they'd turned up. Nell wore a blue dress, high at the neck and cut low down her back. Alistair had raised his eyebrows when she appeared in it. 'New?' he asked. 'I haven't seen it before.'

She told him she'd bought it in a sale. 'Half price.' She lied. May had paid for it.

Two weeks after Alistair had told his family that he wanted nothing more to do with their shenanigans and had walked out of the business meeting, May had turned up at the pen shop. 'Just passing,' she'd told Nell. 'Thought I'd drop in to say hello. Have you had your lunch?' It had been one o'clock.

Nell had shaken her head.

'Well, let's go and get a bite.'

They'd gone to a small café on the High Street. May had ordered sandwiches and coffee. She hadn't asked Nell what she wanted. She'd been sure she didn't need to. She had a natural instinct for other people's nutritional needs. 'Well,' she'd said, 'just because Alistair has fallen out with his family, it doesn't mean we can't be friends. How is he, anyway?'

Nell had told her he was fine. 'Busy at work, but fine.'

'Good. Now, I want you to phone me once a week to tell me how he's doing.'

Nell had asked why.

'Because I'm his mother. I worry about him. It's my job. I need to be told regularly that he's all right.' She'd rummaged in her bag and brought out an envelope. 'For you.'

Nell had turned it over in her hands.

'Open it,' May had told her.

The envelope had contained a bankbook with a single deposit of two hundred pounds. 'What's this for? I already have a bank account. Well, a joint account with Alistair.'

'That's your secret account. A joint one with me. It's your running-away fund.'

'Why would I run away? Where would I go?'

'Most women go to the shops. When you're running away, you don't have to run far.'

The sandwiches had arrived. May had opened them, and peered at the fillings. 'I'm studying sandwiches at the moment. We're going to be serving them at Rutherford's.' She'd fished a notebook from her handbag and jotted down *crab with mayonnaise, cheese and onion, and cucumber with cream cheese.* 'Very nice,' she'd said. 'Every woman should have a running-away fund. I have one.'

'In a bank?' Nell had asked. 'I thought you didn't like banks.'

'I don't. My fund is in cash.'

'So why do you need another one? A joint account with me?'

'Oh, it's your fund. I only put my name on the account so I could pay money in from time to time.'

'Did you ever run away?'

May had taken a bite of her sandwich, and had chewed thoughtfully, 'Cream cheese and cucumber is a good sandwich idea. I'll put it on the menu. Of course, it's a woman's sandwich. Men prefer roast beef or cheese and onion.' She'd taken a sip of coffee. 'I often ran away. You don't know what it's like, alone all day with two toddlers. The little fights, the big fights, squabbles, nappies, loneliness. I needed to get away from time to time. Kept me sane. Mostly I just went to the shops and bought a bar of chocolate that I ate by myself. Sometimes I had a long bubble bath. But that was when we'd no money and my fund was small. Later, I'd go shopping and get a new coat or something. I never actually ran away anywhere. I couldn't. I'd have been on the phone every night checking that the boys had eaten a decent meal and cleaned their teeth before bed. I wouldn't have been able to let go.' She'd sniffed. 'I won't ever let go.'

Nell had eaten a crab sandwich and wrestled with this new information.

'It's just a matter of having secret money,' May had told her. 'It gives you independence.'

'Do you think Harry has a running away fund?'

'Good heavens, no. He's a man. Men don't think

like that. See, women are stoics. Men aren't. They just yell when they're in pain. They don't suffer in silence. Women need the fund for when the suffering and the silence get too much. It's a little escape route. And knowing they have a nest egg put aside for a rainy day keeps them going.'

'Does Carol have a fund? Did you give her one?'

May had shaken her head. 'I expect Carol has worked out something for herself. But I didn't help her. You need things pointed out to you. You're an innocent. If you don't watch out for yourself in this life, you'll get trampled.' She'd put down her sandwich. 'Why do you ask about Carol? What's she been up to?' She'd stared at Nell, scrutinising her face, watching for small movements of the eyebrows or lips that might indicate a lie.

Nell had squirmed, looked down at her coffee and wondered if lunch with the Spanish Inquisition might be more enjoyable. How did this woman know something was amiss with Carol? How did she hone in on it when all she'd done was ask a simple question? Clearly May had a secret sixth sense when it came to matters concerning her family. She'd wondered if she should tell May about spotting Carol doing her famous one-legged kiss in the street, but decided against it. It didn't do to tell tales about your friends, so she'd said she didn't think Carol had been up to anything and had changed the subject. 'Thing is, I don't think I could turn up at home with a new coat. Alistair would want to know where I got it and how much it cost.'

'Yes, Alistair's like that. He notices things. Nothing

gets past him. You'll just have to lie to him. Say the coat's been in the wardrobe for ages. Or if you can't do that, tell him you got it in a sale – a bargain you couldn't resist.' She'd looked at her watch. 'Time you got back to work. Don't want you to get into trouble for being late.'

She'd walked Nell back to the door of the pen shop. 'You can pop some money into the fund if you want. But remember, the time may come when you'll need it, so don't go frittering it away. It's for when misery strikes.'

At the party, May spotted that Nell and Alistair had arrived and teetered towards them. She was wearing an extremely tight floor-length glittering gold dress, the sort of frock Nell had only seen on television, worn by Saturday night singers as they belted out throbbing songs about everlasting love on variety shows. She thought it dreadful.

But May was thrilled with how she looked, even if walking was tricky. She did a shuffling high-heeled twirl, and when she was once again face-to-face with Alistair and Nell, she said, 'Don't I look gorgeous?'

Nell agreed. She didn't dare do anything else.

May coldly handed Alistair a glass of champagne and gave him her best dismissive look. He remembered it well from his childhood – a thin-lipped, icy-eyed glower that told him he'd been a naughty boy and she wasn't speaking to him.

When she had finished being frosty with Alistair, May turned to Nell, put her arm round her and beamed.

'You're looking lovely, darling. Come and have some food.' Leading Nell away, she turned and gave Alistair another glower, just in case the first hadn't registered. He smiled at her, shook his head and said, 'Glower away, Ma. I'm not coming back into the family business. You'll have to take my name off the headed notepaper.'

'Ach, that boy always had a mind of his own.'

'It's his job,' said Nell. 'He has to be a fit and proper person.'

'Implying that I'm not?' May's face darkened.

'Of course not,' said Nell.

'Good girl.' She took Nell by the shoulders, turned her to face the far corner of the room and the dark red grand piano that was standing there. 'What do you think of that?'

Nell said it was beautiful. 'I didn't know you could play?'

'I can't. But I can sing and that's what I'm going to be doing later. Classy, huh?'

Nell said it was, but only because she didn't dare say it wasn't.

The buffet table was mobbed. Undaunted, May shouted, 'Make way for the cook.' People moved aside. 'That's what I like, respect.' She opened her arms at the spread on the table and turned to Nell. 'What about this, then?'

'Dazzling,' said Nell. 'It's like a feast in a fairy story.'

'That was the plan,' said May. 'Help yourself. But next time you come, you'll have to pay.' She looked round. 'Soon this place will be *the* place to come. The most fashionable restaurant in the country.' She smiled, contemplating this, and then patted Nell's hand. 'I have to circulate.' She started to breeze off, but stopped suddenly and whirled round. 'I hope you didn't use the fund to get that dress.'

Before Nell could reply, May said, 'Don't do it again. That money is for when misery strikes. And strike it will.' She pointed at Nell. 'Your trouble is you're too comfortable in your life right now. You know nothing about misery.' She looked round at the gathering at the table and addressed them all. 'But misery is out there waiting to happen. It visits us all. Am I not right, ladies?'

Spooning food onto their plates the assorted women smiled and agreed. May grinned. She knew these women. There was nothing they liked better than eating salmon mousse and salad while reminiscing about miseries they'd endured and exchanging tales of dire things that had happened to other people. And as the stories got more horrific, they'd contemplate the slice of chocolate cake they were about to indulge in.

The evening passed slowly. Nell, clutching her glass, wandered through the crowd, scanning unfamiliar faces, searching for the one she knew best – Alistair's. She couldn't find him. At one point, May took her by the elbow and pulled her to one side away from the throng. 'You're wandering about looking lost and woebegone. Stop it. You young ones have no idea about how to hide your feelings. Step forward with a purpose. Look as if you know where you are going. Look interesting.

That's the sort of people I want here, interesting ones. Now get back in there, mingle, chat, smile, and pretend to be a fun person, even though you're not.'

Chastised, Nell went back to searching for Alistair. Jostling through the crowd, she caught snatches of conversation. Mostly people were complaining about the heat. Some were unimpressed by the grandness of the occasion.

'Wonderful food,' said a woman.

'Bit over the top,' her companion replied. 'The Rutherfords always overdo everything. Show-offs.'

Heading out into the garden, Nell passed two men discussing the new restaurant. 'How long do you give it?'

'A year, if this extravagance is anything to go by,' said critic number one.

'I'd say six months,' said number two.

Nell moved on into the garden, searched the faces there and found Carol. She was leaning against a tree looking bored, but provocative. She was being Brigitte Bardot – sultry. She'd been practising her pout. They trilled their fingers at one another and smiled.

'Haven't seen you in ages,' said Carol. 'What've you been up to?'

'The usual. Working. Coming home, making the tea, going to bed, getting up and going out to work again. Saturday's we go out.'

Carol nodded. 'Sounds a bit boring.'

'I'm happy enough, though. I don't have to ask you what you've been doing. I saw you.'

Carol stopped pouting and asked what Nell meant.

'You were coming out of the Caledonian Hotel with a bloke.'

'When was this?'

'Months ago,' said Nell.

'How do you know it was me?'

'You did your famous one-leg-bent-behind-you kiss.'

'That could've been anybody.'

Nell leaned on the tree beside her. 'It was you. I'd know you anywhere.'

Carol swigged her champagne. 'This is nice. I could drink it all the time. It's better than rum and Coke.'

'I think you've had enough,' said Nell. 'You're looking a bit glazed.'

'You can never have enough champagne,' said Carol. She drained her glass. 'You haven't told anybody, have you?'

Nell shook her head. She didn't tell tales.

'I just want to have some fun,' said Carol. 'I'm due it. I'm making up for all the good times I missed by having a baby when I was too young. I reckon I've lost out on two years of going out on the town. Once I've had them, I'll be ready to settle down. Anyway, it was a goodbye kiss you saw. It was nothing. I'd met the bloke in the bar. He wanted me to come to his flat. You know what he'd have wanted if I'd gone. I said no and gave him one of my famous kisses to cheer him up. I don't cheat on my husband.'

The chatter and small bursts of laughter of other guests sparked around them. Carol looked across at a group of young people, watched them exchange witty remarks, looked with envy at their clothes and their confidence and jerked her head at them. 'See them? They're the real people. The in crowd. I've never managed to be part of something like that. I've never been smart enough. Now I'm just a mum, a nobody, somebody you'd pass in the street and not even notice. Except for when I go out on Thursday nights. Then I'm alive again. I miss my old life. I miss being me.'

'You don't go out to bars on your own?' Nell was shocked at the thought.

'Nah,' said Carol. 'I go with one of the mums from the mother and toddler group. She's the same as me. Got preggers too young, got some wild oats to sow. And we don't do anything much, just drinking and dancing and a little flirting. When a girl is married to a sofa snorer who never speaks to her and never tells her she's lookin' good, she needs to know she's still got what it takes.'

'And have you?' asked Nell.

'I do,' said Carol. She patted her hair, wiggled her hips and grinned.

Nell sighed and told her friend to be careful. 'You never know who you'll bump into when you're out on the town.'

'I don't need to be careful,' said Carol. 'Being careful spoils the fun. I'm only having a laugh. Nothing wrong with that.' She waved her empty glass in the air. 'I'm off for a refill.' Aglow with confidence, convinced she was the best-looking woman at the party, Carol, holding aloft her glass, disappeared into the crowd.

Alone again, Nell resumed her search for Alistair. She found him in the car park at the front of the hotel. 'What are you doing here?'

'Hiding,' he said. 'You know I hate parties, and it's getting a bit lively in there.'

'Is it?' Nell looked longingly at the door. It was open. Noise, laughter and torrents of voices poured out. The party was peaking.

He asked if she wanted to go back in.

Nell nodded.

'Of course you do,' he said, 'but not as an actual reveller. You want to be in your usual place watching from the sidelines.'

'I'm better at looking on than I am at joining in.'

Alistair took her hand. 'A swift ten minutes ogling the goings-on, and then we're going home.'

As evening chill descended, everyone had come inside. May had stoked the fire with a batch of logs and now the heat was insufferable. People gleamed, wiped their foreheads, puffed out their cheeks and complained. The buffet table had been ransacked and ruined – chickens decimated, the huge ornate salmon mousse had turned flaccid, hams were now but shreds and crumbs on their platters, baguettes torn up, lobsters cracked and shells left empty, dollops had been scooped from the cakes. The Eiffel Tower was slowly, sadly dripping, and keeling over to one side. It was a mess, a soggy mess.

But the champagne still flowed. And now some drinkers had abandoned it and were knocking back whisky or vodka from the bar. The alcoholic mix was taking its toll. Nell doubted there was a sober person here. The jostling, the shrill voices, the sudden bursts of ostentatious laughter – it reminded Nell of days gone by. It was like the Locarno without the music, the dancing and the fighting. This is what the Locarno would have been like if old people had taken over. Instead of being a room full of people behaving badly, it was a room full of people who would have behaved badly if their wives or husbands weren't around to see them.

May clapped her hands and addressed the mob. 'Ladies and gentlemen, time for a little entertainment.' She minced across the room to the piano and smiled to the young man in evening dress who was sitting at it. 'Maestro,' she said.

The piano player dragged the back of his hand over his dripping brow, dried it on his trousers and started to play the opening chords of 'There's a Small Hotel'. May leaned casually on the piano, glass placed beside her, took a deep breath and huskily sang the first syllable of the first word.

And from across the floor, a shrill scream, 'Let's twist.'

Carol had cleared a small area of floor and was giving a demonstration of the dance to a group of fascinated onlookers. Pivoting on the balls of her feet, arms bent in a running motion, she was wildly wiggling her body as she lowered and raised herself up and down. Lacking any musical accompaniment, she was getting into the groove by singing 'Let's Twist Again' at the top of her voice. Her audience, mostly men, were appreciative. When she'd finished, she laughed and clapped her hands. 'C'mon, let's twist!'

The whole room turned away from May to watch. 'The twist, how marvellous,' someone shouted. 'What fun.'

'Just twist your body from side to side and up and down you go,' shrilled Carol. 'It's easy. Move to the music.'

One or two people pointed out that there was no music. So someone shouted to the piano player to play some twisting songs. Not wanting to spoil the party, he obliged and thumped out the Chubby Checker number.

A chance to join the young ones and dance the latest craze was too much to resist. Half the room started to gyrate their bodies from side to side while lowering themselves towards the floor. They laughed at how wild and abandoned they were being and joined in the song.

May stopped leaning seductively on the piano, stood up, folded her arms and glared at Carol. Carol grinned and waved. May glared harder, the full electric stare. It could have melted the Eiffel Tower if it hadn't already slumped in a mushy heap onto the table.

The look stung Nell. She gasped. When insulted, this woman was terrifying. But Carol didn't care; she was drunk and doing the twist and having a wonderful time.

Nell saw May turn the vile stare at Johnny. He was

leaning on the bar watching his wife's display looking mildly amused. Sensing his mother's glare, he looked at her, shrugged, caught the bar tender's eye and ordered a beer.

Nell turned to Alistair to see what he was thinking. He was smiling, his eyes aglow, watching Carol with admiration, and something else. Lust. Nell gazed at him. Yes, dammit, that was lust on her charming, mild-mannered husband's face.

Chapter Fifteen
Come In

For some time it had been Carol's morning routine to lock the doors and hide upstairs to avoid May. When she was first married, May had dropped by every day bringing food and offering advice on the business of looking after a man – one man in particular: her son. She offered daily updates on what Johnny liked to eat, wear and watch on television. As she did this, she would sweep round the kitchen gathering breakfast dishes, packing damp towels in the washing machine and giving instructions on how to serve the meal she'd brought for that night's supper. Every so often she would stop, sigh and say, 'He was a beautiful baby. And he's still beautiful. I could just sit and stare at that face of his for hours and hours.'

Later, after Katy was born, May would bring small tubs of puréed food. 'Chicken and carrot, homemade this morning. You don't want to be giving her any of that shop-bought stuff. You don't know what's in it. This—' she waved the tub at Carol '—is pure goodness.'

Eventually, unable to bear this early intrusion, Carol

had taken her baby to the bedroom, crawled with her under the blankets and listened as May rang the doorbell and shouted, 'Hello, anybody at home?' through the letterbox. In time that changed; May would walk round the house peering in through the windows, rattle at the back door, and then return to the front door and shout, 'I know you're in there. You're hiding. You're being silly, behaving like a spoilt child. Nobody hides from me.'

This went on for a couple of weeks. Then it stopped. Carol would spend her mornings sitting, shoulders tensed, waiting for the dread sound of May's footsteps on the gravel path outside. Nothing. It was over. Carol relaxed. The witch had got the message. She wasn't wanted here.

On the morning after the gala opening party at Rutherford's, Carol was feeling seedy. Her head throbbed, her mouth was dry and newly awakened muscles in her legs ached from too much twisting. She fed Katy, put her in her playpen and sat at the kitchen table contemplating last night's foolishness. She'd drunk too much champagne. She'd given a demonstration of the twist. She'd upstaged her mother-in-law. There would be repercussions. She didn't dare think what they would be.

'You forgot to lock the door,' said a voice from behind her.

Carol span round, her hand on her chest to soothe her startled heart. May was standing in the doorway. It was eight-thirty in morning and she was wearing her new navy business suit complete with briefcase and six-inch heels. Her face was made up, a thick layer of blue eye-shadow on her lids, her mouth a slash of scarlet lipstick. She reeked of Estée Lauder Youth Dew perfume. It was scary.

'Who do you think you are, doing the twist at my party?'

Carol opened her mouth to reply. She was about to say she hadn't realised May was about to sing. Though this wasn't true. Her loud offer to demonstrate the new dance had been a piece of mischief. She'd wanted to annoy her mother-in-law.

'You deliberately upstaged me,' said May. 'Nobody upstages me. It was my party and if I want to sing, I'll sing. Rutherford's is mine. It's posh. There will be no teenage nonsense there. It will be a twist-free zone where people can relax and enjoy haute cuisine food and good wine.' She pointed at Carol. 'You are going to learn to behave yourself. You are going to come and work for me. You'll muck in, serve tables, wash dishes, chop vegetables, scrub and sweat with me to make the business a success. We'll be in that kitchen from dawn till dusk. We'll be bone tired; our hands will be raw red. We'll hardly see our husbands and there will be no fun and no twisting for us but it will be worth it. You start tomorrow. Meantime, clean up this house. It's filthy.'

Carol opened her mouth again. This time to say she had no intention of working for May. She hated cooking. She hated cleaning. She hated her life.

May held up a silencing hand. 'Look at you. We're half way through the morning and you're still in your dressing gown. You're nothing but a lazy slut. When I was your age I'd have the nappies washed and out on the line, the house immaculate and the boys fed, dressed and ready for a trip to the park. What sort of wife are you never cooking, never cleaning? My son, my beautiful son, deserves to come home to a sparkling house, a hot meal and a loving wife. Do you know for weeks now he's been bringing his dirty shirts to me to wash and iron? He's a man and men need looking after. That's a woman's job. And you're no good at it. You can't even fry an egg. You're useless.'

She turned and strode towards the front door shouting, 'But don't worry, I'll soon cure you of that.' She slammed the door after her.

Carol slumped in her chair, blew out her cheeks and said, 'Well, that's me told.' She poured herself a cup of tea, looked round and thought that she had to agree with May. The place was a mess. She considered the cups heaped beside the sink. 'Cups. I can't be bothered with cups. I don't want to wash them. Technically, they're not my cups. I didn't choose them. I hate them.' She went over to the playpen where Katy was sucking on a rusk. 'I didn't know I'd have to do all this when I got married. I promised to love, honour and cherish. There was no mention of cups in the deal. Or vacuuming, or making beds, or ironing.'

She picked up the child, and carried her to the living room, 'Look at this place. Isn't it awful? It's hideous – all clashing colours, too much pattern.' She slapped her hand over her eyes. 'It hurts to look at it. This isn't what I wanted. This is what the witch wanted. She chose everything. This isn't where I live. It's where I stay, a roof over my head. That's all. It isn't home.'

The word stilled her. Home, she thought. It's where her mother was – a place of comfort, hot food on the table and a warm bed at night. She wanted to be back in her pink bedroom, a mug of cocoa on the bedside table and a poster of James Dean looking moody. 'Let's go home,' she said. 'Let's just pack up and go where we really belong.'

The notion pleased her. She was suddenly happy. *Happiness.* She grinned. She'd forgotten how it felt. She swept the baby up and ran upstairs to pack. It took a while. Decisions about what to take and what to leave were hard, but two hours later, she walked out of the house and set off along the street shoving Katy in her pushchair, over-stuffed suitcase banging against her leg, singing 'There's No Place Like Home'.

She took the bus to Princes Street and strolled the pavement gazing into shop windows. It was busy, the case was heavy and the child got hot, hungry and fractious, screaming and kicking to get out of her pushchair. Carol crossed the road and went into the gardens where she sat on the grass sharing an ice cream and a bar of chocolate with Katy, and then she held her close and willed her to sleep. She needed peace to daydream.

She imagined, with a sigh, how sweet her life would soon become. In the mornings, she and her mother would potter about the house before taking Katy to the park. In the afternoons, they'd sit by the fire and talk about womanly things. The family would gather round the kitchen table every night at six o'clock when Carol's father got home from work, eating meals her mother prepared. At night she'd sleep in her pink bedroom. It was going to be perfect.

It was after two in the afternoon before Carol arrived at her old home. At the door, she'd doubted herself. Perhaps it wasn't a good idea to suddenly announce she was home to stay. Perhaps she should test the waters. She was sure her mother would be overjoyed to have her daughter and granddaughter living with her, but to give herself time to break the news gently Carol left her suitcase outside on the doorstep.

She barged into the house shouting, 'Hello. It's me,' and was surprised when her mother didn't seem pleased to see her.

Margaret bustled from the living room and stood in the hall looking confused. 'What are you doing here? You might have let me know you were coming. I was just settling down to listen to the afternoon play on the radio.'

'I just thought I'd bring your grandchild for a surprise visit. I thought you'd like to see her.'

'I'm always pleased to see her.' She looked at the child and shrieked. 'For God's sake, Carol, your daughter's filthy. She's covered in chocolate.' Taking Katy into her arms, she said, 'And she's boiling hot. Where's her hat? All babies need a hat in this weather. It keeps

160

their brains cool. She could get heatstroke.' She took Katy into the kitchen. 'Let's get you cleaned up.' She flapped Carol towards the cooker. 'You put the kettle on for a cup of tea.'

Sitting at the kitchen table, sipping tea, breathing in the familiar scents of home – lavender polish, a whiff of bacon from a lunchtime sandwich, the air freshener that was kept in the hall – Carol relaxed. Everything was going to be fine. She was where she belonged.

At five o'clock, Margaret looked at her watch and asked Carol if she shouldn't be getting back home. 'Johnny will be expecting you to have his supper on.'

Carol said he wasn't coming home tonight. 'He's away on business.' She lied.

Margaret sighed. 'Well, your father's going to be late. He's playing golf after work. I wasn't planning to cook tonight.' She saw Carol's disappointment and said she'd rustle something up.

At six o'clock, after a plate of cold ham and salad, Margaret said she thought it time Carol took the baby home. 'She'll be needing a bath and her bed.'

Carol, still unable to find a way to tell her mother she'd come home to stay, went upstairs to look lovingly at her old pink walls and James Dean poster. They were gone. The room had been redecorated. The walls were blue; the poster gone. She clattered back to the living room, 'What have you done to my room?'

'Had it painted,' said Margaret. 'Hated all that pink. And it's not your room any more. It's my spare room. I can do what I like with it.'

'Where's my poster?'

'Threw it in the bin. What do I want with a poster?'

'I liked that poster. I liked to look at it before I went to sleep.'

'Well, get another one and put it in your bedroom at home.'

'This is my home,' said Carol. 'I want to stay here. I've left Johnny and I've come back to live with you.'

Margaret was silent for a long time. 'What does he think of this?'

'He doesn't know. I haven't told him yet. I just decided this morning.'

'You walked out and didn't even leave a note?'

Carol nodded. Leaving – the simple act of walking out of the door for ever – had been so joyous, a note hadn't occurred to her.

'So he's sitting at home right now wondering where you and his daughter are?'

Carol supposed he was. 'But me and Katy are here with you. You'll get to see us every day. I thought you'd be happy about that.'

'Actually,' said Margaret, 'I'm not.' Only this morning she'd been thinking how pleasant life had become now that Carol was out of the house. At first she'd missed the girl. But in time she'd come to enjoy the tranquillity of not having her around. The girl seemed to walk from room to room leaving a trail of clothes, shoes and magazines. And wasn't it lovely to have the phone and bathroom constantly available? Then, there had been the noise. The constant thump of the music she played. No, Margaret didn't miss any of that.

'I thought you loved me,' Carol wept.

'I do. But I never loved the mess you made.'

'But I hate it at my house. I hate my life. It's all cleaning and cooking. I hate cleaning. You clean something and it just gets dirty again. What's the point?'

'Things get dirty. You clean them and they get dirty again. That's life, get used to it.'

'And,' said Carol, 'I'm alone all day waiting for Johnny to come home. Then when he does, he hardly speaks.'

'You talk to him. Tell him about your day.'

'Talk about cleaning and wiping? I don't think so. It's bad enough doing it without talking about it.'

Margaret shrugged. 'So you've discovered that life isn't all about going out dancing and flirting with boys. There's loneliness and drudgery. What a surprise. Every woman in the world knows that. You're a married woman now and a mother. You've made your bed, now lie on it.' She sighed, and slumped into a chair. 'Tell me, what did you think marriage would be like?'

Carol didn't want to answer this. She knew her thoughts on marriage came from magazine adverts for sofas and cookers, and from Doris Day films. She'd imagined herself curled on a huge white sofa in front of a roaring fire, or standing in a pristine kitchen sipping a glass of wine while her husband looked at her adoringly. The husband in this image wasn't actually the man she married. He was gleaned from an advert for soap powder, or he was the man from the photo at the front of a knitting pattern. She had dreamed of living in a beautiful home, the maintenance of which never occurred to her.

Knowing that confessing all of this would be inviting mockery, she instead said, 'So you don't want me.'

'Of course I want you. I just don't want you here. I'm enjoying the peace.'

Carol flounced around the room picking up Katy's toys and stuffing them into her bag. 'That's a terrible thing to say. When a woman is in trouble. When she's tired and lonely she should be able to turn to her mother.'

'When a mother sees her daughter make a mess of her life because she can't put up with a bit of everyday drudgery then that mother has a duty to tell her daughter to come to her senses and make a go of her marriage.'

'Huh.' Carol picked up Katy, plonked her in her pushchair, slung her bag over her shoulder and marched out the door. Then, after gathering up her suitcase, she stamped down the street, head high and battling tears. Her own mother didn't want her.

She trudged towards the city centre, case banging against her left thigh, heaving her down to one side. Eventually, she put it down and picked it up in her right hand. After a while she switched back. The going was tough. She stopped battling tears and wept. In the end, she abandoned her furious march and waited at a bus stop.

On the bus people stared. Tears had taken their toll on Carol's make-up. Rivers of damp mascara stained her cheeks. She was red of face, hot, exhausted and clutching a howling child. But she held her head high. How could any of her fellow passengers know she was a martyr? She was misunderstood and alone in the world. She had walked out on a husband who never showed any love or tenderness, and even her mother had cast her out into the world to make her own way. Well, she would show them all.

She got off the bus at Princes Street and sat on a bench watching the crowds and wondering what to do next. The evening was hotting up – people were on the move, looking for fun. She remembered there had been a time when she, too, had been here strutting her stuff, eyeing the boys. It took a lot of skill to appear aloof, available, desirable and haughty. But she was sure she'd managed it. Now look at her, homeless and unloved. What to do, she thought. And decided there was only one place to go. She hoisted her case onto the pushchair, balanced the child on her hip and set off.

At nine o'clock, she battered on Nell and Alistair's door. When they answered, she sobbed that she'd left Johnny and her mother had thrown her out. 'She doesn't want me. You have to let me in. I've nowhere else to go.'

Nell watched silently as Alistair took the child in one arm, the case in the other, smiled and invited Carol in.

Chapter Sixteen
Make the Place Sparkle

On a rainy morning in early September, May parked outside her restaurant and stared through the splattered windscreen. There, in front of her, was her favourite building in the world. God, she loved it – red roof, green windows and a constant twinkling of fairy lights draped from one side to the other. She thought the lights gorgeous. Beckoning, she thought, inviting people to come in. They promised warmth and comfort.

She climbed out of her car and walked to the front door, opened it and sighed. There was no getting away from it, this place was beautiful. It was red – red walls, red carpets and a single red rose on every table. In the corner, near the fireplace, was the red piano. May thought the place sumptuous and was surprised it was not crowded every night. Takes time, she thought. Word will spread.

When it did, she'd be on her way. She had her future planned. When Rutherford's started to make a profit – and surely that would happen soon – she'd finish the guest rooms upstairs. And in a couple of years, when the business was established, she'd start a second restaurant. She planned to call it Rutherford's In The City. She was sure that by the time she retired – *if* she ever retired – she'd have a chain of restaurants. Of course, she'd keep it in the family. She was doing this for her grandchildren. At the moment there was only one, who May couldn't believe was turning two this month, but she planned for Nell and Alistair to have at least three children. She hadn't mentioned this to them yet. She thought Nell's plan to wait for a couple of years was a good idea. If Johnny didn't get back together with Carol – and she wasn't keen on this – he was bound to find himself another wife. Another three grandchildren there, she thought. That would make seven people to carry on the Rutherford name. She had her heart set on a dynasty.

At eleven o'clock, Annie arrived to help prepare and serve lunch. There were only two customers, who spoke in whispers because the place was so empty. They left after their first course. May wasn't bothered. Early days, she told herself. 'Soon as word spreads this place will be buzzing.' She and Annie ate the chocolate mousses her lunchers had ordered but in their haste to get away had left uneaten. 'Charged them for puddings, anyway,' said May.

Half an hour before May started serving the evening diners, Karen and Sylvie turned up. They were both seventeen, best friends and always arrived with a small group of admirers who were left shouting and jostling at the door. May chased them off, knowing that soon they'd drift back and sit on the car park wall, smoking and bantering, waiting for the objects of their desire to finish work.

Karen and Sylvie set the tables, vacuumed the floor, polished the bar and dusted the piano. 'Make the place sparkle,' May ordered. After that they had the inspection. The two stood side-by-side, hands held out in front of them as May examined their nails and scanned their crisp white blouses and black skirts for stains. 'You'll do,' she said.

She always welcomed the first diners of the evening personally. Gleaming in her chef's whites and hat, she'd show people to their table and hand them a large glossy red menu. Then she'd say, 'I'll leave you in the capable hands of your lovely waitresses for tonight, Karen and Sylvie,' and she'd stride back to her kitchen, her domain.

Running a restaurant surprised May. It was not as easy as she'd imagined it to be. 'It'd be all right if it wasn't for the customers,' she said. 'They keep making demands.' At home, she had always been the demanding one. She'd insisted that the people she fed be at the table as soon as they'd been informed their meal was ready, that people clear their plates and express joy at what they'd eaten. And she wasn't keen on serving pudding to those who hadn't finished their main course.

Here, in her restaurant, she took offence at every uneaten morsel. Not a woman to take insults lightly, she'd often take a plate still heavy with leftovers back into the dining room, put it down in front of the diner and ask what was wrong with the food. 'You haven't finished it.'

It caused emotional stirrings and spoke volumes about matriarchy. Very few people told May that since they were paying it was their business what they did or didn't eat. Mostly they placed an apologetic hand on their stomachs and said they were full up. For an instant they were not addressing a chef, they were being confronted by their mothers.

Harry pointed out that loading peoples' plates wasn't really profitable. 'You could get two meals out of the amount heap on to a single plate.' But May insisted that nobody left her restaurant hungry. 'They've come for a meal and a meal is what they'll get. Food is important. It's life. I can't be doing with those places that serve up a sliver of this and a sliver of that along with a drip or two of sauce and give it a fancy name. Food has to be hearty.' So huge helpings it was.

The best table in the house was constantly reserved for the Rutherford family and friends. Harry entertained business clients here and, since Carol had left him, Johnny ate here almost every night, usually bringing one or two friends with him. That corner of the room was usually noisy, filled with bubbling conversation and bursts of laughter. May thought it brought a convivial atmosphere to her restaurant. It gave the impression that Rutherford's was the place to come for a good night out. Although, since nobody at that special table ever paid, it occasionally crossed May's mind that providing almost thirty free meals a week wasn't very good for business.

Tonight, a Thursday, was piano night, as were Fridays

and Saturdays. A sign on the door read *Musical Entertainment Provided by André Patterson at the Piano*. May was proud of this. As far as she knew, no other restaurant had such a thing. She thought the name – André – sounded musical. Certainly the man looked the part. He wore an evening suit complete with black bowtie. Both these attributes compensated for the manner of his playing. He wasn't awfully good. May knew this, but figured that the noise in the room – crockery clattering, wine bottles popping, people talking – hid his wrong notes. He was paid to play at what May called pudding time. 'When folk are full of good food, feeling mellow and contemplating something sweet to round off their meal.' She often gave out free liqueurs to accompany the music. 'Just a wee drink on the house so you'll remember us kindly and come back to see us soon.'

When the final dish had been cooked and all that was left to do was serve coffee, May would emerge from the kitchen and, still in chef's whites and hat, she'd lean on the piano and sing. She favoured torrid love songs and any song that featured food. Tonight's offering was 'Tea for Two'.

Desperately concentrating on remembering the lyrics, she always sang with her eyes shut. So she never saw Sylvie and Karen holding their hands over their mouths, stifling giggles or shocked diners, holding a spoon loaded with sticky toffee pudding, frozen midway between dish and lips as they tried to come to terms with what they were hearing.

Harry had once suggested that singing to people wasn't an awfully good idea. May had scoffed at him. 'Singing's what you do when you're happy.' She'd pointed accusingly at him. 'Your problem, Harry Rutherford, is that you're not musical. You can't hold a tune, so you don't know a good song when you hear one. My singing may sound off to you, but in here—' she had pointed to her head '—it's lovely.'

Song over, May bowed to her audience and thanked them for their sprinkling of applause. She sat at the special table next to Harry and across from Johnny so she could gaze at him and wonder how someone like her could produce someone like him. As she ate her bacon and eggs – the only thing she could face after cooking so much rich food – she decided that he was her reward. At some time she must have done something good. She couldn't imagine what that might have been.

Watching his mother mop up egg yolk with one of the bread rolls she'd made, Johnny said, 'You want to keep an eye on those waitresses of yours.'

May asked why.

'They giggle. They don't understand a thing about the food they're serving and they spend a lot of time at the window waving to their gang of admirers.'

May said she'd have a word. 'They're rough around the edges, but they're cheap. Cheap is what I need right now.' She sighed. 'I thought the family would rally round. But they're avoiding me.'

It was true. All of May's relatives had suddenly

become very busy when she'd asked if they'd help with the restaurant. In phone calls and gatherings she hadn't been invited to, they'd agreed that May was wonderful, gregarious, generous and a gifted cook. But work for her? In a kitchen? The way she was? They didn't think so.

Johnny said she should get a front-of-house.

'What's that?'

'A meeter and greeter,' he told her. 'Someone to welcome your diners, show them to their tables, ask if they want to order a drink before they eat, and talk about what's on the menu and the wine list. That sort of thing. You get them in posh restaurants.'

'I couldn't afford someone like that,' said May. 'I'm hardly making a penny in profit right now.'

'You could get Nell,' said Johnny. 'She could do it. She's not the mouse she used to be. Not since Alistair got to work on her.'

'But she knows nothing about food and wine,' said May.

Johnny shrugged. 'So teach her. Once she knew nothing about pens and now she can shift about twenty a week. And that's pens. I mean, who wants a pen? I'd have her in the showroom selling cars. But you can't have a woman doing that. Cars are men's business.'

'Nell?'

'Yes, Nell,' said Johnny. He looked at his mother and repeated, 'Nell,' and drifted into his private thoughts. This always made him look sulky. May's heart went out to him. His heart is broken, she thought.

'Are you missing Carol and Katy?' May asked suddenly.

He waved the question away. 'Nah. Well, I'm missing Katy.' He hardly missed Carol at all. In fact, he was enjoying not having her around. He could come and go as he pleased. Now he was planning to sell the house they'd shared so he could buy a flat in town. He wanted a bachelor pad he could furnish with a huge leather sofa, a television, a hi-fi, a fridge and a bed – nothing more. He didn't plan to cook. He'd eat out. He was looking forward to it.

May watched him. She loved him when he looked the way he looked right now. People thought he was sulky, but that was just the way his face fell when he wasn't using it. She thought life must be hard for him. Well, it was probably hard for all beautiful people. So much was expected of them, they never got the chance to be ordinary.

May thought that while life must be hard for Johnny, it couldn't be too hard for Alistair. He wasn't beautiful. He'd gone his own way in life and had become a lawyer because he'd had no hindrances. He hadn't had girls clustered round him. Nobody asked what he was thinking in the way they had of Johnny, who was so beautiful everyone thought he must have been thinking beautiful thoughts. In school reports teachers had called him lazy and sullen. Oh, how wrong they were, May thought. They hadn't understood the trials those blessed with beauty suffer.

There was no doubt in May's mind that Johnny

would need help. He'd left school with nothing. He hadn't passed a single exam. He'd gone into his father's business working in every department, learning the ropes. He'd been useless as a mechanic and Harry said he wasn't much of a salesman. Of course he wasn't. People would be too busy looking at him to listen to a word he said. How awful it must be to be so misunderstood.

Harry was looking strained these days. 'Nothing to worry about,' he'd told her. May knew that when Harry said there was nothing to worry about, there was something to worry about.

Face it, May told herself, she wasn't doing this for the family. She was doing it for Johnny. And if Nell was what he wanted to front this place, then Nell he'd get.

Chapter Seventeen
A Meeter and Greeter

For a moment, a flutter of dread ran through Nell. As her morning bus drew up at the stop a few yards from the pen shop, she thought she'd seen May standing in the doorway. Surely not, she thought. Not that she disliked May. She just didn't want to talk to her at this time of day. A person needed to be properly awake to deal with the woman.

And Nell was not fully awake. She'd been up late last night discussing men, love and relationships with Carol. It had started when Nell asked if Carol was any further towards finding somewhere to stay.

Carol had shaken her head. Flats were pricey and she had no money. 'Johnny's refusing to give me anything. He says he doesn't have to because I left him.'

Nell had looked at Alistair, expecting him to say something about Carol's legal rights and those of her daughter. Katy was also Johnny's responsibility, after all.

However, Alistair had only said that Carol was welcome to stay as long as she liked. 'We enjoy having you around.' Then he'd excused himself; he'd said he was tired after a hellish day and had a feeling the following day was going to be worse.

After he'd gone, Carol had said, 'He's lovely. You're so lucky.'

Nell had agreed.

'Isn't it funny,' Carol had said. 'You're the one who never reckoned on love. And you found it. I always wanted love and in the end I married Johnny for money and security, but mostly because I had to.'

Nell had shrugged. 'Life's unpredictable.'

'I still think that if you never find love then your life has been for nothing.'

Nell had disagreed. 'Lots of people have done wonderful things, lived marvellous lives without ever finding their true love, like Florence Nightingale and Mary Slessor.' She had no idea if either of these women had ever been in love but reckoned Carol wouldn't know either so her theory would go unchallenged. 'And there are people who invented things and people who composed music and people who painted fantastic paintings. You can't say these lives have been for nothing. It's who you are and what you do that matters.'

Perhaps, Carol had agreed. But she'd still thought love was all that mattered. She had gone on to extol Alistair's virtues. What a wonderful husband he was. 'He'll vacuum the floor and he puts Katy to bed. Reads her a story. Johnny never did that.' She'd spoken about how lonely she was, and how she doubted she'd ever find another man. 'Who'd love me now? I've failed at marriage. I've got a child. I'm not a good prospect.'

On and on she'd gone. Life was hard. Men didn't understand how it was to be a woman. And wasn't Nell lucky to have such a beautiful flat. The fire had faded, and the room had turned cold. Nell had yawned. She'd ached to be in bed. It had been after one in the morning before she got there.

Now she was sticky-eyed, grumpy and a little bit sweaty as she hadn't had a bath.

It had been three weeks since Carol had turned up at Nell and Alistair's door and she had established her own routine. She took control of the bathroom every morning. Before bathing herself, she'd bathe Katy, hanging over the side of the bath, splashing the child and singing her favourite songs. At the moment 'Nellie the Elephant' was top choice.

This was irritating. Worse though was the clutter of toys – a family of yellow plastic ducks, a wooden boat, a blue submarine and a large red ball – Nell had to remove every time she wanted to get into the bath. The clutter wasn't restricted to the bathroom. It was everywhere, a spreading of clothes, gaudily coloured toys, baby lotions and potions, and Carol's magazines, make-up and shoes that stretched from the front door to the kitchen. Every night when Nell arrived home, she walked the few yards down the hall to the living room bent double picking things up. There was more picking up and tidying to do in the living room, and then much sighing in the kitchen as she washed the dishes Carol had used during the day. All this and then Nell had to cook the supper.

She was surprised that the clutter and the intrusion didn't also annoy Alistair, but he seemed to be delighted by it. He'd step over any obstacles on the floor as he headed for Katy. He'd sweep her up, saying, 'How's my girl?' He'd ask Carol what sort of day she'd had and listen with interest as she recounted her doings. Carol had a knack of making a day spent reading magazines, doing her hair, going to the park and chatting to the woman in the chemist's shop about the benefits of teething gel sound fascinating. This intensified Nell's annoyance and, as she peeled potatoes and grilled chops, she'd make faces and bob her head from side to side as she silently mimicked her friend.

Going through all this as she walked from the bus stop to the shop door shoved the dreadful, fleeting sighting of May out of Nell's mind. She jumped when the woman appeared at her side, gripped her arm and said, 'I need a word.'

It was May.

'I don't want to be late for work.'

'You'll just have to be late. This is important.' May didn't loosen her grip and led Nell away to a small café round the corner.

They sat at a corner table. May ordered two cups of tea. 'Never ask for coffee in a place like this. They don't understand coffee. Tea they do.' She took a hanky from her pocket and wiped the tabletop. 'Filthy. Can't be doing with germs. Now, you have to come and work for me.'

Nell said she couldn't. She already had a job she loved. 'And, if I say so myself, I'm good at it.'

'I know,' said May, 'that's why I need you to work for me.'

Nell looked at her watch and repeated that she was late for work.

'I'm glad to see you take it so seriously,' said May. 'I like my workers to be punctual.'

Nell said she didn't want to be a waitress.

'Did I not tell you what you'd be doing?' asked May. 'That's not like me. You wouldn't be a waitress. You'd be a meeter and greeter, front of house. You'd welcome people when they arrived, chat to them sort of thing, make them feel at home. Then you'd show them the menu and discuss the dishes and you'd talk them through the wine list.'

'I don't know anything about wine,' said Nell.

'You will when I'm done with you. You'll wear smart clothes – a long black skirt and a white shirt. You'll work from six-thirty to eleven every night, except Sunday obviously, and I'll double your present pay.'

'But . . .'

'No buts. You're family and the family needs you. You can hand in your notice today and start with me a fortnight on Monday. And, of course, when I open up my next restaurant, Rutherford's In The City, you'll be manager. So I'm offering you more money and a chance of promotion. More than you'll get in your present job.'

'I like to be at home with Alistair in the evening,' Nell said. 'I like to spend time alone with him.'

'You'll not be alone with Carol there. Never did like

that girl. She tricked my Johnny into marriage. How is she, by the way?'

'Fine,' said Nell.

'And the little one?'

'Fine, too. She's getting big. Well, bigger.'

'Good,' said May. 'Alistair can come eat at the restaurant any time he likes. We have a special family table set aside. You'll see him then. Don't invite Carol.' She slapped the table and stood up. 'Well, I'm glad that's all settled.'

'But—'

'See you half-past six prompt a fortnight on Monday.' She gathered her handbag, put the money for the tea neither of them had touched on the table and left.

At six-thirty that evening Nell walked in through her front door. There was a new addition to the mess: a huge yellow plastic tortoise. She stepped over it and went into the living room. Carol was lying on the sofa. She put her finger to her lips, and then pointed to Katy fast asleep on top of her.

'Bring me a cup of tea,' said Carol. 'I'm stuck here. Don't want to wake the baby. She's been howling all day.'

Nell sighed, turned, headed for the kitchen, tripped over the giant tortoise, hit her head on a pile of building blocks, cracked her knee on the floor and yelled in agony. The child woke and howled. Carol shouted, 'Can you not watch where you're going?'

Nell heaved herself from the floor and, clutching her wounded knee, hobbled to the kitchen. She sat at the table, one hand on the knee, the other on the rising bump on her head. Carol appeared at the door, carrying the child. 'Don't bother making tea. I'll do it myself now.'

'I think you should make an effort to clear the toys away. It's dangerous leaving them lying around,' said Nell.

'Well, that tortoise is big enough. You should have seen it.'

'Well, I did when I came in. I didn't when I went out again. Where did you get it? It's hideous.'

'I saw it in a shop and I just knew Katy would love it. And she does. That's all that matters.'

'Where did you get the money? I thought you didn't have any?'

'Took it from that jug.' Carol pointed to a blue jug on the dresser. 'There's usually a few pounds in there.'

Nell said that the money in that jug was for the milkman and the paperboy. 'We pay them on Saturday mornings.'

'Well,' said Carol. 'You'll just have to pay them with money from your purse. The jug's empty now.' She looked at Nell. 'That's quite a lump coming up on your forehead.'

'I think it's time you found a place of your own.'

'Are you throwing me out?'

'No. Not exactly. But sometimes me and Alistair like to be alone together.'

'So you are asking me to leave? You're putting me and my child on the streets? We have no place to go. We've no money. We'll be wandering about in the cold and the rain, sleeping on park benches.'

'Johnny should give you money. He should provide for you. Have you asked him?'

'You know I have,' said Carol, 'but he'll only give me enough to feed Katy. He says he owes me nothing since I left him. I told you that.'

Actually, Johnny had told Carol she was welcome to stay at the house she used to live in with him. He'd said he planned to sell the place, but when he did that, he'd offered her half the profit so she'd be able to find somewhere comfortable for Katy. 'Somewhere with a garden,' he'd suggested. But Carol wasn't going to tell Nell about this. She liked it here. She loved this flat. She enjoyed seeing Alistair play with her daughter.

A stab of loathing for her friend sliced through Nell. She thought, it's her or me. And since Carol had showed no interest in finding somewhere else to live, Nell decided: it'll have to be me. She'd take the job May was offering – anything to get away from Carol.

Later Nell realised working for May in the evenings would leave her at home all day with Carol. She decided to keep her day job. She'd be out of the house from half-past eight in the morning till after eleven at night. Tiring, but perfect.

*

A fortnight later, Nell started her evening job. May supplied her with her work outfit – a long black skirt, white shirt and black waistcoat – discussed the menu and showed her the big book: a leather-bound tome that was kept on the desk at the door for bookings. Nell leafed through it. 'It's empty. The pages are blank.'

'For the moment,' said May. 'Once we take off, when word spreads, that book will be full. It's only temporarily empty. When people arrive, you ask their name and check the book even though the pages are blank. It makes us look efficient.'

It seemed to be remarkably easy. All she had to do was show diners to their tables, hand them a menu, chat about the dishes and ask if they'd like something to drink as their meal was being prepared. When the diners had finished eating, she'd prepare the bill in the beautiful handwriting she'd perfected during slow times at the pen shop and take it to them on a silver platter.

The wine was tricky. The only thing she knew was that red was usually drunk with meat, white with fish. Usually when asked to recommend something, she'd excuse herself and go into the kitchen to ask for May's advice. May would always tell her to pick something with a flashy label and display it with reverence to the customer. It usually worked.

'Remember to sniff the cork when you've opened the bottle,' May said.

When Nell asked why, May said, 'It lets the customer know you're checking to see if the wine is corked.'

'Corked?' said Nell. 'What's corked?'

May said she wasn't sure, but that it had something to do with the cork not sealing the bottle properly and the wine being off.

'How will I know?' said Nell. 'It all smells like wine to me.'

'The cork smells of old underpants,' said May. 'Pour the wine anyway. If the customer notices bring them another bottle. If not, carry on. And—' May waved a spatula as she spoke '—look superior and knowing so that when you give them a little smile to let them know they've made an excellent choice, they'll feel smug. Even if they've made a terrible choice.'

It was all a matter of looking serene, Nell told Alistair, who hadn't been entirely happy when he'd heard that Nell had started working for his mother. 'I walk about with my head up and smile and get paid for it.'

At the end of her first week, May had given Nell a brown envelope containing her first week's wages. It was several pounds short of the amount she'd been promised. When asked about it, May had explained that the shortfall was simply the money used to buy her work uniform. 'I'll see you all right next week.'

Nell put her earnings into the running-away fund account. She told Alistair she was keeping this money separate from their joint account savings. 'I'll be able to dip into it now and then without touching our savings.' She didn't mention anything about not paying tax. She knew he wouldn't approve.

Nell was happy. She was back in the bosom of the Rutherford family. Harry would put his arm round her, and kiss her cheek every night when he arrived. Johnny grinned to her. May clapped her hands and told her she was doing a great job. And, every night, when she climbed into bed, Alistair was waiting for her. He'd put his arms round her, hold her and say, 'At last, you're home. Couldn't sleep without you here beside me.' Nell thought life couldn't get better than this.

Chapter Eighteen
The Singing Chef

Life did get better. By January, Rutherford's had become fashionable; it was *the* place to be seen. The pages in the big book were no longer blank. Every table was filled. Late in the evening, when May emerged from the kitchen, people would nudge one another and nod towards the piano, anticipating a little light entertainment.

Nell realised that this was why people came. Word about the singing chef had spread and everyone wanted to say they'd been to Rutherford's and had heard her.

Perhaps she wasn't so terrible after all. Or maybe it was her warmth and enthusiasm that enraptured people. After all, Nell thought, Marlene Dietrich can't really sing, but her audiences love the way she performs a song. Nell decided May had charisma. That was what it was all about. May nodded to the piano player, cast her eyes round the room, taking everyone in, making them all feel she was their friend and she sang. It was simple. People loved her because she made them feel loved.

Sometimes, Nell would stare at André, the piano player, trying to remember where she'd seen him before. He was very familiar, but she couldn't place him. In the end she supposed his face was just one of the faces she'd seen about. It's like that in cities, she thought. People hang out in bars and cafés and eating places, and you recognise them even though you don't know who they are.

It was exhausting. Nell's working hours whizzed past – she ran from table to table and from bar to table and kitchen to table.

'Stop running,' May said. 'You make people nervous. They're here to enjoy themselves. They mustn't know it's bedlam behind the scenes.' She was, at the time, scooping a peppered steak from the floor. It had fallen as Nell, plate in hand, had whirled round as she headed out of the kitchen towards the dining room. May had picked up the steak, examined it and put it back on the plate. 'They'll never know.' She scowled at Nell. 'Don't run, glide.'

'I'm too busy to glide,' said Nell.

'Glide quickly, then.' Then as Nell slid away, she added, 'I need a word with you later.'

It spoiled Nell's night. Shouldn't have whirled, she told herself. Whirling's not good, not with a plate in your hand. She worried that May was going to fire her. At half-past ten, May burst out of the kitchen and took a bow. A small cheer rippled round the room – this is what they'd been waiting for. May nodded to André. 'Maestro,' she said. André started to play. Tonight's offerings were 'Mountain Greenery' and 'Life is Just a Bowl of Cherries'. She resisted the calls for an encore, telling the crowd she was absolutely bushed, tired out, exhausted. 'Time for a wee sit down and a little something to drink.'

She went to the special table where her bacon and eggs were waiting for her, along with a large glass of Burgundy. 'Excellent.' She took an enormous swig. 'Been needing that.' She signalled Nell over to join her. 'Take a seat.'

Nell sat opposite.

'What I need you to do is give up your stupid day job,' May said. 'I can see that working in two places is getting too much for you. You're doing too much running and whirling and not enough gliding.'

Nell nodded.

'You're to come in at lunch times. We need the extra hand now we're getting busy.'

Nell said she'd think about it.

'No need to think,' said May. 'The deed's done. I phoned your shop this afternoon and told them you wouldn't be back.'

'You what?'

'I told you. I handed in your notice for you. I haven't time to wait for you to think about things. You'd take too long. You're indecisive.' She reached for the bottle of wine on the table, refilled her glass, and continued, 'You've been at that shop for years now and you're no further forward. You'll be teetering in when you're ninety and you'll still be behind that counter. I'm offering you opportunities. I'm offering you a life. In two years you could be running my next restaurant. After that, the sky's the limit.'

'Gosh.' It was all she could think of to say.

May winked. 'Stick with me, kid.' The matter of Nell's employment done with, she turned to Harry and started to talk about finances at the garage.

Nell wasn't interested and stopped listening. Instead, she drifted into a small fantasy of her future. She'd manage a restaurant. It would be in the West End. She'd wear a smart business suit and carry a leather briefcase with her initials engraved in gold letters on the side. She'd have an office with a large black desk that would be polished to a glisten and would have a fresh bunch of white roses placed on top every day. They'd sit next to the white phone. She'd work hard. She'd push her staff to perform well but she wouldn't bully. I'll be firm but fair, she thought.

It was a comfort to have someone like May who'd take her hand and lead her through life. She no longer had to worry. She had someone to lean on. May was wonderful. Nell stared at her, noticing for the first time how beautiful she was. Oh, she wasn't gorgeous like Sophia Loren or Marilyn Monroe; May had a painful beauty. Every single thing she'd gone through in her life was written on her face. Nell could see it all: May's early poverty; her struggles; her love of Harry and her children; her determination; her generosity; her ambition. It was what made May truly beautiful.

Sensing the stare, May turned. 'What are you looking at?'

'Nothing,' said Nell. 'I was day dreaming.'

'Well, don't. It won't get you anywhere. So you'll

turn up here to help with the lunches on Monday and on Sunday you'll also be here to learn about cocktails. I'm going to be serving them. They're sophisticated.'

'Who's going to teach me?' asked Nell. 'A cocktail tutor? Some sort of master of mixing drinks?'

'Don't be daft,' said May. 'I've bought a book. We'll get all we need from that.'

Chapter Nineteen
The Love Speech

'We're not going to offer a range of cocktails,' said May. 'Just one rum and one whisky.'

'But,' Nell protested, 'some people prefer gin.'

May agreed. 'OK. One rum, one whisky and one gin.'

Johnny said that a lot of women drank vodka these days.

'Fine. One rum, one whisky, one gin and one vodka,' said May. 'That's four.'

Nell said she thought champagne cocktails were posh.

'Oh yes. We've got to have them. So it's one whisky, one rum, one gin, one vodka and a champagne one. Five. No more.'

She put the book on the bar counter and thumbed through it. 'We want drinks that people have heard of. A Manhattan, that'll be good. It's the sort of thing film stars drink in the movies.'

'Martinis,' said Nell. 'They have them in films.'

As each cocktail was chosen, May placed the required bottles on the bar. They would start with martinis as she considered them to be the classic cocktail. 'Shaken, not stirred,' she said.

They each took a cocktail shaker and measured the gin and vermouth into it along with a splash of bitters and a dash of lemon. They shook the mixture, and Nell quickly got a ticking off for being too flamboyant.

'You're not playing the maracas. You've got to look professional.'

They poured their drinks into cocktail glasses, added ice and an olive, and drank. They exchanged glasses, drank again. Exchanged glasses once more, drank again and all agreed Nell's was best. Nell admitted she'd skimped on the gin and added more vermouth than the recipe recommended.

'This is what we want,' said May. 'Cutting costs is a priority. We'll be giving these cocktails away. Though only on Tuesdays and Wednesdays, our quiet nights. Anything to bring the punters in.'

They worked their way through Daiquiris, Moscow Mules and Manhattans, working out just how little alcohol and how much lime juice and sugar syrup made a reasonable drink. By the time they started on the Champagne Charlies – a mix of champagne and apricot brandy – nobody was sober.

Johnny said it was time to go. He had a date tonight and wanted to shower. Nell wondered if perhaps he ought to order a taxi. 'You might not be fit to drive, and the roads might be frosty.'

But May said if there was one thing about Johnny, it was that he was an excellent driver. 'That's one thing he does really well.' She started to clear up, washing glasses, putting bottles away. 'I'll put the cocktail spirits apart from the normal spirits. We'll be watering them down a little. Saving money, that's the thing.'

'Isn't that against the law?' said Nell.

'Not when the drinks are free,' May said. 'Besides, who's to know?'

'I just think it's wrong,' said Nell.

'Nonsense,' said May. 'It's business and all's fair in love and business. I'm not selling anything that isn't what it purports to be. I'm giving away something that isn't what it purports to be. There's a difference. I'm not a cheat.'

Nell nodded. She was impressed. May was such an astute businesswoman, Nell thought her a wonderful role model. One day, she'd be like that.

She asked, as she dried the glasses, how Harry was. 'He looks a little down these days.'

'Oh, he's got his worries. Who hasn't? Life isn't easy. If your life is easy, you're doing something wrong. It's overcoming the difficulties that make a man of you.'

Nell decided not to mention that she wasn't a man and asked what Harry's difficulties were.

'Oh, just a little hiccup with the Inland Revenue. They think he hasn't been paying enough tax. Well, nobody pays any tax if they can avoid it. My money is for the family, not the government. I don't like governments and I don't like politicians. I want my loved ones to benefit from my work. I mean, what does the government do with my money? It builds nuclear bombs. Well, that's not on. Nobody asked me if I wanted nuclear bombs. I'm not paying for them. They can't tax you on what they don't know you have.' May looked about the room, embraced it with a sweep of her arms. 'All this is about love. My love for you, Harry, Alistair and Johnny.' Her voice softened as she said that last name. 'He needs this. He needs a mother to protect him.'

Nell said nothing. May was plainly on a roll.

'These cocktails, this restaurant, the food, the wine, the singing, the plans for the future – it's all for love. I love my family. This is what I do for my boys.' She looked at Nell. 'You know nothing about poverty. You know nothing about being hungry. Well, I do. I remember when we had no food and no money to buy food. Harry and me and us not long started out – hadn't sold a car in months. I had two boys at the table and not a scrap to give them.'

'What did you do?' Nell asked.

'I went out and stole two tins of beans and a pack of sausages. I'd do it again if I had to. I stole and it was love made me do it. So only my family gets my money. Nobody else. I work my fingers to the bone, charge reasonable prices and people go away happy. Same with Harry. He works all the hours God sends. And, when people drive out of his garage in a car, they're happy. So maybe the car's done a little more mileage than is on the clock, and maybe the rust has been glossed over and a few holes in the bodywork have been patched up with this and that, but the car's shiny and smells of being new and they're happy. That's what Harry and me do – we make people happy. And we do it for love.' She plonked a glass on the bar, filled it with gin and just a splash of tonic. 'Love,' she said, sniffing and wiping her eyes with the back of her hand. 'Love, it's all for love. I love my family.'

Nell stopped drying the glasses and stared at May, eyes aglow. This woman was marvellous. She was more that a businesswoman, she was the complete woman: a mother; a cook; a wife; a lover; a woman of many opinions and passions who gave her family everything she had. Nell wanted to be like that. She wanted to live in a big house, dote on her children, lavish money on clothes and food and furniture. She wanted to boldly start new businesses, come up with innovative ideas that would push them forward. She wanted to wear extravagant styles. She wanted to be May.

A car drew up outside. May perked up and smiled. 'That's Harry now, come to take us home.'

In bed that night, Nell said, 'Your mother's remarkable.'

'Is she?'

'Yes. She told me that everything she does, she does—'

'For love,' said Alistair. 'Oh God, she gave you the love speech.' He pulled the blankets over his head. He squirmed remembering it.

'I think it's wonderful,' said Nell. 'She works her fingers to the bone for her family. For love of the family.'

'Did she mention not paying taxes because the government used her money to build bombs?'

'Yes,' said Nell. 'I think she's right. Except it's illegal not to pay taxes.'

'Too true,' said Alistair. 'Did she mention stealing two tins of beans and a pack of sausages?'

Nell said that she did. 'Endless amazing devotion. She risked everything for you.'

'The first time I got pocket money I bought beans and sausages and went to that shop and put them on the shelves. I think stealing is wrong. I think just about everything my mother does is wrong.'

'But she does it for love. She does everything for love. I think it's wonderful don't you?'

Alistair sighed and said he didn't. 'I think the woman loves too much. I think she loves to love and doesn't know the guilt it causes. I never asked to be loved that much. It's embarrassing. It's tiring. I feel weak just thinking about it.' He turned away from Nell, pulled the blankets over his head, shutting her out, and tried to sleep.

Nell settled herself into her sleeping position and pulled her pillow down so it met the top of the sheet and eliminated all draughts. She didn't sleep. She didn't want to, not yet. She had plans to make. In a year, maybe two, she'd be managing a restaurant. She had to make a go of this; she had to prove to May, a woman she now found inspirational, that she was worthy. She wondered what she'd wear when the day of the new job came. A suit, she thought. The sort of thing Doris

Day wore in *Pillow Talk*, business-like but feminine. And a hat, a neat perky, witty number that would perch nicely on the side of her head, 'A hat,' she said out loud.

Alistair heard and turned, but couldn't think of anything to say on the matter of hats.

Nell said, 'Do you think we ought to ask Carol to go? We could give her the money for the deposit on a flat of her own.'

Alistair didn't answer. He liked having Carol here. He had someone to talk to in the evenings. He loved his niece. He loved watching her grow, listening as she started to speak, watching her wonder at the world. When she discovered a butterfly, he felt he was discovering one too. He thought the child a marvel and didn't want her to leave. So rather than reply, he let out a soft snore and pretended to be asleep.

Chapter Twenty
Born With a Disadvantage

The phone woke them. Alistair jumped from bed, ran to the kitchen and answered it. Phone calls that came in the night never brought good news.

It was May. Johnny had been in an accident. 'His car's a write-off. He drove it into a tree. He's broken his leg and several ribs. They had to cut him free. His beautiful face is all swollen and bruised. I think he's broken his jaw. He's lucky he didn't break his neck.'

'You're at the hospital now?' asked Alistair.

'Yes. How did you know?'

'Because you're sounding sane.' May only fell apart in private. She'd wait till she got home before she started weeping.

'How well you know me. You've got to come. I need you here.'

Alistair said he was on his way.

He found May sitting on a plastic chair in the corridor outside the ward. Her handbag was on the floor beside her. She had her hands folded in her lap and was staring at the wall. She looked suddenly unusually small. Her face, stripped of its usual enthusiasm, looked gaunt. He sat down next to her, took her hand and squeezed it. 'How are you doing?'

'Bearing up,' she said. 'They've set his leg and his jaw. He's sleeping now.'

Alistair asked if his brother had been drinking.

'Cocktails,' said May. 'Him and Nell and me were testing out which ones we'd serve.'

'Ah.'

'I told him not to drink them. "Just taste," I said. But no he knocked them all back. He's like that. Never knows when to stop.'

Alistair suspected this wasn't true, but that May had made it up to ease her conscience. He thought it was likely she'd encouraged Johnny to drink, but by now she'd have convinced herself she'd told him just to taste. In time, when Johnny's accident became part of family lore, it would be true. There would be no doubting the story the way May would tell it. He looked round.

'Where's Dad?'

'Sleeping,' said May. 'He's had an awful day. Hours and hours with the accountant planning what to say to the tax inspector at the meeting tomorrow. Now this.' She sighed.

Alistair didn't ask why his father had a meeting with his tax inspector. Instead he asked May how long she'd been here.

'Since six this evening. Sitting here smelling that

hospital smell, worrying and waiting for the doctor to come and tell me what's happening.'

'I think it's time we took you home,' said Alistair.

'I'm not going home. I need to be here in the morning when Johnny wakes.'

'I don't think they'll let you see him till visiting time.'

'There's no visiting time for me. I don't do visiting times. Soon as he wakes I'm going into the ward to see him.'

He draped her coat over her shoulders and took her arm. 'You'll do what you're told. You'll go home and get some sleep.'

She didn't resist. She walked with him to the car park, and insisted he drive her home. 'I'm too upset to drive. Leave your car here. You can pick it up later.' She gave him her keys.

'What are we going to do about Johnny?' she asked. 'He was born with such a disadvantage.'

'He was?' This was news to Alistair.

'Oh yes, he's beautiful. Not like us people who have ordinary faces. His is perfect. That's why I called him Johnny. He needed an easy name, but one that was also romantic. His beauty might be ruined now. Glass from the windscreen. He'll be scarred.'

It started to rain. Alistair switched on the screen wipers and said that scars heal.

'Yes, but they leave their mark. You and me were blessed to be born ugly. If you'd been beautiful you'd never have become a lawyer.'

'I think I would have.'

'No. Coping with beauty would have worn you out.'

Alistair said he hadn't known being beautiful was exhausting. 'Anyway, I don't think I'm ugly. Plain, perhaps, but not ugly.'

'Yes, plain,' said May. 'I saw that the minute you were born. I was so relieved.' She looked out at the rain. 'I like being in a car at night. The streets are empty. Everyone is sleeping and I'm out here, safe and warm and nobody knows I'm here. I get a little respite from my worries.'

'If you paid your taxes you wouldn't have so many worries.'

May said she always had worries. 'If it's not one thing it's another. You get one dilemma sorted out and you think, well that's that. I can get on with living now. I can have a little peace of mind. Then another thing comes along and whams into you. Life is never ordinary. Life is full of whams and bumps. When does all this whamming stop?'

'When you start paying taxes.'

'I already pay taxes, just not as much as those in power think I should. But that's their problem.'

Alistair said nothing. He wasn't prepared to argue with May about governments, politicians, nuclear bombs and taxes. He'd done it often before and not once had he won.

He pulled up outside the family house, got out of the car and went round to help May climb out. She leaned on him as they walked to the front door.

'You're a good man,' she said. 'I sometimes wonder how that happened. I'm sure it had nothing to do with me.'

Once inside, she said she was going straight to bed. 'Too tired to make a cup of tea. Too tired to drink one. But you help yourself to anything you find in the kitchen. You'll stay here tonight. The bed in your room is made up. It's always ready for you.' She kissed his cheek and started her slow climb up the stairs to her bedroom.

Alistair went to the kitchen, put on the kettle and leaned against the unit waiting for it to boil. Why did he have a mother like May? Why couldn't he be the son of some quiet, gentle soul like Nell's mother – a woman who delighted in her ordinariness and demanded nothing more than the odd visit when she'd take pleasure in dishing out plates brimming with egg and chips? He sighed, made a pot of tea and carried it to the kitchen table.

There was no point in going to bed; he wouldn't sleep. How familiar it was here. He listened to the house. He knew well every click and shift and small movement. These noises had been part of the sound-track of his childhood. He remembered lying in his darkened bedroom as a boy and being comforted by the sounds of water in the radiators, the creak of the stairs, the windows rattling and the low murmur of his mother and father talking. Back then, he'd wait till May and Harry had gone to bed, then he'd creep downstairs to poke through the drawers. The details of his parents' life had always fascinated him.

It was almost Pavlovian; he heard the same old noises, and his mother and father were asleep upstairs. He got up from his chair and started to do what he'd done as a young boy. He rummaged. He wondered what he'd find if he had a look around tonight. Maybe, he thought, there'll be no evidence of recent dodgy dealings and my making a stand has made a small difference. He ignored the recipe drawer where May put cuttings from magazines and newspapers, and started towards the drawer at the far end of the kitchen. The dreaded drawer, May called it. It was where she stuffed all the bills and other things she didn't want to think about. He could hardly open it. Slips of paper, envelopes, and letters tumbled out.

He gathered them, spread them on the kitchen unit and started to read. There were bills, final demands and threatening letters. The worse the threat, the further down the pile it had been shoved.

Alistair was well aware of Harry and May's attitude to money. If they had it they spent it. If they hadn't they still spent it. He remembered his mother saying that she didn't take money seriously. 'I don't reckon having it and I don't reckon not having it.' She'd thought a moment before adding that on the whole she'd rather be rich than poor. 'Being poor is draining.' Now, he wondered how seriously she was taking this financial mess. It was worse than anything she'd gone through before.

There were phone bills, electricity bills, bills from her suppliers, bills from Harry's suppliers along with several alarming letters from the Inland Revenue. A quick totalling of the sums owed made him gasp. Thousands and thousands, he thought.

Of course, it had happened before. There had been tough times in the past. Perhaps they hadn't been as dire as this, but there had been scary moments. He remembered hiding upstairs with his mother and brother when a couple of men (probably debt collectors, he thought now) battered on the door. May had clamped a hand over his mouth when he'd started to ask why they were here and why weren't they letting the men in.

'Ssshh,' May had hissed, and her hand pressed over his mouth so he could hardly breathe. She'd been wearing Chanel perfume. He could smell it still; he hated that scent.

From time to time, the electricity had been cut off. May treated this as an adventure. Eating tinned corned beef by candlelight and going to bed early to keep warm had been a test of the family's pioneering spirit, she'd claimed. 'You'll never keep a Rutherford down.'

Alistair had long realised he'd spent his young years being frightened. Of what, he didn't know, but he'd always had the feeling that doom was nigh. He'd known it had something to do with money, so he'd saved. He'd put all his pocket money and any cash he'd got his hands on into a small piggy bank he'd bought. Any coins he found lying on the pavement went into the china pig along with money retrieved from down the side of the sofa and change he might have left over from any message his mother sent him on. When the day of doom arrived, he'd be ready. He might even have a whole five pounds to hand over in triumph to his parents.

He snorted; fat lot of good that would have done. His piggy bank savings were pathetic. He never did get the chance to come to his parents' rescue. If, during worrying times, Alistair went to the pig to fish out his savings, he'd find it empty. His mother had raided it. She had a nose for money. Alistair was convinced she could smell it. To be fair though, when good fortune returned, she always paid him back.

It was her flamboyance that was the problem. May's extravagance was legendary. When the good times rolled she'd come home glowing with joy from a shopping trip laden with goodies: toys; clothes; sweets, books; records; anything she thought her beloved boys might want. She entertained lavishly. She bought lamps, rugs, cushions and bed linen for the house. She filled her wardrobe with coats, shoes and handbags. She booked the family on trips to expensive hotels. Saving never occurred to her.

Alistair saved. He went over his bank statements with a fine toothcomb. He always knew exactly how much money he had and only parted with cash if he absolutely had to. He knew his mother thought him mean, but he didn't care.

He wanted to be free of the fear. He'd been scared all his life and he was tired of it. He'd been scared to leave home in the morning and spent his time at school imagining what might be happening while he was away. Then again, he was also scared of going back home at the end of the day; he didn't want to find out what have happened in his absence. He worried that the men had come knocking again and this time taken his mother away.

This was part of the reason he'd married Nell. Not really to be with her, but to be nearer to her mother and father. Their home was calm. In the evenings, the couple would sit by the fire watching television. They rarely spoke, but then it seemed to Alistair that they didn't need to. Each knew what the other was thinking. Every time he visited, Alistair felt the tension drain from his shoulders. He relaxed. Everything was in order here. There would be no sudden terrifying phone calls; the electricity was not going to be cut off. There was a constant undersmell of bleach. This was a secure place to be. It made him want to curl up on their ancient creaking very uncomfortable sofa and sleep.

He shoved the bills, final demands and foul letters back into the drawer and crossed the kitchen to check the money cupboard. May had forgotten to lock it in her earlier distracted state and Alistair saw it was almost empty; just a few forlorn notes scattered at the bottom.

He knew what had happened. His mother had blown the lot firstly by paying the workmen who renovated her restaurant in cash, and then buying crockery, table linen, cutlery and furnishings. Oh, what a time she'd have had. He pictured her buzzing round the supply warehouse selecting only the best copper pots and Irish linen. How she must have been welcomed with her handbag bulging full of cash. In his imagination his mother became balletic, wafting up and down aisles, picking things up, twirling, laughing and dipping her hand into her bag to pull out fistfuls of notes. God, the woman was a fool.

Well, he wasn't going to hang about here pondering the foolishness of his mother. He'd walk back to the hospital and pick up his car. Walking helped with the worrying. It was always better to worry when on the move. Doing so when lying in bed staring into the silent dark was likely to drive you insane.

He pulled on his coat, shoved up the collar and stepped out into the night. This was better: fresh air and rain. He thought there was nothing better than a long walk through wet streets when the mind was clogged with gloom. But no matter how fast he walked or how wet he became, he could not dispel the feeling of dread. He had butterflies in his stomach. Horrible things were about to happen.

It was after six in the morning when Alistair finally got back to the flat. Nell was still sleeping but Carol was up; she was in the kitchen preparing breakfast for Katy. She looked at Alistair and pointed out that he was dripping on to the floor. 'You should have a bath and put on some dry clothes. I'll make you something to eat.'

Half-an-hour later, warm and wearing jeans and a sweater, he was at the kitchen table eating bacon and eggs. Carol sat across from him as he told her about Johnny.

'He'll live,' Alistair told her. 'He'll probably be scarred. My mother thinks his beauty will be ruined and he won't be able to cope with that.' He dipped a slice of toast into his egg and sighed.

'I never thought he was beautiful. Handsome, definitely that. When we first met I saw him as my handsome prince. But beautiful is different; he was never that.' Watching Alistair eat, she asked, 'What do you think?'

He sat back and ran his fingers through his hair. 'It's all such a mess. Everything's a mess. My mother's a fool. She's spent all the family money. There's hardly anything left. God knows what's going to happen there. My father's in deep shit with the taxman. Johnny's in hospital with a broken jaw and a broken leg. Nell thinks she's going to be a manager of a restaurant in town and a glittering career lies ahead of her. She's imagining herself in a big office with a gleaming desk and a white phone. She's always been a dreamer; head in the clouds. She's my wife and I hate to say this, but she's naïve. I'm surrounded by clowns who don't see what's coming. Well, I see it. The shit is about to hit the fan and it scares the hell out of me.'

Carol took a sip of her tea, told him all that was very interesting, 'But I just wanted to know what you thought of the bacon and eggs.'

She leaned over and put her hand over his. 'You'll be fine.'

Chapter Twenty-one
I Saw You

'I need your help,' May had said. 'I'm moving a few bits and pieces from my house to Johnny's house. Carol's not living there anymore. And he'll not be needing it, being in hospital.'

When Nell had asked why May was moving her things into another house, May had said, 'Making room for a few new things. Might get the decorators in while I'm at it. Don't want my crystal glasses getting broken.'

They had worked all afternoon packing and had driven round to the empty house a couple of streets away with all the cardboard boxes.

It had unsettled Nell to be here. The place had been eerily empty. Usually when Nell had visited, there had been noise – the radio blaring – and clutter. Instead it had been immaculate, uninviting and totally lifeless.

'Gave it a good clean up,' May had told her. 'Had to, the mess Carol left.'

For the first time, Nell had noticed how truly awful the décor was – the clash of patterns and colours. She would have hated to live in this house.

May had looked around. 'There's a nasty feel to this

place. There's no love here. Never has been. Thought it every time I came.'

'Carol was lonely.'

'Well, she'd no right to be. She had everything – a good-looking husband, a beautiful daughter and a home to die for. And what did she do? She went out on the town taking up with men in bars.'

'You know about that?'

'She was seen. Harry was driving past the Caledonian Hotel and there she was, kissing a man. The girl's nothing but a hussy.'

'She was looking for some fun. She's changed, though. She cleans up the flat. She even cooks for Alistair. I'm always leaving for work when he comes in.'

'I'd watch that one if I were you.'

Nell had said she had nothing to worry about. 'Alistair would never do anything to hurt me. Besides, it will all change when I'm managing my own restaurant. I'll be in town. I'll see more of him. I can't wait. I'm already planning my wardrobe. I thought I'd get a hat.'

'A hat? Is that all you can come up with? I'm looking for a manager that does more than wear a hat. You'll need to know the catering game inside out. You should be watching and learning, not planning your wardrobe.' She'd pointed at Nell. 'You dream too much. Your head's in the clouds. You need to stop sighing about the future and start to live in the now. You should be enjoying the moment and not looking too far ahead. And, another thing, you're too trusting.'

Nell had asked what was wrong with trusting people.
'They'll let you down. People do that.'

'You won't let me down, though. I trust you.'

'Don't. Don't trust anybody. That way you won't
get disappointed. All I'm saying is you should enjoy
what you have – a lovely flat and a loving husband.
Now let's get off to work, and on the way we'll have
to stop and shop for vegetables. My supplier's let me
down. You'll have to pay; I've forgot my purse.'

It was the kind of evening Nell loved. The place was
busy, but not too busy. She had time to stand behind
the bar and observe the goings-on. The room glowed:
candles on every table; an intriguing display of bottles
behind the bar; a fire roaring in the hearth. It smelled
of conviviality: food being prepared; cigars being lit;
brandy being sipped; wine being appreciated. Nell
sighed; she never imagined that one day she'd be part
of such a scene.

She loved to speculate about the diners – their jobs,
the décor of their living rooms and their relationships.
Some people she imagined were on a first date and
about to embark on a passionate romance. Some were
having affairs. Some were still in love after years of
marriage. And some had been together for so long
they'd run out of conversation. Nell thought these last
couples tragic and vowed this would not happen to her
and Alistair.

She walked slowly past the tables catching snatches

of conversations, noting silences, refilling empty glasses from the wine bottle on the table, smiling and asking people if they were enjoying their meal.

She shoved the swing door, stepped into the kitchen and was welcomed by a searing blast of heat, the rattle of pans and a hiss of steam as May added a generous glug of wine to the sauce she was making. Nell loved this. May and Annie were talking loudly – as they always did – about their sex lives.

'To be honest, I don't have one right now. I'm just too tired for a cuddle. When I get to bed, all I want to do is sleep. I'm out like a light. Harry is complaining. Also he says I smell of cooking fat.'

'Cheek,' said Annie.

'I know! I mostly use butter.'

'A man needs sex more than a woman so I just do it,' Annie said. 'Doesn't take long. And he always sleeps well so he's in a good mood next day. Men need sex and praise and a good supper.'

'There's that,' said May. 'Mind you, I'm not averse to a spot of you-know-what. It's good for the complexion.' Her voice rattled as she spoke. She was shaking a pan at the time. She turned to Nell. 'Two Chicken Kievs coming up. Table eight.'

Nell took the plates, hit the swing door with her hip and backed out into the dining room. She put the plates before the diners at table eight, told them to enjoy and slid politely away.

Across the room Harry was sitting alone. He was pale and he wasn't eating. Nell thought that recently he'd shrunk. He certainly didn't seem as tall as he'd been a year ago. He was thinner, paler and he certainly wasn't the hearty chap he'd been when he'd first come into Nell's life.

Right now, after hearing May's remarks about Harry complaining about his lack of cuddles, Nell wondered if that was the cause of this shrinkage. She vowed not to let that happen to Alistair. She must always be available to love him in bed. Sex, praise and a good supper, she thought. She wasn't around to cook supper these days. And, now that she thought about it, she too had been too tired for cuddling when she got to bed. Must put more effort into my sex life, she decided. Then there was praise. Nell couldn't remember when she'd last paid Alistair a compliment. Better do that tonight as soon as I get home, she promised.

She hadn't seen much of Alistair recently. He was in bed when she got home. There had been a time when he'd reach out for her saying. 'At last, can't sleep without you.' Now he complained that her way of heftily slumping onto the mattress woke him. 'Can't you just slide in gracefully?' He'd always left for work before she got up. And she was usually on her way out to work when he came home again at six in the evening. Well, tonight when she got home, she'd make sure they had a proper conversation about all this. They'd find a way to be together, to make love, to be the couple they'd once been.

Table six had finished their puddings – a peach melba and a black cherry gateau – and were leaning back waiting to have their dishes removed. Nell obliged, asked if they wanted coffee and on her way to the kitchen told Karen to stop hanging about the window waving to her admirers.

As she passed table eight, she overheard a snippet of conversation. The two Chicken Kiev eaters were discussing the new British cinema. 'It's gritty. It's real. It's what film should be about. I identify with everything.'

'Miranda, darling, your father owns a bank. What do you know about life in the back streets of Liverpool or Nottingham?'

'I know about heartache, loss and loneliness.'

Nell thought she could talk about the new British cinema to Alistair when she got home – after she'd flattered him and before sex.

In the kitchen, May had moved on from talking about cuddles and was waxing lyrical about mushrooms. 'They're beautiful. Perfect. When you slice them they look sculptured and have many shades of brown. They make you sigh.' She took a swig of wine, leaned on her cooking range and added, 'I was almost thirty when I had my first mushroom. We didn't have such fancy things where I came from.'

Annie, now washing the dishes, said, 'My mother used to make lovely mushroom tarts.'

'Really? Your mother was a cook, then?'

Nell put the pudding dishes next to the sink for Annie to wash and lingered over pouring two coffees, eavesdropping.

'My mother loved to cook. She made wonderful soups and her pastry was light as a feather,' said Annie.

'That'll be why you're the right size. You got fed proper when you were young. I didn't, so I'm not the right size. This me you see is an optical illusion. I'm really meant to be taller.' She took another large swig of her wine, which Nell noticed was an expensive Margeaux. 'I was destined to be really tall, but I didn't get the nutrition when I was a child. So my bones are compacted. All the natural growth is still in them waiting to come out, only it won't happen now because I'm too old to grow any more. That's why I get pains in my hips and elbows when it rains.'

Annie said it was a pity. 'I've never heard of compacted bones before.'

'It happens. Only the doctors don't recognise it as a condition, so there's no cure.' She topped up her glass and swigged some more.

It dawned on Nell that May wasn't sober. In fact, now she thought about it, May was often a little worse for wear these days. Perhaps she was worried about Johnny and guilty about not cuddling Harry enough. It was tough being a businesswoman, a wife and a mother.

Nell put two cups, a bowl of sugar cubes, a jug of cream and a small plate of petit fours on to a silver tray and carried it into the dining room. Poor May, she thought, she's had a hard life. She served the coffee and asked if anyone wanted a brandy or liqueur. She was told no, and she smiled and moved away, noticing that the Chicken Kiev and film buff eaters were leaning back, plates shoved aside.

Nell brought two dessert menus to the table, handed one to each diner and removed the main course plates noting that Miranda, the lover of gritty films, hadn't eaten anything. Nell asked if she was sure she'd finished and was waved away.

'I'm not in the mood,' said Miranda, 'but I'll have pudding. I love pudding.'

In the kitchen, May stared at the unfinished plate. 'What's this?'

'The customer said she wasn't in the mood. She's having pudding, though.'

'Oh no, she's not.' May took the plate and stormed out into the dining room. She stood, holding the plate, glaring round at the diners, looking for the brazen one who'd rejected her Chicken Kiev. Table eight. That was her. Thin as a pin, spoilt and brainless. May went over, shoved the plate under the brainless one's nose and demanded to know what was wrong with it.

'Nothing,' said Miranda. 'Perhaps a bit heavy on the butter. But nothing really.'

'It's Chicken Kiev. Of course it's got butter. Butter's the whole point of Chicken Kiev.'

'I'm just not in a buttery mood,' said Miranda.

'Do you know how tricky this is to make? Stuffing the chicken, dipping it in flour, then beaten egg, then breadcrumbs, making it so the butter doesn't burst out before it's served. It's not easy. And you've turned up your nose at it. There's people in the world would be glad of a dish like this. There's people starving in Africa.'

'Well, send it to them, then.'

'Don't you get cheeky with me. This is good food and I'm proud of it.'

'Well, good for you,' said Miranda. 'I'll have the butterscotch ice cream with chocolate sauce.'

'You'll have nothing of the sort,' said May. 'No pudding for those as don't eat their main course. Pudding's a treat.'

The room was hushed. Every diner had stopped eating to watch. A few women were looking in despair at their plate knowing that they could never finish the heaped pile of food it contained. They feared this ticking off would soon happen to them.

Miranda stood up. 'What did you say? Did you just refuse to serve me pudding? Are you forgetting that I'm the customer here? I can eat or not eat as I like.' She turned to her companion. 'We're going. Nobody talks to me like that.' She swept her coat from the back of her chair, picked up her handbag and headed for the door.

'Hold on,' cried May. 'You haven't paid.'

'You expect me to pay for being told I don't get a pudding because I didn't eat my main course? I don't think so.'

'You drank a bottle of Chablis,' shouted May.

'It was overly chilled,' said Miranda as she walked out of the door.

May took the plate back to the kitchen. 'Some people

have no manners,' she said. She filled her glass. 'I cook and I cook and I sweat and I slave and then some spoiled brat turns her nose up at my efforts. It's just plain rude not to eat the food you're offered.'

Annie agreed. 'Just a few mouthfuls to let the cook know their hard work is appreciated. That's all it needs.'

Nell said nothing. She was confused. She thought if people didn't want to eat the food they were paying for, it was their decision. Then again, it must be hurtful to serve up a delicious meal and have it rejected.

She made up her mind to handle such a tricky situation tactfully should it happen when she was in charge of her own restaurant. If the meal hadn't been up to snuff, she wouldn't charge for it. If it had been all right and the diner hadn't felt like eating it, she'd offer them a free glass of wine. She imagined herself putting a glass of the best house red in front of a reluctant eater and saying, 'A little something to cheer you up.' That would keep the customer happy.

'Leaving without paying,' said May. 'That's mean. People should pay for what they order. I do. Well, I don't at the moment but as soon as this place is turning a profit, I fully intend to pay my bills.'

Looking out into the dining room, Nell saw a young couple who'd arrived not long before the pudding dispute finish their free cocktails, put on their coats and leave. And the group at table two – prawn cocktails and steak au poivre all round – were shifting in their seats, looking round for someone to give them the bill while gathering their jackets. Plainly, they'd decided to give pudding a miss. She went out to make up the bill which she'd take to them on a silver platter and hand over with a smile. That was the way to do it. Surely when they saw how polite and friendly she was, they'd come back. But no, as they heaved on their coats and headed for the door, one of them said, 'Well, I'm never coming here again.' The others agreed.

Nell lingered that night at the special table, drinking coffee and listening to May, who was working her way through a second bottle of wine, justifying her outburst.

'I'm not just a cook,' said May. 'I'm an artist. I create dishes. I give people pleasure with my imagination. Every dish comes from my heart. I'll not put up with rejection.'

Nell nodded.

'What I do is on a par with Van Gogh or Da Vinci.'

'Is it?' Nell asked.

'Oh, I'm not a genius like they are, but I put my soul into my creations, just like they did. All I want is a bit of recognition for my art. Not some spoilt brat saying she's not in the mood for it.'

'Of course.' Nell was by now numb with tiredness, and wanted only to lie down and sleep. She longed for her bed.

It took May some time to notice this and stop her long flow about being a misunderstood artist to turn to Harry and tell him it was time the poor lass was in her bed. 'She's tired out.'

In the car, half asleep in the back seat, hearing, but not making out, the soft murmur of May and Harry's conversation, Nell realised that May had not cooked the Chicken Kiev. Annie had. In fact, since Johnny's accident May had spent every afternoon and evening visiting him, leaving Annie to prepare all the shrimp cocktails, steak au poivres, Sole Véroniques and chocolate mousses, as well as everything else on the menu. May put the prepared chicken into a pan and noisily, flamboyantly cooked it with flares of flame and clouds of steam. But all the hard graft was done by Annie. Nell supposed that was how it was when you were boss: you delegated.

The flat was quiet when Nell got in. She went straight to the bedroom, and, without switching on the light, took off her coat, hung it up and said, 'I hope you're not sleeping. I think we should talk. We never talk these days.' Nothing. She reached for the switch and snapped on the light. The bed was empty.

Nell went into the hall, called Alistair's name and stood listening, waiting for a reply. Nothing. In the kitchen there was an empty bottle of champagne on the table along with a crumpled pile of fish and chip wrappings. Someone's been having fun, Nell thought. Shouting, 'Hello, I'm home,' she went into the living room.

It was dark, but the fire was glowing. There was enough light from that for Nell to make out the two sleeping people lying entangled on the sofa. There was no doubt about what Carol and Alistair had been up to. Neither of them was wearing anything. She was sprawled across his chest. He had his arms round her.

The wine and the physical activity that had gone with it had sent them both into a deep stupor. And Nell's presence, standing gazing at them in horror, did not wake them.

She didn't cry out. She just stood, hand over mouth, shocked. They looked comfortable, content, like the pictures in a book she'd loved when she was little – *Babes in the Wood*. She hated them. But she couldn't move. She noted that Carol slept with her mouth open and she'd had her hair cut in the latest style; there was a mole on the side of her right breast; her nails were bitten. Alistair had his hand spread over Carol's hip. He still had his wedding ring on.

Nell slipped from the room. She shut the door quietly behind her, tiptoed up the hall to her bedroom and sat on the bed, arms wrapped round herself, rocking back and forward thinking, how could they?

She didn't know what to do. If she stayed Alistair and Carol might gang up on her in the morning. 'What do you expect?' they'd say. 'You're never here. We were lonely.' Then again, they might be horribly apologetic. Beg for forgiveness. They might swear it was a once-only thing. It hadn't happened before, and wouldn't again. Nell doubted this. She knew the allure of naughtiness. After all, when she and Carol first went to the Locarno they'd vowed they'd only stay for half an hour. Just to see what it's like, they'd said. But they'd stayed all night. And they'd gone back again and again. They hadn't been able to resist it.

She decided to leave. She packed the white suitcase

her mother had given her to take on her honeymoon. It was only as she was walking up the hall towards the front door that it occurred to her to leave a note. In the kitchen the only thing she could find to write on was the envelope of a gas bill. She stood chewing the end of her pen. What to write? Something scathing? Something nasty – *you bastards*, perhaps? Something to make the adulterous pair feel guilty? In the end she wrote just three words: *I saw you.*

Chapter Twenty-two
Comfortable's All You Want

It was five in the morning, and Carol and Alistair were in the kitchen. He was making tea; she was sitting at the table reading and re-reading Nell's three word note. They had woken, stiff and cold, looked round in alarm wondering momentarily what they were doing on the sofa.

'What time is it?' Carol had asked.

'Late,' said Alistair. 'So late it's early.'

'How long have we been sleeping?'

'Hours,' said Alistair.

'Where's Nell? Is she home?'

Alistair got up and went through to the bedroom. 'She's not here.' He went into the kitchen, put on the kettle and found the note. Carol came through to read it.

"Three words, that's all. What does she mean *I saw you?*'

'She means she saw us,' said Alistair. 'She knows what we've been up to,' said Alistair.

'So why didn't she wake us up and demand an explanation?'

'Nell wouldn't do that. She hates confrontation. She'd walk to Peru to avoid a fight.'

'But she left a note. She wanted us to know she knows.'

'She wanted us to feel guilt and regret,' said Alistair.

'And do you?'

'Guilt, yes, but no regret,' he told her.

She agreed. 'Not that I planned it or anything. It just happened.'

It had happened slowly. At first, when Nell had started working for May, leaving the pair alone together every evening, they'd avoided one another. When Alistair had arrived home from work, Carol would be busy bathing Katy and putting her to bed. After he'd eaten, Alistair would take some work to the small desk he had in the bedroom, leaving Carol to watch television.

This had been their routine for several weeks, with Carol aware that Alistair had been feeding himself on baked beans and fried eggs as he'd been too tired to cook anything else. Thinking he was looking pale and underfed, she'd cooked him a steak and had sat opposite him drinking coffee as he ate it. She'd already eaten. He had been so grateful, she'd cooked for him again the following evening and the evening after that. Soon she'd taken to exploring Nell's cookbooks and planning meals.

Mostly, they had spoken about Nell: how lovely she was; what a good person but such a dreamer.

'Not in touch with reality,' Alistair had said, 'but you have to love her for it.'

224

Carol had agreed. 'She drifts off. You can see it happening – a faraway look in her eyes.'

'Yes, she looks glazed. It can be annoying sometimes, though.'

'Yes. Sometimes, I think she doesn't really take in what's actually happening. She lets the dream take over. Still, you have to love her.'

It hadn't been long before Carol was preparing a meal she and Alistair could enjoy together as he put Katy to bed. They'd linger at the table chatting. Their conversation had become intimate enough for Carol to tell Alistair that she hadn't been able to believe how much she now liked him. 'I used to think you were boring.'

'Thanks for that.'

'Actually, it's Johnny who's boring. He doesn't talk much. That's good, really. He's got nothing interesting to say. He spends hours looking at himself – can't walk past a mirror. When we went out, he was the one who took ages to get ready. I was the one waiting by the door with my coat on.'

'I used to think you were a bit of an airhead,' Alistair had admitted.

'Me? I have done some stupid things, I suppose.'

'What stupid things have you done?' he'd asked.

'Got pregnant too young. Married your brother. That was stupid. Then going out at night looking for fun when I should have accepted that part of my life was over. I wasn't ready to settle down.'

He'd nodded.

'Everyone needs a little slice of their life when they can be a little bit wild. Mine didn't last long, so I went out to bars to recapture the abandon I'd felt when I went to the Locarno. I wasn't looking for men. I just wanted to know I still had what it takes to attract them. I wanted to flirt. I'm ashamed of it.'

'I never really understood flirting. I'm no good at it.'

'Doesn't matter. You're good at lots of other things. I suppose I got forced into marriage, my mum and your mum arranged it. And one day I looked at Johnny, thought he was gorgeous but not my type. I didn't love him. Do you love Nell?'

'Love,' he'd said. 'Never thought about it much. One day my mother came into the living room where me and Nell were watching television and said she'd set the date. We were getting married. We giggled about it. I thought it was a good idea at the time. But love . . . love's tricky. It comes at you out of nowhere.' He'd looked at his watch. 'So, what's on telly tonight?'

'Dunno. Are you trying to change the subject?'

'Definitely.'

By now they'd come to watch evening television together, sitting side by side on the sofa, laughing at the same comedy programmes, being bothered by the same documentaries. But, come bedtime, they'd always go their separate ways. Alistair would lie in the dark, thoughts of Carol lying in her own bed keeping him from sleep.

On Saturdays, when Alistair wasn't working, he'd

hang about the flat waiting for Carol to come back from taking Katy on her afternoon walk. He'd sigh, and wait by the window watching for her, unable to do anything about the surge of joy that ran through him when he saw her walking towards the front door. Eventually, he'd started going with her. They'd gone to the park or the zoo when the weather allowed. If it rained, they'd gone to the museum. He'd carry Katy on his shoulders, laughing when she bounced up and down, not minding at all that she gripped his hair. Both he and Carol had known that people around them thought they were a young family – man, wife and child. This had delighted them both, though they'd never admitted it to each other.

The night of the fish and chips and champagne had been a celebration. He'd won a victory in court. His client, a serial shoplifter with a previous conviction, had been given a year's probation rather than the custodial sentence he'd been fearing. He was jubilant, although he was sure he'd soon be seeing the woman again; she just couldn't resist helping herself to things on shop shelves that took her fancy. Still, feeling his career had taken a step forward, he'd phoned Carol and told her not to make supper tonight. He'd bring in a treat. He'd be home after he'd visited Johnny in hospital.

It was the first time Alistair had visited Johnny without May being there. They'd been alone. They'd been able to talk. Alistair had asked what the hell Johnny had been doing, steaming top speed around the countryside. 'Were you drunk?'

Johnny looked a little ashamed. 'Probably. I'd been drinking our mother's cocktails. I was thinking about everything, and I was mad. My life selling Dad's dodgy cars, and then the plan to give away watered down cocktails at the restaurant. I don't want this. The more I thought about it, the harder I put my foot down. I took a corner without braking and it was a bigger corner than I thought it was. I lost control and here I am in hospital.'

Alistair had nodded.

'Our parents are rogues. And they don't see it. They really believe they're making people happy,' said Johnny.

'I know.'

'I'm not going back to it. When I get out of here, I'm not sticking around. I'm not going back to the back lot. I hate it. I want to see a bit of the world. Tell me, how did you manage to get out of working for Dad?'

'I just refused. I think the lawyer bit appealed to Dad. He guessed he might need one. He thought I'd work for the firm. But not me. There's only so much of our mother I can take. There's too much of her for me. Too much emotion, too much gushing, too much spending money on too many hideous things.'

Johnny had agreed. 'There's that. She smothers me. Drives me crazy. She says my beauty will be ruined because I'll have a scar.' He'd touched his cheek. 'I always wanted a scar when I was a kid. Thought it would make me look interesting.'

'So did I.'

They'd grinned at one another.

'So,' Johnny had said, 'will you lend me some cash?'

'Why? Don't you have any?'

'Nope. Dad stopped paying me weeks ago. He said I should have saved for tough times and tough times were here.'

'How much?'

'A hundred?'

'I'll give you five.'

'God, you must really want rid of me.'

'Nah. I just think you need time away from our ma.'

On the way home, Alistair had stopped to pick up some food. He'd originally planned to buy a Chinese takeaway, but had changed his mind for fish and chips.

'Fish and chips?' Is that your idea of a treat?' Carol had asked.

'It is, especially when it's washed down with this.' He'd produced the champagne.

The wine had its effect. They'd become giggly. They'd flirted.

'Are you going to be a great lawyer then?'

'Probably not, but I might have my moments.'

'Are you going to be rich?'

He'd shaken his head. 'Comfortable.'

'Comfortable's all you want. It would be good not to worry about money.'

They'd poured the last of the champagne into their glasses and taken them through to the living room. They hadn't switched on the television; instead they'd sat side by side, sipping occasionally and watching the fire.

'We're like an old married couple.' Carol had put her head on his shoulder. Then, thinking she was being overly familiar with her friend's husband, had removed it.

'Oh, don't do that. I like your head there.'

So she'd put it back again. With the closeness, the warmth, the wine, the electricity between them, a kiss had been inevitable. As was what had followed – urgent fumblings, hastily discarded clothes, wilder and wilder kisses, the joy of skin on skin and the passionate relief of doing what they'd both been longing to do for weeks.

They'd woken at nine o'clock. Both of them had been shivering as the fire had died out. Alistair had fetched a blanket from his bed and spread it over them. They'd agreed that what they'd just done was wrong – very wrong – but they hadn't been able to resist doing it again, more slowly this time, savouring one another. Afterwards, entwined and warm under the blanket, they'd fallen asleep again, wrapped in each other's arms.

Nell ran the length of the street. She didn't look back. Carol and Alistair might be coming after her; they might catch up and persuade her to come back to the flat. There would be an argument – two of them against her. She wouldn't win. Breath heaving, heart pounding, she turned the corner and stopped. She was out of sight.

Now she could walk. She headed for the West End, where she could find a taxi.

Oh, she could imagine all the things Carol and Alistair had said about her. They'd probably laughed at her behind her back. They'd think she had a stupid job, welcoming people into a restaurant, bringing them their bills, pouring their wine. Carol would have said that anyone with half a brain could do that. They'd have joked about how useless she was in bed. Nell stopped, put down her case, sniffed and wiped her eyes on the back of her hand. She crossed her arms over her stomach to quell the churnings. Then told herself to walk on, to walk away from it all.

She found a taxi, climbed in and gave her mother and father's address. Hold on, she told herself. She would be brave. From now on she would have to be a strong, independent woman of the world. She'd be on her own.

She hammered on the door of her mother and father's home, and when her mother opened it, Nell burst past her, dropped her case in the hall, ran into the kitchen, sat at the small Formica-topped table and broke down.

Nancy stood at kitchen the door, watching her, thinking someone had died. 'What's happened?'

'I needed to come. I've nowhere else to go.' Nell reached for a tea towel and blew her nose.

Nancy folded her arms. It didn't sound like someone had died. 'If you've had a fight with your husband, you can go right back and sort it out. You're a married woman. You can't come running to me when something goes wrong.'

'I can't go back. I'm never going back. Alistair doesn't want me anymore.'

Nancy put on the kettle. 'Don't be silly. Of course he wants you back. You've had an argument. All couples argue at first. It's the way of things.'

'You don't understand,' Nell wailed. 'I found them naked on the sofa.'

Nancy turned. 'You found who naked on the sofa?'

'Alistair and Carol. They were all cuddled up together and she had her hand on his chest and he had his arms round her and they were sleeping.'

Nancy abandoned her tea-making and sat at the table opposite Nell. 'They were naked? On the sofa? Carol and Alistair?'

'Yes!' Nell started to sob uncontrollably, heaving, coughing, and gasping for breath.

Nancy hadn't seen such anguish in years. Her life had become so calm, so routine, that she'd forgotten what raw emotion looked like. She wasn't one to put her arms round other people. It had been years since she'd last cuddled Nell, but she reached out and took her daughter's hand and patted it. 'I didn't know Carol was still staying with you.'

Nell blew her nose and nodded. 'She's been with us for ages. She just settled in and made herself at home.'

Nancy looked down at Nell's hand, soft in her own. It was a good hand; a young hand. Not like hers:

creased; worn; liver-spotted. She thought of all the things her hands had done: wiping; scrubbing; wrapping up cakes in the shop; baking; rubbing embrocation into her husband's back. These hands had held the child that this young woman across the table from her used to be. They had dried her crying eyes, dabbed her cut knees with disinfectant, changed her nappies, washed her clothes, and combed her hair. It occurred to Nancy that it had been a long time since she'd used these hands to show love.

Looking at her daughter in floods of tears, Nancy realised she had never wept like that in her life. Nothing this bad had ever happened to her. She'd spent her life getting on with things, noting tragic events in other peoples' lives, hoping that nothing heart-stopping ever happened to her. Nancy supposed crying helped; better than holding all the pain in.

'Oh, Nell,' she whispered. She went back to the kettle, made tea and brought two cups to the table. 'So Carol and Alistair were alone in the house when you went out to work?'

'Yes. Well, Katy was there, but she's little. She goes to bed at seven o'clock.'

'You never thought anything about them being together every evening?'

Nell shook her head. 'Not really. Maybe at times I did wonder but really I was just glad Alistair had some company.'

'But evenings is when a couple sits together, plans their holidays, shares their dreams, chat.'

'I know,' said Nell, 'but I have such a good job. I have prospects. I never had prospects before. I'm going places. One day I'll be managing my own restaurant. I'll be making good money.' She blew her nose heartily into the tea towel.

Nancy couldn't deny her daughter was a fool. Always dreaming with no notion of what life was about. 'The books you've read, films you've seen . . . why, you've even been abroad. I've never ever dreamed of going to another country. All the things you know – and you know so much more than I do – but you're not wise, love, are you?'

Chapter Twenty-three
How Does The Taxman Know About Me?

May was rummaging down the side of the sofa looking for stray coins. Today she had to fetch Johnny from the hospital and she was short of cash. The letterbox rattled and mail thumped onto the mat. She went to the front door, picked up the pile of letters and put them all, unopened, into the drawer in the kitchen where she kept all the mail she didn't want to read. Then she returned to her sofa search.

When the doorbell rang, she'd moved on to the armchairs and had a fair pile of coins on the coffee table. She ran upstairs and peered down at the front step, checking who was there. It was Frank Harris, the family accountant.

He was a tall man, slightly balding, with a passion for clothes. Today he wore a grey suit, pale olive shirt and pink tie. He left a thin waft of Old Spice aftershave in his wake as he walked past May into the living room.

'I won't stay long,' he said. 'Just need a quick word.'

He sat on the sofa. May noticed him noting the pile of coins, told him she was having a bit of a tidy up, and then added that Harry wasn't there. 'He's at work.'

'I actually came to see you,' said Frank. He shot her a discouraging look that May dismissed. She didn't like him. Then again, he didn't like her. May assumed that was because he didn't like women. Well, not ones that worked, anyway. His wife stayed home, cooked, cleaned and always had a hot meal waiting for him when he got home. 'Got her well trained,' he'd once told Harry. May had hated him the moment she'd overheard that remark.

Frank took off his glasses and rubbed the bridge of his nose.

'The Inland Revenue are asking about you. They've written to you but haven't had a reply.'

May nodded. The letter would probably be in the drawer with all the other unopened letters. She said she didn't know why the taxman would want to write to her. She'd done nothing.

'They want to know where you got the money to open a restaurant.'

'Savings,' said May.

'Where did you keep these savings?'

'None of your business.'

'I'm your accountant. It *is* my business. Do you have a bank account you haven't told me about?'

May shook her head. 'Don't use banks. I had the money in the cupboard.'

'Please don't tell me this money was undeclared earnings.'

'Of course the earnings are undeclared. If I declared them the Inland Revenue would want them.'

'Only a bit of them,' said Frank.

'A bit's more than I'm prepared to let them have. I don't believe in taxes.'

Frank said that nobody likes taxes. 'Thing is,' he said, 'they want to know where the cash for all the building work came from. And they also want to know why you pay your staff and suppliers in cash. They want to see your accounts.'

'Don't have accounts. Keep everything up here.' She tapped her head.

Frank sighed.

'How does the taxman know about me?'

'Someone must have told them. That's usually the way of it. An anonymous phone call or letter.'

'I've been betrayed?'

Frank nodded. 'Someone has told them you renovated a restaurant using cash. A huge amount of cash.'

'Who?'

'I don't know. That information is secret. They'll never tell you.'

'Betrayed,' said May again. 'And me just trying to make people happy. I provide good food. I sing to them. I employ people. What's wrong with that?'

'Nothing, except you're doing it with money you haven't declared to the Inland Revenue.'

'I told you I don't believe in taxes.'

'It doesn't matter. The law states you must pay them.'

'What happens if I don't?'

'They'll demand the money, plus interest, plus a fine and perhaps a jail sentence.'

'What if I don't have the money?

Frank looked round. 'You have this house. You have all the stuff in it. They'll sell it off and keep the money.'

'I had a suspicion they might do that,' said May. 'It's nasty. I work hard. I put my heart and soul into my restaurant and that's what they do. I hate them all. And mostly I hate the person who shopped me.'

After Frank had left, May sat in the kitchen and stared out of the window. Wishes and curses tumbled through her. If only people would hang on and stop demanding cash all this would be sorted out. At the moment, since they'd stopped giving her credit, she was paying suppliers with the takings from the night before. This meant she hadn't enough to pay her staff. Annie hadn't been paid for weeks. No doubt she'd quit soon. Her piano player had told her he wouldn't be coming back. Not that this mattered because the people who'd supplied the beautiful red piano were coming tomorrow to take it back. Should've paid for it, thought May. Nell hadn't been paid for a long time, not that she knew. May had told her she'd paid the money into the running-away fund. Nell hadn't checked, but then Nell wouldn't. The girl's a fool, May decided.

She slapped her palms on the table. No point in sitting here; there were things to do. She phoned the restaurant and told Annie to do the lunches today. 'A few things have cropped up that I must attend to.'

Annie told her it wasn't a problem but May detected a certain coldness in her voice.

After that, May packed her favourite handbags, shoes and jewellery in a box. She knew what was going to happen. Something she suspected weeks ago would happen when she'd stashed her crystal glasses at Johnny's house. As she could not pay the taxman, sheriff's officers would be appointed to come to the house and sell the furniture and pretty much everything else. Well, she could make sure there were some things they couldn't get their hands on.

She drove round to Johnny's house and dumped her goods in his hallway. She'd bring some more things tomorrow. Right now, she had to find some more money. Back home, a rake through the pockets of Harry's coats and jackets brought her enough to buy half a tank of petrol.

She drove to the hospital. Johnny was sitting on his bed, dressed and waiting for her. 'Where have you been?'

'Busy,' she said. 'No matter, I'm here now.' She picked up his case and headed for the door.

He followed on crutches, complaining that she was walking too fast.

'Lots to do,' she called.

She took him to her house, telling him it would be easier to keep an eye on him here. 'You'll be needing looking after.' She brought him a sandwich and a glass of milk.

'Milk?' he said, holding up the glass in disgust.

'I'm out of beer,' she told him. 'Besides, milk's good for you. Good for the bones.' She put her hand under his chin and lifted his face, considering it. 'Not bad. They've done a good job on you.' She ran her thumb along the scar on his cheek. 'You'll be marked for life, but it's a fine scar. Gives you a bit of character. Before you used to look beautiful but—' a bit thick, she was about to say, but stopped herself. 'Now you look beautiful *and* interesting.'

He smiled and nodded. May noticed how easily he took the compliment, but then supposed he would: he was used to them. She bustled across the room, picked up a vase and a bowl and said she was going out. 'Have to talk to Harry, and then I'm off to work. Got dinners to prepare for tonight.'

He asked why she was taking the vase and bowl with her.

'I've been betrayed. Someone close has shopped me to the taxman. They're wanting unpaid taxes that I can't pay. Like as not, they'll requisition the furniture and sell it off to get the money. I'm getting as much stuff out of here before that happens.' She sighed. 'I'll be fined. I may get jail. Not that I'll go.' She slumped down on the sofa beside him. 'Who would so such a thing? Who would betray me?'

Johnny said it could have been anybody. 'Perhaps there was a reward. People will do anything for a reward.' He stared ahead for a moment, turning this news over in his mind. 'What about me? Will they come after me?'

May said it was a possibility.

'And Alistair?'

'Probably not,' said May. 'He's got nothing to do with the business these days.'

'Do you think it was him?'

'What? Alistair? He'd never do such a thing. I have

to go. Drink your milk and have a little sleep. Sleep and milk is what you need.'

As May drove to see Harry, she thought about Alistair. It couldn't have been him, could it? No, she shook her head. Oh, he disapproved of the goings-on, but not that much. Still, the doubt had seeded in her mind.

Harry was in his office, sitting at his desk, looking pale.

May sat opposite him, folded her hands on her lap, and also looked pale.

Harry said, 'Well, what do you think?'

'I think we're done for. The sky has fallen.'

'Our solicitor phoned. I'm going to be charged.'

'What with?' exclaimed May.

'You know what with. Selling dodgy cars. Turning back the mileage. Fiddling the books. God knows what else.'

'What will happen to you?'

'I'll get bail till the case comes up. Then a huge fine. Prison, perhaps. Won't be able to sell cars again. Then there's the earnings I didn't declare. A fine for that, too. Huge fine. And we've no money. I've had to close this place down. Told everyone this morning.'

'Well, it looks like the tax man is doing a job on us,' said May. 'Frank came round and told me they want to know where I got the cash to start the restaurant.'

Harry sighed. He pulled some coins from his pocket, threw them on the desk along with a five pound note from his wallet. 'This is what I'm reduced to.'

May said she was the same. 'The electric and the phone will be cut off soon enough. It's not right. We only turned back the clocks a little and covered some rust. Nothing much.'

'We've been doing it for years and years. It's a bit more than nothing much.'

'The cars were lovely. All shiny. People drove out of the back lot happy. And maybe we didn't declare all the money we made. But what did we do with it? We started a restaurant. Employed people to fix the building. And now we employ people to serve and prepare the food. We're contributing to society. We're making people happy. And that fifty thousand we kept from the government didn't go to building nuclear bombs, so that should make people happy, too. I'll say it again, we've done nothing wrong.'

'It's against the law to keep the facts of your earnings from the taxman. Simple as that.'

'Well, the law's wrong,' May said. 'People should get to keep the money they earn.'

Harry put his head in his hands. He felt sick. His life was filled with dread. He dreaded going to prison. He dreaded the scandal that would follow when the truth of his back lot activities came out. Mostly, he dreaded sitting in court watching May giving evidence in the dock. She'd be wearing a pink suit and all her jewellery. She'd be smelling of Chanel. No, she'd be reeking of Chanel; wafts of it would drift to the far reaches of the courtroom. Her face would be overly made up. She'd repeat what she'd just said, boldly admitting her guilt. Oh, how delighted the prosecutor would be.

He decided he'd have none of that circus. 'Don't worry,' he said. 'We're not going to court. I'll think of something.'

Slightly reassured, May drove to the restaurant. Lunch was over. Nell, Karen and Sylvie were sitting at a table discussing Rutherford's In The City.

'I've got it planned,' Nell was saying. 'I know exactly what it will be like. Plain white walls with huge posters in thin black frames. Wooden tables with a checked or crisp white cloth, lights hanging from the ceiling and a simple menu. It'll be classy but not so classy as to frighten off people who don't often eat out.'

Sylvie said it sounded lovely.

May breezed past thinking they sounded like a bunch of silly schoolgirls and noting how puffed Nell's face looked. If she's coming down with the flu, she shouldn't be here.

Annie was in the kitchen ferociously chopping onions. May always marvelled at the speed Annie worked up; the knife was a blur. 'You could cut your fingers off doing that,' she said.

'Always chop like this,' Annie said, 'My mother taught me.'

May asked how the lunches went.

'Only a couple of tables. People passing by stopped for a bite to eat. Only three reservations tonight.'

'We won't be making our fortunes anytime soon,' said May. 'What happened? We used to have a full house every night.'

Annie said it was the way of things. 'People are curious about a new place and give it a try. It takes time to build up some regulars.'

Actually, she thought the empty tables had a lot to do with the article that appeared in the local paper a few weeks ago. Miranda Cartwright-Jones wrote a regular column called 'Where to Go at the Weekend', recommending new restaurants, exhibitions and plays. This time, there had been an extra section – 'Where Not to Go. Ever' – and the only restaurant mentioned was Rutherford's. She'd mentioned being berated for not eating her Chicken Kiev and being refused pudding. *It was like being loomed over by a bullying school dinner lady. The décor is hideous. And the chef apparently embarrasses the diners with a song. Perhaps she thinks music eases the digestion of her absurdly heavy food. So, don't go to Rutherford's, life's too short for misery you actually have to pay for.*

Plainly May hadn't seen this review and Annie had no intention of mentioning it to her. Instead she said, 'Give it time. Maybe a year.'

I don't have a year, May thought. She opened a bottle of wine, poured a glass and sat watching the wonder of Annie's chopping and mulling over her suspicion that Alistair was the one who had betrayed her. The more she thought about it, the likelier it seemed. After all, he did know everything about her business, and he'd told the family he wanted no more to do with it.

'I need to be seen as a fit and proper person,' he'd said. 'And some of the things that are going on at the back lot are not what a fit and proper person would do.'

I'm a fit and proper person, thought May. There has never been a fitter or properer person than me. She finished her drink and started work, preparing the dough for the small parsley and rosemary dumplings she would put in her stew, which was tonight's special.

Annie stopped what she was doing when she heard what May was making. 'Stew? People coming out to eat want something fancy, not stew. That's what they'd have at home.'

'It's got wine in,' said May, 'and it's good hearty food. That's what people want. It'll make them happy. That's my job, making people happy.'

Annie sighed and continued her chopping.

May gazed down into her pot. Scents of garlic, onions and browning meat steamed up to her, bringing memories of stews past. They always reminded her of cold days. Her children coming home, blowing on their fingers, noses red, complaining about the chill outside. She'd stand in the kitchen chopping vegetables – celery, carrots and peppers – adding them to the pot, watching them mix with oil and the vegetables already in there and as she did, listening to Alistair and Johnny playing in the living room. They'd mock fight, speculate about their teachers, film heroes and pop stars, and then sit on the floor side-by-side, watching television. Sometimes she'd slip away from her cooking to watch them. She'd never known she could love so much.

Harry always accused her of preferring Johnny, but this wasn't true. She knew Alistair would be all right. The people who go through their childhood being a little overshadowed by a brother or sister usually found a way to make their voices heard. Alistair was bright, he had a strong sense of right and wrong, he knew what he wanted. Offered a choice – a toy or a book, an apple or a pear, a biscuit or a cake – Alistair never had any trouble deciding what to pick. It was always the book, the pear and the cake. Johnny always hesitated, watched what Alistair did, and then copied him. May decided that the people who were fussed over, and told they were good-looking never thought to fight to have their voices heard. It barely crossed their minds that they had a voice.

And Alistair had always instinctively known all the things Johnny had to be taught: not to cry when you lose a game; offer a plate of cakes to the guests first; don't sulk; be brave when you've fallen and skinned your knee; always say please and thank you.

And now Alistair had phoned the Inland Revenue and told them about her secret cash. He'd decided it was the honest thing to do. How could he? How could he betray his own mother and see his family ruined? It was heartbreaking. My boy, May thought, my lovely, lovely boy hates me. Slow tears slid down her face, dropped into the pot, mixed with the browning meat and melting vegetables. This would be a sad and salty stew. She must remember to watch the seasoning.

It wasn't a good evening for Rutherford's. Only three tables were taken. May grouped them close to one another, hoping this would make the place look busier. It made the diners self-conscious. They spoke in whispers and left as soon as they could. Nobody lingered and nobody ordered May's stew.

'They don't know what they're missing,' she complained. She shrugged on her mink coat over her chef's whites. 'I'm going home. I'm tired.'

She breezed through the empty dining room, noting that Nell was lounging behind the bar with nothing to do. Daydreaming as always. Oh, she couldn't be bothered with her company tonight. Let the girl make her own way home. She patted the red piano in passing, saying goodbye to it. She'd miss it. She went to the cash register, opened it and sighed. The takings weren't good: about twenty pounds in cash and a cheque. She took ten pounds and the cheque, shouted, 'Goodnight all,' and left.

Harry was in the kitchen when she arrived home. He had the contents of the dread drawer spread on the table in front of him. 'Do you want the good news or the bad news first?'

'The good news.'

'The good news is things have got so bad, they can't get any worse.'

'Well, that's something,' said May. She looked round, 'Where's Johnny?'

'Haven't seen him since I got in. I thought he'd gone to bed and I let him sleep. Lying in bed in hospital is tiring.'

'Let him sleep. Best thing.'

Harry waved his hand over the letters on the table. 'Oh boy, are we in trouble. You were meant to go see the Inland Revenue, but because you didn't open the letter, you didn't know to go. I've been hit with a huge back payment, but because I didn't open the letter, I didn't pay it. No matter, I couldn't have paid it anyway. Fact is, sweetheart, I don't think I can talk my way out of this.'

May slumped on the chair opposite him.

'The sheriff's officers are coming to requisition our possessions and sell everything off,' Harry told her.

'I hate this. It's all worry. I feel like I'm walking through black. Everything black. Can't think. Can't eat. My stomach's a mass of nerves and all I feel is dread. I dread the phone ringing. I dread the sound of mail dropping through the letterbox. I dread the knocking on the front door. The shame of it. After all our hard work, we'll be back to having nothing.'

Harry took her hand. 'But wasn't it grand? Didn't we have fun? It was a rollercoaster. And we will rise again. You can't keep a Rutherford down.'

'But my things. My furniture, my handbags, my shoes.'

Harry leaned over and put his face close to hers. 'We'll get more. We'll get better things.'

May was surprised. 'You don't seem bothered at all.'

Harry leaned back, hands behind his head, and told her it was a challenge. 'Us against them. It's an opportunity. We're starting over and we can do anything. We've proved that.'

May pointed out that bankrupt people couldn't start their own business. 'We'll be homeless. Penniless.'

'We'll be free. No furniture to dust. No bills to pay, because we can't pay them. It's a fresh start. Think about it. Daydream. Just let your mind go. We've got no ties. The boys are all grown up. We can do whatever we want. What's your secret wish? A wee B&B in the Highlands? We could breed horses.'

'No, we couldn't. I don't like horses. Besides, we've got no money!'

Harry flapped his hand at her. 'Ach. You've got to learn not to take poverty so seriously. It's temporary. C'mon, what's your dream? Something exotic, I hope. Something with glitz and sparkle and exciting.' He leaned towards her. 'Whisper it.'

May took a deep breath. 'Well, what I like best about having a restaurant is singing. I'm not so fond of the cooking as I thought I'd be, but standing at the piano and singing is a treat. What I'd like to do is have a bar with lots of booze and chat and no food except nibbles.'

Harry thought that sounded good. 'Pity about the no money, though.'

Suddenly May smiled, 'Well . . .'

Chapter Twenty-four
Left in the Lurch

It took some time for Nell to realise that May wasn't going to drive her home. The woman had breezed past her with hardly a glance, stroked the piano, helped herself to some money and shouted goodnight. Thinking she'd come back, Nell stood staring at the door. Bloody hell, she thought, I'll have to get the bus. Bummer. She'd been planning to tell May about Alistair and Carol. She'd been sure May would have given her good advice. May was a woman of the world. She'd know what to do.

A voice rose from the kitchen. Annie waltzed out, moving between the tables singing 'Magic Moments'. She saw Nell watching her, and stopped, embarrassed. 'I thought you'd left with May.'

Nell shook her head. 'You sound happy.'

Annie said she'd just had a little burst of happiness. 'Just came over me and I had to sing.'

Nell asked what had brought this burst of happiness on.

Annie shrugged and told Nell there was nothing wrong with feeling happy for happiness' sake. 'Mind you, I'd be happier if I got paid.'

'You haven't been paid?' Nell was surprised.

'No, not for a few weeks,' said Annie. 'May promised me a big bonus if I'd stay with her through this sticky patch. Have you been paid?'

'Yes,' Nell told her. 'May told me she'd put it into my bank account.'

'But you haven't checked?' said Annie.

Nell shook her head. It hadn't occurred to her to check.

'Well, I'd get myself to the bank as soon as possible and find out,' Annie advised. Changing the subject, she asked why May hadn't given her a lift back to town. 'Left you in the lurch, has she?'

Nell said she did seem to have forgotten her.

'She's got a lot on her mind these days.'

'Has she?' This surprised Nell.

'She has,' said Annie. She looked at her watch. 'You better go, the last bus leaves in ten minutes.'

On the bus to town, Nell reviewed her troubles. Trundling through the dark, all she could see in the window was her own reflection: a face contorted with worry. She had been trying not to think about her troubles. But here, alone on a bus, it was no longer possible to push them out of her mind.

Flashbacks of the moment she'd seen Alistair and Carol lying entwined on the sofa kept coming to her. She relived the moment, imagining what she ought to have done. Running away – sneaking off into the night terrified of confrontation – seemed foolish now. She should have challenged them. 'And just how long has this been going on?' she should have said. Or, 'You are welcome to each other. You deserve one another, you cheats.' Pointing at Alistair, 'You no longer have a loving wife.' And to Carol, 'You don't know the meaning of friendship.' Then, she'd have left, head held high, dignity intact. In this imagining she was wearing a smart black suit with a high collar white blouse, though she did not possess any such clothes. As she left, without turning back, Alistair and Carol would watch her filled with guilt and humiliation. Then, they'd argue, each blaming the other for what had happened. Their relationship would flounder. They'd part. And they'd both come to her begging forgiveness, which she may or may not grant. She hadn't yet conjured up this part of her daydream.

'What are you going to do?' her mother had asked this morning.

Nell had said she didn't know. 'Divorce, I suppose.'

'You can't do that. People in this family don't get divorced. Once you're married, that's it, happy or not. You've made your vows and you stick to them – richer or poorer, in sickness and health. That's the deal. You go to Alistair, you tell him you forgive him, you get Carol out of that flat and you and him start afresh. That's what you do.'

'Perhaps.' She'd had a feeling her mother's tactics wouldn't work. She knew Alistair. He wouldn't be tempted into a swift fling with his wife's best friend. No, this was serious. He'd want a divorce.

The bus trundled on. In the seat in front of Nell, two young girls were discussing the Beatles. Paul was cute, Ringo funny, John deep and probably difficult. 'You'd go out with him, but George is the one you'd marry. He's reliable,' said one.

Her friend agreed. 'You couldn't take John home to meet your mum, but Paul would be OK. My mum would like him.'

Nell remembered how she and Carol had similar conversations about Buddy Holly. She'd had a fantasy that he'd turn up walking along the street where she lived and as he passed her, he'd smile. She'd smile shyly back. He'd ask if she lived round here. She'd point to her house. He'd nod and say it was homely, and that she was just the kind of girl he was looking for: down-to-earth and not interested in his wealth or fame. She'd tell him it was the person inside who interested her.

She sometimes fantasised about famous actors coming to Rutherford's and being attracted by her simple charms. She could get whisked off to live in Hollywood in a fabulous house with a swimming pool and a white phone by the bed. It could happen.

Divorce, she thought, wasn't such a scandalous thing really. There had been a divorced woman lived across the road when she was young. Mrs Morton. She'd worn stiletto heels and pencil thin skirts. She'd worked at the make-up counter in a big store and drove a pink car. Eventually she'd married a rich man and had moved into a huge house in the country. It's not *all* bad, Nell thought.

If she divorced, she'd rent a small flat with two rooms and a kitchen near the West End; not that she'd use the kitchen much as she'd be working. She'd be an experienced, sophisticated woman. She'd have affairs. Not that many, and just with worldly wise stylish men who'd lean against the bedroom wall drinking whisky, watching her dress as she got ready to go out to a fashionable restaurant for dinner. They'd have witty grown-up conversations about life and art. Perhaps, one day, she'd remarry, but she'd always retain an air of mystery and quiet drama. She'd be a woman who'd experienced tragedy. And survived.

It was after eleven o'clock when Nell got off the bus. She walked from the bus station to the stop where she could get a second bus to take her home. She waited for fifteen minutes and then decided to walk to the next stop to keep warm. The number forty-two passed her midway between stops. Not knowing if there would be another one at this time of night, she decided to walk home.

It was a route littered with memories. This was where she and Carol had jived in the middle of the pavement singing an Eddie Cochrane song. And here was the spot where she and Alistair had seen Carol and Johnny share their first kiss, with Carol doing her one-leg-behind-her stance. It was the walk she'd done with Alistair when he'd taken her home after they'd been introduced at the Locarno. She'd decided on that night that she'd marry him. How foolish it all seemed now. How young she'd been. All this was too painful, so she turned her thoughts to May, wondering why she hadn't paid Annie. Certainly the restaurant hadn't been making money recently but, still, people didn't work for nothing. May knew that. Nell decided it was a glitch. May had been worried about Johnny and had let the business of making up the wages slip. Still, May had promised Annie a big bonus. Perhaps she'd get one too. It would all be sorted out soon.

By the time she reached her parents' house, Nell was adding up the pros and cons of being back home. Well, there wouldn't be the same privacy. Her mother would want to know where she was going when she went out and at what time she would be back. Then again, her laundry would be taken care of. And her mother had promised she'd leave a flask of cocoa on the kitchen table for her to drink when arrived home. Nell was looking forward to that.

Her father was waiting for her when she got in. 'Where the hell have you been? You left work hours ago. I've been phoning.'

Nell told him she'd walked home.

'Your mother's died. She was making a cup of tea and I was watching television and heard this awful clatter. It was her dropping to the floor.'

Nell stared at him, paralysed.

'I got the doctor, but it was too late. Heart attack, he said. Could've happened any time. She's in the living room. Undertaker will pick her up tomorrow.'

Nell felt numb.

'She's gone,' her father said. 'Just like that. Gone.'

Chapter Twenty-five
Gone to Visit
Aunty Dot

May was in the kitchen making scrambled eggs for breakfast. She was wearing her fur coat over her night-dress. 'It's a comfort with all this misery going on.'

Harry, sitting at the table, told her everything would be fine. 'Just hold on. Don't pick up the phone and don't answer the door.'

'Wasn't going to,' said May. She buttered three slices of toast, poured the tea, piled the eggs onto the plates she'd laid out and brought them to the table.

'Where's Johnny? He's usually at the table soon as he gets the first whiff of food.'

She got up, went to the foot of the stairs and shouted, 'Johnny, breakfast's on the table.'

Nothing.

'God,' she said, 'that boy can sleep.' She climbed the stairs, still shouting, 'Johnny. Food's up.'

She stood at his bedroom, knocking on the door. 'Johnny?'

Nothing.

She went in. He wasn't there. His bed was made up. Didn't look as if it had been slept in. The plaster

256

cast that had been encasing his leg was lying on the floor.

'He's not here,' she shouted. 'Is he down there?'

Harry left the table and looked in the living room, the dining room, the bathroom and then peered out into the garden. He shouted to May that there was no sign of him.

Harry went upstairs, picked up the plaster cast, looked round and saw May's carving knife and her kitchen scissors. 'He's cut this off himself. Bloody idiot.'

They went to the bathroom, peered in, and then searched the remaining rooms, opening doors, calling Johnny's name.

'He's gone,' said May. She opened his wardrobe and peered in. 'His clothes are gone.' She turned to Harry. 'Where's he gone to?'

'Just done a bunk, I suppose.'

Back in the kitchen, they noticed a small note. *Gone to visit Aunty Dot. The leg's fine. Don't worry about me. Johnny.*

'Is that it?' said May. 'Not even "love Johnny" or a kiss at the end?'

'That isn't his way. He'd never write love. Doubt if he's ever even said the word. Besides, he was doing a bunk. He'd have been in a hurry.'

May snorted. 'Aunty Dot's in Australia. How's he going to get there?'

'In an aeroplane, I should think,' said Harry. He looked at his watch. 'He'll be well on his way. Might even be there.'

'It's not right. He's not able to look after himself. He never has been.'

'No more, May. You're about to say he's too beautiful. He's cursed with beauty. Stop it. Let him go.'

'But what if I never see him again? He's my boy. My best boy.'

'You'll see him again. And if you don't, you'll always know you did everything for him. Stop looking out for Johnny. Time to look out for May and Harry.'

May said she'd never stop worrying about him. 'It'll be part of my life for the rest of my life. You know what I think happened. Alistair was the one who shopped me to the taxman, and then he tipped Johnny off and told him to do a runner before things got hot.'

'You've been watching too many old films. Alistair never told anybody about us. He's not like that.'

'He's the only one who knew.'

'He may have been the only one who knew, but plenty must have guessed the way you were splashing cash about.'

May admitted she might have got a little carried away. 'But I was only doing good. I was employing people.'

'I know. You were making them happy. And you emptied the money cupboard doing it.'

'How was I to know you'd get closed down? How was I to know the cash would dry up? I thought in time I'd be adding to the cash.'

'Well, it's happened.'

May's face crumpled. She hid it in her hands and wept. All she could say was, 'Awful. Awful. Awful.'

Harry dug into his pocket, fished out a hanky and gave it to her. 'C'mon. No tears. You have to see this as the end of one thing and the beginning of something new. We've got to look forward, think about the future and forget all this.'

Blowing her nose, May said, 'I suppose.'

Harry nodded and leaned towards her. 'Tell you what, let's fill a flask with coffee, make some sandwiches and have a picnic.'

'It's March. We'll be freezing,' said May.

'So we'll put on our coats,' said Harry. 'We'll go to Princes Street Gardens and watch the world go by. We'll dream and plan.'

'Dreaming and planning are the best bits of life,' said May.

She phoned Annie and asked her to hold the fort. 'Got one or two things to tie up at this end. Can you manage the lunches?'

Annie said it wouldn't be a problem. This was because there were no bookings but she didn't mention this.

'Where would I be without you? This has bumped up your bonus big time,' said May and put down the phone. She turned to Harry. 'Let's go. I feel naughty doing that. It's like skipping school. Used to do that all the time. Never felt so free as when I was walking the streets watching the world, enjoying myself when everyone I knew was sitting at a desk learning their times tables.'

They prepared their picnic, left the house and used some of Harry's tiny remaining funds to take a bus to Princes Street. They held hands as they strolled the Gardens. May held up their entwined fingers and looked fondly at them, 'Haven't done this for years. It's nice.'

Harry reminded her that this was where they'd first met. 'You were walking with your pals and I was walking with mine. I saw you and said to myself, "There's a girl I've got to get to know."'

'You and your mates started walking behind us whistling and asking our names.'

'"Hello, beautiful." That's what I said.'

'I thought you were talking to someone else, not me.'

'It could only have been you. You were the loveliest of the bunch.'

They found an empty bench, sat on it and unpacked their bag. May unwrapped the sandwiches as Harry poured the coffee. 'You wouldn't talk to me.'

'I was playing hard to get. That's what you did in them days.'

'You weren't that hard to get, thank goodness.'

'Didn't want to put you off. I fancied you. You were such a dandy.'

'Still am,' said Harry.

'Who'd have thought then that we'd end up where we did? Two kids from the wrong side of the tracks like us. The Christmases we used to have – everything lit up, huge tree, huge turkey and fairy lights all over the garden. Oh, it was lovely.' May gazed into the distance, smiling slightly, drifting into fond memories.

Harry sighed. 'It was lovely.'

'To think we were almost posh,' said May.

'We were posh,' said Harry. 'We *are* posh.'

May shook her head. 'Us? No, we'd never make it as posh. I was never one to wear a twin set and pearls, and your ties are too loud. And we have a naked-boy peeing fountain in the garden and we laughed too much and played music late at night. I'm a bottle blonde with a brassy laugh who drinks too much gin and tells dirty jokes. Harry, we're not posh. We were born to be cheap and snazzy. And I love it.'

Annie watched four men lift the red piano and heave it out of the restaurant and into the back of a van. Well, that's that, she thought, and locked the door. She looked at the empty space the piano had once occupied and at the dead embers in the fireplace. The place looked forlorn. There wasn't a lot of food in the kitchen, and certainly not enough to cook any of the dishes on the menu. Then again, these days there was hardly anybody to cook for.

Back in the kitchen she made a pot of tea, and then sat at the special table where May and Harry had entertained their guests with free meals to consider her future. Nell had phoned to say her mother had died and she wouldn't be at work today. Shortly after May had called to say she wouldn't be in today either. After that several suppliers had phoned demanding to know when they'd get paid. The butcher had called in person and hadn't been polite about the amount he was owed. 'Thirty years I've been in business and never have I been owed so much by one customer. I must have been mad to keep delivering to her, but that May would give me a whisky and tell me how well she was doing and how good my meat was. I've been duped. I want my money now.' Annie had apologised and had told him it was really nothing to do with her, saying, 'In fact, I haven't been paid either.'

Annie heard a car pull into the car park outside. She went to the window, saw two people get out and head for the door. Annie slid to the floor and crawled under the table. She'd had enough.

The two people rattled at the door, peered in, decided the restaurant must be closed and walked back to their car. Annie found a sheet of paper at the bar and wrote a note.

Closed due to family ~~beere beree~~ breav. How did you spell bereavement? She scored out her last attempts and instead wrote *disaster.* She pinned the note to the door, helped herself to three bottles of whisky and as much wine as she could cram into her shopping bag, thinking this would help cover some of what she was owed. Then she put on her coat, went out the back door and fled.

Harry and May finished their picnic and walked arm-in-arm to Princes Street. They gazed into shop windows.

'Isn't the world changing,' said May. 'Skirts are getting shorter. Everything's for the young these days. I feel I didn't get the chance to be young.'

Harry said that was true. 'When we were young, we were expected to be old. Live the same lives as our parents.'

'Yes,' said May. 'I feel like I only had a few weeks of being young. Then I got married and had to get stuck into being a wife and mother – cooking, cleaning, and working my fingers to the bone. Worrying.'

'Shoplifting,' said Harry.

'That was only to survive,' said May, defensively. 'I never stole anything I wanted. I just took food for the kids.'

'I know that. You took risks for your family.'

'Exactly,' said May. 'If I'd had a proper youth, I wouldn't have had children and I wouldn't have had to do that. I want my youth. I'm going to have it now.'

'Too right,' said Harry. 'We'll start being young and we'll stay that way for the rest of our lives, though I'm not going to grow my hair long and wear tight trousers and pointy toe shoes.'

'Of course not,' said May. 'That's for proper young people. They only dress that way so us older young people can disapprove. If we liked it, they wouldn't do it. They'd do something worse to shock us.'

'True,' said Harry. 'Still, I like the idea of starting being young after being old for such a long time.'

At six, when the shops were closing, Harry said that it was time to go home. May didn't want to go. 'There's too much there. Too many happy memories that I'm sad to remember, and too many worries. All those letters in the drawer – bills, final demands, threats, court orders and God knows what else. Also, it's cold without the heating.'

Harry suggested they light a fire.

'We've no coal and no logs,' said May.

'But we've got bills, final demands, court orders, threatening letters galore. That'll make a fine blaze. It's what a young person would do.'

'Harry, you're a genius,' said May. 'I'd never have thought of that. First, though, Alistair.'

Alistair had been banished from the kitchen. Carol had taken up cooking, moving between the cookbook on the worktop and the cooker, mumbling about ingredi-ents as he'd watched. She'd told him to go away. 'I can't do this with you looking on.' She flapped him out of the kitchen with a dishcloth. 'Take Katy with you.'

He picked up the child and took her to the living room where he stood at the window. He was wrestling with his guilt. Nell had phoned him earlier in the day telling him her mother had died. His heart had gone out to her. Poor soul, he'd thought. She'd told him she wanted a divorce. 'I expect you do, too,' she'd said. 'Don't think it'd work. Not with me seeing you and Carol like that. I can't get it out of my head.'

He'd agreed and apologised sincerely for what she'd

gone through. He'd told her he cared for her, wished her happiness and would take care of everything. 'If you ever need anything, anything at all, call me.' But she'd already rung off. He wished she'd been angry. But she'd been depressed, diffident, almost as if she was in the wrong. Anger was easier to cope with. A shouting match might have cleared the air. It certainly would have helped the guilt. He could have accused her of being submissive, naïve, too dreamy to live with. 'I can never get through to you,' he could have said. 'You were never here. You practically threw me at Carol.' But no. She hadn't quite apologised to him for his sleeping with her best friend, but she'd come close.

He was plagued by his vision of her discovering him entwined on the sofa with Carol drunkenly snoring, and he banged his head on the window pane to get rid of it.

'What the hell are you doing?' Carol asked. She'd come through wiping her hands on the back of her jeans, having finished making the stew.

'Giving myself a severe reprimand for how I treated Nell. Shouldn't have got drunk, shouldn't have fallen asleep.'

'Shouldn't have slept with me?' asked Carol.

'Should've done it sooner,' he said. 'Should've have broken it gently to Nell.'

He opened his eyes, and saw a garishly dressed couple walking towards the flat. The man was wearing a pin-stripe suit, pink shirt and outrageously floral tie. The overly made-up woman mincing beside him in six-inch stilettos wore a fur coat that was flapping open revealing a matching pink skirt and jumper. For a few blissful seconds he didn't recognise them. Then he said, 'Oh, God.'

'What's up?' asked Carol. 'More scoldings?'

'My parents are heading this way.'

'Hide.'

'They've already seen me.' Still holding Katy, he took her hand and made her wave to them. May waved back.

Alistair watched them reach the steps to the main door. They were arm-in-arm, moving jauntily. He wondered why. Considering their present problems, he thought they ought to look miserable.

They knocked and, without waiting for anyone to answer, walked in.

'We were just passing and thought we'd drop in and say hello,' said May. She looked round and took in the scene – Carol standing by the fire, Alistair in shirtsleeves, shoes kicked off, holding Katy, coffee cups on the table, a newspaper on the sofa, something savoury cooking in the kitchen – and said, 'Very homey. I suppose Nell's at work.'

Alistair shook his head. 'Nell's at home. Her mother died.'

May sank onto the sofa. 'Poor soul. It's awful when your mother goes. You feel alone. A huge hole in your life. Things happen and you think, I'll phone my mum. Then you remember she's gone. It keeps coming back at you.' She sighed. 'I'll feel that way about Johnny. Though he's not dead. He's gone.'

'To visit Aunty Dot,' said Alistair.

'You know?' May was surprised.

'I gave him the money.'

'Without telling me,' said May.

'He was afraid you'd dissuade him from going.'

May said she would indeed have tried to keep him here.

'I know,' said Alistair. 'Your beautiful boy. Your best boy.'

'You never really understood how hard it was for him.'

Alistair sighed. 'He needed to get away.' He wanted to tell May that Johnny actually needed to get away from her, but he held his tongue. 'He needed some sunshine, so I gave him the money for the fare. He's my best boy, too.'

'I suppose you know about all the trouble we're in.'

'I know,' said Alistair.

'Somebody told the income tax people about me.'

Alistair nodded.

'It wasn't you, was it? You knew.'

Alistair shook his head. 'I wouldn't do that. You're my ma and pa. I love you. Actually, I even like you which is harder. The love comes naturally.'

'Fair enough,' Harry said, slapping his knee. He wanted this conversation to end. He hated this kind of chat; keep things jolly was his motto.

'I had to ask. I needed to be settled in my mind,' May said. She got up, crossed the room and touched Alistair's cheek. 'You're a good boy. We're proud of you.' She heaved on her coat. 'Although sometimes I wonder where you came from – you're so upright and honest.' She busied herself putting on her gloves. 'We better be going. Got a lot to do.' She turned to Carol. 'Take care of my granddaughter. And your stew's burning. The smell's turned dark. It'll be sticking to the bottom of the pan. Probably you put it on too high a heat.'

Carol swore and ran to the kitchen. May grinned.

Alistair watched them walk arm-in-arm down the street. They're up to something, he thought. They always were. They planned, schemed and came up with new ways of making a buck. They put their money in the kitchen cupboard and were often seen standing side by side, looking at it with joy.

He remembered his mother running into the flat the family lived in when he was young carrying a pack of sausages. She had slammed the front door, leaned on it panting and had chucked the sausages to him. 'Quick, cook them and eat them. Once they're gone, they're gone. Eat the evidence.' Sometimes he thought she was magnificent.

'What was that about?' asked Carol. 'The stew's burnt, by the way.'

'Just add a spot of wine and swish it about,' said Alistair. 'That's what she does. And I've no idea what that was about. Perhaps they were saying goodbye.'

'You didn't tell your mother about us.'

'No need. She knew.'

'How?'

'She's a nosy, interfering, bossy mother. It's her job.'

'And she doesn't mind?'

'Oh, she minds. She just knows when not to mention it. She's awfully fond of Nell. Well, Nell is a gift for bossy, nosy, interfering mothers, isn't she?' He put his arm round her, and kissed the top of her head.

'You told her you loved her,' Carol said. 'Do you?'

'Of course I do. She's my mother. I just don't approve of her.'

Chapter Twenty-six
Time to Move On

There was quite a crowd at Nancy's funeral. Nell was taken aback; she hadn't realised her mother had known so many people. After the ceremony, as mourners, friends, neighbours and work colleagues lined up to shake Nell's hand and sympathise with her loss, she thought miserably that she only knew about ten people who might come to see her off, should she die soon. Carol was included in the total and Nell wondered if she'd come along. She certainly wasn't here today, though Alistair was. He smiled sympathetically at her and repeated that if there was anything she needed, she should give him a call. Nell said she'd have to go to the flat and pick up the things she left behind.

'Anytime,' Alistair said.

He didn't come to the gathering at a small hotel afterwards, saying he had to get back to work. Nell had wanted to throw a more glamorous celebration of her mother's life than the drab affair that her father insisted upon. She'd suggested they serve canapés and wine.

'Canapés,' he father sneered. 'I've never eaten such a thing in my life and neither has your mother. Plain food is what we'll have – ham sandwiches and fruit cake. We're ordinary folk and proud of it. Plain is what we like.'

People milled around, sipped the sherry provided, nibbled on the sandwiches, and then left. When the last guest had gone, Nell's father went to the manager, took out his chequebook and paid. 'Don't worry about funeral bills,' he'd told her earlier. 'Nancy and me have all that covered. When my time comes, you'll find the details in the cabinet beside the bed upstairs.'

By two in the afternoon, she and her father were home. He sat on the sofa, sighed and said, 'That's that, then. I don't know what I'm going to do. Always thought I'd go first.'

Nell didn't know what to say. She longed to get back to work to help distract her. She'd phoned several times but got no reply. This was bothering her but she consoled herself by thinking they must be too busy to pick up the phone. Perhaps there was too much to do with her being off so they let it ring.

Two days after the funeral, Nell told her father she thought it time she went back to the restaurant. 'I can't just leave people to cover for me. I have important work to do, and as I'll be managing my own place soon enough, I have to show May how responsible I am.'

Her father told her she didn't have to show May anything and that he needed her at home, so Nell stayed. She shopped, she cooked, she lit the fire, she massaged her father's aching back with a foul-smelling embrocation, but none of it was good enough for her father.

'You don't have Nancy's touch,' he told her. 'You don't ease the sore bits the way she did.' And she didn't light the fire properly, or buy the right things. 'That's not the right kind of cold meat. I only like ham.' Her cooking didn't come up to scratch, either. 'These chips aren't crispy like your mum's. And the egg's too hard. I like it runny.'

In the evenings, he sat staring blankly at the television. He rarely spoke to Nell. He despaired.

He lasted three weeks. He died in his sleep. Nell had made breakfast and had called that it was ready from the foot of the stairs. When her father didn't appear, she called again before going up to his bedroom. She knocked and then stuck her head round the door. She'd known even as she went to the bed that something was wrong. His stillness was disquieting. On tiptoe, holding her breath, she crept up to him, touched him and jumped back. She stared at him for a long time before calling the doctor.

The doctor told her it was quite common: one partner dies and the other follows soon after. 'These old hearts don't cope with grief.' He smiled to her. 'Still, your mum and dad – it was quite a love match, wasn't it?'

'Was it?' Nell was surprised.

'Oh, yes. I couldn't help but notice how close they were. In fact, your dad had your mother's photo under his pillow. He must have missed her terribly.' He told her to look after herself, and left.

Nell made a second announcement in the deaths column of the local paper and organised a second funeral. This time, in an act of defiance, she booked a room at the best hotel she could think of – the Caledonian – and ordered canapés and wine. Her father proved to be a lot less popular than her mother. There were six mourners and nobody touched the food. Mrs Lowrie, a neighbour Nell had rarely spoken to, had clutched her hand as she made her way out. 'We're plain folk, lass,' she said. 'Ham sandwiches and fruit cake would have been fine.'

Alone at home, Nell sat in front of the fire. Not knowing what to do, she got up and walked into the kitchen, looked round, realised she wasn't hungry and went back to sitting by the fire. How suddenly silent this place was. Even the clock in the hall had stopped ticking. It must know he's gone, Nell thought.

She went upstairs, looked in her father's bedside cabinet. In it she found a bottle of embrocation, a pair of false teeth, his spectacles, a couple of handkerchiefs and his insurance policy. She'd send that off tomorrow along with the death certificate to claim the money that would cover the undertaker's bill and the hotel catering. There wouldn't be much left after that.

In her mother's cabinet, she found a pair of stockings, knickers and the romance novel she'd been reading. Nell looked over her shoulder, afraid that somebody might catch her prying.

She started searching; what for, she didn't know. In the cabinet in the living room were Christmas cards going back fifteen years, a photograph album with snaps of the only holiday the family had ever taken. There was Nell aged seven building a sandcastle on a beach in the Highlands. In the kitchen were the same old pots and pans and utensils Nell had been familiar with all her life.

Is this is? Nell thought. Ancient things, false teeth, Christmas cards from people long forgotten – is this what love brings? Two lifetimes reduced to this. She rummaged some more, then at the foot of her mother's wardrobe she found an old shoebox, lined with blue tissue paper. Carefully preserved were Valentine cards, years and years of them, all dated and all written in her father's careful hand. *To my lovely Nancy. To my sweet-heart. You're still the beautiful woman I married all those years ago and you make the best cup of tea in the world.* Pressed between two sheets of pink paper was a violet. *I saw this and thought of you. It's sweet and tender and it was flowering in the snow.* Nell hadn't known her father was such a romantic. She felt she'd never known romance. Alistair had never sent her a Valentine card. 'It's crass commercialism,' he'd said. No doubt he'd send Carol one. She'd make his life hell if he didn't.

It hadn't occurred to her how much her parents had loved one another. To her they'd just been her mum and dad. Just there, that's all. Maybe love was something more than passion. Maybe it was warm and comfortable and the two people involved reached a moment when each knew what the other was thinking – like when to make a cup of tea.

She wished she had someone to talk to. Usually, she'd discuss dramatic moments in her life with Carol, but now the idea of seeing Carol was too painful. She thought of Alistair, who'd said if there was anything he could do, she should ask, but she was pretty sure that by that he'd meant money, not listening to her misery.

She went back to the sofa and considered her life. A tear for her dead parents slid down her cheek, but beneath the shock and grief was a glimmer of relief. At last she was free to go back to work. It was time to leave this small house with its faded wallpaper and tired furniture and find a place of her own, time to start being the sophisticated, independent, working twenty-one-year-old woman she'd decided to be.

Chapter Twenty-seven
Walk Away

Nell didn't start her new life the next day, nor the day after that. She was numb. She lay in bed till midday, got up, moved from room to room and went back to bed again. Pictures of her mother and father filled her mind. Moments she had forgotten reappeared – her father pulling her along the street on the sledge he'd built for her. She remembered how cold it had been and looking back at the tracks they'd left in the snow and his serious face looking down at her telling her to hold on. She remembered sitting on her mother's knee listening together to a story on the radio; standing on a chair helping her mother bake a chocolate cake and licking the bowl afterwards; Christmases when they decorated the living room with paper chains – all that, and oh-so-many other things. She cursed that she'd dismissed them as boring. She chastised herself for being rude to them as she grew up. Sometimes the memories pained her so much, she doubled up as the emotional became physical.

She struggled through three days of this grief. On the fourth morning she told herself that many people had suffered misfortune and had not only survived but had gone on to great things. Charlie Chaplin, she thought. Marilyn Monroe. What about Buddy Holly's widow? How she must have grieved. I can get over this. I can carry on with my life. I am a woman who has opportunities. I must stop my daydreaming. I'm addicted to it. It makes me happy to float away into a fantasy world. It's time to face reality. If I don't I'll never be a sophisticated, independent woman of the world like May.

She bathed, drank a couple of cups of tea, dressed and set out for work.

The restaurant was deserted and the doors were locked. Nell knocked but nobody answered. She went round to the kitchen door at the back. It, too, was locked. She peered in the window. Nobody. She looked at her watch – quarter to eleven. Really, someone should be here preparing lunches. She waited, pacing the car park. Something was wrong.

Every so often, she would step out into the road, stare one way, turn and stare the other way, hoping someone would come, but nobody did. After a couple of hours she set off towards the village nearby where Annie lived. It was a cold April day. She pulled her coat collar up and moved carefully. There was no pavement; the road was rough and her shoes delicate. She tripped and stumbled, cursed and fretted. Occasionally she would turn and walk backwards, staring down the road, watching the car park in case somebody turned up.

Once she reached the village, Nell went into the post office and asked for Annie. 'Annie who?' said the woman behind the counter.

'Annie who works at Rutherford's. She's my friend,' Nell said.

The woman came out from behind her counter, led Nell out into the street and pointed to a cottage on the opposite side of the road. 'That's our Annie.'

It was chocolate-box perfect. The garden was a tumble of late-spring blooms. There was a log pile at the side. Nell was charmed. As she walked up the brick path, she imagined herself living here. She'd live the simple rustic life. She'd be 'Our Nell' to the folks in the village. She could wear a yellow frock but jeans would be best when she was chopping logs. She'd bake her own bread and the local squire would court her. She thought she'd be like Doris Day in *Calamity Jane*, except without the horse.

She stopped herself, clenched her fists and thought, 'Quit the daydreaming, Nell.'

She knocked on the door, and after a minute Annie answered, stared at her and asked what she was doing here.

'I wanted to find out what's going on. I've been off for a few weeks, come back and Rutherford's is locked up. What's happening?'

'Nothing as far as I can tell,' said Annie. 'Nobody's been near the place for ages.'

Nell asked why.

'As far as I know, May's broke. Can't pay any of her bills. She certainly hasn't paid me. I stopped going in to work a while ago. I figured the big bonus wasn't going to happen.'

'So Rutherford's is shut down?'

Annie nodded. She stepped back, invited Nell inside and asked if she wanted a cup of tea.

'Please.'

Annie waved Nell into her living room and told her to make herself comfortable while she put the kettle on. The room was small; the furniture was old, comfortably worn. The far wall was covered with bookshelves. A log fire burned in the hearth. Tucked behind the sofa was a pile of toys.

After a few minutes Annie appeared with a tray bearing two mugs of tea and handed one to Nell. In this light, Annie looked different: slimmer and younger. Up till now, Nell had only seen her in her cooking whites. Today she wore jeans and a long jumper. Her face was lightly made up. Nell had always thought Annie was old, but now could see she was probably only in her early forties.

'You have children?' Nell asked, pointing at the toys.

'Standard two, both girls,' said Annie. 'They're at school at the moment.'

'I didn't know,' Nell admitted. 'What does your husband do?'

'He's a musician. Plays the piano.'

'Oh, like the piano man at Rutherford's.'

'That's him.'

'Really, I didn't know you and he were married. Gosh. Do you know, every time I looked at him, I thought I knew him from somewhere? Only I can't place him.'

'Oh, he remembers you. Did you used to go to the Locarno?'

Nell flushed. 'In my stupid youth, I did. God, that place was wild—' she stopped. Emerging through the mists of her memory was the moment she'd seen André, the piano man. 'Oh,' she said. 'It was the last time I ever went there. A goodbye-to-all-that-silliness outing. He was fighting with another man in the passage outside the lavatories.'

'My husband has never got into fights. He's the sweetest man alive. He was helping his friend who was epileptic. He'd had a fit and passed out. André ran for help and to phone for a taxi to get his friend home. The taxi came, and you and your friend took it. He was furious.'

Embarrassed, Nell put her hand to her mouth. 'Oh my God, I'm so sorry. I didn't know. Oh God, I took his taxi. I thought—' She didn't finish the sentence. She cringed and wished the ground would open up and swallow her.

Blushing furiously, she changed the subject. 'I—I—I like your house.'

'I was born here,' said Annie. 'I inherited it after my parents died. I like it. So May hasn't been in touch?'

Nell shook her head. 'My mother died, and then

my father. She probably thought I had enough on my mind.'

'I'm so sorry for your loss, Nell. That must have been tough, losing them so close together.' She paused. 'As for May, I should think she's got a lot on her mind, too. That woman's in a lot of trouble. The taxman's after her for unpaid taxes.'

Nell said she knew May was against paying tax, 'But how did the Inland Revenue find out?'

'Somebody informed on her.'

'Who would do such a thing?' said Nell.

'Me,' said Annie.

Nell couldn't believe it. 'You're joking.'

Annie shook her head. 'No.'

'Why would you do such a thing to someone like May?

'That woman is a pain. I got sick of her. Singing to the customers, who all looked startled. Feeding all her friends and Harry's clients for free at the special table, laughing, drinking and me in the kitchen cooking her bacon and eggs and scrubbing up.'

'She's a wonderful cook,' said Nell.

Annie shrugged. 'Being a good cook doesn't make you a chef. She knows nothing about menus. She served heaped plates that came back to the kitchen still heaped. Nobody could finish their portions. Waste, free food, free cocktails – that's the profits getting thrown away, and my wages come from the profits. I don't take kindly to being told there's not enough money to pay me. I don't take kindly to working my backside off, then not having enough to feed and clothe my kids. I got sick of that woman so I told the taxman about her. I put a stop to her.'

'You've done a terrible, terrible thing,' Nell said.

'Maybe, but I don't feel guilty. In fact, I feel quite good about it.'

'What will happen to Rutherford's now? I loved that place.'

'Someone will buy it and run it properly,' said Annie. 'I'm sure of that.'

Nell pointed to the bottles of wine on the dresser. 'Aren't these from Rutherfords?'

Annie followed Nell's gaze. 'Indeed they are. They cover some of what I'm owed. Not all, mind you, but it's a start.' She looked Nell up and down, the full critical gaze, 'I bet you got paid, being one of the family.'

Nell said she hadn't checked yet, 'May paid my wages into the bank. It's a joint account so she could put money in.'

Annie looked at Nell over the rim of her mug and raised an eyebrow.

It took Nell over an hour to get back into town. As the bus rumbled over narrow country roads, she realised how little she'd known about Annie. She'd been so besotted with May, she had hardly noticed the other woman in the kitchen.

But there was something about that look Annie had

given her just before she left – something disbelieving, cynical, almost mocking. It had been unnerving. Nell urged the bus on. She had to get to the bank and check on her money. Surely May wouldn't have emptied the account. Nell comforted herself that May was kind, open-hearted and generous. She'd given Nell the account, a little something to fund her independence – a running-away fund. It'll be fine, Nell told herself.

In town, she jumped off the bus and ran to the bank. She handed over her bankbook and asked to withdraw twenty pounds. She wasn't sure how much money she had, but there had to be hundreds of pounds in the account.

'The book's not up-to-date,' said the cashier, and asked her to wait.

She watched from across the counter as he filled in the pay-in column. Nell sighed, everything was fine.

The cashier took her withdrawal slip, compared it to his updated figures and told her he was sorry but she didn't have twenty pounds in her account. He slipped the book back across the counter. 'You appear to have withdrawn all of your cash a few days ago, Mrs Rutherford.'

'No, I didn't.' Nell looked at her book. She'd hadn't had it made up for a while but though she should have a few hundred pounds in there what with her wages going directly in. But four days ago, she'd had five thousand pounds, and three days ago all but one pound had been removed 'I never had this much money – and I never took any out! This is a mistake.'

The cashier assured her it wasn't.

Twenty minutes later, she was sitting in the manager's office weeping and saying there had been a dreadful mistake with her account.

The manager, a small, dapper man with a bushy greying moustache, said that his bank rarely made mistakes. 'I have all the pay-in and withdrawal slips here. You've been making regular deposits – cheques and cash.'

'No, I haven't. I hardly ever come in here. This was my private savings account. My. . . .' She was going to say running away fund. But thought perhaps not.

The manager pushed some of her bank slips over the desk. 'See, you signed them.'

'I never signed anything' said Nell.

She examined the slips, which were signed Mrs N Rutherford, but the handwriting was May's. The final stroke in the M in each case hadn't been completed. They looked like Ns.

'You phoned us and said you wanted to empty your account. I took the call myself. I made the arrangements.'

Nell stood up. 'I should go. I'm sorry I bothered you. There's been a mix-up. I share this account with my mother-in-law. I work with her. Obviously she's withdrawn the money without telling me.'

She fled. Ran the length of George Street. Stood in Charlotte Square, panting, weeping, trying to figure this it all out. May had been putting cheques and cash from the restaurant into the bank using her name. How could she do that? And why clear out the account now, not even leaving Nell the wages she was owed. 'My God.'

She walked down to Princes Street and caught a bus out to May's house. It was time to confront the woman and demand an explanation and her wages at least. Heart pounding, stricken with worry and fear, Nell strode the familiar short route from the bus stop to the Rutherford's front gate.

The house was busy, thronging with people. The front door was wide open. May's furniture was on the lawn and cluttering the garden path.

Nell stopped to watch. She approached a man who was leaving carrying a pair of vases that had taken pride of place on May's mantelpiece. 'Excuse me, who are these people?'

'Dealers,' he said. 'Second-hand furniture mostly. Few antiques people.'

Nell asked why they were here.

'Sale of goods to cover debts.'

'What?'

'Sheriff's officers have put the stuff in this house up for sale. The money goes to the folks the people who lived here owed money to. Must have been a hell of a lot. Go see the guy over there if you want to look round.' He pointed to a balding man in a grey suit.

Nell said she didn't. 'I just wondered what was going on.'

But the sheriff's officer had spotted her. He came over. 'Do you live here? Are you Mrs Rutherford?'

Nell shook her head. 'No.'

'Did you know the Rutherfords? Were they friends of yours?'

'No,' said Nell. 'I was passing and saw all this. Stopped to look. Just being nosy, I suppose. And, no, I've never heard of the Rutherfords. Don't know them at all.'

She walked away and didn't look back.

Chapter Twenty-eight
Just Who Are You Running Away From?

Nell phoned Alistair. It was seven o'clock in the morning and she knew he wouldn't yet have left for work. She'd lain in bed in her old room in her parent's house all night sleepless and shocked. Her only comfort had been the light from the hall. That little glow from beyond the room eased the torment. Pitch dark deepened it. She didn't count her troubles, or even tackle them; her mind was a jumble of fears – humiliation, poverty, homelessness.

'Your mother's robbed me,' Nell said when Alistair picked up the phone.

'How did she do that?' Alistair asked, shocked.

'She emptied our bank account, which had my money in it.'

'*Our* bank account? You and my mother had a bank account?'

'Yes,' said Nell.

'You had a joint account with my *mother*?'

'I told you, yes. She paid my wages into it. Or said she would. Now she's emptied it and taken what was mine. I went to see her yesterday. Only she wasn't there and some sheriff's officers were selling all the stuff from the house. Did you know that?'

'Yes, they announce all warrant sales in the newspapers and I saw it, but I'd guessed before then that it would happen.'

'You did?'

'They were up to their eyes in debt.'

'They were? Where is your mother anyway?'

'I have no idea, but I suspect she and my dad aren't even in the country anymore.'

'What do I do about my money?'

'I don't know. Listen, I'll come and see you at lunchtime. Are you at your mother and father's house?'

Nell told him she was.

'See you around one o'clock,' he said, and rang off.

Nell slammed down the receiver. 'Damn your mother. Damn all the bloody Rutherfords.'

Alistair arrived just after one. Nell had been pacing the house, stopping at the front-room window to watch for his arrival every time she passed it.

'You're late,' she said. She noted how well he looked. He was wearing a new suit, charcoal grey with a dark blue shirt and red tie. He had a different haircut. His shoes were polished. Carol had smartened him up. He didn't look older; he just looked more mature – handsome, even.

'Only five minutes late.' He refused a cup of tea. 'I just had lunch with Carol before we came over here.'

'We?' said Nell. 'Where is Carol?'

'At her mother's. She's got a lot to tell her.' He took off his coat and sat down. 'So you and my mother had a secret bank account.'

'It was her idea. She set it up. She said women needed their own bank account these days. She called it my running-away fund.'

He asked what she might be running away from. 'Me?'

'No. She said it was for when things got rough. You know, it was for an emergency. When I might need to get away.'

'What from?'

'I don't know,' said Nell. 'May said that women needed a running-away fund. She always had one. Only she never ran away. She treated herself when she was feeling low.'

He asked why it had been a joint account.

'She said it was so she could pay money in.'

Alistair sighed. 'You don't need to have your name on the account to pay money in, only to take it out.'

Nell looked surprised. 'I didn't know that.'

He smiled, 'So my mother *did* have a bank account. I always wondered what she did when her customers paid by cheque. How much was in the account?'

'Five thousand. That included my wages.'

'You should have told me. I was your husband.'

'You still are,' said Nell.

'I won't always be. Carol and I want to get married.' Alistair changed the subject. 'You can't trust my mother with money. If she's got it, she'll spend it. She always thinks she can get more.'

'She tricked me,' said Nell. 'She planned it all.'

Alistair said he doubted that. 'She would have known she had to have a bank account. But she wouldn't have planned to run off with the money. She was desperate, saw an opportunity and took it. My mother's philosophy is to live for the moment. She rarely thinks beyond that moment. If things go wrong she'll say that it seemed like a good idea at the time.' He looked round. Something wasn't quite right here. 'Where's your dad? He's usually about.'

'He died.'

'Oh, Nell, I'm sorry. What happened?'

'He died in his sleep. A heart attack, the doctor said. Actually, he said his heart was broken. He missed my mum so much. I didn't know they were so in love.' Her eyes glazed with tears. 'I miss them. It hurts.'

'God, Nell. I didn't know. You've been through a lot.'

Nell said she knew that. 'Among all the other things my best friend stole my husband.'

'Nobody stole anybody. It happened. Perhaps it wouldn't have if you hadn't left us alone together night after night.'

'I was pursuing my career. And I trusted you both. How could I have imagined you were both sneaking around and betraying me behind my back?'

'The only time we slept together was that night when you discovered us.'

'And that makes it OK? Do you love her?' asked Nell. The only question she dared. The ones she longed to ask – is she prettier than me (answer, yes) more fun than me (yes), a better cook than me (yes), better in bed than me (oh, probably) – remained unasked.

'Yes. I do love her.'

'Didn't you love me?'

'I thought I did. We really just got married because May arranged it. It was easier than not getting married.'

Nell said she supposed that was true and nodded sadly.

Alistair stood up, put on his coat. 'I have to pick up Carol and get back to work.'

'Of course.'

'If you want to get in touch,' he told her, 'you'd better do it through my office. Carol and I are moving. She doesn't want to live in the flat we shared. She's after a fresh start.'

Nell asked where they were going.

He shrugged. 'I don't know yet, but it'll be some-where with a garden for Katy.' He took his wallet from his pocket. 'I'm assuming you don't have any money.'

'Everything was in that account.'

He gave her thirty pounds. 'That's all I have on me.'

'My wages amounted to a lot more than that.'

'Nell, *I* don't owe you anything. My mother does. This is to help you out.'

'You'll owe me alimony when we divorce.'

'True, but it won't be much. We've only been married for just over a year. We don't own a house or

291

have children together. I paid our rent. And you earned your own living so you weren't dependent on me.'

Numbly, Nell took the money he offered. She'd need it. She had her parents' rent to pay, and there was no food in the house.

All Carol's mum could say was, 'Poor Nell.'

'It just happened,' said Carol, defensively. 'We didn't plan it. In fact, we didn't want it to happen. But it did.'

'That girl has just lost her mother and now her father and you do this to her. How do you think she feels?'

'Pretty bad,' said Carol, meekly. 'But you don't understand. You met Dad, fell in love, married him and had me. You were lucky.'

'Oh, was I?' Margaret said that wasn't the way of things at all. 'We worked at our marriage, and made it what it is today. You ran away from yours. And took up with your best friend's husband.'

'I love him and he loves me. That's all there is to it.'

Margaret snorted. She wondered if she should tell her daughter the truth about her real father and how, after his death, she'd spent her life feeling grateful towards the gentle, considerate man who'd rescued her from disgrace. She would never have left him or hurt him. Besides, love of a kind had come in time. No, she thought, I can't tell her. There's too much going on right now. Later, she decided, knowing that later wouldn't ever come.

'He's wonderful,' said Carol. 'I didn't know a man could be the way he is. He cares for me. He helps in the house. He adores Katy. He takes her out so I can have a rest. Johnny never did anything like that.'

'What does he think of all this?' asked Margaret.

'He's gone to Australia. I'll get a divorce eventually. He's just glad to get away.'

Margaret snorted again. She went to the kitchen to put the kettle on.

It always helped in dramatic moments to do something, anything. Carol picked up Katy, slung her onto her hip and followed her. 'Alistair took me out to buy some clothes. He chose them for me. A suit with a checked waistcoat that makes me look smart, and a summer dress in plain dark blue that I wouldn't even have looked at. Not too much colour, he told me. And he's right. He knows about being stylish.'

'He knows about making you look like the sort of woman he wants to be seen around with,' said Margaret. 'What's wrong with the way you dress?'

'He thinks it's a little cheap. And he took me to a foreign film. I didn't want to go but it was wonderful. He's given me books to read. I'd never read books before but now I've read *Bonjour Tristesse* and *Catcher in the Rye*. They're really good. I can discuss them with him. He's helping me expand my mind.'

Margaret poured boiling water into the teapot. 'Well, if there's any mind that needs expanding, it's yours.'

'I'm going to go to night school. I'll do English and History and probably French. Then, once I've passed my exams, I'll apply to university. See, Johnny would never have approved of me doing that.'

Margaret stared at her. 'University? What about Katy? Who'll look after her?'

'She'll be at school by then. So will the other children. It's our long-term plan.'

'Other children?' Margaret poured two cups of tea.

'Two,' said Carol. 'Alistair wants to have three kids. He thinks that's a proper family.'

Margaret felt a stab of regret. She'd wanted more children. It hadn't happened. 'They won't all fit into that flat,' she said.

'Oh, we'll have a big house by then. One with a garden. We're looking for somewhere now. Alistair knows exactly how it will look – big lamps, a couple of sofas and rugs on polished floor.'

'Is that what *you* want?'

'Now that he's told me about it, yes. I'd never have thought of it.' Carol said she was happy. 'Happier than I've ever been.'

'I'm glad for you, love. I just hope it works out and that you know what you're doing.'

'I do. Alistair really, really cares. He's opening up a new world to me. I'm going to be a whole new person.'

'I can see that. I don't see what was wrong with the old Carol, though. I liked her.'

'I'll still be me,' said Carol, 'but I'll know more. I

intend to be the woman Alistair wants me to be. That'll make me happy.'

Margaret shrugged and said happy was the thing to be. Then added quietly, 'poor Nell,' though she thought 'poor Carol' might be more appropriate.

Chapter Twenty-nine
Crystal Glasses

'You've lost weight.' Carol looked at Nell, a piercing head-to-toe glare.

'You haven't.' Nell was pleased to note Carol was, in fact, putting it on.

'It's the cooking,' said Carol. 'I've been experimenting and all the tasting you do as you go along – not to mind the actual eating – takes its toll. But Alistair likes me this way.'

'Well, that's all you want,' said Nell.

She'd come to pick up her remaining clothes.

'I'll take my stuff and leave you in peace,' she said. 'You won't want to have to take any of my belongings with you when you move.'

She headed for the bedroom, but Carol stopped her.

'I moved your things. They're in the spare room.'

Nell sneaked a swift peek into the main bedroom as she passed. It was different, and much sexier than before. There was a new eiderdown on the bed, sheets Nell hadn't seen before and matching lamps either side of the bed. 'Didn't take you long to make your mark,' she said.

Carol shrugged. 'Didn't like it before. It reminded me of you.'

'Thanks for that,' said Nell.

Carol was embarrassed. 'I didn't mean that I didn't like it. Just I don't want to be thinking of you when I'm in bed.'

'With Alistair?'

Carol didn't answer that.

Nell gathered her clothes from the wardrobe in the small bedroom at the back of the flat. She shoved them into her suitcase and headed for the front door.

'Won't you stay and talk?' said Carol. 'Have a cup of coffee.'

'Why? Have you got new cups you want to show off?'

Carol shook her head. 'I just think we ought to talk.'

'What about? Are you going to give me handy hints on seducing other women's husbands?'

Carol said there was no need to be like that.

'Isn't there? said Nell. 'Isn't this what always happens? You've always copied me. You've always wanted what I had. You lost your own husband so you took mine.'

'It wasn't planned. It just happened. We didn't mean to hurt you.'

'And that excuses you both? Nell sniffed, held her head high and said she hadn't been hurt. 'Anyway, I'm grateful. You've set me free to go my own way and . . . start a new life somewhere else if I want.'

'Where?' Carol scoffed.

Nell said the first place that came into her head. 'London,' It was as much a surprise to her as it was to Carol. It had only this moment popped into her head. 'There's lots going on there. The Beatles live there. There are all sorts of fascinating shops and galleries. I'll find my way, get a job and when I'm on my feet I'll get a flat. So don't worry about me. I'll be fine. I'll let you know how I'm getting on so when you inevitably copy me and go off to London on your own, you'll be aware of any pitfalls.' She picked up her suitcase and stomped out of the door. And not a tear fell till she was round the corner and out of sight.

At home that night, she sat wrapped in blankets. She lacked the energy to light a fire. She cursed her luck. She'd lost everything. Her life had crumbled to nothing while she wasn't looking. How could this have happened?

She'd been pursuing an opportunity. Who wouldn't have done the same? She might have been manager of a restaurant in town. She'd have had smart clothes and an office of her own. She'd have been making good money – if May had paid her.

May had once told her never to regret anything. 'Life's too short. What you've done, you've done. Don't regret, don't apologise and don't complain. Just move on.'

Nell, however, was awash with regret. She should

have listened to her mother. Don't go to the Locarno. Well, she'd been right there. If I'd never gone to the Locarno, I wouldn't have met Alistair or any Rutherford and this wouldn't have happened to me, Nell thought. I'd have married someone else and I'd be happy.

She didn't regret meeting Annie, but wished she'd taken more interest in her at the time. The woman seemed interesting and astute. Nell cringed to think of herself wafting about the restaurant, showing people to their seats, laughing at their feeble jokes and bringing them bottles of wine. 'Margaux is an excellent choice, sir. It's bold and full bodied. Just the thing to go with your steak au poivre.' Yet she'd never drunk the stuff herself, and wouldn't be able to distinguish it from a glass of Vimto. Pretentious cow, she derided herself.

She couldn't bear to think about her mother and father. Bringing them to mind was like touching an open wound, checking if it still hurt. 'Oh,' she cried out every time. She had an unfinished relationship with her parents. All the things she should have said and done to show her love for them remained unsaid and undone. She should have been kinder. It was guilt she'd have to live with.

'Married in January's hoar and rime, widowed you'll be before your time,' her mother had warned. And Nell had mocked her. Well, Nancy had been full of such sayings. Rhymes about sneezing: *One's a wish, two's a kiss, three's a disappointment, four's a letter, five's something better and six is a appointment.* There were rhymes about haircuts: *Best never enjoyed if Sunday shorn. And likewise leave out Monday. Cut Thursday and you'll never grow rich, likewise on a Saturday. But live long if shorn on a Tuesday, and best of all is Friday.* And rhymes about thunder, how did it go again: *Sunday was an omen of death of a learned man, judge or writer. Monday was the death of a woman. Tuesday was the sign of plenty of grain. Wednesday was the death of harlots or news of bloodshed. Thursday plenty of sheep, cattle and corn. Friday the death of some great man or battle. Saturday forebode pestilence or illness.* There were so many of them; Nell wondered where her mother had learned them all. At her own mother's knee most likely. These verses probably went back through the generations to the beginnings of her family. Nell knew it was her duty to hand them on to her children, should she ever have any.

Well, the one about the winter bride seemed to be true. Not that she was widowed, but she might as well be. Most likely the rhyme appeared in the dark times before divorce. *Marry when January cruel winds doth send, and your husband will sleep with your best friend.* There was a new one to add to the list. She'd definitely teach her children that.

Where would she be when they came along? She didn't know, but she'd told Carol on the spur on the moment that she was going to London to start a new life and now the idea had taken root. Going away, suitcase in hand, to a new place, to breathe new air and mix with new faces seemed like the thing to do. Only, all she had to her name was thirty pounds. It wasn't much to cover her expenses.

Two days later, the parcel came. Nell opened it and read the note: *A little something to make amends.* It wasn't signed but Nell recognised May's dreadful scrawl. Nell remembered thinking when she first saw it that a good pen with a broad nib might help.

She dug into the parcel, pulled out something tightly wrapped in newspaper. It was a gold-rimmed crystal glass. The box contained five others – May's treasures. Nell laid them out on the kitchen table. 'Glasses, I don't want glasses. I don't even like them. What good are they to me?' She picked one up and threw it at the wall. 'Go to hell, May.'

When she'd calmed down, she took the remaining five to the pawnbroker. He held one glass to the light, pinged it with his finger, swore it wasn't real crystal and offered her fifteen pounds for the lot. Nell refused. They must be worth more than that. Why would May have treated them with such reverence if they weren't?

In the antique shop – *antiquities bought and sold*, it boasted in the window – the man behind the counter looked bored when Nell walked in carrrying her box. However, she noticed the glee that flickered momentarily across his face when he lifted out a glass. He turned it over in his hands. 'Georgian,' he said. 'Very nice. Lovely, in fact.' He held it out to Nell. 'Beautiful vermicular collar and conical foot. Do you have the full set?'

She told him no, she only had five.

'Pity, I could offer you a lot more if you had six. Still, I'll give you eighty pounds for what you have.'

Nell smiled. She knew that pawnbroker had been trying to cheat her. I'm a lot smarter these days, she told herself. Not so trusting. She told the dealer she'd take his money.

'Good girl. I knew you were sharp. I could see you wouldn't take any kind of nonsense offer.' He opened his till, withdrew eight ten-pound notes and handed them to Nell. He wished her a good day and watched her leave the shop. Then he unpacked all the glasses. 'Oh my God, you beauties. You lovely, lovely things.' They were perfect. No chips, no scratches. They had been loved. He could easily sell them separately for over a hundred pounds each or, perhaps, eight hundred for the lot. 'Nice,' he said.

At home, Nell laid out her money on the kitchen table. She had just over a hundred pounds. She searched the house for more. She dug into pockets, emptied her mother's handbag, peered into drawers and came up with a further five pounds. She had a tidy little running-away fund. She'd go tomorrow.

She couldn't sleep that night. Fear plagued her. London was a huge and worrisome place. Where would she sleep tomorrow night? A small hotel, she decided. Then she'd find a job, possibly in a shop or a bar. After that she'd find a bedsit. 'I'll be fine,' she said. It helped to speak out loud. She almost convinced herself.

But arriving alone in the big city, almost penniless, certainly friendless, was the stuff of big adventures. People did such things. Nell had seen this story often in the movies and it always ended in success – glory, even. Good things happen to people; why shouldn't they happen to me? It's my turn, she told herself.

But still when she let her imaginings rip, the streets she walked were dark and strangers lurked; night came and she had nowhere to stay; windows were lit; people in glistening rooms pulled their curtains shutting her out in the cold. Buildings loomed large. And, somehow, she was smaller.

If she listed the things she wanted, it wasn't money or friends or success that came out top. It was safety. More than anything else, she wanted the pain of recent events to stop. She wanted to stop fearing what would happen next because she couldn't stand another shock, another thing to add to her aches. She wanted to be safe.

Chapter Thirty
Safe

It was Mrs Lowrie who planted the notion of going on holiday in Nell's mind. Nell had always been wary of the woman. Mrs Lowrie had always given her the most peculiar of looks, as if she knew something about Nell that Nell didn't know herself. It had happened again at the funeral when Mrs Lowrie had said everyone would have been happy with sandwiches and fruit cake.

Nell didn't know that Mrs Lowrie was responsible for her very existence. Without Mrs Lowrie she would not be on the planet. This was the woman who'd set the seeds of guilt in her mum's heart when she'd mentioned that it was a woman's duty to let her husband have his way with her, especially during wartime. If Nancy hadn't taken this seriously, she'd never have submitted to Nell's dad's desires on that fateful night when Nell was conceived. Now she was about to have a hand in Nell's destiny for a second time.

Nell was walking down the path, suitcase in hand. She'd looked round the house and said goodbye to it. She had the keys in her pocket and would hand them in at the council office before going to the station. She was awash with trepidation and joy: the first because she was afraid of what might happen to her; the second because she was saying goodbye to everything. Walking away gave her hope. It was an act of defiance.

She met Mrs Lowrie at the gate and they exchanged good mornings.

Mrs Lowrie noticed the suitcase. 'Going on holiday, Nell? Just what you need after all you've been through. A few days to blow away the cobwebs and relax.'

Not wanting to discuss her plans, Nell agreed: she was going on holiday.

'Where are you off to?'

'London.'

'On your own? Oh, I wouldn't go there on my own. It's too big. You could get lost and if you do you need someone with you. And what about eating? You can't go into a café or restaurant on your own.'

'I'll manage. There's lots to do in London, galleries and cinemas. I'll be fine.'

'No, you won't. Trudging through busy streets all alone. Getting jostled, looking out for pickpockets – London's full of them. That's not a holiday. You want to go somewhere quiet. Somewhere where you can rest, gather yourself after all your woes, eat and sleep. That's a holiday.'

Nell said she liked cities. 'All I need is to get away.'

'Oh, well, if that's what you want. London's not for me. I like quiet. I like peace. And if you ask me peace and quiet are what you need right now. Still, have a lovely time.'

All the way to the council offices, Nell thought about this. She handed over the house keys, paid her rent and walked to the station. A holiday, she thought. I haven't had a holiday in ages. In fact, she'd only had two holidays in her life. One, when she went on honeymoon with Alistair. The other, when she went to a Highland village, Catto, with her parents when she was little. It had only lasted a week.

Memories of the holiday in the Highlands with her parents swam in her head. Remembering that time soothed her. She had snapshot memories – her father, trousers rolled up, paddling in the sea with her; her mother sitting on a deckchair watching, eating fish and chips at the harbour; breakfasts of porridge and a boiled egg at the B&B where they'd stayed. What was the name of that place?

Nell stopped, put her case down on the pavement and thought. It had been the combination of the names of the husband and wife who owned the house. Nell sat on her case. This bothered her. She would not move till she remembered. Their names were Kelvin and Byrony. *Kelby*, that was it. They used to put out cakes and chocolate biscuits at breakfast time, she remembered. God, no wonder I thought it a wondrous place. She got up, took her case and headed for the station.

'Why "Kelby"?' Nell's mother had asked. They had been in the small dining room at the time.

Bryony, a small woman with long black hair, had laughed and explained. 'But it is an actual word. It means "place by flowing water" in Gaelic.'

Nell had wished she lived there, in that house with those lovely people. The bedroom had had a sink where she could clean her teeth last thing at night and then jump into bed. One morning, instead of porridge, she'd had cornflakes for the first time in her life. She'd thought them exquisite.

She'd thought that if she'd lived there she could have them every day. She could go to the beach in the mornings on her own. She might have a boat she could row to her own secret island and have adventures.

Struggling down the Waverley steps into the station, Nell realised that even then, all those years ago, she'd been dreaming her life rather than living it. It was time to stop. Time to have a holiday and celebrate the start of a new life and a new Nell.

Chapter Thirty-one
Greek Gods

It was seven o'clock when Nell arrived in the Highland village of Catto. If she'd bought a ticket to London, she'd have been there already. She had no idea the journey was so long – four hours on a train, an hour on a bus, then two hours on a second bus – but then she couldn't recall coming here before or going home again; she only remembered being here.

All the way, desperate to reach her destination, whooshing sometimes, trundling sometimes, through spectacular countryside, heathered mountains, rambling rivers, she had urged the train and buses on. Catto was where she had to be.

The place hadn't changed much. At least, she didn't think it had. The air smelled ozone fresh, though as she walked the main street there were wafts of booze from the pubs. Seagulls floated above the harbour. Windows were lit. Bubbling conversations sparked with laughter drifted from each of them, but there was nobody in the street except her.

A rush of nervy panic swept through her. What was she doing here? She had nowhere to stay. There were several public benches along the opposite side of the street, facing out to the sea. Nell dreaded that she might spend the night on one of them. If this is the new me, she thought, she is even sillier than the old me. Why didn't I phone in advance and book a room?

Catto's main street consisted of a long row of houses, mostly painted white and facing the water, a narrow beach, a harbour with three or four fishing boats, an ice cream shop, a fish and chip shop, a general store, a chandler's and the three pubs. There was also small café; inside was a group of teenagers sipping frothy coffee, and the Beatles blared out 'I Wanna Hold Your Hand'.

Nell stopped and listened. It was a new sound. The sound of a new generation. If the Locarno hadn't closed down, that's what the band would be playing. The singer would be ruining it with his eyebrow movements and his BBC newsreader accent. God, she thought, it's three and a half years since I last went to the Locarno. Three and a half years and I married, left my job, lost my husband, my job, my best friend and my parents. I should have been more careful. She resisted the urge to run into the café to warn the kids in there about the dangers of life. The teenagers inside were all staring back at her as she dithered on the pavement. They were sneering. Ha, she thought, you call that sneering? I can out-sneer the lot of you.

She turned and walked to the corner, the way to the B&B where she'd stayed all those years ago slowly coming back to her. She'd walked this route from Main Street to the house so often with her parents, it was engrained in her memory. Round the corner, up the hill, then along Springfield Street and there was Kelby. It was up a short drive behind a giant monkey puzzle tree. Nell rang the bell.

An older, greyer Byrony opened the door.

Nell coughed and asked if there were any rooms vacant. 'I know I should have phoned and booked, but it was a spur of the moment thing.'

Byrony stood still, staring at Nell.

'See,' said Nell. 'I stayed here years ago. With my mum and dad. Only they died recently. First Mum, and then Dad. He couldn't live without her. And I thought it would be wonderful to come here where we were happy. You know, return to where memories were made.' She wished this woman would say something. The more she kept her mouth shut, the more Nell spoke. 'I mean what's the point of staying in that house where we lived. I was alone and thinking of them. I was so sad I could hardly breathe.'

Byrony invited her in. As Nell stepped into the hall, Byrony stepped out and looked down the drive. 'Are you on your own?'

Nell said she was.

'No matter,' said Byrony. 'I'm not busy.' She led the way upstairs. 'The room has a view of the garden and over the rooftops to the sea. It's one of our best. Ten shillings a night, breakfast is at eight, but you've missed supper. Bathroom's across the hall.' There was a large double bed, a small button-down chair and a desk by the window. It was perfect.

'Where have you come from?'

'Edinburgh.'

'Well, that's a way to come. Did you drive?'

Nell shook her head. 'Train and a couple of buses.'

Byrony said she'd leave Nell to settle in. At the door she stopped. 'I expect you're hungry. I'll make you a sandwich. It'll be in the sitting room in ten minutes.'

It wasn't a sandwich. It was a heap of sandwiches on a platter, along with a slice of coffee cake, a selection of biscuits and a pot of tea.

'Thank you,' Nell said. 'I don't think I could eat all that food.'

'Just take what you want.' Byrony sat watching Nell as she bit into a sandwich. 'Just when were you and your mum and dad here?'

'About seventeen years ago,' Nell told her.

Byrony stared. 'Don't remember you. Sorry.'

'I was just a kid. We only stayed for a week.' She looked round. 'Where are the other guests?'

'There aren't any,' said Byrony. 'I stopped doing bed and breakfast ten years ago.'

Nell put down her sandwich. 'I'm sorry. I should go. I didn't know. It's just this is where I stayed before. I didn't think.'

Bryony raised her hand to silence Nell. 'When I saw you there at the door looking pale and worried and nervous, I couldn't turn you away. Poor lost soul, I thought. Never mind, I'll enjoy the company. Haven't had any paying guests since my husband ran off with the postmistress. It wasn't the same without him.'

'Kelvin?' said Nell.

Byrony nodded.

'I remember because of the name of the house,' said Nell.

Byrony said she always meant to take down the nameplate. 'Never got round to it. I really should go back to being plain old number six. It's this place, it makes you procrastinate. You never do today what you can put off till tomorrow. I think that's the local hobby, procrastination.' She stood up. 'Bedtime for me. I'm an early riser. Busy day tomorrow. I've a whole lot of procrastinating to be getting on with.'

Nell finished her sandwiches, ate the coffee cake and went to her room. She unpacked her case, cleaned her teeth in the bathroom across the hall, undressed and climbed into bed. It was soft and spacious. She spread herself out, sighed and slept.

When she woke, Byrony was leaning over the bed, peering at her.

'By God, you can sleep.'

Nell rubbed her eyes, looked round and wondered for a moment where she was and what was happening.

'You're at the bed and breakfast house with me,' said Byrony. 'You turned up on my doorstep last night.'

'Right,' Nell said. 'Of course. What time is it?'

'Three o'clock.'

Nell lay back. 'It's the middle of the night.' She'd sleep some more.

'It's the middle of the afternoon. I was worried about you. Thought you might have died. I came up to check you were still alive.'

Nell threw back the blankets. 'I should get up.'

'You're on holiday. You've nothing to do. I'll leave you to get washed and dressed; there will be some sort of breakfast for you when you come downstairs.'

Nell spent what was left of her day looking round the village. It didn't take long. She bought a pair of walking shoes at the general store, stared at the boats in the harbour, looked at piles of rope and lobster creels, threw a few pebbles from the narrow beach into the sea, and then went back to the B&B where Byrony had prepared an evening meal.

'I only ate a couple of hours ago,' Nell complained.

'No matter, you can eat again. You need it. There's nothing of you. Also, you can sign the visitor's book. It's in the hall.'

Nell stood, pen in hand, debating what to write. Eventually she decided to use her maiden name. *Nell McClusky,* she wrote. She was done with the Rutherfords.

Byrony invited her to eat in the kitchen with her. 'No point you eating in one room, me in another. Your food's on the table.'

The kitchen was large and cluttered, with a cooking range, plants on the windowsill, and a long pine table in the centre. Nell and Byrony sat either end. Then Byrony decided they were too far apart for comfortable passing of the bottle of tomato ketchup and conversation. She moved nearer to Nell. 'Dig in. Fish is good for you. Helps your weary brain.'

'My brain isn't weary. It's functioning as normal.'

'I doubt that.' Byrony pointed at the ring on Nell's left hand. 'Where's your husband?'

'He left me for my best friend.'

'Well, with that and your parents dying your brain's definitely weary. It'll be struggling to cope.'

They ate in silence for a while, till Nell asked what people did around here.

'They get up in the morning, eat, work, come home again, eat some more, watch television and go to bed. They meet their friends, drink, worry about bills and make love. Just like anywhere, really.'

'I mean, what sort of work do they do?'

'There's the fishing, hotel work, bar work, shop work. They work in the doctor's or the solicitor's. There are farms round about. But actually, there's not a lot of employment for young people. Mostly they leave. Go to cities.'

Nell said that was a shame.

'It is,' said Byrony, 'but it's the way of things. A lot of the people here are newcomers. Not born here. Not local. They come here, on the run, looking for a new life.'

'From the law?'

'No. From jobs they hated, or a broken marriage, businesses that failed, lost loves. They're looking for shelter, for a bit of peace. Like you. They're hiding from themselves.'

'I'm not looking for shelter,' said Nell. 'I'm fine. Actually, before I decided to come here for a holiday, I was on my way to London.'

'To do what?'

'To work. To live.'

'You're not nearly ready for London. You're too wobbly.'

Nell suspected Bryony might be right.

'What you want to do,' Byrony told her, 'is walk. There are good walks round here. Just moving along at your own pace, thinking and then not thinking. That'll fix you.'

Next day, Nell put on her walking shoes and set out to fix her wobbliness. On the far side of the harbour, she saw a telephone box, bright red against a grey sky. She cheered. She could phone her mother and father and tell them where she was. That would surprise them. Then she remembered. Oh, the sudden pain came. She couldn't. They wouldn't be home.

She walked past it.

About half a mile past the village boundary, there was a wide track leading, as far as Nell could tell, into the mountains. She decided to take it.

She walked looking towards the mountains for an hour and then stopped. On either side of the track was an expanse of dense heather. Beyond that were pinewoods and beyond them hills that spread into mountains. It was silent. A small wind blew, ruffled her hair. It was all so huge, she felt suddenly small. She stared ahead, turned and looked back the way she'd just walked. Nobody. She felt insignificant and scared in the vastness. The world could have ended and she wouldn't know about it. She hurried back to the road, panting and desperate to see another human being.

Back in the village, she went into the café for a cup of coffee and a doughnut. Caffeine and sugar was what she needed.

After that, she walked to the other end of Catto. The path led along the shore, the sea on one side and a scattering of houses on the other. This was better, she thought. She wasn't far from humanity. There was a fishing boat on the water and washing flapping in the gardens of the houses. She sat on the verge and watched the water.

Late in the afternoon, she went back to the B&B where Byrony was preparing supper.

'Stew tonight,' she said. 'Have you had a good day?'

Nell said she'd walked. 'First one way out of the village, and then the other along the shore.'

'You walked towards the forests first?'

'Yes, but I turned back. It's a bit lonely.'

'That's the big walk. I did that every day after Kelvin left me. I loved the loneliness of it. You'll not be up to that yet.'

Nell said she wasn't. 'It scared me. I felt like I was the only person in the world.'

'Ah, yes. You feel conspicuous and vulnerable at the same time.'

Nell said she wasn't used to open spaces. 'I like to have buildings either side of me, and people passing by.'

'In big cities it's the people passing by that make you lonely. It reminds you that you're alone.'

'I like looking at people,' said Nell. 'I hated being out there alone.'

'You'll get used to it. You might even come to love it. There's something comforting about being in the wild with nothing but your thoughts and the prospect of wonderful views not far ahead.'

Nell laughed. 'I'm a townie, simple as that. Some people don't like the countryside as much as cities.'

'Oh, I know that. I also know that until you make peace with what's happened to you, you won't be ready to move on. You'll make mistakes. Like going to London.'

On Saturday night, Byrony suggested that she and Nell went to the pub for a drink. 'We'll go to the Anchor. It's the quietest.'

For a May night, it was chilly out but diamond bright. Stars clustered the sky and a fat moon floated above the sea. Byrony said it was a night for things to happen. 'There's mischief in the air. Babies will be made tonight.' She pointed upwards. 'A shooting star. That's lucky. Did you make a wish?'

Nell said she didn't. 'I don't believe in wishes anymore.'

'Oh, that's just silly. It's an insult to the universe not to wish on a star. You don't have to wish for riches or for a flash car to appear at your door. You could wish for illness to be cured or for starving people to be fed. It won't happen, of course, but it shows you care.'

The Anchor was crowded. Nell and Byrony squeezed to the bar where Byrony ordered two glasses of whisky. 'Twenty-year-old malt. It'll do you good.' She started a conversation with the barmaid. 'Busy tonight.'

The barmaid said that the local football team had won a game against a neighbouring village. 'Six–nil. There are celebrations going on. The team are doing the Catto Crawl.'

'Well, there will be some sore heads in the morning,' said Byrony.

Nell asked what was the Catto Crawl?

'They start at one end of the village, have a drink in each of the three pubs, plus the Fisherman's Hotel at the end, then they drink their way back. Sometimes they do it all again. There will be drunken doings tonight.' She poked Nell's arm, 'Your round. Same again, then a walk along the harbour and home.'

The moon was higher by the time they left the Anchor. They walked towards the harbour and sat on a bench overlooking the sea. Paths of light on the water. A seal rose from the deep to look about. From further round the bay, they could hear them call, a long hungry sound.

'Randy seals,' said Byrony after a while. 'It's that sort of night. Brings out the wild in you.'

The noise from the pub got bawdier. There was chanting. The cries of people being egged on.

'Mischief,' said Byrony.

Suddenly the door of the Anchor burst open. People poured out. From the midst of the throng came four young men, all naked. As the crowd yelled, 'Go, Go, Go,' they sprinted along the street, rounded into the harbour and ran past Nell and Byrony.

They were slim-hipped, tight-bummed and broad shouldered. Byrony clapped her hands and shouted, 'Wonderful!'

The men reached the lighthouse at the end of the harbour, smacked the wall, turned and hurtled back past the two women. They were panting, each trying to push past the others to be first back at the pub.

Nell looked on, mouth open. She turned in astonishment to Byrony and said, 'They'll catch their death running about like that on a night like this.'

Byrony was shocked. 'You don't have a woo or a wolf whistle in you, do you? You see young men, beautiful young men, Greek gods, stark naked and magnificent, running in the moonlight and that's all you can say? Girl, you are definitely not ready for London.'

Chapter Thirty-two
This Will Do

In keeping with the spirit of Catto, Nell procrastinated. She kept putting off going to London and six months later she was still living with Byrony. She was safe here. She walked and no longer felt conspicuous and vulnerable alone in a huge landscape. She enjoyed the loneliness and relished the vastness she was moving through. There was comfort in insignificance. This vast place had been here long before she arrived and would endure long after she'd gone.

She listened to her breathing and pursued her thoughts till she was no longer thinking, just moving and noticing the scenery. One day, she realised she hadn't thought about Carol and Alistair for weeks. That moment when she'd discovered the pair lying entwined on the sofa no longer crept uninvited into her brain. She didn't wonder what they were up to, where they were living, and if they'd moved into a fabulous new house. It didn't matter. She didn't care.

She could pass the telephone box without thinking she should phone home and tell her parents where she was. She didn't have to fight the urge to fall on her knees and weep. Her mother and father were gone. She was learning to accept that. She thought they'd be happy for her. They'd smile if they knew where she was.

She was still furious with May. If I saw her right now, she thought, I'd punch her nose. Striding up the path and into the forest, she cursed the glasses May had sent her. Months and months of work, and what do I get? Six bloody glasses. The cheek of the woman.

She hadn't gone to London, but London came to her. It was there on the radio that played all day, every day, in Byrony's kitchen The Beatles, the Rolling Stones, the fashions, the new crazes – she followed it all. It was almost 1964, she'd be twenty-two in a few months, and she decided she was a new sixties woman. She took up the hems on her skirts, grew her hair long and told herself she was happy. Well, as happy as it's possible to be.

Her funds, however, were dwindling. Every night, she took her money out from the drawer of the cabinet beside her bed, laid it out and counted it. It was becoming obvious she'd have to do something. She could go to London or she could stay here, find a job, replenish her cash supply and then go to London.

She took a job as a receptionist at the Fisherman's Hotel. It suited her. She could watch the world from behind her desk and make up stories about the guests. Some she imagined were having affairs, some were on the run from their life and some were simply on holiday. She answered the phone, 'Good morning, Fisherman's

Hotel. How can I help?' She handed over keys, took orders for room service, organised fishing trips, advised guests on the best walks, and, when the dining room was busy, helped serve the food.

It always surprised Nell how often she said hello these days. It was part of the village custom to acknowledge everyone you met. She counted fifteen hellos one morning on the way to work and a similar amount on the way back. 'I'm accepted here,' she said to Byrony one night. She hoped she might become 'our Nell' one day soon; she wanted to belong.

The hotel was owned and run by Hamish Watson, a tweed-clad man who lived in a house he'd built in the grounds. With the guests, he was warm and hearty. With his staff, he was curt. Nell thought him intimidating. He reminded her of her physics teacher. For years she'd sat at the back of his classroom barely understanding what he was talking about. He'd never once spoken to her or she to him.

Once, after she'd left school, he'd come into the pen shop. She'd smiled to him and he'd stared at her blankly. 'You used to teach me physics,' she'd explained.

'Did I?' he'd replied. He shook his head and told her he didn't remember her. He'd left without buying anything. Like Hamish, he had the knack of making her feel insignificant.

Hamish Watson breezed past Nell every morning, giving her a curt nod. He checked the register, and gave another curt nod. When Nell left work to go home, she got a third curt nod.

There were rumours about him. He'd fought in Korea, and had won many medals. He was fearless. His wife had died of cancer ten years ago. He drank too much whisky. He played the violin when alone at home, but he only played exquisitely sad music because his heart was broken. He was lonely.

Nell dismissed these rumours. She figured in a place like this there were rumours about everybody. Along with procrastinating, believing and spreading rumours was a hobby. It passed the time. She knew the rumour about her was that she was the woman who'd appeared out of the blue while suffering a little bit of a break-down. She didn't deny it.

One morning, just after nine, Nell was at the front desk pouring over an article in the newspaper. Hamish walked past and said his usual curt, 'Good morning, Miss McClusky.'

'Good morning, Mr Watson,' she said, without looking up.

He stopped. 'Staff are not to read the morning papers before our guests.'

'I'm really sorry. It's just that something caught my eye.'

He joined Nell behind the desk to look over her shoulder at the newspaper.

Nell put her finger on a photograph. 'My husband.'

The article spoke of this promising lawyer who had helped with the successful defence of two schoolboys who'd been accused of writing and distributing porno-graphic material. They'd sold their alternative magazine in Edinburgh pubs. Along with music reviews it had contained parodies of fairy tales that were not in the best of taste. 'It was innocent schoolboy fun,' Alistair had said. 'That's all.' The newspaper piece concluded that Alistair Rutherford was a great lawyer in the making: *'erudite, wise and witty – he's definitely one to watch.'*

Hamish stared at the picture. 'I didn't know you were married.'

'He left me for my best friend. I'm single now.'

'Divorced?'

Nell shook her head. 'Not yet. No doubt I will be. I don't think of myself as Mrs Rutherford anymore.'

'Ah,' said Hamish, and went to his office.

A week later Hamish invited Nell to a concert. 'Got two tickets. It should be an excellent evening.'

It wasn't, as Nell had hoped, a gig by the Rolling Stones making a rare appearance in a far-flung spot. It was a small chamber orchestra playing Mozart's Clarinet Concerto. But, much to her surprise, she enjoyed it.

'Excellent stuff, didn't you think, Miss McClusky?' said Hamish as they drove home.

Nell agreed.

'I have a suspicion you are more of a rock and roller than a classical music aficionado. But never mind, we'll soon fix that.'

Nell said she didn't want anyone to fix that. 'I like what I like. My choice.'

Hamish apologised. 'I don't have any intention of

changing your tastes. I rather like the Beatles as a matter of fact. I just hoped I might show you some of the joys of Mozart and Beethoven.'

Nell said she'd like that. 'But I am who I am. Nobody's going to change me.'

Hamish said that was good. He wouldn't want her to change.

The next week they drove to the cinema forty miles away to see *Lawrence of Arabia*. The week after, they had a Chinese meal and after that went to another concert. By their fifth date they were tentatively calling one another by their first names. On their sixth date he invited her back to his place.

His home was not as Nell had imagined. It was practical, and absurdly practical. In the living room there was a television, and opposite it was a single armchair. Beside that there was a crate of beer. One wall was taken up with shelves of LPs and a hi-fi.

'Is this is?' asked Nell. 'One chair. That's all.'

'It's all I need.'

'What about visitors? Where do they sit?'

Hamish said he never had visitors. 'You're the first person that's ever been here.'

She told him that wasn't very sociable.

'I see people all day. I'm very sociable at work. At home I tuck myself away.' He asked if she'd like a cup of coffee. She followed him into the kitchen saying she'd keep him company as he made it.

There was nowhere to sit here. There was a neatly ironed shirt draped over the back of each of the four chairs round the table. An ironing board took up the area between the table and the cooker and meant Hamish had to shuffle sideways to reach the kettle. He explained that he left the board up because it was easier. 'If I fold it down and put it away, I only have to get it out and put it up again.'

He had a laundry routine. He had six shirts. 'All identical,' he said. When four were dirty, he had one clean one and one he was wearing. He washed the dirty shirts, ironed them and draped them on the chairs. 'Ready to wear. It works.'

He pointed to the cooker. 'One pot is all I need. Porridge every morning. Eat it, clean up, fresh shirt and off I go to work. All my other meals I eat at the hotel. I have everything worked out.'

'Everything except comfort,' said Nell.

'I have a very comfortable bed. In fact my bedroom's quite luxurious.'

Nell said that was good to know.

'Would you care to join me in it? We could drink our coffee there. It would be easier than sharing the armchair.'

'My goodness,' said Nell. 'You certainly know how to woo a girl.'

He hung his head, and confessed that wooing and flirting baffled him. 'I have no idea where to begin with such things. To be honest, women baffle me.'

'I thought you'd been married?'

'I was but I'd known my wife all my life. She lived a few doors down from me. We were childhood sweethearts, teenage sweethearts and it was always assumed we'd marry one day, so we did. Wooing didn't come into it.'

Nell told him about Alistair. 'We'd settled into a comfortable relationship. No demands. Then his mother announced she'd booked the church and the hotel for the reception. She thought it was time we grew up and settled down.'

'But did you love him?' asked Hamish.

'Love,' said Nell. 'I don't know about that. I loved the notion of having a steady boyfriend, someone I got along with. I loved his family and wanted to be part of it. I loved the idea of being in love. We probably both assumed we'd marry one day, but neither of us mentioned it. I thought he was a suitable candidate for a husband. I thought I'd be safe with him. I wanted security.'

He said that was understandable.

Nell confessed some more. 'I'd envisioned a glamorous life with a famous lawyer. Looks like I was right. He will be sought after. He will have a glamorous life, but without me in it.'

He asked if she minded that. She shrugged, shook her head and told him, no. 'I don't think of him that often.'

Hamish poured two cups of coffee, picked them up, headed out of the kitchen, jerking his head as an indication that she should follow.

Nell walked behind him through the sparse living room into the hallway, past the row of useful things stored there – golf clubs, a spade, a lawnmower, several pairs of shoes, a length of electric cable and a pair of skis – and up the stairs to the bedroom. It was, as he said, quite luxurious. It was spacious and thickly carpeted with a large bed, which Nell soon discovered was as comfortable as he'd said.

At first the love they made was awkward. They were both shy. But, as moments passed and they pursued pleasure, there was passion. They were, Nell thought, two lost, lonely and hurt souls reaching out for one another. They were both seeking comfort.

It will do, thought Nell. This man will do. This new life will do.

Chapter Thirty-three
The Flash

Nell settled into a routine of seeing Hamish twice a week. They went to the local pub, to concerts, and often they walked, talking sometimes, sometimes just companionably breathing together as they covered miles of rough tracks. They didn't discuss past lives. They never mentioned love.

Once Nell came across a violin at the back of Hamish's wardrobe. 'I've never heard you play.'

He told her that was because he didn't. 'Can't play any instrument. That was my wife's. Catherine's. She played professionally.'

'But people say they've heard you playing beautifully when they were passing by.'

'That would have been Yehudi.'

'Yehudi?'

'Menuhin.'

She stared blankly at him.

'Probably the greatest violinist ever. The people passing by would have been hearing a record. Funny they didn't wonder why I had a full orchestra playing with me. Rumours and gossip are marvellous.' He put the violin back into the wardrobe. 'She's gone from me. I'm learning to let her go. Have you let Alistair go?'

'Yes, I do believe I have. Him and his family.'

It was a surprise, then, when, a few days later, Byrony told her there had been a man at the house asking for her. Nell asked what he looked like.

'Tall, fiftyish, quite plump,' said Byrony.

So it wasn't Alistair. Nell said she had no idea what it was about. She tried to forget about it but over the next few days she had the notion she was being followed. Walking to and from work, she'd whirl round and stare behind her. There was never anybody there. She eyed strange cars parked in the street outside Byrony's house with suspicion. Eventually, remembering the truth about the murder she had convinced herself she'd witnessed at the Locarno, she told herself she was being absurd. It was time to stop imagining dramas. There was nobody following her. There was nothing to worry about.

It was a Wednesday in January and the hotel was quiet. Nell and Hamish took the afternoon off and walked. Hand in hand they strode up the long track to the forest and beyond. They scanned the horizon for deer and saw two in the distance. Once an eagle soared high overhead; they stood watching it, entranced. Nell said it would be wonderful to fly, to just take off and move through the sky. 'I'd love that.'

Hamish agreed. 'Freedom,' he said. 'It's all about freedom.' Then he said, 'Let's go home. I've got steaks for supper. I'll cook.'

They held hands again, each enjoying the feel of palm against palm. They breathed in unison. No need to speak. They'd reached to point of relishing companionable silence. But as they walked back along the track, just before they reached the main road and civilisation, he kissed her. 'An outdoor kiss,' he said. 'I like the taste.'

Nell said she liked indoor kisses. 'In the warmth by the fire. And the bedroom's handy for anything that might come next.'

He agreed. She had a point. 'But when I kiss you out here, I can taste the country you've walked through and the air you've been breathing and the sweat from your upper lip, the essence of you.' He kissed her again. When they pulled apart, she looked round. 'We're being watched.'

'No, we're not. There's nobody for miles. Look, we're the only people here.'

She stared in one direction and then the other. Nothing. 'I just had the feeling somebody was watching us. Weird.'

He told her she was being silly. 'We're alone. And if we are being watched, what of it? We're kissing and it's wonderful.'

At the house, Nell sat in the kitchen watching Hamish cook. He'd changed his shirt routine – now he hung them upstairs in the bedroom – and he'd bought a second armchair for the living room. 'Soon,' he told her, 'I'll get a sofa so we can snuggle.'

She approved. The lawnmower, spade, hose and

gardening tools had been relocated outside, but the skis and golf clubs remained. Nell thought that fine.

After they'd eaten, Hamish made coffee. 'I thought it might be more comfortable if we drank it in bed,' he said. It had become a private joke between them.

They didn't close the curtains. They never did. They could see the stars from where they lay. It made them closer when they considered the wild vastness beyond the window. To the south, as the night wore on they could see the Plough. The room was dark. She moved into his arms. She wasn't wearing anything.

The flash stormed the room. They sat up, looked at the window, both shocked. 'What the hell was that?' There was a second flash. Hamish jumped out of bed, thrashed about looking for his trousers, and then ran downstairs and out the front door.

The ladder he kept at the side of the house was propped against the wall. He looked round the garden, looked up and down the road outside, walked round the house, and then went in again.

Back in bed with Nell, he told her there was nothing to be seen. 'Except the ladder against the wall.'

'It was a photographer,' said Nell. 'Why would anyone want to take a picture of us?'

He told her he didn't know, but he did know, and he also knew that Nell would find out soon enough.

A week later, Nell was on her way home from work. It was early evening and not quite dark. As she walked through the gates at the end of the hotel drive, a man stepped out of a car and called her name. It was Alistair.

'You're a hard person to find,' he said.

She told him she didn't think anyone would be trying to find her.

'I had to hire a private detective. He spoke to your neighbour who said she hadn't seen you since you went on holiday last year.'

'That would be true,' said Nell.

'You told Carol you were going to London.'

'Well, I didn't.'

'You came to the place you'd been on holiday with your parents. And you took your maiden name. I figured it out. Took a while.'

'So you found me. What do you want?'

He suggested they go somewhere quiet where they could talk. She pointed towards the main street. 'The Anchor. It's quiet there at this time of day.'

He wanted to drive, but she insisted they walk. 'I'm walking a lot these days.'

They selected a table in the corner. The barmaid waved to Nell, shouted hello and gave Alistair a curious look. Nell didn't introduce him. He was part of the life she'd left behind. When Alistair asked what she wanted, she went for a twenty-five-year-old malt. She rarely drank whisky, but this was expensive and she reckoned he owed her. 'No ice.'

He had the same. He put both glasses on the table and sat opposite her. 'So, how are you?'

'Well,' she said. 'Living quietly. You?'

'Well,' he said. Then, 'You left a bit of a mess when you went away. The council tracked me down and I had to pay to have your parent's house cleared.'

She shrugged. She didn't care. 'How's Carol?'

'Pregnant,' said Alistair.

She congratulated him.

'I want a divorce,' he said. 'I want to marry Carol. She divorced Johnny a while ago. He came over from Australia.'

She asked how Johnny was.

'Happy,' said Alistair. 'He's a beach bum. Surfs most days. He's starting a school to teach tourists. He's tanned and looking more handsome than ever.'

Nell sighed and thought it was true: you never could keep a Rutherford down. 'So divorce me,' she said. 'I thought we'd discussed this already.'

'It's different now.' He pulled an envelope from his inside pocket and placed it in front of her.

Inside were several photographs. The first showed her walking hand in hand with Hamish. In the next they were kissing. In the third they were in bed, arms round one another. The fourth she thought the worst photo she'd ever seen. She and Hamish were sitting up in bed, looking in horror towards the window. Her hair was rumpled. She was pulling up the sheet to cover her nakedness. His mouth was open. He looked like he was shouting, 'Hoi.'

'Very salacious,' she said. 'I look like a trollop.'

He said he was sorry.

'So I'm having a relationship. It happens. People

move on. Anyway, you started the whole thing when you slept with my best friend.'

He said once more that he was sorry. 'The thing is, my career's going well I don't want a scandal.'

'Perhaps you should have thought of that before you had it off with Carol.'

He shrugged. 'It was bad enough when the police came after May and Harry. I had a struggle coming through that with my reputation intact.'

'They should have paid their income tax like everyone else in the world.'

'You can hardly talk, Nell. My mother paid you in cash.'

Nell flushed. 'I know. I hadn't thought about that, though she didn't often pay me. I never loved money the way your mother did.'

He agreed. 'May liked to look at it. On Thursdays she'd bring out all the cash and put it on the table so she could savour it. It was one of her collections along with her handbags and shoes.'

'That's what happened on family nights. I thought you talked business.'

'We did. But it was also May's way of keeping us together. We'd sit round the table – just the family. She loved that. The family and the money all together. But we did talk about how to make more money. One of May's ideas was to spray a dozen cars pink and have a ladies' day. She'd noticed women were buying more cars.'

'Where did the piles of money come from?'

'Cash sales,' Alistair told her. 'They'd always have several really cheap cars in the lot and offer them at a discount for cash.'

'Your parents were crooks.'

'My mother always believed they were making people happy. She worked hard. For years, she went into that back lot and cleaned and polished old cars. She saw customers proudly driving off in their gleaming Rovers and Alfas and Triumphs and it made her happy to see them happy. She just didn't want to share the profits with the government.'

'Then she lost everything in the restaurant,' said Nell.

'She gave away cocktails, entertained people at the special table, plied customers with free drinks, served enormous helpings and spent a fortune doing the place up.'

'And then she scarpered when it went wrong,' said Nell. 'With my money.'

'I know,' said Alistair, 'but she was very generous to you – all the presents, the cashmere sweaters, the watch, the handbags. She loved you in her own way.'

Nell supposed she did. 'Do you miss her? Do you even know where she is?'

'I have no idea where she and Harry are. I imagine them in some sunny country walking arm-in-arm along a beach, watching the waves and planning how to make their fortune. Of course I miss May. She's my mother. And when she was around you never knew what would happen next.'

'Like she might come into the room and announce you were getting married,' said Nell.

'Exactly.'

They smiled. Couldn't help it.

'God, we were fools,' said Nell.

'I know,' Alistair agreed. 'But my mother wasn't a woman who ever took no for an answer.'

Nell said, 'There's that.'

She looked out of the window. Boats lit against the dark were drifting into the harbour. People passed by on their way home now the working day had ended. She knew all of them. She was at home here. 'So, what do you want?'

'I want you to take the responsibility in the divorce. I want you to admit adultery.'

'So you can avoid a scandal? So it looks like I'm the nasty one?' asked Nell.

He nodded.

Nell picked up the photographs and scrutinised them. 'You have the evidence. And I have none. Except that you are living with Carol – and she's pregnant.'

'I am Mr Rutherford who is living with Mrs Rutherford. Nobody knows she's not my Mrs Rutherford.'

'That's a good point, but it's easy to prove that Carol isn't your Mrs Rutherford. I have the marriage certificate.'

He agreed. 'I'd pay you.'

'A bribe?' said Nell. 'That's a very Rutherford thing to do. Keep your money. I don't want it. And I don't want any alimony, however small the sum might be.'

He looked shamed and took out a newspaper article. *A glamorous, go ahead couple,* it read. The picture showed Alistair and Carol together. She wore a loose silk gown, he was at his desk, shirtsleeves rolled up, collar open. He had his arm round her waist. Nell remembered the scene well. It had been one of her early daydreams. My best friend has stolen my life, she thought.

'Oh hell,' she said. 'I'll do it. Why not? I suppose I don't have so much to lose. But when it's over I don't want to see you or Carol again. Too many painful memories.'

Alistair said he could agree to that. 'Though it's a pity. I'll never know what's become of you.'

'You'll miss finding out about my fabulous life.' She tapped the newspaper article, 'But, I expect I'll be able to follow yours.'

She finished her drink and asked for another. Only because it's so expensive, she thought.

He fetched it, put it in front of her and thanked her. She took a sip and considered him. The old Alistair, the one she married, had gone. This Alistair was wearing an expensive bespoke suit, a pale shirt and dazzling pink tie. Who does that remind me of? Oh God, she thought, he's turned into Harry. He's the image of his father. That's what Harry was wearing the day he tried to sell me a car.

'Does Carol pick your clothes?' she asked.

'Sometimes, but mostly I buy them myself. Actually, I help to pick hers.'

'Ah,' she said, and then smiled, 'When did you fall for Carol? Was it always her? Right from the night we met at the Locarno and you walked me home?'

He shrugged.

'On the night of the opening of Rutherford's, when Carol did the twist, I saw you looking at her. The lust in your eyes shook me to the roots.'

He blushed. 'I'm sorry.'

'You know what I think?'

He shook his head.

'I think I should have listened to my mother and never gone to the Locarno. If I'd done that none of this would have happened. And I do believe I would have been happy.'

He smiled, reached over and took her hand, 'Be happy, Nell. You deserve it. I have to go. You'll be hearing about the divorce. Dates for the court case, everything. It'll be quiet, no big fuss.' He got up to leave.

Nell asked about the restaurant. 'What happened to it?'

'Annie bought it. She sold her house to raise the money. Annie's Place, it's called. White walls and framed posters. Very plain, very stylish. She lives in the rooms above the restaurant with her husband and kids. She's doing well. She's going to open up a second place, Annie's In The City. Carol and me are invited to the opening.'

Nell nodded. 'Enjoy it.'

After he'd gone, Nell finished her drink, gathered the photographs and headed home. She stopped by a bench under a street light, sat down and looked at the pictures. She dismissed the sleazy shots of her and Hamish in bed and stared at the one that showed her and Hamish walking together. It intrigued her.

Hamish was walking in the slow, almost relentless way he always did. It was a stump of a movement, one reluctant foot after the other. He was looking at her. She knew that expression. She'd worn it herself not that long ago. She could see, in this captured moment, what he was thinking. This life will do. This place will do. This woman will do. And then he'd kissed her.

Chapter Thirty-four
You Know

It was over quickly. Nell admitted adultery. The divorce was granted. Alistair paid the costs. Outside the court-room in Edinburgh, they shook hands and parted. He told her he was marrying Carol the following week; the baby was due three weeks after that. 'So it will be legal,' he said. 'That still matters. You'd think we'd have left all that behind in this enlightened age, but no.'

She congratulated him, refused his offer to pay her train fare and walked to the station. On the train back to Catto, she told herself it wasn't that bad. She'd done a noble thing. She'd helped her husband – well, ex-husband – escape a scandal and freed him to marry the one he really loved. And being the guilty party in a divorce wasn't that bad. Why, look at Elizabeth Taylor. She'd cheated on her husband with Richard Burton and the world was shocked, but everyone knew it was a grand passion. She was the same, but without the grand passion. Still, she was free.

She thought about going to London. Now was surely the time. She was single; a woman with a mysterious past. She convinced herself she had no reason to stay where she was. No strings, she decided. But she did stay. She continued her routine, staying with Byrony for most of the week and spending a couple of nights with Hamish. It was comfortable. And she couldn't deny there was passion. In fact, the passion was getting deeper and deeper. She was enjoying it.

Byrony changed things. She announced she was selling her house. 'Lived here too long. It's time to move on.'

Nell asked where she was going.

'London,' she said. 'I was brought up there. It was you gave me the notion to go back. Got me thinking about busy streets, cafés, cinemas. I have family in London. I've a hankering to be near them again.'

'Are you ready for London?' Nell asked with a smile. 'If Greek gods go whizzing past you, every one of them stark naked, what would you do?'

'I'd whistle and stamp. I certainly wouldn't be thinking they'd catch their death storming about with nothing on. I'd enjoy the view.' She watched Nell's dismay. 'Nothing stays the same, Nell. Everything changes. Everything always changes.'

'But where will I live?'

'You can rent a cottage. There's always plenty available. Or you could move into the hotel. I'm sure there's a room. My goodness, the work you put in there, Hamish should be glad to let you have one.'

It was true. Over the past months, Nell had taken on more responsibilities. She ordered stock for the bar. She'd brought in a range of malt whiskies, encouraging guests to try each one over the course of their stay. She'd persuaded Hamish to have the lounge redecorated. 'Make it like an old country house,' she said. 'Comfy sofas, a small library and a huge roaring fire.' She'd reorganised the menus. 'Scottish beef and local seafood,' she'd said.

When she told Hamish she was looking for a cottage to rent, he asked why she didn't move in with him. 'It's not as if we don't get along,' he said. 'My house is so handy for work; you'd be home in no time. I'm sure we won't get in each other's way. I do like you, you know. You know that, don't you?'

Nell said she did know that and she was glad about it. He smiled.

He'd made it sound as if she'd be more flatmate than lover, but she accepted the offer. It saved her the bother of looking for a cottage. And he wouldn't charge her rent so the new running-away fund would benefit.

Nell moved in on the day Byrony left for London. Kelby was still on the market but Byrony was convinced it would sell. 'There's always people looking to start a new life in a new place. It's a popular dream to buy a place you could run as a B&B and live a quiet, undemanding life by the sea. Of course, they're all wrong.'

At the small farewell dinner they'd held for Byrony at the hotel, she had leaned over to Nell and said, 'Have you noticed how Hamish is walking these days? He doesn't slouch any more. And his legs don't look like they resent the small business of moving one in front of the other. He doesn't look as if he's in the doldrums. In fact, I do believe he's happy. You've done that.'

Nell had said that Hamish hadn't mentioned anything about being particularly happy to her.

'He's changed. And so have you. You've become more cynical. And you've stopped daydreaming. I think you should take it up again. I think you've lost your wonder.'

Nell had told her she didn't think daydreaming and having a sense of wonder did her any good. 'I no longer trust people. This will stop me getting hurt.'

'Ah, but nothing will stop you getting hurt. It's part of life. I wish I had daydreamed a bit, it would've helped when Kelvin left and I was suddenly alone.' She sighed. 'Better to daydream than to fall on your knees when walking to the forest. Better to daydream than to want to bang your head on the ground and weep.'

'You know about that?'

'I know,' said Byrony. 'I did that.'

Nell took her hand and squeezed it, 'You poor thing.'

'It was hard. One day Kelvin was there. Next day he was gone. He left a short note saying he was sorry, he loved someone else. That was that. Looking back I wish I had daydreamed. I wish I'd had your sense of wonder.'

Nell said, 'Do you? I thought I was a bit naïve.'

'Well, you were. But losing your sense of wonder may also stop you accepting how marvellous it is that you are loved. And you are. It's plain to see Hamish loves you. And I think you love him. But you hold back. You don't trust. Plus, you are not in touch with your feelings.' She had sighed. 'I don't think you ever have been. Perhaps that's why you daydreamed so much. You were hiding from what you felt.'

In time, as guests saw Nell arrive with Hamish and leave with him in the evening, they assumed they were married. People who came to the hotel and stayed for a few days called her Mrs Watson. Nell never bothered to correct them. It was easier to accept the mistake than explain the truth.

These days, Hamish strode through the hotel beaming at everyone he came across. He'd greet guests with open arms. 'Hello and welcome,' he'd say. 'Have a wonderful stay and please, if you want anything, anything at all, just ask. We're here to help.'

He delighted in having Nell around permanently. He'd follow her about the house, smiling to her. 'Just want your company,' he'd say. From time to time, she'd catch him staring at her as she did the most mundane of tasks, like peeling potatoes or wiping the sink. 'What are you staring at?'

'You. You look lovely standing there peeling potatoes.'

'Nobody looks lovely peeling potatoes. They look bored.'

In bed, in the middle of the night, he'd wake her as he reached over to touch her.

'What are you doing?' she'd say, grumpy at being awake.

'Just checking you're still there.'

'Of course I'm still here. Where else would I be? It's three in the morning.'

'I don't know. You could have slipped away and left me. I like to know you haven't gone away.'

She'd turn over, pull the blankets round her and pursue sleep.

In March, Hamish closed the hotel while refurbishments were made. At Nell's suggestion he was installing en suite bathrooms in most of the rooms in advance of the summer season. 'It's what people want,' she'd told him. 'They hate sharing a loo with strangers.'

At first Hamish had been against the idea. 'We'll have to shut the place down. We can't have people staying while a bunch of plumbers crash around banging and whistling. Besides, they'll have to shut off the water. We'll lose money.'

'Think of the money you'll make by being modern,' said Nell. 'You'll be ahead of the game. That'll be a first for you.'

Two days later Hamish said that since the hotel was going to be shut, he'd booked a holiday.

'Valencia,' he said. 'Always fancied going there. It's the home of paella, you know. I'll taste the dish as it is intended to be eaten and see how they make it differently to how I've had it here. Fabulous architecture as well. Got a room in a lovely little hotel not far from the Plaça de la Verge.'

'It sounds wonderful. I hope you have a great time,' Nell said carefully.

'You're coming too,' he said. 'I booked for two. Got two seats on the airplane.'

'You could have asked me before you booked. You could have said, "Do you fancy a few days in Valencia?"'

'But then it wouldn't have been a surprise. This is a surprise. OK then, do you fancy a few days in Valencia?'

'Yes, but the way you said it at first, made it sound like you were going alone.'

Hamish asked why he'd do that now he had her in his life. 'We're a couple.'

'Ah. People who are part of couples say "we" not "I".'

Hamish smiled. 'I'll remember that. *We* can sample paella as it's intended to be eaten.'

They flew to Barcelona and drove to Valencia in a hired car. Hamish sang opera most of the way. 'Do you like Verdi?'

'I used to, before I heard your rendition of *Aida*,' said Nell. 'Actually, I'm more of a Beatles woman. And the Rolling Stones. I loved Buddy Holly.'

'God, yes, Buddy Holly,' said Hamish. 'You're taking me back to my wasted youth with that name. I had all his records.'

'What did you do with them?'

'Left them behind when I moved north. Left everything – all my books, all my furniture. Wanted to walk away from the life I'd had with my wife and start afresh. Couldn't bear the memories. Could've taken my Buddy Hollys though – they were from the time before I met her.'

She asked if he'd had the horn-rimmed glasses.

'Oh, yes. The complete Buddy Holly outfit. I even did a fair impression of him.' He gave her a swift burst of 'Raining in My Heart'.

'That's really good,' said Nell. 'Takes me back to the Locarno in Edinburgh.'

'I only went to Edinburgh once as a lad. Had an uncle and aunt lived there. But I went to the Locarno with my cousin. That was a rough place. Wild. I didn't stay long. You never used to go there, did you?'

'Yes, but only because my mother told me not to. She said it was heathen. Well, after she'd said that I had to go and find out what it was like.'

'You have to be careful what you say to children. When I have kids I'm going to sit them down and explain everything to them. And if they do things I don't want them to do and get into trouble, I want them to feel they can come to me. Understanding is all.'

Nell wanted to ask when he'd like to have kids but she let it go. She told him she agreed with him.

The hotel was perfect. Their room was snug, had a large bed and a small balcony that overlooked the Plaça de la Verge. 'What more could you want?' said Nell.

'Nothing,' said Hamish.

Over the next few days they became tourists. They wandered the streets, marvelling at the architecture, stared into shop windows and sat in cafés watching people pass by. They drove out to the Malvarrosa beach, sauntered round the Institute of Modern Art, visited the Botanical Gardens and went to see the Goyas at the Cathedral Diocesan Museum. They ate paella. 'It's the saffron,' said Hamish. 'Though I've been told they put colouring in.'

'It's wonderful. We could do it at the hotel. There is the local seafood.'

'Good idea,' he said. 'I'll look into Spanish wines to wash it down.'

Everywhere they went, Hamish kept his arm round Nell. 'Protecting you from the world,' he said. Every day, he told her she looked lovely. They both wished they'd booked for longer than five days.

'Isn't this marvellous?' said Hamish. 'Aren't we wonderful? All this time together in a strange new place and we haven't argued once. Most couples argue when they're on holiday.'

'Do they?' asked Nell, though now she thought about it, she and Alistair had argued about having children on their honeymoon.

'Oh, yes. We're doing fine. Getting along like a house on fire.'

In retrospect, Hamish wished he hadn't said that. The big fight came on their last night in Valencia. They were on the balcony planning where they should go to eat, and, as they did, watching a young couple with a little girl. The child was between them, holding a hand of each parent. Every few steps they'd hoist her into the air and swing her forward. The girl screamed with glee.

Hamish was entranced. 'I want one of them. Well, two or maybe even three.'

'With who?'

'Why, with you, of course,' he said. 'Who else?'

'Don't you think there should be a few polite preliminaries first, like saying you love me, or telling me you want to marry me? Actually getting married so our children wouldn't be illegitimate?'

Hamish was upset. 'But you know me. You know I, well, you know. And you must know I want to . . . well, you know.'

'No, I don't know anything. It's always "you know this" and "you know that" with you. What are you talking about?'

Hamish said, 'You know.'

'Too many you knows,' said Nell.

'I just don't know how to say it,' Hamish told her. 'I have all this going on inside. These emotions, these feelings and I try to express them, bring them into the open, and say them out loud, but when I open my mouth all that comes out is "you know".'

'Try harder,' said Nell.

Hamish looked pained, he spread him palms and looked pleadingly.

After a few seconds of him saying nothing at all, Nell picked up her coat and stormed out.

She clattered down the stairs and into the street. It

was busy. Boiling with frustration, she pushed through the crowds. Why were men so awkward? She remembered what May had once told her: that they thought in straight lines as opposed to women who thought in curves, which was why women were wiser. Hamish probably thought in straight lines and made the mistake of thinking she did too.

She turned into the Plaza de la Reina. It was full of bars and restaurants. She and Hamish had eaten at a few of them but had been too busy visiting museums, gardens and the beach to explore it properly. Tonight, she wandered further than she'd been before.

It was starting to rain. Nell knew she should go back to the hotel, but she wasn't yet ready for that. Her anger hadn't subsided enough. She saw a bar, its name lit up in blue neon. The Locarno. Oh my, she thought, it's an omen. She'd never in her life gone into a bar alone, but hey, this was Valencia. Perhaps women did that here. She went in.

It was crowded. It seemed to Nell that the place was full of men in crumpled linen suits drinking brandy and puffing cigars. Of course there were women, too. They wore low-cut dresses and sipped from long-stemmed glasses. The walls were painted dark red, the bar glistened with rows and rows of bottles and in the corner a young, handsome man was playing a baby grand piano.

A woman in an absurdly tight dress came forward, put her glass on the piano and leaned on it. She nodded to the man, grinned round at the assembled customers who all clapped, and started to sing 'Fly Me to the Moon'. It was May Rutherford.

Nell stepped further into the room. She couldn't believe this. What was May doing here? Of course, she was safe here. She couldn't be extradited back home. Nell remembered reading that many British criminals ended up here. But, my God, *May Rutherford* here in Valencia, leaning on a piano and singing in her throaty voice. Who'd have thought it?

Nell scanned the room, looking for Harry. He was behind the bar, wearing an immaculately ironed pale-blue shirt and dazzling pink tie. Perched on his head was a floppy linen hat. He was pouring drinks and holding one finger to his lips, hushing anybody that dared speak while his wife was singing.

Nell stood frozen like a statue in the centre of the floor staring at May, even though she knew it would only be a few seconds before she was noticed.

May stopped singing. 'Nell,' she shouted. 'Oh, Nell, it's you. I always knew you'd come one day.'

Nell said nothing.

May turned to Harry. 'It's our Nell. Isn't this place just like Piccadilly Circus? Stay here long enough and in time everyone you know will come by.'

Harry looking stunned, recovered, smiled and waved.

May started her long, twinkling mince towards Nell. The tightness of her dress made anything other than tiny, shuffling steps impossible. 'Nell,' she said with her arms spread wide, reaching out to her. 'This is lovely. It's made

352

my day. It's made my month, my year. You've got to have a drink. Harry, pour Nell a glass of champagne. And me too, come to that. We've got to celebrate. A glass of champagne on the house for everyone . . .' Nell found herself clutched in May's embrace, 'How long are you staying? There's a job for you here if you want it,' she whispered fiercely in her ear. 'You're more than welcome. Have you got my glasses? They're worth a fortune.'

For a moment, Nell's mind drifted off. Her first daydream in a long time. She could stay here. She could have a small apartment, nothing fancy, just two rooms and a balcony where she could drink thick, black coffee in the morning watching the world go by. She could work in this bar. She wouldn't wear anything tight like May. Perhaps wide silky trousers that flowed as she moved and a dark pink shirt with a high collar, but unbuttoned to show just a hint of a curve of her breasts. She could flirt with these men in crumpled linen suits. Maybe they were all criminals, gang leaders on the run from the law. It was a bit Lauren Bacall and Humphrey Bogart. She could learn Spanish, and spend her days in this fabulous, beautiful, ancient city.

As May finally released her, Nell took a step back and studied her ex-mother-in-law. She could see that she'd got older. Her face was etched with lines, thick with make-up. Her eyes were caked with blue eye-shadow. Her lips were terrifyingly scarlet.

Nell clenched her fists and felt repulsion and fury. This was the woman who'd yelled at customers who hadn't eaten their greens. This woman had deposited secret cheques in her bank account so she could hide it from the taxman. And then run off with the wages she owed her. She had caused that awful afternoon at the bank when Nell had learned her account was empty. This woman had booked a church and a hotel without bothering to ask first if Nell had even wanted to marry her son. This woman was awful.

Nell turned and fled.

'Nell,' she heard the thick throaty cry, 'Nell, what's got into you? Come back.'

But Nell ran. Back to the Plaça de la Verge and there was Hamish standing with his hand clasped to his forehead looking first this way, then that way, stumbling back and forth not knowing where to go. She called his name.

He came to her and took her to him. 'Where the hell have you been?'

'Just for a walk to clear my head.'

He held her at arm's length, scrutinising her with a concerned look on his face, 'Are you all right? You look like you've seen a ghost.'

'I'm fine. I just needed to get back to you.'

He held her again. 'Nell, you know I want to marry you. You know I . . . Well, you know—'

'Yes, I know,' Nell said.

Chapter Thirty-five
Go On, Say It

It was six years before they married. They'd procrastinated. There were so many other things to do. The hotel was busy from May to October, and then again at Christmas and New Year. At quiet times there were repairs to see to, accounts to update and bar stocks to check. They kept saying, 'Next year, we'll do it then. We'll have a big party and invite the whole village. It'll be fun.'

Then Nancy came along. Nell refused to walk down the aisle when pregnant. 'I'd be waddling. Nobody wants to waddle down the aisle. We'll do it later.'

Hamish said, 'You said you wanted to get married before you had children. You wanted to do things in the right order.'

'I did,' said Nell. 'But that was before I knew about waddling. I want to be a beautiful bride.'

But Nancy was followed by Ben, so it was the waddling excuse again. After that, Nell was busy helping in the hotel and looking after the two little ones. 'I've no time. It'll have to wait.'

In truth, she didn't mind. She was happy with how things were. In summer she'd take the children to the beach, watch them play on the sand, stare into the rock pools and jump the waves as they rippled towards the shore. From time to time she'd see dolphins slip by, moving effortlessly several yards out to sea. They made her heart leap. 'They're a sign of good weather,' Hamish told her. Sometimes she and Hamish would take the children up the long track to the forest. They'd find a spot where they could eat sandwiches and scan the horizon for deer. Every time they passed their kissing spot where they'd been snapped locked in an embrace they'd catch one another's eye and smile. They had secrets. They had a history.

In winter the deer came down from the hills and wandered the hotel grounds looking for food. Nell loved to watch them. Sometimes the snow came so thick and deep, plodding to the log pile at the side of the house was tough going. The chill numbed her face and hands. Nell would complain bitterly about the biting cold and the endless whiteness of everything. 'It's a trial getting to the village and it's only a step away.' Yet, there was the beauty of it, the silence and the sudden isolation was a wonder. At times like this the hotel was empty as nobody could get through. Nell and Hamish would spend hours together when the kids were asleep, sitting by the fire, feet up, drinking tea, planning their summer and napping. Hamish thought napping with someone was the most intimate thing you could do. 'It's a trust thing,' he said. 'Slipping off into sleep feeling warm and relaxed, knowing you'll wake together is calming. It's comfortable. I like it.'

Nobody in the village bothered that the pair weren't married. It was the way of things. Oh, at first there had been some gossip, but as time passed, they'd moved on to fresh sources of chit-chat and discussion. The two became 'our Hamish and our Nell who can't be bothered getting married'. This pleased Nell. It felt like she belonged.

Once she saw a newspaper article about Carol and Alistair. It was a feature on their new home, which was a delight. *Modern furnishings, but with an old-fashioned homey twist. Beautifully crafted tables and sofas from Italy mixed with junk shop finds make the Rutherford's home a joy.* Carol had completed her university course, gained a degree and was planning to teach. Gosh, Nell had thought, who'd have thought it? She always seemed pretty thick to me. She hadn't finished reading the article because some guests from America had arrived and she'd had to check them in. When she'd looked for the newspaper intending to finish reading about the two people from her past, she'd discovered that Hamish had used the paper to light the fire in the lounge. It was gone. Oh well, she'd thought. Doesn't matter.

Every so often Byrony wrote with news from London and asked if Nell would visit, and each time Nell would say to Hamish, 'I think I'll go see Byrony. One day.'

Hamish agreed it would be good for her, 'One day,' he agreed.

'One day,' they'd say in unison. Procrastinating again.

The village changed. Houses were built, all tacked

on at the end of Main Street. Fresh faces arrived, every one of them creased with tension and worry. 'People on the run,' Nell said. In time, these faces would relax as the worries drifted away and the procrastination kicked in.

Some people arrived looking hopeful and fled months later. They found the pace too slow. They couldn't stand the weather: sudden storms; lashing rain followed by splashes of sunshine. They didn't know what was coming next. They missed pavements, city smells, shops, restaurants, and the array of strangers to ponder. Nobody stayed a stranger for long here. These people hated the intimacy of this place. Everybody knew everybody. Everybody knew everybody's business. What they didn't know they assumed and turned into gossip. It seemed to Nell that these people ran away, screaming and waving their arms in the air.

Hippies turned up in their Volkswagen camper vans. They'd park near the shore and sit in groups playing guitars and smoking pot. They called one another 'man' and spoke of a new world of peace and love. Some of them moved into abandoned cottages miles into the hills. They wanted to grow their own food and raise their kids away from the hustle and demands of bureaucracy. Nell was sure they all lived on lentils and beans, so, now and then, she'd take them leftover food from the hotel. They always thanked her and invited her in to sit by their smoky fires and drink coffee. She liked their clothes and their music. She liked their banter. She ordered a copy of Jimi Hendrix's *Electric Ladyland* from the local shop. When it arrived it was put in the window with brown paper over the cover and a note that said *Our Nell's weird LP*. Nell was so enamoured she left it there for weeks before picking it up.

Nell never forgot the Rutherfords. Things happened to make them sneak back into her mind. A waitress on a busy night in the dining room barged past her, whirled round to apologise and a steak slid from the plate she was carrying and landed on the kitchen floor. 'Don't barge and whirl. Glide,' said Nell. 'Our guests are here to unwind and they mustn't know it's mayhem in here.'

The waitress blushed and Nell bit her lip. Oh, God, I sound like May Rutherford.

Proud at seeing his guests leave relaxed and glowing after their holiday, Hamish boasted that they made people happy. 'That's what we do, and we do it well.'

Nell told him not to say that. 'It reminds me of someone I'd rather not be reminded of.'

'Who?' asked Hamish.

'My old mother-in-law, May. She was a wicked witch and I got caught up in her spell.'

Hamish said that was absurd.

'No, really,' said Nell. 'I adored her. I actually wanted to be her. She was so wildly generous and glamorous, if you like scarlet lips and violent blue eye-shadow. She threw herself at life and I loved that. Of course she was a rogue as well. She and her husband sold really dubious cars and, in her restaurant, she'd refuse to serve pudding to people who didn't finish up their main course.' She shrugged and said, 'Ho hum, I don't think about her much these days. I ended up hating her, but now I think she never got over her impoverished childhood. She threw money around. She loved expensive things. I think she only ever wanted to be loved. Sometimes, I almost feel sorry for her, and wonder what must she have been feeling inside. Sometimes I almost forgive her, but only sometimes, and only almost.'

In the end it was Bella who forced the marriage. Nell was three months pregnant with her and decided that this child ought to be legitimate. 'And it'll make honest children of the other two, as well. We'll do it before I start to waddle.'

They married in January. Nell jokingly complained about being a winter bride for a second time. But this time it was her choice. She'd found the perfect outfit: a simple empire-line dress in a dark – almost black – satin that skimmed over her blossoming stomach. Nell could almost hear her mother whisper in her ear, 'Marry in black, you'll wish yourself back.'

Hamish thought this excellent news when she shared the old rhyme with him. 'I'm going to take it to mean that you'll wish yourself back to me when you've been away. You'll always come back to me.'

The party afterwards included most of the village, hotel guests, anyone who happened to pass by, and Byrony, up from London. They ate from a buffet prepared by the hotel chef and just about drank the bar dry. They danced to the music of Beautiful Insight, a local hippy band who specialised in Creedence Clearwater Revival numbers. They planned to honeymoon the following year, taking their children with them. 'Anywhere but Valencia,' said Nell. 'People I don't want to run into ever again live there. Or Florence. I don't want a second honeymoon there.'

They would decide on a honeymoon location later. One day.

It was just after midnight on the night of their wedding; the newlyweds were outside cooling off. The night was bitterly cold, thick frost on the lawn, a damp chill mist hung in the air. As Nell and Hamish spoke to one another steamy breath burst in small clouds from their lips. Hamish said they'd better get inside soon or they'd catch their deaths out there.

The front door of the hotel burst open, and Byrony shouted that it was time for the official march past. 'The ultimate wedding celebration.'

Half-a-dozen young men burst out into the night and steamed down the drive to the gate. All were naked but for red bow ties. The wedding guests gathered to watch them run, all shouting, 'Go, Go, Go.'

Nell said she thought they only did that to celebrate winning at football matches.

'This is just for you, Nell,' Byrony said. 'A treat.'

'Oh . . . And it is,' said Nell, laughing

Hamish said he thought it a bit crazy. 'They'll catch their death running like that on a night like this. It's about four below out here.'

Nell and Byrony looked at one another and smiled.

'He's not ready for London,' said Nell.

Hamish said he never was and never would be. 'I love living here.'

He pulled Nell to him and whispered, 'You know.' It was something he said to her every day. Nell replied, as she always did, 'Yes, I know.'

Bella was born at twenty-past-three on the morning of the third of June in the local hospital. She weighed seven pounds and eight ounces, had a shock of black hair and seemed to look round at the world with a bemused expression. The midwife said she was going to be a dreamer. Oh no, Nell thought, anything but that. But at least I can warn her about the pitfalls.

Hamish held the child put his lips to her head and said, 'You know.'

'No,' said Nell. She was tired and spoke softly. 'You tell her properly. And say it to her and to all our children every day. They must grow up knowing they are loved. They must have confidence so they can go into the world and do what they please, and be the people they want to be. No drifting into daydreams, no hiding. Go on, Hamish, say the words. Say them out loud.' And he did.

He started with Nell.

IZZY'S WAR
ISLA DEWAR

A country at war, a young woman in love . . .

Izzy has joined the Air Transport Auxiliary and can't believe her luck. She's getting to do the thing she loves most: flying. On the ground she is a woman who longs to be independent, but who is lying to her family about the job she does. But, in the thrill of the air, she can be free.

Izzy's heroine is her friend, Elspeth, who, on an impulse, signed up to do her bit as a lumber-jill and has been regretting it ever since. While Elspeth dreams of simple comforts: hot baths and home cooking, Izzy dreams of being more like her friend and finally standing up to her vicar father. But when Izzy falls for the charms of an American doctor, she ends up only adding to the list of secrets she's keeping . . .

'Appealingly spirited' *Mail on Sunday*

Turn the page to read an extract . . .

Chapter One
Three Women Cycling to Work

There was rapture in Izzy's life. It came when she was flying, when she had such a view – God's view, her father called it. Well, he would. She thought she could write a book about the things she'd seen from above: herds of deer, hundreds of them rippling across hilltops. She saw houses, gardens; washing flapping on the line; people small as matchstick men, moving through streets and stopping, sometimes, to look up at her hovering above them, and point. Once, she'd seen a couple entangled in their own not-as-private-as-they-thought rapture on a sun-soaked moor. She saw the shape and glide of rivers, was shoulder to shoulder with mountains. It took her breath away. She was addicted to the air. Removed from earthly worries and demands, she was truly happy.

It had been her friend Elspeth's idea to learn to fly. Such a fashionable thing to do, 'Women are taking to the sky,' she'd said. 'They are the new adventurers. Flying to Australia, across the Sahara, looking for a new kind of romance.' Elspeth had taken lessons, Izzy watched. Then, unable to resist, had taken it up, too.

1

She had never been ambitious. Had no desire to become a new adventurer, cruising the heavens was joyful enough.

In time, Elspeth had moved on to new pursuits. She abandoned flying when she became obsessed with her new accordion. She dreamed of forming an all-woman accordion band that toured the country playing wild, stomping music. But then, Hitler invaded Poland and ambitions were abandoned, everything changed.

Izzy felt that rapture, though it was a lesser joy, every morning when she cycled with Julia and Claire to work. Pushing through the morning contemplating the possibilities of the day ahead. Where she might fly to, and in what?

It was always the same, the rattle of bikes and the hum of tyres, hissing today over the glistening November frost, thick over everything, a stiff sparkle. A lone crow in the field beyond the hedge hopped over hardened ground. Above, a scattering of seagulls silently cruised the still air. Right now, apart from them, the sky was empty.

The bus had passed five minutes ago. Everyone on-board banged on the window, waved and mocked the three cycling. They were late. When were they not?

It was a problem, three women sharing a cramped cottage with one tiny bathroom. Mornings were a flurry. Downstairs, in the kitchen, the kettle would be coming to the boil, quietly steaming and singing, the wireless would be on. Upstairs, Julia and Claire, in their silk dressing gowns, getting ready to face the day, jostled in and out of the bathroom, bumped into one another and did polite sidestepping dances in the narrow hallway.

Izzy always made porridge first thing, standing by the stove wrapped in a voluminous thick flannel tartan robe, tied firmly round her waist with a bright red cord. It was an embarrassing garment, she knew, but comfortable and comforting. A gift from her mother and, indeed, exactly the sort of thing her mother would deem an ideal and useful thing to own. Izzy couldn't deny its warmth, and often, on the winter nights when three thin blankets did little to stave off the cold, she slept in it.

They were all used to having space. Claire and Julia had grown up in large country mansions, Izzy a manse. They were also, all of them, used to working alone. They couldn't share a kitchen. They clattered, banged, spilled tea and burned toast. And bumped into one another. Izzy was always surprised when the others refused a share of her porridge.

Claire and Julia would sit at the table, eating charred toast, drinking weak tea. Neither of them could cook. Izzy would eat leaning against the sink, saying this was the way to eat porridge. 'It's to be taken standing up.' When the weather report came on they'd fall silent and listen. Weather was important to them.

While Julia put on a fresh layer of lipstick, Izzy would run upstairs, wash in tepid water, run her fingers through her hair – a thick black curly mass – and put on her uniform. Then they'd bustle out into the day, leaving damp towels lying on the bathroom floor, beds unmade and the kitchen in chaos. At nine o'clock Mrs Brent would come in and clean it all up.

Today had been worse than usual because the Pole had been there. Jacob, one of Julia's waifs – she'd met him the night before – had sat silently, watching. His only comment was a surprised, 'You fly?' when Izzy had pulled back the curtain, pressed her head against the window and said that it was a good flying day. She had nodded, and he'd nodded back. And smiled. This had surprised Izzy. Often, when she told people, especially male people, what she did, they didn't believe her.

Still, Jacob's presence, his bulk, his stillness, the quiet way he drank his tea, made the three feel uncomfortable. They were glad to get away.

'It's been lovely to meet you,' Julia had said. 'Please shut the door behind you when you leave.'

They had collected their bikes from the side of the cottage and cycled off. Only Izzy turned to wave goodbye.

Julia cycled up front, her usual place, face into the breeze, shouting about the temperature. 'Bloody, bloody cold. I hate it.' She sat upright in her saddle, her face flushed with chill. Her coat flapped at her thighs, revealing fleeting flashes of scarlet lining.

This lining was not, strictly speaking, part of the Air Auxiliary uniform. It was her own little flamboyance. She never could resist a little bit of scarlet silk.

When she'd first joined the ferry fleet, Julia had

loved the thought of being in uniform, especially one that was blue with gold bars. She'd been so tickled, she'd had one specially made up for her by her father's Savile Row tailor. The resulting outfit was not quite the chic ensemble she'd hoped for.

The gentlemen who'd measured her had never measured a woman before and the business with the measuring tape and where it had to go had made their cheeks redden. They'd coughed a lot. They had left some distance between the tape and Julia's body when measuring any sensitive area. Their recordings of Julia's bust size and inside leg length were wildly inaccurate.

The result of all this was that Julia's jacket was lumpily generous from shoulder to waist and baggy at her rear. She was always hitching up her trousers. She worried about them falling down. In fact, it bothered her a lot that if ever she got into difficulties when flying and had to bail out, her trousers might slip past her knees as she parachuted to the ground. And if she landed badly, and died, she'd be found in a tangled heap, trousers round her ankles and flappy silk knickers made from old parachutes in full view.

Pedalling along now, her breath steamed short bursts of vapour before her as she spoke. And really her complaint about the cold was half-hearted. This morning, she was happy.

Izzy envied her. She wanted to be Julia – crisp bobbed hair and scarlet lips. Julia didn't walk through life, she bounced; she always drew a crowd. Evenings, she never stayed in.

Last night she'd eaten at Bertram's, a small, dingy place in Blackpool. No, it wasn't a place. It was a joint, a dive. She loved it. It had been busy, smoky, noisy, filled with the clamour of swaggering voices. In the corner a wind-up gramophone played Billie Holiday records that some GIs at the next table had brought with them. Billie crooned silkily about the glorious and exciting things a little moonlight could do. Oooh, it was wonderful.

Julia had been with Charles, her number-one boyfriend – she called them her beaux – and the only young man she knew who wasn't in the RAF. He'd joined the Royal Artillery – mostly, Julia thought, to annoy his family. His father had flown in the First World War, and now both his brothers were pilots.

Charles had brought along Jacob, a morose Pole he'd met on the train. Charles was always taking strangers under his wing. The Pole, however, hardly spoke, but tapped his fingers on the side of his whisky glass in time to the music.

Charles and Julia had laughed, smoked, drunk too much, swapped favourite stories, toasted absent friends and tried not to mention the awfulness of the ragout they'd ordered.

Julia said she'd heard that the food there had always been pretty bad. 'So in a way, it's comforting to find something that hasn't been changed by the war.'

Charles said that was one way to look at it.

Julia told him not to think about it. 'Just eat it. One just can't think about what might be in things these days, darling. I've even heard of people eating guinea pigs. Yuck.' She made a face.

She had a habit of calling people darling. It was a word she liked, also it pleased her to note that it irritated the Pole. She'd started to dislike him.

Charles asked where Julia had been last night when he had phoned.

'You know better than to ask me that,' said Julia. 'But I was stuck out. Still, got back this afternoon. And here I am, darling.'

They never spoke in detail about where she'd been. Careless talk cost lives, everybody knew that – posters in the railway stations, messages on milk bottle tops.

Julia had often been 'stuck out'. She hated the frustration of finding herself caught at some distant airfield flunk-hole as fog deepened, impenetrable, dense, yellow. Often, she'd sat drinking thick stewed tea, watching the sky darken as delays kept her grounded, knowing she could not beat the sunset and she wouldn't have time to fly home before dark descended. There would be a blackout. From above you would hardly know there were houses, streets, pubs, cinemas and factories in the world below.

When she first started flying, it had been to take Tiger Moths and Puss Moths that had been requisitioned at the start of the war, but were now taking up valuable hangar space, north to Scotland. It had been winter and all the planes had open cockpits. She had never known cold like it. She'd worn several layers of jumpers under her flying suit, and a jacket under the flying jacket plus a couple of thick woollen scarves, and still the chill had bitten into her. Often, numb, rigid with cold, she'd hardly been able to move. Ground engineers had lifted her out of the cockpit. She'd felt her face frozen into a stiff macabre grin, a mix of shocked horror at the extreme chill she'd just experienced and relief that it was over.

The journey, technically, took just over four hours. But often the weather had closed in and she'd had to land to wait for it to clear. So, sometimes it took four days to fly from Southampton to Perth.

She had slept in strange small hotels, dormitories, in the huts of WAAF night operations officers whose beds were empty when they were on duty. These beds, only recently vacated, were often still warm. Once that would have appalled her, now it was a comfort.

She remembered nights spent on the train rumbling home to London. Hours and hours sitting on her hard parachute bag in a packed and noisy swarming corridor when there were no available seats, trying to sleep, jostled by loud bantering soldiers and airmen, none of them particularly sober, who smoked, sang and shoved past her.

Later, the ATA had sleeping cars set aside at the back of night trains. Then, she had been hauled from a deep and swaying sleep by gunfire or bombs as they chuntered through the Midlands. She'd leave the train at King's Cross, have breakfast, take another train back to Hatfield, where she was based, then start the whole gruelling trip over again, exposed to the elements in another frail and rickety Puss Moth.

Thinking about it now, humming through this icy but glorious morning, she wondered how she'd done all that without collapsing into an exhausted coma.

But, really, when she thought about it, how hellish it had been, she knew she wouldn't have missed any of it for the world.

She loved this life she was leading. Though now she was posted at Skimpton, it was mostly short flights, sometimes three or four a day. And it was usually Spitfires and Blenheims she flew. But once she was in the air, the decisions she made were hers alone. She was living, now, in the moment, no plans for the future. And, for the first time in her life, the money in her pocket was money she'd earned.

She sang as she rode along, joining Billie Holiday in her celebration of moonlight.

While Charles was her number-one beau, Jeffrey was number two. Her reserve lover, she thought. Though she hadn't seen Jeffrey in months, since he'd been posted to North Africa.

'Why two?' Izzy once asked. 'That's not very nice, two lovers. One of them is going to get hurt.'

'Both of them might get hurt,' Julia told her. 'They offset each other. Charles is rather moody but gorgeous to look at. Jeffrey is not so gorgeous, but he's fun. So I have a handsome lover and a fun lover. I have everything I want in a man from two men. And that stops me falling in love with either of them.'

'What's wrong with falling in love?' Izzy wanted to know. She had always thought falling in love was what every woman wanted to do. It was what life was about. Well, that was the message in all the songs she knew.

'Oh, darling,' said Julia. 'You don't want to go and fall in love. It will be the end of you. You fall in love, next thing you get married and once you're married your mother and his mother and probably the man himself will start wanting you to have children. So you have a baby. All you'll talk about is baby this and baby that and baby has its first tooth and baby smiled. And that's that. You'll never fly again. Oh no, darling, you must never let yourself fall in love. Just a little lust to keep you smiling is plenty.'

Last night she'd been angry at Charles for bringing the Pole with him. 'He's a gooseberry,' she'd hissed. 'I wanted to have you to myself.' She'd wanted to snuggle and kiss.

He'd told her not to be selfish. 'That man has been through hell, absolute hell. His wife is still in Poland. He has no idea what has happened to her. It's your duty to be kind to him. Besides, he's a stranger here. Knows nobody. And, he's starting work at your base. Be nice to him.'

Julia had hung her head, ashamed. 'I'll try.'

After the club, they had walked, arms linked, along the pier. Julia sang that Billie Holiday song, and broke her step from time to time with a little skip. Jacob had come with them. Though he didn't link arms, he walked behind, hands in his pockets. Julia thought he lumbered after them, like a huge stray dog. She still didn't like him, but now she felt guilty about it.

Thing was, she thought she'd seen him take the tip Charles had left for their waitress. It had been such a swift movement of hand from table to pocket, she wasn't sure. Jacob had been so quietly still, standing looking at the dance floor, that Julia had decided she'd been mistaken, and didn't mention it.

In fact, Jacob had become so attached, he'd come back to the cottage with her and Charles. He'd slept in the spare room. 'Make yourself comfortable, old chap,' Charles had said. Jacob had thanked him, 'It's kind of you.' He'd nodded to Julia. 'Tomorrow I report to your base. They'll sort me out with somewhere to stay.'

Julia had smiled, relieved.

Upstairs in bed, in Julia's small bedroom with the sloping roof, Charles had told her she was too judgemental. He pulled her on top of him. 'I like to see you making love to me.' He held her face. 'A good face,' he said. 'Verging on beautiful. But I don't see a lot of kindness in it. You have to learn to be kind. There's a war on, we must all be nice to one another.'

He'd run his hands over her breasts. Kissed them. Julia had reached over and switched off the light. She was more comfortable with intimacies in the dark.

Afterwards, just before she slept, he'd told her he'd be gone when she woke up. 'Got to get back to camp.'

But he'd be back soon. His regiment was going abroad, he'd have a week's leave before he sailed.

He leaned back, hands linked behind his head. He started to expound on the absurdity of war, the things he'd seen at Dunkirk, men queuing to be hauled onto a ship, drowning as they waited. He moved on to talk about his socialist principles, his admiration for George Orwell, theories he'd come across while studying history and politics at Cambridge. He stopped when he heard Julia snoring.

Claire always cycled in the middle of the group. Izzy was always last. She was a slow starter, but, in time, she'd gather strength and come from behind to take the lead and be first to arrive at the base.

In the mornings, Claire complained about the others complaining. She wished they would shut up. This time of day was precious, a time when she could think about her husband and her children. She'd shut her eyes as she pedalled along, trying to precisely conjure up their faces.

It had been over a year since she'd seen her husband Richard. He'd been shot down over France and was now a POW in Stalag Luft 1. Nell and Oliver, her children, had been sent to live in South Africa with her brother-in-law, Joe, at the start of the Blitz.

There had been tantrums when Claire told Nell and Oliver where they were going, and further tears and tantrums when she'd seen them off at Southampton docks. Two tear-stained children dressed in their Sunday best, standing beside their luggage, lips trembling and looking in disbelief at their mother. How could she banish them like this? And why was she packing them off to a distant land with only their Nanny Green to look after them on the trip? Why wasn't she coming too?

Claire had suggested she go to South Africa. But Richard had been adamant. 'I don't think so, old girl. We need you here.' He had joined up when war was declared, and was now a squadron leader in the air force. He had wanted Claire at home when he was on leave.

The childrens' first letters home had been filled with the longing of two small people out of their depths in a strange land. Slowly, slowly, the mood of the letters changed. There were hints about the good life out there – swimming every day, riding their uncle's horses. In time, there was no more hinting. Neither Nell nor Oliver remembered the holidays in Cornwall, picnics in the garden, walks with Willy, the retriever, on Hampstead Heath. Their memories of London were of rain and dirty yellow fog. Now, they didn't want to come back. The sun shone, they'd made new friends. Uncle Joe had given each of them a pony.

A pony, Claire thought, how could Joe do that? He knows Ollie won't want to leave it. And how it belittled the knitted red socks and leather football she'd sent him.

Even Nanny Green had decided not to return to Britain. She was, as Claire put it, on the wrong side of forty and was to stay with the children for six weeks to

13

ensure they were settled. She'd written to Claire telling her she'd made up her mind to stay put. She'd met a man, a delightful widower in his fifties, and, well, there was romance in the air.

God, even Willy the dog was happy. He'd been sent to stay outside Edinburgh with Claire's sister, Virginia, and her husband, George. Bounding around chasing rabbits, Virginia had told her.

Initially, Claire had believed that the war would end, and life would return to how it had been before it started. Now, she doubted that was going to happen. A family of strangers would reunite in that house in Hampstead. The two children wouldn't want to be there. She and her husband would be different people. She had a dreadful feeling they wouldn't fall into one another's arms. They wouldn't know what to say or do. It was going to be awful. She doubted they'd make it.

At night she studied the most recent photographs of Nell and Ollie that Joe had taken with his Box Brownie. She ran her fingers over their faces, pained at the changes she hadn't been around to witness. She wondered if they remembered what she looked like. She wrote letters to Richard, not knowing if he got them. His letters to her were heavily censored with thick black lines.

Thing was, at work, she was having the time of her life. She was enjoying this war, and that wasn't right, was it? She loved flying. She felt useful, fulfilled. This was new to her.

Richard had no idea what his wife was up to. Claire didn't worry about him as she cycled to work. She saved that slice of fretting till she was alone in her room at night, lying in the dark listening to the sounds beyond her window – bombers on their way down the coast, the river that was yards from their front door pushing against the shore, a heron calling a long desperate cry. She knew how it felt.

She was tired and lonely. She felt she'd spent the last year flying and running. There was an urgency about the job. If she wasn't in the air, following the curves and lines of railways and roads below, she was running across windy airfields, delivery chit in hand. Once it was signed, she was off, running again, to a new plane or to the taxi plane that would take her to another airfield, and then, she'd be running once more. Factories were churning out planes faster than they could be delivered.

Nights, she would write letters to Richard and to the children, fill in her logbook or sit by the fire working on the quilt she was making and listening to the wireless. If she was alone in the cottage, she'd look at the empty chair across from her and wish there was someone sitting there she could talk to about the jokes on *I.T.M.A.* Sometimes, she'd go into the hall and stare at the phone, willing it to ring. It would be Richard, escaped from the camp, back in the country and on his way to see her. In bed, she longed for him. She wanted him lying beside her, holding her hand as they spoke, low voices in the dark, about their plans for the future.

She wanted someone to hold her. She wanted long deep kisses. 'Face it,' she told herself, 'you miss sex.'

She considered that and revised her longing: 'I miss a hand in mine under the sheets at bedtime.' She missed a body next to her, someone to spoon into in that quiet moment before sleep came. Though, she had to admit sex was everywhere these days. She supposed people were far from home. They'd fetched up in places they'd never heard of, mixing with all sorts of people they might never have met if the war hadn't started. They were scared, lonely and homesick, though some, far from disapproving mothers or spouses, were tasting a bit of freedom they'd never imagined possible. Everyone was grabbing any pleasure that was on offer. And now she thought about it, sex was just about the only thing that wasn't on ration. Still, it wasn't really sex she missed. 'I miss the closeness of another being. Hearing someone next to me breathe. Sharing thoughts, worries and little bits of gossip.' Intimacy, she thought. Yes, that's it, I miss intimacy.

Izzy, coming along behind, also had family worries. Two weeks ago she'd received a letter from her father. He said he hoped that living away from home hadn't turned her head, made her abandon her morals. He told her that she'd been given a good Christian upbringing and he trusted she wasn't doing anything that would disgrace her family.

'Jeepers,' Izzy had said. A word she'd picked up from Dolores, one of the Americans at the base, and a word she liked, used as often as she could. She knew

16

what this warning meant. Her father had read 'The Letter'.

Allan had been killed in North Africa. Before the war he'd been a history teacher in Perth and Izzy's boyfriend. Their affair had turned physical after he'd been called up. Fearing he might die in some foreign country, alone and still a virgin, he'd turned to Izzy. She'd said there was nothing she could do about the alone-in-a-foreign-country bit, but she could help relieve him of his virginity.

After his death his things had been sent to his mother, who'd found The Letter and, not knowing Izzy's present address, had sent it on to the manse at Fortham, where she'd been brought up. He father had obviously opened and read it. 'Sorry, didn't notice this was for you, opened it by mistake,' said his curt note that accompanied it when he sent it on.

'Jeepers,' Izzy said again.

'Darling Izzy,' The Letter read, 'I think of you all the time. I love to think of you naked, coming to me from across the room, slipping into my bed, lying with me. I ache to feel you touch me again. Memories of your body are with me always out here.'

'Jeepers,' Izzy had said once more.

She had written to Allan's mother, thanking her for sending on The Letter, and telling her what a wonderful person he was, that she'd miss him. She would remember him always.

Nights, she would lie in bed thinking of him. She could hardly believe he was dead. She'd shut her eyes

17

and try to conjure up his face. When she couldn't, she'd take out the few photos of him she had and examine them. She wept for him.

They'd been better at being friends than they were at being lovers. They'd both been shy and inexperienced. There hadn't been time before he left to learn to be relaxed with one another. Still, Allan might have died alone in a foreign country – and that was awful – but at least he hadn't died a virgin. Izzy was glad she'd done what she had done. There hadn't been anyone since those few stolen nights with Allan.

But now her father knew she was a wanton woman. She'd given herself to a man without first going through the holy vows of marriage. He would be furious. 'Sex outside the sanctity of marriage is a sin,' he'd told her often. It pained her that she must be a disappointment to him when he was the man she adored.

She didn't want to lie to him, but lie to him she did. Not exactly lies, she thought, just a little fiddling with the truth. I keep things back to stop him worrying. One thing she'd kept from her father, the big thing, was her job. Oh, he knew she was in the ATA, but he didn't know she flew. She'd given him the impression she was an assistant operations officer. It made life easier.

She loved her father dearly. She'd love him more if he didn't have such fixed ideas about a woman's place in the world. 'Flying's a man's job,' he'd said. 'Women don't have the brains for it.' Then seeing Izzy's horrified expression, he'd added, 'Don't get me wrong. I'm not saying women are stupid, far from it. There are some pretty clever women in the world. But flying takes logic, quick thinking, making calculations. Women run on their emotions, and thank heaven for that. The world needs their shrewd nurturing natures, their unquestioning love, their beautiful soft hearts.'

He'd given sermons on the role of women in society. 'We should fight for their right to femininity. A woman who dresses as a man is to be reviled. Women are like flowers in winter – a primrose, a daffodil in the snow, bending with the terrible travails of weather, never breaking and always beautiful. Women are wonderful and mysterious beings, strong in heart and mind, but fragile and gentle in their ways. They should not undertake the labours of men, they should not wear slacks and try to look like men.'

Obviously, Izzy hadn't mentioned to him that she was a pilot and, therefore, dressed in pilot's clothes. There would have been an argument. Arguing with her father, and winning, was impossible. This was why she lied to him. She'd been doing it since she was eleven.

It had started with her faith. She'd started to doubt there was a God and couldn't bring herself to discuss this with her father since his belief was his reason for living. She fancied he'd mock her.

Later she lied about where she'd been and what she'd been doing. 'Just out,' she'd say, 'talking to my friends.' She'd been kissing Rory McGhee and sharing a secret cigarette. How were her piano lessons going? 'Oh, very well.' She and Elspeth, her teacher and new best friend, would lie in Elspeth's garden on good days, on the sofa in her sitting room on not-so-good days and sigh about life's endless possibilities.

In Izzy's eyes, her father was a wonderful man. He adored her. He'd sweep her off her feet and dance her down the hall in the manse. He'd buy her chocolate and toys. He'd sit her on his knee when she was small, put his bearlike arm round her and read her stories – *Treasure Island* and *Kidnapped*. She adored him back. She lied because she could not suffer to be the cause of his displeasure.

She'd written to Elspeth, who was working in a forest north of Inverness, and told her about The Letter. 'I worry,' she wrote, 'because he might come to hate me. I am no longer lying to him about little things. I'm lying about my whole life.'

Thinking of Elspeth relieved her from the ticking-off from her conscience when she imagined her father's horrified face – the pulled-in lips, the heaving eyebrows – when he'd read Allan's letter. Even here, even now, hundreds of miles away from him, she could hear the thunderous silence of his disapproval.

She imagined Elspeth singing as she chopped down trees, Elspeth whistling as she strode the forest tracks, axe slung over her shoulder. Elspeth – a lumberjill, who'd have thought it?

After fondly thinking of her friend, Izzy started to contemplate her day ahead. In less than an hour she'd be flying. If the weather holds, she thought.

Right now, Edith, the ops officer, would be on the phone finding out about conditions at the airfields the pilots were expected to deliver to that day. She'd be working out who was to fly what and where and who was to be today's duty pilot, flying the taxi plane picking everyone up and bringing them back so they could do it all again the following day.

The CO would be in his office, dealing with matters of the day. Irene, the nurse, would be in the sick bay, getting ready for any physical examinations and any pilots who might be sent to her with flu or to be assessed after some sort of trauma.

Nigel, the met man, would be in touch with the central met office checking on any fronts coming in, making up his charts. It seemed to Izzy that Nigel, Edith, Nurse Irene and the CO had proper jobs with a desk, a pen, someone nearby clattering at a typewriter and a phone always ringing. The people who did these jobs looked strained and a little bit flustered.

She, on the other hand, flew aeroplanes. The pleasure this brought her made her doubt she should get paid. It was a sin to take money for doing something that thrilled her. She'd get her comeuppance for this, she was sure. Life should be filled with onerous duties, guilt and shame. It was not to be enjoyed.

In the upper reaches of her thinking, she was sure this wasn't true. But guilt was deeply rooted in the murky fathoms of her psyche. She had breathed it in on her childhood Sundays, sitting in the front pew of her father's church, listening to his searing hellfire sermons.

She remembered hearing that the Lord was watching

her, knew her and all her thoughts and that she would pay for her sins. Her father, Reverend Hamish Macleod, used the word 'vengeance' a lot. She would sit next to her mother – a diffident woman in a dark-blue, fur-collared coat and skull-hugging red hat – vowing to avoid such sins as pride, envy, greed and lust. She would, according to her father, pay threefold for indulging in such things. Gluttons, fools and proud people were all doomed.

Izzy drank it all in. She'd look down at her shiny patent leather Sunday shoes, fiddle with the velvet buttons on her green Sunday coat and silently promise to be good, kind and meek. The subliminal message, the constant undertow in her father's ardent preaching, was that she would pay dearly for enjoying herself.

Life, at the moment, was very thrilling. Oh, how she would pay.

After her weekly verbal scouring, she'd return with her family to the manse for the routine Sunday lunch of roast beef, potatoes and carrots. By now, her father would have resumed being his usual affable self. Every week, he'd step into the pulpit and rant hellfire and damnation, then step back out again, greet his parishioners at the church door, shake hands, joke, ask after the sick and elderly, and go home for a hearty meal with his family. He was loved.

Away from the pulpit, Hamish enjoyed spending his free time tinkering with his MG sports car. Often, on Saturday afternoons, he'd take Izzy for a run, roof down, through the Perthshire countryside where they lived. They would thunder and rattle through Crieff towards Loch Tay, wind sweeping their hair from their faces, yelling their sparse conversation above the din of rushing air and roaring engine.

So, her father had given Izzy a conscience that she kept in prime condition, and a passion for speed and wind. He was her hero.

When she'd read about the ATA in *The Aeroplane* magazine, she'd applied, thinking she wouldn't be accepted. But she was invited for a test flight at White Waltham near Maidenhead. She'd flown round the airbase following the orders her instructor, seated in the rear cockpit, hollered down a Gosport tube. To her, and her family's, amazement, she'd passed.

Her mother had been horrified. 'But you can't go flying aeroplanes all over the country, you'll die,' her mother said.

'I'll just be on the ground planning the routes and making sure everyone gets home at night. Same sort of thing I did for Betty Stokes Flying Show.'

'Don't mention Betty Stokes Flying Show to me. I don't want to hear that name again. You, a well brought up minister's daughter, joining a show like that. It's a disgrace.'

I suppose I am a disgrace, Izzy thought. But she rattled along smiling. She'd told her parents she was a back-room girl at Betty Stokes Flying Show, making tea, selling souvenirs. But she'd been flying. Happy days, she thought. Flying over towns and villages, a long red and yellow banner trailing behind her Tiger

Moth – ARRIVING TOMORROW, BETTY STOKES ALL-GIRL FLYING SHOW. People below would stop and point, and she'd heave a batch of leaflets over the side, watch them flutter down. God, she'd loved doing that. It would have been better, though, if she'd been paid.

'You'll be miles from home,' her mother had said. 'And what about the other girls? How will you get on with them? They'll be rich, and you're not.'

Izzy hadn't answered this. But, in time, she'd found this to be true. It wasn't wealth that bothered her. She'd never dreamed of being rich. In fact, she wasn't bothered when her new colleagues spoke about their huge homes. She didn't want a vast mansion. Who would clean it? She wasn't comfortable with the notion of servants. Certainly, she did have Mrs Brent cleaning the cottage she shared with Julia and Claire. But Mrs Brent wasn't really a servant. She was an opinionated tour-de-force who had a way with dusters. The thing was, Izzy knew that if she had servants, she'd be on their side. She imagined herself getting up in the middle of the night to wash dishes and sweep floors so they wouldn't have to do it. In her mind, she was sure that if she hadn't learned to fly, she'd probably have ended up as someone's maid.

No, it was the self-assurance of her fellow pilots that worried her. She was mixing with women who had ostentatious accents, loud voices and oozed confidence. They made her feel emotionally dowdy. Failure never occurred to these women. Izzy was sure none of them had ever experienced such a thing as doubt. They surged

24

through their lives busy being right about everything. She, on the other hand, tiptoed. She entered rooms quietly. She thought she was just . . . just Izzy. I'm only me, she thought, nobody much. She went through life looking over her shoulder, expecting to be discovered for what she was – just Izzy who did not belong among these poised women.

'I thought that was what you're meant to do, follow your dreams,' she'd once said to her father.

Her father had placed his folded hands on the table, 'Following your dreams is one thing, making rash decisions is another.' He'd looked across at his wife. 'I fear that we have somehow produced a child that is prone to rash decisions. You must promise us, Izzy, that when you're far from us, you'll behave in the same way you do when you are near us. You'll not forget your faith, and you'll be true to your upbringing.'

Now, puffing as she skimmed along, Izzy shook her head, dismissing this. Memories, she thought, mustn't linger in the past.

Her bike rattled more than the other two, and was too big for her. She had to stretch to reach the pedals. It was heavy and black, and had belonged to a local policeman. He'd sold it to her for two shillings and sixpence.

'I think he saw you coming,' Julia had said when she saw it. 'You got rather ripped orff, I'm afraid, darling.'

Thinking that soon she might join the sky, Izzy cycled faster and caught up with Claire, who shot her a scathing look. 'Don't chat. You'll interrupt my worrying.'

That was it, Izzy thought. Claire just said she didn't want to chat out loud. Izzy would just have thought it. Claire said what she wanted – peace to worry – and didn't give a fig what anyone felt about that.

Izzy said, 'Sorry.' She cycled past to catch up with Julia. 'We're bound to get up today.'

'Absolutely,' said Julia.

Izzy allowed herself to feel the rapture that came when contemplating flight, and the guilt and fear that always went with it. 'Do you think this is wrong?' she said. 'To be enjoying this war? People are dying and I'm having the time of my life.'

Julia said she knew, but what could you do? 'If they weren't paying me to ferry planes, I'd do it for nothing. It's such bloody fun. Anyway, it isn't all good. There's always the chance we could get bumped orff.'

She always put an 'r' in her 'off's.

At first, Izzy had been troubled by Julia's attitude to death. It seemed flippant. But, as time passed and colleagues had been killed, she'd seen this as a way to deal with it. Considering her own mortality and the likelihood of an accident in foul weather or in a mechanically faulty plane, she decided she'd rather not die, just get bumped off. It was jollier.

Izzy said, 'Don't you worry about what you'll do when the war ends?'

'Depends on how it ends. But we're sure to win this thing. After the Blitz and Dunkirk, it's in the way of things that we should win. It's our turn. Besides, we're in the right, we didn't start it.'

Izzy said she didn't think that not starting a war necessarily meant you'd win it.

'Of course it does,' said Julia. 'Greedy, arrogant little dictators never win in the end, they always get what's coming to them.'

This struck a chord with Izzy. Of course Hitler was doomed, vengeance was coming his way. It was a pity, she thought, that he'd never attended that little hillside church outside Perth and heard one of Hamish Macleod's scathing Sunday sermons, he'd never have dared to invade Poland after that.

They were both a little breathless, faces pink with effort.

Izzy asked, 'Who was that man this morning?'

Julia shrugged. 'Don't really know. Some Polish chap Charles met on the train and invited along. He thought he looked a little lost. He'll be gone when we get back, Mrs Brent will see him orff.'

They grinned. Mrs Brent was a force to be reckoned with.

By now, they were almost at the base. Skimming along beside the long wire fence towards the gate, they could hear it and smell it – the rumble of engines, the shouts of ground engineers, the heavy leaden reek of petrol.

Nerves shifted and heaved through Izzy's stomach.

'Aren't you scared?' Elspeth had asked her once. 'I mean, don't people die doing what you do?'

'Yes, they do get bumped off, sometimes,' Izzy had agreed. And was she scared? 'Sometimes, a little.'

Elspeth had looked at her sceptically, eyebrows raised. She didn't believe her.

Izzy had looked down at her feet. There wasn't a day when she didn't know fear.

The other pilots felt it, too. Though nobody spoke about it. For, really, it didn't diminish the rapture she felt.